SHATTERED DREAMS

ELLIE JAMES

Quercus

First published in the US in 2011 by St Martin's Press,
175 Fifth Avenue, New York, NY 10010

First published in Great Britain in 2012 by
Quercus
55 Baker Street
7th Floor, South Block
London
W1U 8EW

A CIP catalogue reference for this book is available
from the British Library

ISBN 978 0 85738 822 3

1 3 5 7 9 10 8 6 4 2

Printed and bound in Great Britain by Clays Ltd, St Ives plc

SHATTERED DREAMS

'A word to the wise – this tale of love, betrayal, and stalking evil is best read with the lights on'

Jana Oliver, author of *The Demon Trappers*

'Well-written and filled with both dramatic and romantic tension, *Shattered Dreams* is an exciting debut you won't want to miss'

Jenna Black, author of *Glimmerglass* and *Shadowspell*

'A haunting and engaging story with characters who will stay with you long after you finish the book'

C. C. Hunter, author of *Born at Midnight*

For my four favorite girls: Brittany, Victoria, Grace and Elizabeth . . .
Follow your dreams. They'll take you far.

ACKNOWLEDGMENTS

This book would not have been possible without the insight, support, and encouragement of so many people:

My awesome agent, Roberta Brown, for belief, wisdom, and inspiration.

My fabulous editor, Holly Blanck, for sharing my vision, and knowing how to make it so much better.

My super talented friends, Catherine Spangler and Linda Castillo, for always being there to answer questions and give advice.

Faye, for all things New Orleans.

Jeffery, for all things *Halo*.

My sweet friend Dawn, for gracing me with an early read.

And most of all, my husband and children, for overlooking all the things that didn't get done while I was happily lost in Trinity's world, and loving me anyway!

SHATTERED DREAMS

ONE

"I heard this place is like . . . haunted."

Stepping around a huge old oak, I lifted my flashlight . . . and saw the house. Everyone else kept tromping through knee-high weeds, but something held me there, totally still, while Spanish moss slipped against my face.

The abandoned Greek Revival rose up against the moonlit sky like something ripped straight from the picture book my grandmother used to keep on her coffee table. Surrounded by seriously old trees and nearly covered by vines, it was big and boxy, with massive columns and wide porches. Once the place had probably been white. Even at night I could tell that. But now it was dirty and worn out. Tired.

Alone.

It was an odd word, but there you go. Alone. The old place with its dark windows and peeling siding looked like it was . . .

Waiting.

A warm breeze blew off the river, but I hugged my arms

around myself as I watched them—Jessica, the stupidly beautiful cheerleader; her way-too-skinny best friend Amber; Jessica's little sister Bethany; and the guys: Chase, the quarterback (and my chemistry lab partner); Drew, who rarely said more than two words at a time; and the massively tattooed Pitre—making their way toward a broken window. They weren't that far away, but they might as well have been in another state.

At the steps leading to the porch, Jessica swung back to me. She was the one who'd invited me to tag along. "What's the matter, Trinity? You're not scared, are you?"

My throat tightened. I wasn't scared. That wasn't the right word. Just . . . uneasy.

Waiting.

"Just taking it all in," I said, forcing my legs to move. Beneath my flip-flops I felt stuff crunch. I didn't want to know what.

Amber made it to the window before she turned back. "Last year," she said, her eyes glowing, "these two seniors came here—"

"Amber!" Jessica shot her friend a *shut-up* look. "What are you trying to do? Make her leave?"

That would be a yes. I was the new kid, after all. On the first day of school when the teacher had said Trinity Monsour, everyone had turned to stare at me, obviously sizing up the new girl. Being from Colorado made me an outsider, but at least I looked like I belonged. With long dark hair and dark eyes, skin my grandmother called olive, a T-shirt and low-rise jeans, I could have been Jessica's twin.

But still. Starting a new school junior year pretty much sucked.

"Leave?" Amber said. "No way." And with that she slipped into the darkness beyond the broken window.

Two of the guys—Drew and Pitre—followed. Jessica waited until I reached the big bushes obscuring the porch before taking Chase's hand and tugging him toward the darkness. Bethany shot me a nervous look, but followed anyway.

"You coming?"

I recognized the voice as belonging to Amber. Sidestepping broken glass, I reached the tall window and lifted my flashlight, looked inside. They all stood there, waiting.

There was that word again. *Waiting.*

And with it my throat tightened.

Or maybe that was because of what I saw behind them, neat little piles against the far wall. *Ashes.*

"Of course," I said against a slap of warm air. Until New Orleans, I'd never known air could be so thick. Breathing was hard enough, but my hair! It had been straight in Colorado. Here it was a frizzy mess. My aunt kept saying I would get used to it, but I think she was just saying that.

She does that a lot, tells me I'll get used to things. But I've seen that look she gets in her eyes, the worry.

"Then what are you waiting for?" Through a mass of perfect, coffee-colored ringlets, Amber's smile looked more like a smirk. "Want Chasey to hold your hand?"

Jessica's eyes narrowed, invisible claws coming out for the thousandth time since she'd discovered her boyfriend and I were chemistry partners. Just because we had an out-of-class assignment—

But that was another story.

She eased closer to him, inserting herself between him and me. Through the play of shadows his eyes met mine anyway, forcing me to look down at an empty fast-food bag trapped by a rock.

I so knew he was taken.

I also knew I did not want to go into that house. Everything inside of me screamed for me to stay right where I was. But I rubbed my palms against the amazing Rock Revival jeans I still couldn't believe Aunt Sara had bought for me, and stepped to the broken window.

(If anyone had told me back on my birthday in April, that six months later I'd be breaking into a deserted mansion in the Garden District of New Orleans in the middle of the night with a bunch of teens I barely knew, I would have thought they were on serious drugs.)

The cold hit like a punch to the gut. I must have staggered from it because Chase lunged for me, his arms reaching out. The warmth of his hand practically seared through the invisible blanket of ice suddenly covering every inch of my body.

No, I told myself. *No!* Not now.

Not here!

Not in front of these people . . .

The last time I'd felt the icy veil—

I stopped the thought, knowing I couldn't just stand there like an idiot in a trance. No one else heard the buzz. No one else felt like they stood in a freezer. My flashlight showed the sheen of sweat on Chase's forehead. Everyone had on tank tops—Jessica's was plastered against her chest. No one was shivering.

Only me.

And only on the inside.

Kind of like the old house.

With a pretend laugh, I stepped from the warmth of Chase's hand and again rubbed my hands against my jeans. I didn't bother looking at Jessica. I knew she'd be glaring in that she-animal way of hers.

"Holy crap." I gagged on my first full breath inside. Mud and smoke and stale whiskey mixed with something else, something really foul. "How old *is* this place?"

"Real old," Chase said. "Civil War, I think."

"Wow." The beams of our flashlights jumped through the pitch-black room, creating a strobe-light effect. I could only catch pulsing glimpses. Floor. Darkness. Empty water bottles. Darkness. Peeling walls.

Darkness.

By the time I caught detail, it was gone.

Refusing to let my hands shake, I played it cool and lifted my light to the far wall, and saw the tattoo. Well, not really a tattoo, graffiti was more like it, intricately painted over the faded image of a paddleboat on the river.

The heart was done in black. A red cross ran through the top, with some kind of weird swirl design and grid through the middle, like something you'd see on someone's arm.

Actually, I was pretty sure I *had* seen it.

"Before Katrina," Amber said, strolling over to dominate the circle of light, "you could still see the blood."

Blood? Inside, mine ran cold.

"You still can, dimwit," Jessica said. "This place didn't get any water."

"Omigod—" That was from Bethany. I twisted around, found her staring at the back corner. She was really pale—and really glued to Chase. His eyes were narrow, his dimples gone. "W-what's that?"

With my light I followed her line of vision to a small collection of sticks piled on top of each other.

Except they weren't sticks.

"Bones," Amber whispered.

I swallowed hard as Bethany let out some kind of strangled sound. "I don't think—"

"No one's making you stay," Jessica pointed out before her sister could finish. "If you want to leave . . ."

"Probably an animal." Chase's voice held absolute calm. "They like to die alone."

Bethany, a smaller, less sexy version of Jessica, looked up at him as if she wanted nothing more than for him to be right. It was so painfully obvious how badly she hung on his every word. His smile was warm as he gave her a brotherly pat on the back.

I was quite sure it broke her heart.

Around us darkness throbbed, and with every warm breath of wind, the old house groaned. The place was huge. I had no idea how many rooms there were, or who (or what) else could be inside.

Waiting.

The urge to move was strong. To leave. The stillness felt . . . wrong.

Everything felt wrong.

. . . still see the blood . . .

"I thought everything flooded," I said, stepping toward the wide hallway that cut through the middle of the house. I'd only been a kid, but my memories of the hurricane were vivid. My grandmother had been glued to the coverage, her eyes worried, her hands fisted together. I'd never seen her like that, and it had freaked me out.

It wasn't until Gran died that I understood why.

She'd never been one to talk about the past, had always said, *Triny, ain't no point lookin' backwards.* But I'd never really thought much about it. Maybe because I didn't have much to look back at. My parents died when I was little—I didn't even have any pictures of them, didn't have any brothers or sisters. I had never been anywhere besides the Colorado mountain where Gran raised me, had never even seen an ocean.

Gran always made everything sound simple.

Never, not even in the aftermath of Katrina, had she mentioned that she'd been born in New Orleans and had lived there for fifty-one years, until my parents died.

I still didn't know why she'd left. Aunt Sara, Gran's youngest, said her mama had needed to make a clean break.

I guess that made sense. That was, after all, sort of why I was in New Orleans. Of course, being an orphan and having no living family besides an aunt I'd rarely seen was the much bigger part.

Nothing prepared me for how totally my life was going to change. And even though Gran had watched nonstop news coverage of Katrina, nothing prepared me for how wounded the city was.

At sixteen, I was coming to realize there were some wounds you never got over.

The old house knew, too.

". . . Garden District and French Quarter are on higher ground," Chase was saying. His voice was warm, like some kind of drugging anchor I wanted to grab, but I knew how disastrous that would be.

"The roads were like rivers," he explained, "but most of the houses were okay."

Through the beam of Drew's flashlight, Jessica's smile glittered as she dragged her finger along the grid superimposed on the heart. "Which is why the blood is still here."

They were practically begging me to ask. "What blood?"

Jessica looked away, down toward a pile of . . . corn? I tensed, trying to focus on the faint sounds of the city drifting on the night, sirens and the horn of a tugboat, music. Laughter.

Crying.

In New Orleans, if you listened closely enough, you could always hear something.

At least I could.

The low buzz threatened to drown it all out. Still cold, I swung my flashlight toward the broken glass, but saw only the shifting shadows of the huge trees beyond.

I would have sworn someone had been watching.

"No one knows for sure," Jessica said, and I could hear the deliberate drama in her voice.

"But they say when the moon is full . . ." Like it was tonight. I doubted that was a coincidence.

"The walls start to bleed." That was Amber.

"And that you can hear a girl crying from one of the rooms upstairs."

"And smell whiskey . . ."

My heart bumped hard, even though it was obvious what they were doing. They were like lame, wannabe actors reading the script for some low-budget horror flick. And while I hadn't spent tons of time with kids my age, I wasn't stupid.

Jessica and Amber had been friends forever. Chase and Drew were cousins. They'd all grown up together. I was the new girl.

That, apparently, made me fair game.

But the cold was real. And the tomblike darkness. The disgusting smell.

Still, I swallowed hard and tilted the flashlight to shine on my own face. "I want to see."

Sometimes I really regretted my smart mouth. Now was definitely one of those times. Jessica led us through the shadows of the kitchen to a closed door. She pulled it open to a blast of stale air, revealing a hidden staircase.

"This is what the servants used," she said, taking the first step.

"You mean slaves," Amber corrected, lingering at the bottom as the rest of us started up.

Her friend huffed. "Whatever."

"The blood is theirs," Amber just had to say. "Some weird voodoo—"

Her terrified scream stopped me cold.

"Amber!" Jessica cried as we all swung our flashlights behind us. We saw them immediately, Pitre pressing Amber against the graffiti-polluted wall, his hand over her mouth. Her eyes were wide—*furious*.

"Jerk," Jessica muttered.

But Pitre only laughed. "Sike!"

"Let her go." That was not Chase, as I expected, but Drew. Three words strung together.

There's a first for everything.

Pitre's lip curled as he stepped back from Amber. She recoiled from him, slinking up several stairs while barely seeming to move. All the while she looked at him like he was one of those disgusting cockroaches Louisiana specialized in.

Apparently she was a lot more over the night they hooked up than he was.

"I think it's time for you to go," Jessica hissed, shining her flashlight into his face. "No one wanted you here to begin with."

His mouth curled. "Now who's scared?"

Her eyes got narrow. "*Chase*. Make. Him. Go."

Chase moved between them like a referee, and in that moment I felt so bad for him. I mean, putting him in that position, making him choose between his girlfriend and his All-State receiver.

"I wanted him here." Chase's words surprised me as much as they surprised everyone else. I stepped back, but couldn't stop staring at the way his blue eyes glittered. "If he goes, I go."

The walls pushed closer. Jessica didn't move, though. No one did. I'm not sure anyone even breathed.

It was Jessica who moved first, after a long hot second, glancing beyond Drew to her best friend. Their eyes met. Understanding flared.

"It's cool," Amber said, even though it was obvious she was lying.

The awful drone grew louder, and the walls wouldn't stop watching. If someone got locked in here—

I needed to move. "Then come on," I said. Standing in place made me feel like a sitting duck.

"Need me to lead?" Pitre asked, obviously needling Jessica. "Because I'd be happy to show you where to go—"

"Oh, shut up." With the words she took off.

Flashlights in front of us, we all followed, Chase and Bethany behind Jessica, Amber and Drew behind them, me with Pitre. He said nothing, but I would have sworn I saw a flicker of respect in his quick glance. Or maybe that was gratitude.

Upstairs, doorways lined each side of an ultra-long hallway, all closed, like in a hotel. Except this had been a house. Actually, was still a house. Just empty.

Except for the presence that hummed like invisible blood through invisible veins . . .

Oblivious, Jessica swung open the second door to the left, and vanished inside.

Again we all followed. My heart pounded hard as I crossed into the room—the mattresses stopped me. Surrounded by the remains of little white candles and an unbroken chain of dead flowers, they dominated the center of the room, like . . . an altar.

Crouching beside them, Jessica glanced up through a tangle of dark hair, and smiled. "You wanna see?"

TWO

No one moved. Through the crisscross of flashlight beams they all looked at me, as if some massive gauntlet had been hurled at my feet.

Probably because it had.

Challenge glimmered in Jessica's eyes, but it ran so much deeper than the mattresses. They were just a prop, everyone else the audience. This was about her, and me. And Chase.

Actually, it was all about Chase.

She was staking her claim, daring me to make a move. I was supposed to back away, to run, giving her the satisfaction of scaring me away. Not from the house.

But from Chase.

Open door number one; open door number two. Life was about choices. Take a different path—dream a different dream. Even the road not taken led somewhere.

I'll never know what would have happened if I'd just turned and walked away.

But I'd never been very good at that.

Determined not to buckle, I stepped deeper into the room—and saw. Lightning flashed in from a cloudless sky, replacing shadows with a harsh silver light. And in that one cruel flash, everything came into horrible focus. *Filth littered the warped wood floor. Some kind of greasy grime coated the windows. Dark copper smeared against the walls. And on the mattresses, something really red.*

A single pink flip-flop lay upside down.

A cell phone in the corner.

On the bed . . .

I gasped. *The girl lay limp as a rag doll, long legs barely covered by short denim shorts. And the hair, long, dark—*

I recoiled, tried to breathe. My throat burned. My chest hurt—

"Jesus."

I grabbed onto the oath, the familiar voice, used it to pull me back. Somehow I managed a forceful blink, returning the shadows to the room and revealing everything exactly as it had been: Jessica and Amber crouched among the candles by the mattresses, a scowling Drew a few steps away, Bethany hovering close to Chase, Pitre beside me. They all stared as if I was crazy.

There'd been no lightning. Not for them.

Only for me.

"You're eff'in cold as ice," Pitre muttered.

Only then did I realize he'd grabbed my hand.

I yanked back from him, willing the stupid images to clear. There was *no* light in the room, *no* blood. *No* knife on the floor.

I wasn't lying discarded on the bed . . .

Nonsense, Gran had told me the first time she'd found me frozen by that horrible, invisible lightning. *It's all nonsense.* Shaken, I'd buried myself in her arms and clung to her, held on as tightly as I could.

I missed having someone to hold onto. Aunt Sara was awesome, but it wasn't the same. *She* wasn't the same. She didn't know.

She couldn't.

Gran had made me promise to never speak of what I saw.

"A nice shade of pale, too." Amber smirked, exposing me with her flashlight. "What's the matter? See a ghost?"

Say something! I told myself. *Don't stand there like some kind of freak.*

"Maybe," I said with a hint of smart-ass I didn't come close to feeling. Forcing my own smirk, I kept my eyes on the girls, absolutely refusing to look at Chase. It was bad enough that I could feel him watching me.

"Don't *you* feel it?" I played innocent, crossing my arms to fend off the shiver I felt—but they did not.

"Feel what?" Bethany asked, and the real fear in her voice made me feel kinda bad. I didn't look at her, though. Because looking at her would mean looking at Chase.

"The cold," I said.

Pitre laughed. "Sorry, babe, but it's hot as hell in here."

"Like a meat locker," I said, edging closer to the mattresses. "Like on those ghost-hunter shows."

Jessica pushed the hair back from her face, rolling her eyes. "Uh-huh. That's why my shirt is sticking to my chest."

No, but heat and humidity weren't the reasons, either. Buying clothes a size too small . . .

But I wasn't going to go there.

"Wait a minute." Amber closed her eyes and opened her arms in welcome. "I think I *do* feel something."

Bethany edged closer to Chase.

"The candles, the mattresses," she purred, opening her eyes. "It's *perfect*!"

"Perfect?" I echoed.

Through the play of shadow and light, she literally glowed. "For a séance! We could do one, see if there really are ghosts here."

Around my throat, a nonexistent scarf pulled tight.

"Anyone got a lighter?" she asked, kneeling to pick up a candle.

"I-I don't think this is a good idea," Bethany said.

But her sister joined Amber, lining up the votives in two little rows. "Come on," Jessica said. "Don't you have anyone dead you want to talk to?"

The wave of grief hit so hard, for a second I couldn't breathe. *Mom* . . .

It was a weird time to think about a woman I didn't even remember. But New Orleans had been her town, and sometimes I'd swear I could feel her . . .

Was she here? Would she come if I called?

Driven by something I didn't understand, I ignored the heaviness in my chest and approached the altar of mattresses. They were old and dirty . . . stained.

Going down on one knee, I leaned in for a better look, counting to ten before twisting toward Jessica. "I dare you to touch it."

Gran hadn't been much for television or movies, but she'd been a mean poker player. Early on, she'd taught me the beauty of the bluff—and the rush of calling one out.

The surprise in Jessica's eyes felt good. Beautiful and popular, the oldest child of two rich doctors, she was one of those people so used to calling the shots, it never occurred to her that sometimes the tables could get turned. "Touch it?"

Something dark drove me. Challenging Jessica was not the smartest way to get accepted, but she'd started the game. And when you started a game, you had to be prepared to play.

"The blood," I said as the others bunched closer. "I dare you to touch it. I mean, if we're gonna have a séance . . ."

Pitre laughed. "Yeah, babe," he drawled in what I'd learned was a Cajun accent. "Touch it."

Maybe it was the way he said "touch" . . . or maybe the way he said "it" . . . but daggers shot into Jessica's eyes. I just knew she was going to tell Chase to make Pitre leave.

Instead she glanced at her BFF, then looked down to where I crouched.

"If I do," she said quietly. "What will *you* do?"

I think that was supposed to scare me or make me back off. And while little warnings did ping through me, I wasn't going to be the one to back down. "Clap?"

Someone gasped. Bethany?

It was Amber who spoke up first. "Truth or dare," she answered before Jessica could. I wondered if she realized the way her fingers closed around the silver cross dangling from the chain at her neck. "If Jessica takes your dare, you *owe* her."

The room got crazy quiet. The stillness vibrated.

Walk away. That's what common sense told me. This was Jessica and Amber's territory. I was the outsider, the newcomer. I had no way of knowing—

"Trinity."

Chase's voice, the tense undercurrent, stopped me.

"You don't have to do this," he said.

But I did. "I'm not afraid." Yeah, that was so a lie.

Jessica got down beside me, whispering, *"Maybe you should be,"* before leaning over the mattresses. She made a show of lifting her hand toward the copper stain, then lowering her palm to the center of it. She held it there, the beam of her sister's flashlight highlighting the contrast between the black polish on Jessica's nails and the pale skin of her fingers.

"Happy?" she asked.

That wasn't exactly the word I would have chosen. My eyes met hers, but I said nothing. I didn't need to. We both knew the game we were playing.

"Give me your flashlight."

My heart slammed—I didn't need to look down at my death grip to know my knuckles had gone white. *Game,* I told myself. *Game, game, game!*

But the buzz no one else heard rang like a bullhorn in my ears.

"You're not scared, are you?" Amber asked.

"That's enough—" Chase started.

But I cut him off. "What if I'd rather a truth?"

I'd grown up believing smiles were reflections of happiness. Smiles made you feel good. Smiles held warmth, love, compassion.

Jessica's held none of that. There was only triumph. "Then a truth it is." Her voice was very quiet.

"Jessica." Chase broke toward her and took her hand, yanked her to her feet. Away from me. He led her to the corner—the same corner where I'd seen the discarded cell phone.

There was an edge to his voice, sharp, angry, but the words were lost to me. He stood stiff and rigid, like he wanted to drag her out of there. But his girlfriend held her head high, letting her perfect hair fall down past her shoulders. Her black tank top had ridden up, exposing the intricate chain of Celtic crosses tattooed to her lower back. A tramp stamp, Aunt Sara called them, but despite how much Jessica irked me, I thought it looked pretty cool.

"Trust me," I heard her whisper as she pushed up to give him a quick kiss. Then she was crossing back to me, standing so close she looked down at me.

"Who in this room," she began in a measured, singsong voice, and suddenly I so knew where this was going, "do you most want to hook up with?" I saw Chase frown as she added, "—and what, *exactly,* do you want to do with him?"

I felt myself still as her words slipped around me. I'd asked for this. I knew that. I'd issued the first dare. I'd requested a truth.

But that one was far too venomous to indulge.

Mouth dry, I looked up at Jessica. Everyone else faded from my awareness.

"I'm not here to hook up with anyone," I said, pushing to my feet. It was better standing. At least that way, she wasn't looking down at me. In flip-flops, we were pretty much eye-to-eye.

"Most," she repeated. "Who do you *most* want to be with?"

There was absolutely no winning with that question. So I returned to her dare, and held out my flashlight. "A dare for a dare," I said as my cell phone buzzed.

Jessica's hair fell into her face. It was sticky now, no longer quite so shiny. "Sorry, Trin," she said, taking my flashlight and letting it fall to the ground. "You already got your do-over."

Which meant I was left with the truth I could never give. Mind racing, I looked through the shadows to Chase, saw the horribly still way he stood watching me. The worry still lurked in his eyes, but something else gleamed there, as well. Something that shifted the roar within me to a hum.

"You better check that," he said, with absolutely no emotion in his voice. "Unless you want your aunt to freak and call the cops."

The virtual lifeline fell into the silence like an unexpected gift. He was right. There were only two people who could be texting me, and I knew it probably wasn't my friend Victoria. She was with her boyfriend, and Lucas didn't like it if her attention slipped elsewhere.

Downstairs, wind blew through the broken windows, but up here it was as still as a cemetery on a cloudless night, and ten times as hot. I could feel everyone watching as I slid the BlackBerry from my pocket and flipped it over. Sure enough, Aunt Sara had texted me. Three times.

Not sure how I missed the first two.

I'll be home round midnite.

The first message had arrived a little after eleven. We'd still been in the Quarter.

Home now . . . will wait up n case u forgot key.

The second had come shortly after twelve.

Worried, Trin. Let me no u r ok!

That was the most recent, sent at 1:16, and even though my aunt and I were little more than strangers linked by blood, the thought of her worrying made me feel bad. Plus, her ex was a cop. The last thing I needed was for her to send him out looking for me.

"Hang on," I said as I keyed in my response. I was pretty slow compared to everyone at school, but I was getting the hang of it. There'd been no reason for a cell phone on the mountain.

Everything OK. With friends. Home soon.

Only a few seconds passed before her response:

U sure?

I could hear Jessica and Chase arguing in the corner as I typed out my response, but couldn't make out their words. Drew had positioned himself behind Amber, with his hands on her hips. Pitre hung back, watching.

Y. Chase is here.

Aunt Sara liked Chase.

Good. CUITM

See you in the morning. I recognized that one. I returned the phone to my pocket.

"Any day now," Jessica said, still draped all over Chase. I couldn't see his face, but the press of their bodies gave me a sick feeling in my stomach. And suddenly I wasn't sure why I cared whether or not these people liked me. Chase had really been the only one . . .

Abruptly I shifted my focus to the right. "Amber," I said, and seemingly on cue, Bethany's light found her sister's friend on the far side of the mattress. Drew, not much taller than she, still stood behind her. "I most want to be with Amber."

I loved the flash of surprise in her eyes. Maybe she and Jessica weren't as untouchable as they wanted everyone to think.

"Amber?" Jessica scoffed. "But—"

"And as for what I want to do with her . . ." With a deliberate smile, I let the words dangle. "I'm thinking a dare."

My words fell into dead silence, save for the slow, labored breath of the room itself.

"Now we're talking," Amber whispered, and over the scratch of a branch along the window, I would have sworn I heard Jessica growl.

"What," I started, dragging the word out for effect, ". . . were you doing . . . after the football game last Friday night—"

Just like that, the room quit breathing.

"—in the backseat . . ." Hesitating, I toyed with one of the small silver hoops at my ear. I'd never actually played the game, and while I'd wanted to make Amber squirm, the way her mouth worked made me second-guess myself. I would have sworn she was silently begging me to stop.

Jessica moved closer to her.

". . . of Pitre's car?" I made myself finish. And as far as bombs went, mine sucked the air right out of the room. Amber stiffened. Drew's hands fell away. Jessica let out a strangled noise.

Against my earring, my fingers froze. Sometimes games were fun. And sometimes they weren't.

Amber's eyes met mine. Her voice faltered. Clearly she hadn't realized Victoria and I had seen them.

"You said a dare," Jessica snapped. "That's a truth."

Either way, everyone knew the answer. "It's all the same to me," I said.

"Then I dare her to tell the truth," Pitre said. I couldn't tell whether it was possession I saw burning in his eyes—or contempt.

"It's not your turn, jerk-off," Jessica snapped, as Drew took another step away from Amber.

Bethany's light, the last one still on, shifted toward me, and even though I could no longer see against the glare, I knew they all watched. Would I give Amber a new dare, or dare her to tell the truth?

It was an unexpected moment of power, but it came with consequences. I got that. Jessica and Amber had brought me to this nasty place as some kind of initiation, but I'd held my own. And while we would never be BFFs, I didn't want to be a total loser, either.

Games were one thing. Punishment was another.

"I dare you . . ." I hesitated before obliterating the point of no return. ". . . to lie down on the mattress." Maybe Amber didn't deserve a do-over, but giving it to her had more to do with my sense of right and wrong than anything to do with her.

Pitre muttered under his breath and stormed from the room, leaving Amber hugging bony arms around her body while Drew hovered nearby—but no longer touched.

Like a virgin (as if!) sacrifice, she moved to the mattresses and lowered first one knee, then the other. Then she dropped from her knees to lay with her back covering the stain.

Through the darkness, her eyes met mine. *"My turn,"* she whispered. And I knew my reprieve was over.

"So what's it going to be?" she murmured, stretching like a centerfold. "Truth, my friend?" And before the word could really register, she shifted, smiling at Jessica. "Or dare?"

Stunned, I stood there so very, totally still, trying to figure out what had just happened. Bethany's light swung to her sister, who negligently twirled a strand of dark hair around her finger. *"Moi?"*

"Toi," Amber confirmed. "Unless, of course, you're too scared."

"Have you ever known me to be too scared?"

"Truth?" Amber asked.

Her friend's eyes gleamed. She glanced at Chase, then back at Amber. "Let's find out."

What was it with these people and the truth?

Amber was on her feet now. "Walk down the hall," she said. "Alone." Then she held out her hand. "Without any light."

"No." The flash came with the word, invisible like before, a spear straight through me. The room shifted as everyone twisted toward me.

"No?" Amber asked.

"It's not *your* dare," Jessica pointed out.

But the nonexistent scarf choked off my breath. "I . . . I just . . ." *Breathe,* I told myself. *Breathe.* But I saw it all again, this time through the darkness. *The walls. The blood.*

"Trinity—" Only then did I realize Chase had left Jessica's side and was moving toward me.

I shook him off. "I don't . . ." *Tangled dark hair.* ". . . don't think it's a good idea." *Long legs.* "What if someone else is here?"

"Puh-lease." Jessica yanked the sole remaining flashlight from her sister and handed it to Amber, along with her Maglite. Then she flashed a bright smile and trotted from the room in the same way she took the field to cheer during half-time.

Twenty-two seconds later she screamed.

THREE

We ran.

"Jessica!" Chase reached the hall first. "Stay here!" he shouted, clicking on his flashlight as he broke toward the staircase we'd used on the way up. Drew, Amber, and Bethany veered left, taking the other two lights with them. *"Jess!"*

On instinct I went after Chase, but he was already gone. I had no light and couldn't see two inches in front of me. Behind me, the others had disappeared. I could hear Amber, though, shouting.

There weren't even shadows to guide me.

I took off anyway, using my arms to feel my way toward the end of the hall.

"Jessica!" My feet ran out of floor. "Chase!"

In response, the silence breathed.

Heart pounding, I slid my hands along the wall. There was a door there. I knew there was. I'd come through it—"Chase!"

From downstairs, I could hear him shouting for his girlfriend.

I fumbled for my BlackBerry, turning it over to reveal a faint glow. The door had to be somewhere!

"Jessie!" That was Amber. The burst of footsteps sounded like running.

Another scream.

I thrust my phone in front me as if it could protect me, almost crying with relief when I found the small knob. Fumbling, I yanked the door open and staggered through—never saw the wall of shelves. I slammed into them, forehead and waist plowing in simultaneously. The impact stole my breath. Pain sang hard. I fell back, doubled over and tried to breathe. "What the—"

My hands shook. I lifted one to my face, my fingers stilling at the stickiness. *Blood*. And everything started to spin.

I gasped for air, gagged on the smell. Stale like before, rancid now. Coppery. I went for the light from my phone, but realized I no longer held it.

Darkness took everything. I lifted my hand but could see nothing. I dropped to my knees, feeling my way through the grime for the opening.

Behind me, something moved.

I made myself keep going, refusing to think too much about anything. The webs my fingers ripped through, the spiders that had to be somewhere. The sound of shuffling.

The smell of whiskey—*and worse*.

Through the darkness everything throbbed, bringing with it a low mewl . . .

Me, I realized with a start. The barely human sound was coming from my own throat.

The wall stopped me. I twisted . . . found another.

Tried to stand.

Couldn't.

Tried to breathe, swallow.

Gagged instead.

Think, I begged myself. *Think. Find the phone. Call someone.* Aunt Sara would come.

But the darkness pressed from all directions, sucking the oxygen from my lungs.

The bright flash blinded. Recoiling, I sat frozen, once again in the unsettling room with the dirty walls and grimy windows, the cell phone discarded in the corner, the girl on the bed . . . the dark tangled hair.

Not me, I finally realized. Not me.

Jessica.

And finally, the scream burned my throat.

Immediately something whooshed to my right, and the darkness let go. This time the stab of light did not come from the confused corners of my mind.

"*Jesus*—Trinity."

"Pitre . . ." I managed, but the sound that crawled from my throat was no more than a whisper.

Flashlight in hand, he lunged inside what looked like a large closet and reached for me. "What the hell—"

The instant his hand touched mine, he looked like he wanted to hit someone. To hurt them. Bad. "*Jesus*—you're like ice."

I fumbled for words. "*. . . bad place.*"

With a gentleness totally at odds with the rough-around-the-edges veneer, he helped me to my feet.

But around me, everything kept right on shifting.

"Easy," he muttered, stepping beyond me, toward the walls of shelves that had not been there before. They hadn't. I was sure of it. All the while he didn't let go, kept his hand curled around my wrist.

Then he blew my mind. Slipping his hand under the fourth

shelf from the bottom, he pushed something, and the shelves creaked open, revealing the vat of darkness beyond.

My heart slammed, hard. *"Omigod . . ."*

"Come on!" He jerked his flashlight from me to illuminate the staircase we'd used on the way up. "Let's get out of here."

My mind struggled to process everything. The staircase was secret, hidden. The heavy door must have closed after Chase ran through it, accidentally trapping me . . .

My legs felt like rubber, but I made it to the kitchen. With the muggy night air rushing me, the stench of mud welcomed. Never letting go, Pitre led me to the gaping room where we'd started, where broken windows stood like the most amazing welcoming committee in the world. I scrambled through to the backyard, where Spanish moss swayed with the breeze—and three girls stood watching.

I stopped.

"Jessica." She looked . . . fine. "What—"

She and Amber beamed—Bethany looked away.

And in that fractured moment, another kind of flash went through me, uglier than before. And I knew. I understood.

The dare Amber had given her friend hadn't been for Jessica at all. It had been mine. She and Amber had planned everything, long before we'd reached the awful mansion. They'd goaded me, played me, gotten me to give them my flashlight. When Jessica screamed, everyone had run, taking their lights with them. Leaving me alone.

They'd closed the door to the secret staircase. *They'd* waited until I was inside the fake closet.

They'd shut me in.

They'd been on the other side, waiting, knowing I was inside. In the dark. That I was scared . . .

"Trinity!"

Something dark and vicious took control of me. I spun toward Chase's voice, found him emerging through the gaping darkness. "You're okay!" he said, vaulting through the window.

I didn't wait for him to reach me. I charged him, catching him off guard as I slammed my hands against his chest. "You knew!"

The others I could understand. But him . . .

"Easy," he said, reaching for my hands.

I twisted back from him, hating the tightness in my chest. "Game over," I whispered.

He went so very still, looking beyond me to where his girl-friend stood like a vision of saintliness. "No—" he muttered.

"Liar!"

He shook his head, eyes darker than usual. "No, I swear!"

"Bullshit!" My hands were tight fists. I wanted to hit him. "You pretended to be my friend! You pretended I could trust you!"

That he was different . . . *special*.

"Trinity." His voice was softer now, lower. "This isn't what it looks like. You have to—"

"I don't have to do anything." Except leave. I very much had to do that.

"Let me explain—"

"What, you think I'm an idiot? That because my grandmother homeschooled me I'm stupid?"

"No—I didn't know—"

"Save it." I spun and started toward the front of the house, my flip-flops crunching down on broken glass.

I'm pretty sure I wouldn't have noticed if any had sliced straight through.

"Wait!"

From his voice, I knew that he was right behind me.

I kept going, didn't turn back.

"You can't just—"

This time I did stop, spin. "Don't."

From beneath a sweep of bangs I'd once fantasized about brushing from his forehead, he stared hard at me. "Let me take you home."

I laughed. I really did. It was a hard sound, ugly. "Not in this lifetime," I said as I noticed Jessica strolling toward him.

I didn't wait. I twisted back around and made my way to the street. The cars we'd come in were by the cemetery around the corner.

I walked in the opposite direction.

The night settled around me, darkness broken by puddles from the streetlamps. The house on Prytania Street was deserted, but around me manicured lawns and cars parked in the street told me life went on. I wasn't scared. Not for me, anyway. Walking down the old cracked sidewalk was peaceful in an odd sort of way. A major intersection was only a few blocks away. There I could find a taxi.

Instinctively my hand went to my back pocket, but my Black-Berry was gone.

I was so not going back for it.

Away. That was all I could think. I had to get away from them, Jessica and Amber, Chase . . .

My heart gave a cruel little thump. *Especially* Chase.

From that place—the ugliness.

From what I'd seen.

Because while the frantic search for Jessica had been staged, while me being locked in a small pitch black room had only been a joke, the strobe-light images I'd seen were *real*.

They always were.

I'd been seven years old the first time. It was my earliest memory. We'd been in Colorado by then, living in a nice little house on a huge piece of property. There'd been lots of trees, pine and aspen, towering up toward the always-blue sky. I'd been outside playing with our golden retriever, Sunshine. She'd run into a thicket after a pink ball—and I'd started to scream.

The flashes scared me, like a lightning storm dancing around me. I remembered falling, blinking, crying for Sunshine. Through the flashes I'd seen her lying on her side, so horribly still. I'd heard the whimper . . .

That's how Gran found me, curled on my side, crying. I dove into her arms and held on tight, clung to her as I tried to breathe. I was trying to tell her about Sunshine when the big dog came bounding out of the trees, running up to slobber us with doggie kisses.

Two days later we'd found her dead.

Even now, all these years later, the memory made me shiver.

The things that I saw . . . happened. They always, always happened.

I didn't notice the headlights until the car was right beside me. I tensed, prepared myself to tell Chase or Jessica or whoever it was exactly where they could go.

The shiny black Lexus stopped me. One darkly tinted window lowered, and Aunt Sara looked like she wanted to cry.

She also looked like she'd rolled straight from bed. Her long dark hair, so like my own, fell softly against a face with no makeup, making her look much younger than thirty-three. I could tell her shirt was the huge New Orleans Saints Championship tee she always slept in.

"Hey," was all she said. Maybe it was something in her voice—or maybe something in her expressive eyes—but my throat got all tight.

I don't really know what I felt. Surprise, maybe relief.

"How did you know?" I asked.

Her smile was sad. "Chase called me."

I hated the sudden salty sting in my eyes. He must have called the second I walked away. The Warehouse District where she lived wasn't that far, but still, she clearly had not hesitated.

"Come on, *cher*," she said. "Let's go home."

Home. I wasn't sure where that was anymore. I stood there a long moment, looking at this stranger who was my father's sister, my grandmother's daughter, and though we barely knew each other, something warm swelled through me. Quietly I walked to the passenger side of her gorgeous brand-new car and pulled open the door, saw the photograph.

"I found that earlier," Aunt Sara said. "Not sure why I grabbed it on the way out . . ."

But I was. Because somehow she understood. She knew. She knew how badly I needed to connect.

Numbly I picked up the faded black-and-white image, and for the first time I could remember, saw my mother.

FOUR

All my life I'd wondered. I'd dreamed. A picture, that's all I wanted. A story, a piece of jewelry, a memory. *Anything.* Something to connect me to them, my parents. Something to make them *real*.

But nothing prepared me for the faded image.

I wasn't sure what I expected. A stranger, I guess. Someone I didn't recognize, didn't know. But her . . .

My heart slammed so hard it hurt. There wasn't much light in the car, only quick flashes from the streetlamps we zipped past, but it was enough. It was enough to realize that the woman in the picture was no stranger. *I knew her.* I'd seen her before, this woman with the long dark hair and haunting, wide-set eyes, the sad, knowing smile, so many times. At night, when my eyes closed and the images took over, and my parents came to visit. I'd thought they were only dreams, fantasies of the perfect childhood I'd never had.

But as Aunt Sara cruised down Magazine Street, I realized my mother had been with me all along.

"She was beautiful," I whispered.

The lights from outside the car faded as we neared Aunt Sara's Warehouse District condo. "She was."

I was aware of the car turning, but didn't look up. "Gran said . . ." Without thinking, I lifted a hand to feather a finger along the side of my mother's face. "Gran said there weren't any pictures." I'd asked so many times. "She said they were destroyed."

"Not all of them."

I glanced up, saw that we were pulling into the private parking garage. "Do you have more?" I asked as Aunt Sara rolled down her window and slid her access card through the scanner.

"I might."

Against the picture, my fingers tightened. And even though it was just October, excitement ran through me like a kid on Christmas Eve. They were my parents, but I knew little more than their names. John Mark and Rachelle had been married less than a year when they had me. Two years later they'd both been dead. Gran had acted so odd when I asked questions, that eventually I'd stopped.

"What was she like?" The question practically shot out of me. I'd gotten the occasional story out of Gran about her son, but nothing about my mother, her daughter-in-law.

The car stopped. I looked up, realized we were parked. The engine idled. The lights shone up against a dirty concrete wall. Next to me, my grandmother's Buick waited. And Aunt Sara, well, she stared straight ahead, silky dark hair falling against her face and hiding her eyes. I saw her shoulders rise and fall.

Time slowed. It was weird. We sat in what felt like suffocating silence, even though the radio played. You would have thought I'd asked her to reveal some major secret, rather than a simple question about my mother.

It felt like forever, but it was probably a minute before she looked at me. Her eyes were dark, faraway as they met mine.

"You," she said, and her smile was soft. Kind.

Sad.

"Your mom was a lot like you."

It was weird how I jerked. They were words that should have made me feel happy. My mother, this stranger who sometimes appeared in the darkest vestiges of my sleep, was more than just a figment of my imagination. We were alike.

Connected.

But I felt like someone had thrown rocks at me. "Me?"

Aunt Sara killed the engine, plunging us into near total darkness. "There were ten years between me and your dad," she said. "I was your age when he brought your mom home."

Which meant she'd been nineteen when they died.

"But I always liked her," she said. "She was good to me." An odd sheen moved into her eyes. "Sweet, kind of quiet."

Through the dim lighting, I squinted at the faded picture of the woman in the gauzy sundress, standing next to one of those massive old live oaks that sprawled all over town. I'd never seen anything like them in Colorado. But here . . . they stood like living statues, surviving for hundreds of years. It was weird to see the huge trees thriving in areas where the storm had destroyed everything else, almost as if they were . . .

Eternal.

The word jammed into my throat, and just like at the awful old house, I shivered. It was still pretty hot outside. I knew that. But even when Aunt Sara opened her car door, the warmth didn't touch me. If I hadn't known better, I would have thought I was stepping into a Colorado night.

Numbly, I climbed from the car and followed my aunt through the dimly lit garage, where there were more open spaces than those occupied. New Orleans was recovering, but Aunt Sara said a lot of people had yet to return.

Through the shadows I was aware of the echo of our footfalls, of the brief wait for the elevator, of stepping inside and waiting while Aunt Sara entered her access code. All I could think was . . . what if? What if my parents had lived? What would it have been like if I'd been raised by them? Here? In this town?

The answer was easy. Tonight would never have happened.

The elevator opened and we crossed the short distance to Aunt Sara's condo. A hundred years before, the brick building had been a factory, then a warehouse. For a long, long time, it had sat empty, abandoned like the house on Prytania. Even now, despite the luxury condominiums on all six floors, the exposed brick hallways felt cold.

In the heat of summer, that was probably a good thing.

At the door, Aunt Sara fiddled with a series of dead bolts, which seemed odd to me, considering you had to have a code and key to get inside the building in the first place.

"How did they die?" The question blurted out before I could stop it.

With the door partially open, my aunt stilled. I appreciated that she didn't play games or ask who. "You don't know?"

Her hair shielded her expression, but I heard the caution in her voice. "Gran never liked to talk about it."

She stood still for a second or two, then shoved open the door and breezed inside. She threw on a few lights and tossed her purse on a small table, as if I wasn't waiting for an answer. So much for that appreciation I'd had a moment before.

"You don't want to tell me, either, do you?"

She kicked off one flip-flop, then another. "It's not that," she said, still brisk and matter-of-fact. "It's just . . ." She turned, and before she even spoke, I saw the change—and knew there would be no more answers tonight. *"Trinity."*

The way she said my name made me feel like someone had pointed one of those big police searchlights at me.

"Don't you think it's time to tell me?"

Automatically, I felt my throat tighten. "Tell you what?" I asked, but had a bad feeling I knew.

She frowned. "It's almost two o'clock in the morning. Chase calls me and tells me—" She broke off, sucked in a sharp breath. "Do you have any idea what I thought—" She squeezed her eyes shut, obviously struggling for control. "He asks me to come get you. So I do. And I find you walking by yourself. Do you even realize—"

The coldness bled harder, and with it came guilt. Here she was, this beautiful, successful, single woman with whom I'd had little contact for fourteen years, and suddenly she's responsible for me. She didn't ask for this.

She didn't ask for *me*.

"My God," she whispered, and then she was closing in on me, lifting a hand to my—

I stepped back and lifted my own hand.

"You're bleeding," she whispered.

Tentatively my fingers found the stickiness at the side of my forehead.

I saw it all register in her eyes, through the soft light of an old Tiffany lamp: the filth on my jeans and the tear at my knees, the copper splotches on my flip-flops. And my hands, the nails broken and palms scraped raw.

"My God." Her voice was barely more than a horrified breath. "He hurt you. That boy—"

"No," I said, not needing her to finish to realize where she was going. Teenage boy, teenage girl . . . late at night. *"No."*

But she was already reaching for her phone. "I'm calling the police—"

"No!" This time it was a shout. "That's not what happened," I practically screamed, and finally, finally she looked up from digging in her purse. "He didn't . . . *No*," I said for the fourth time. Words jammed in my throat. "He didn't touch me."

Frozen there, she looked at me. "Then what?"

"I—we—" Dangerously close to cracking, I backed away. "Just a game," I murmured with another step toward the hall. "Just a stupid mistake!"

I shouldn't have run. Even as I turned, I knew that. But I couldn't stand there one second longer, not with the way she was looking at me.

"Trin—" she called, but I slammed the bathroom door before she could finish. The hall was short, but my heart pounded as if I'd been running forever. Closing my eyes, I leaned against the hard, solid wood, willing my breath to slow—and hating the hot salty moisture stinging my eyes. No way would I let it fall. No way would I cry. They weren't worth it. None of them.

Not even Chase.

My throat burned. *Chase.*

Through the darkness of my mind, I could see his smile, the warmth in his heavy-lidded blue eyes and the curve of his mouth, how incredibly hot he looked when he didn't shave for a few days. Even in chemistry goggles, he had a way of looking drop-dead—

Drop. Dead. They were good words. Because that's all he would ever be to me again. Dead.

Sucking in a deep breath, I opened my eyes, and saw the blood. Through the glow of the wall-mounted cherub sconces, the antique oval mirror revealed everything: the blood on my forehead and the bruise already forming; the dark hair I'd meticulously flatironed earlier that evening, stringy now, matted with sweat and mud and I didn't even want to know what else. The makeup I'd carefully applied, gone, revealing scratches and the cluster of freckles I tried to cover up.

Jerking, I ripped off my clothes and stepped into the shower. It took a while for the hot water to come, but when it did I let it rain down on me for a long, long time, plastering my hair against my face and washing away every trace of grime and blood and disappointment. Of shame, and foolishness.

When the scorching water went cold and I stepped from the shower, I found a different girl staring back at me, long dark hair combed slick and clean, face flushed from the heat, eyes dark, bright, and confident. This time they were *her* eyes, my mother's eyes, and somehow that made me feel stronger.

"Trinity?" Aunt Sara's voice startled me. For a few minutes there, I'd forgotten.

"Chase is here."

FIVE

My heart pretty much leapt. I hated the reaction, I did. It was foolish and totally emo, but one hundred percent involuntary—and five hundred thousand percent devastating.

Hurrying across the slate floor, I yanked open the door and almost plowed into my aunt. "I don't want to talk to him."

She stepped back when it became clear I wasn't stopping, somehow not spilling a drop from the big mug in her hands. "He's downstairs, Trin . . . he's been here about five minutes."

The flash of relief almost knocked me over. *Downstairs,* of course. No one could get upstairs without card access. "Tell him to go away."

"I told him you were asleep," she said, trailing behind me. "But he said it's important."

I didn't know why I moved into the main room of the condo. And I totally didn't know why I went to the window, where through the slats of the wood blinds I could barely make out a shadow on the porch below. He stood so very still, crazy still for a guy like Chase, who was always in motion.

The salty sting in my eyes surprised me. So did the stab of longing. *Chase was here.* All I had to do was buzz him up and—

And what?

I was not his girlfriend. I wasn't even his friend, for that matter. I was just the new kid in school. His lab partner.

The night's entertainment.

"Trinity?"

I spun toward my aunt, saw the lingering sheen of concern and confusion. I knew what she thought, still, even though I'd denied it. The grandfather clock was about to chime two in the morning, and now Chase was downstairs, wanting to talk to me.

I was lucky she hadn't already called the cops.

"Please," I said, and if my voice thinned a little on the word, we both pretended it didn't. "Just make him go away."

She frowned. But it was tender somehow, and the compassion in her eyes touched me. For so long, there'd been only Gran, and while I'd loved her with all my heart, she'd always been pretty closed. And a whole lot older than me.

Aunt Sara was, well, she was young and beautiful and . . . cool. I really wanted her to like me.

"Okay," she said, and as she crossed to the intercom, I knew that when she came back, I had some serious explaining to do.

"Chase," she said in that thick drawl of hers, as if she caressed each word as it came out. I'd heard Southern accents on TV, even alleged New Orleans accents. But they'd seemed hokey. I'd thought if people in the South really talked like that—

They didn't. At least, not Aunt Sara. Her voice was . . . The only words I could come up with were warm and rich.

"You need to get on out of here," she said.

"But—" He looked up and I froze, although I knew it was too

late. He saw me standing there, silhouetted through the slats of the blinds. ". . . just . . . she's okay?"

I winced, wrapping my arms around my body and hugging tightly. All I had to do was ask my aunt for five minutes—

"She's with me," Aunt Sara said.

But she did not say that I was okay.

"Then . . ." Unsure, I realized. Chase Bonaventure, star quarterback of the Our Lady of Enduring Grace football team and Mr. Everything, sounded unsure. "Tell her I was here."

From my perch five stories up, I watched him kick something.

". . . and that I'm sorry."

Words were just that. Words. A whisper of breath. They had no form or substance. They weren't supposed to touch.

But I would have sworn something soft and aching settled around me.

"Good-bye, Chase," Aunt Sara said with complete and total authority, leaving no doubt the conversation was over. But he didn't move, just stayed on the top step, tall, contained, while I did the only thing I could. I counted, making it all the way to ninety-seven before he turned and disappeared into the darkness.

I made myself swallow, hating that tearing feeling deep inside, as if I'd just lost my best friend.

"I'm ready when you are."

I turned to find Aunt Sara near the breakfast bar separating the kitchen from the main room. The whole place was an odd combination of industrial and Old World chic, exposed brick walls with heavy furniture in dark woods, wrought iron and delicate china, crosses and fleur-de-lis hanging adjacent to huge, almost angry, modern art. Art my aunt had created. Somehow it all worked.

Part of me wanted to pretend I had no idea what she was talking about. But already I knew her well enough to know that wasn't an option.

"I made you some cocoa," she said, tracking me as I made my way barefoot across the wood floor.

With stainless-steel appliances and dark granite, the kitchen should have felt cold. But Aunt Sara had transformed the space into something cozy and welcoming. Maybe it was the rich fabrics, or maybe the stylish canisters and eclectic collection of French chefs in all shapes and sizes, the scattering of gardenia votives.

Or maybe, in that moment, it was the two mugs of hot chocolate topped with Cool Whip and sprinkles of cinnamon.

"Thank you," I said, slipping onto the stool next to hers. On the counter, I noticed her laptop open to a spreadsheet. A real estate agent, she was always doing something on the computer.

Her hair was long and wavy like mine, but softer, the color of pecans. A few layers framed her face, a sweep of long bangs slipped against her right eye. Pushing them back, she gave me one of those *I'm-still-waiting* smiles, then reached for her mug and drew it to her mouth.

I did the same. Whipped cream came first, followed by an explosion of cocoa. And for that one little moment, my world felt totally and completely right.

"Trinity."

So much for the moment.

"I get that we don't know each other that well," she said as I looked up. "But I made my mother a promise, and as long as I'm responsible for you . . ." She set down her mug. "I'm on your side, you know."

I tensed.

"You said it was just a game," she said quietly. "But Chase did not sound like he was playing." She hesitated for a long, awkward moment. "I want to know why."

Everything played back in my mind, every single moment,

every single lie. "Because I know who he is now," I whispered. "And he knows the game is over."

"What game, *cher*? What game is over?"

"The one where I believe everything he says."

"Trinity." Her eyes darkened. *"What happened?"*

I stared at the remains of whipped cream melting into the chocolate. Funny how quickly it could all just . . . go away.

"We were hanging out in the Quarter," I murmured. "On Bourbon." Dancing to the music spilling from the clubs. Laughing. Daring each other to have our palms read by the psychics in Jackson Square.

Maybe the way the woman with the long silver hair crossed herself before hurrying away should have warned me.

"I thought we were killing time," I said, as Aunt Sara once again dragged her cocoa toward her mouth. "We went to this old house—"

She stilled. "What old house?"

"In the Garden District . . . close to where you picked me up. It was big and beautiful—"

The mug hit the granite. Chocolate sloshed onto her hand.

She made no move to wipe it away, even though I knew how hot the cocoa was.

"The house on Prytania Street," she whispered.

"You *know* it?"

She nodded, dark hair sliding in to cover the strange glow in her eyes.

"How? Is it famous or—"

"Everyone knows that place."

She was so not telling me something. "They said it's haunted," I said, fishing. "That people died there."

She looked away, down to where the spilled chocolate puddled on the granite. And all I could wonder was *why*? Why did she look so pale? Why wouldn't she look at me? What did she know?

"They should have torn that place down a long time ago," she murmured.

I sat a little straighter. "Why? What happened?"

Without warning she looked up. Hair hung in her face, but she made no move to push it away. "It's not what happened," she said. "It's what *could* happen."

Lights glared all around me, but for a second the darkness returned, and with it the image of Jessica strewn out on the dirty mattress.

"What?" I pressed. "What could happen there?"

What had I seen?

Maybe it was the stark contrast between her dark hair and cheeks many hours removed from fresh makeup. Or maybe something altogether different. All I knew was that for a second there, my aunt looked like she'd come face-to-face with something that terrified her.

"Anything," she said. "Anything could happen there." Her eyes were narrow, probing, as if somehow she, too, saw.

Somehow she, too, knew.

"I want you to stay away from that place," she said, standing. "I mean it, Trinity Rose." The words were sharp, the use of my middle name a first. "Don't go back there again."

This time, it was she who walked away, leaving me staring after her.

What in God's name was that about?

I'm not sure how much longer I sat there, a while, long enough for the cocoa to go cold. The lights still hummed around me. I was in my aunt's ultra-funky, ultra-secure condo. I was safe. I knew that.

But that was just my body.

The rest of me . . . I was back at the house on Prytania, where in the darkness, cold bled. And the shaking wouldn't stop. Not because of what Jessica and Amber had done. Not even because of

Chase, and how badly it hurt to know that every time he'd smiled at me, inside he'd been laughing.

And not because of my aunt, and the terror I'd seen in her eyes.

No, I shook because of what I'd seen.

And what I knew was going to happen.

There was no way to avoid him.

The second I walked onto campus Monday morning, I saw him, standing in the shade of an oak just beyond the main walkway.

If I hadn't known better—*which I totally did*—I would have sworn he was waiting for me.

Once, Our Lady of Enduring Grace Academy had been a place of solitude and reflection. Built as a monastery over a hundred years before, the sprawling campus seemed an unlikely place for a high school. The old, Gothic-like brick buildings looked as if they belonged in the French countryside. Statues dotted the courtyards. Everywhere you turned, there was either an angel or a saint, or some beautiful old fountain.

Every morning during the first week of school the fountains had been like giant bubble baths—apparently, adding detergent to the water was a time-honored tradition.

The campus was huge, but the old stone wall encircling the buildings allowed for one point of entry in the front and one in the back. That meant there was no getting to homeroom without him seeing me.

Of course, he'd be in homeroom, too. True, he sat two rows over, but Chase was my lab partner . . .

Now he stood in the shade of a massive oak, this one with a big swooping branch a foot off the ground, making a perfect bench. Nearby, the angel atop the main fountain lifted her arms to the clouds drifting across the ridiculously blue sky, as if invoking some higher power.

In that moment, I could relate.

He looked . . . well, he looked like Chase always looked—hot. I hated that. I really did. I didn't want to feel that little twist in my stomach that I'd felt the second he walked into homeroom back on the first day of school, when the warm blue gleam of his eyes had found mine, and those dimples had flashed. I didn't want my throat to tighten, or my palms to sweat.

But they did. It was different, though. This time it was different. Because despite my unwanted reaction to how good he looked— even in the drab school uniform of navy pants and a white golf shirt—disappointment and betrayal ran through me like ice water.

Pushing away from the tree, he started toward me, his eyes on mine, making it impossible to look away. And, even though he was still fifteen feet away, he held me somehow, held me so very still, preventing me from so much as breathing.

"Tell her I was here . . . and that I'm sorry."

"Trinity."

I barely had time to glance over my shoulder before Pitre jogged up beside me.

"Hey." Despite how tough Chase's favorite receiver looked with the coiled snake tattoo around his bicep, he hesitated, as if not sure what to say. "Almost called you yesterday—"

I found a smile. It was tight, but real. "No need," I said.

His gaze flicked down to a faint scrape visible just below my skirt, then back up. "Wasn't sure—"

I cut him off. "I'm fine."

"If I'd had any idea," he muttered, frowning, "I would have stopped her."

Him, I believed. He was one of the last people Jessica would have drawn into her vicious little game. "No harm."

"One of these days it's going to catch up with her. She's going to screw over the wrong person," he said, his gaze fixed beyond me.

"Somehow," I said, turning to see what he was looking at, "Jessica doesn't strike me as being too worried about—"

The girls stood in a tight, closed group beside the angel fountain—Jessica and Amber and several others—laughing, whispering so that their voices carried, but the tinkling of the water drowned out their words.

"Karma," I muttered.

The sun shone, but for a split second everything turned cloudy, distorted like a smeared watercolor painting.

And the water turned red.

I stood frozen as the crimson tide gathered, spilling over the angel with the lifted arms and streaming down her robes, splashing all over Jessica. She kept talking, kept laughing, made no move to step away or wipe away the blood . . .

"Trinity?"

I blinked and the fog cleared, and Pitre was staring at me again, much like the night at the house.

"You can't let them get to you like that," he was saying, and with his words I looked beyond him, to the girls by the fountain. There was no red. Once again the water ran clear, trickling gently against the angel.

". . . better get going," Pitre said. "Can't afford another tardy."

I made myself smile, because despite his tough-guy exterior and the fact he sometimes drank too much, on the inside I was pretty sure he was a cupcake. I'd heard about a dad in prison and a mom who worked two jobs to keep him in school, a brother who was a rookie cop, but I didn't know if they were true. I hoped they weren't. Pitre had been one of the first to make me feel welcome.

Maybe that's because, like me, he was an outsider.

The bell rang, and Jessica and her friends scattered. I knew I had to get going, too, but had no desire to—

I turned back toward the beautiful old oak, with its draping branches and swaying Spanish moss.

Chase was gone.

Relief, I told myself. That's what I felt. But the sharp edges felt more like disappointment.

Annoyed, I hurried to Building A and retrieved my chemistry text from my locker before heading to homeroom. The routine was starting to feel familiar, even if I still saw more strangers than friends. Until Enduring Grace, I'd never stepped in a school, public or private. In Colorado, the nearest had been over thirty miles away, so Gran had taught me herself. She'd done a pretty good job, too. According to the state of Louisiana, I was a junior. But I could have tested out of high school altogether.

I didn't want that. I didn't want to be a prodigy, or special. I wanted to be like everyone else. And that meant going to high school even if I'd already learned most everything they were teaching. I wanted to hang out with kids my age, to walk the crowded halls and eat in the cafeteria (even if the food sucked), to go to football games on Friday nights and—

Have a boyfriend.

It was ridiculous all the things I'd never done, considering I would turn seventeen in the spring.

My steps slowed as I neared homeroom. But my thoughts didn't. Because I knew who would be in there. I'd gotten lucky in the courtyard. I'd managed to avoid him. But once I stepped inside the classroom, there'd be no escaping the inevitable.

Instinctively I lifted a hand to shift my hair over a small cut at my temple. Makeup hid the greenish bruise. Then, as the final bell rang, I raised my chin and swung into Coach Cameron's room.

SIX

"Lucas said he got hurt."

I looked up from my backpack as Victoria, the first person who'd invited me to eat lunch at her table, dropped down beside me on the concrete bench. She was in Coach Cameron's homeroom, too. Her on-again, off-again boyfriend Lucas played tackle on the football team.

"That's why he wasn't in homeroom," she said. "Lucas said Coach C. wanted Chase to get treatment."

I absorbed the information, tried to play it cool. The last thing I wanted was Victoria to know how hard my heart started to pound.

But despite how many times I told myself I didn't want to see him, despite all the ways I'd fantasized about blowing him off, the second I'd swung into homeroom and found Chase's desk empty, it was like someone had let the air right out of me.

"Oh."

Victoria took a swig from her water bottle. With her long

blond hair and killer green eyes, she was one of the most beautiful girls I'd ever seen. She had this exotic look to her, and from what I understood, she was an amazing gymnast.

"Oh?" she repeated. "That's it? That's all? '*Oh?*'"

I shrugged. "What else would I say?" I wasn't about to ask any of the questions tripping through me, like when did he get hurt and how bad was it?

"Oh, I don't know. Maybe you'd give me a few details, since you were with him when it happened."

A warm breeze blew through the oaks crowding the courtyard. The trees here were a little smaller, not as old, but they still had moss dangling from them. Even on the few occasions I'd been alone, it was always as if someone else was there—or a lot of some-ones. Because of the shifting moss, I told myself. It created an . . . energy.

"I don't know what you're talking about—" I started, but Victoria's wide smile stopped me.

"Come on," she said. "I *saw* the pictures."

I felt myself still. "Pictures?"

"On Jessica's Facebook page. That's where it happened, right? At that old house?"

I blinked. Tried to focus. Didn't know what question to ask first.

Victoria spared me that decision. "I can't believe you went there," she said in a rush. "I mean, there's just no way. You couldn't pay me a million dollars to go there—"

"Why?" Watching Victoria, I fumbled for my thermos. The water inside would be warm enough to break the growing chill.

"Oh, I don't know . . . because people who go there die?"

That got me. I mean, that really *got me*. I found my thermos and unscrewed the lid, pretended like my heart was not hammering so hard it hurt. "That's a pretty blanket statement."

"Chase got hurt, didn't he?"

"Hurt isn't the same thing as dying."

"Then why was everyone running?"

Clearly I needed to see the pictures Jessica had taken it upon herself to share with the world. "We were just playing a game," I said.

"Ha-ha then. Looks like it was so much fun."

I took a swallow, waited for the warmth. I mean, holy crap. This was New Orleans. It was early October. The temperature was hotter than the dead of summer in Colorado, and the humidity made everything feel like a steam bath. I was so-o-o tired of being cold. It made no sense. I could hang with subfreezing temperatures and blizzards, but here in the sauna of the Deep South, I couldn't stop shaking.

"Don't look now, but there he is."

What was it about someone telling you what not to do? As soon as someone says not to turn around, that's exactly what you do. Foolishly I looked toward the gym as Chase, Drew, and Victoria's boyfriend Lucas came around the corner. And for the first time, I noticed the limp.

When had *that* happened?

And why hadn't *I* noticed?

"What's with you two anyway?" Victoria asked.

I looked back to the knobby roots of the old oaks. Chase had been running, I knew that. Through the darkness, I'd heard him shouting, seen him come rushing from the house . . .

"Nothing," I said.

"Yeah, I guess that's why he won't stop looking over here, huh?"

I would not let myself look. If I had, I would have seen Jessica closing in.

"Trinnie!" she said, descending on me like we were long lost friends. "There you are! I've been trying to find you all day!"

Jessica Morgenthal was the last person I wanted to see, but no way would I give her the satisfaction of acting like I cared one way or the other—or to remind her that she'd already seen me at least four times.

I stood.

"I'm so glad you're okay," she shocked me by saying. Then she blew my mind. She wrapped her arms around me, smothering me in the thick scent of hair spray and expensive perfume. "I was so worried."

I focused on the sky. It was blue, a really vivid blue, with thin, swirling clouds. I focused on that, on the song of the birds from somewhere unseen, determined not to allow the—

But even as the edges blurred, I knew it wouldn't work. Once the visions began, once the invisible lightning struck, they never went away.

Not until what I saw happened.

No one knew. Despite the disturbing images playing through my mind, I went through the right motions, pulling back from Jessica and taking the phone she offered me—my BlackBerry, which she allegedly found when she'd gone back inside the house. I even think I said "no big deal" when she apologized for freaking me out.

"It was just a game," she'd said with a beautiful, model-perfect, fake-as-her-tan smile. "Truth or dare. I thought you knew that."

Twelve hours later, I wondered what she'd been trying to prove—or who she'd been trying to impress.

Aunt Sara was already in bed. She had a meeting in the morning and wanted to be at her best. I had a history test and should have been asleep, too—or at the very least studying—but I couldn't stop looking at the pictures. The social network thing was crazy addictive.

I'd been playing on Facebook ever since Victoria insisted I join. At first, she'd been my only Facebook friend. But gradually my list had grown, so that it now included over two hundred people I didn't even know.

How did *that* happen?

Anyway. I didn't post much, didn't really know what to say:

Trinity Monsour . . . saw Brad Pitt on Magazine Street.
Trinity Monsour . . . had the most amazing dream last night.
Trinity Monsour . . . wishes things were different.
Trinity Monsour . . . can't get warm.
Trinity Monsour . . . knows something bad is about to happen.

I couldn't see myself announcing any of that to the world.

But Jessica didn't have the same misgivings. She posted *everything*. And I do mean everything.

Jessica Morgenthal . . . is having a bad hair day.
Jessica Morgenthal . . . loves kissing Chase Bonaventure.
Jessica Morgenthal . . . got a new pair of jeans.
Jessica Morgenthal . . . can't wait to go out.

And, her most recent post, from early Sunday morning:

Jessica Morgenthal . . . just had some serious fun.

The pictures were all there, in an album titled, TRUTH OR DARE PRYTANIA STYLE. She must have taken them with her phone—that's why I hadn't realized what she was doing. Some I recognized. The rest I was pretty sure she'd taken after I left. And I'm not sure what unnerved me more, the pictures of the votives surrounding the bloodstained mattresses—or those of me and Chase.

All along I'd been telling myself it was nothing. Just a casual flirtation, an unreciprocated crush. He was the big guy on campus, a gifted athlete and good student, totally hot, but oddly approachable. Because of his movie-star smile, the way I imagined that he looked at me.

Saturday night, I'd realized my mistake.

Now I had to wonder. And apparently, Jessica was, too.

It was all there in her photo album, for me and her two thousand other "friends" to see:

1.   Chase standing close to me, his hand brushing mine.
2.   Chase looking at me with quiet apology in his eyes. (Realistically, no one else would know he was looking at me, because I wasn't in the picture. But I knew. I remembered. And I bet Jessica did, too.)
3.   Me, unable to hide the longing on my face (again, most people would have no way of knowing I'd been watching Chase . . .).
4.   Me running from the house, pale and terrified.
5.   Chase standing still as a statue, with murder in his eyes. (In truth, I had no idea when this picture was taken, or what was going on. But sitting cross-legged on my bed with my laptop dragged close, I had this little fantasy . . .)

I'm not sure when I drifted off. One minute I was staring at Chase, wondering, and then the next thing I knew I was in the upstairs room of the house on Prytania.

The candles were lit. They were white, giving off flickering light.

They surrounded the mattresses and smelled of vanilla. That was odd. Amid all the darkness and grime, the scent of vanilla. Then she screamed.

I spun. Or at least I tried to. My body didn't want to move. It was like an invisible spiderweb held me in place, and no matter how hard I struggled, I couldn't move. Couldn't turn. Could only stand there, trapped, listening to her scream . . .

"Help me! Please! Someone help me!"

I fought harder.

"I'm sorry," she sobbed. "So sorry . . ."

"Hang on," I tried to whisper, but the words didn't make it past my throat. Hang on!

"Don't leave me here," she cried, and her voice, thin and terrified, broke. "Please . . ."

I couldn't take it. I couldn't stand the horror in her voice one second longer, knew I had to turn, had to find some way to get to her and—

I twisted. The web broke. And my body, not ready for the unexpected release, dropped to the floor. I fell, landed on my knees, and looked up.

She was there, on the mattress, just like I'd seen over and over again. Her feet were bare. Her skin was pale. Her eyes . . . dark. Terrified.

Slowly they met mine, and what I saw in them chilled me to the core.

"Jessica!" I surged to my feet and lunged for her, but the ground gave way and I fell through the shadows, while the air turned thick, and the cold swallowed me . . .

"Trinity!"

I fought, flailed, searched for something to grab onto. Tried to breathe . . .

"Trinity!"

The voice came at me through the watery haze, and like a life-line, I reached for it, grabbed it.

"Wake up, *cher*. Wake up!"

The command registered, and I made myself blink, gasp. And with the sweet rush of breath came the grainy image of my aunt leaning over me, the feel of her cold hands, one against the side of my face, the other holding my hand.

"That's it," she said in that thick, wonderful voice of hers, the one that reminded me of honey. "That's my girl. Come on back to me."

I blinked again, and this time focus returned, and detail registered. I was in my bed. The lamp was still on. My laptop was beside me, the screen dark. On the small table, green numerals on my clock glowed 5:26.

I took it all in, knew that I was safe. But my body wouldn't stop shaking, and even though I was cold, my oversized T-shirt clung to me as if I actually had fallen through water . . .

"Oh, God," I whispered, coughing on the sudden rush of oxygen. "I was there . . ."

"Oh, *cher*." My aunt pulled me into her arms and held me, running her hands along my body as if it was vitally important that she touch me, all of me.

From the moment my grandmother died, from the moment I'd stepped into this strange world of New Orleans—my parents' world, the world I'd been born into but had no memory of—I'd been trying to be strong. I'd been smiling at all the right times, doing all the right things, trying like crazy to ignore the cold mist that kept seeping deeper into my bones. If I ignored it, it would go away. If I ignored it, nothing bad would happen.

But in the chilling predawn of that Tuesday morning, there was no ignoring the dream or the shaking, or the knowledge that something bad had happened.

"It's okay," Aunt Sara promised, and for the first time I quit fighting, quit pretending, just sank into her arms and drank in the feel of her hugging me. "You're okay!"

"I was there," I said again. *"I was there."*

She pulled back and framed my face with her hands. "You're here, Trinity. You've been here all night."

I shook my head, knew she would never understand. "No." My throat constricted on the word. "I was . . . *there*."

Through the side-swept bangs, Aunt Sara's eyes met mine. "Where, Trinity?" The question surprised me. "Where were you?"

I swallowed. Tried to breathe normally. "The house . . ."

"On Prytania."

It wasn't a question. She knew. And when she spoke again, her eyes glowed like black diamonds. "Were you alone?"

"No."

"Did someone hurt you?"

At the time, the weirdness of her questions didn't register. "I fell . . ."

"Did you get hurt?"

"Water." That's what it was. Water. I'd fallen through water. ". . . so cold."

Against my arms, Aunt Sara's hands began to rub. "Trinity, honey, listen to me. Whatever happened, wherever you went, you're with me now, okay? You're safe."

She didn't think I was crazy. Can I tell you how amazing that was? "But she's not," I whispered. "She's hurt."

Aunt Sara stilled. "Who, sweetie? Who's hurt?"

I didn't want to say the name. I didn't want it to be true.

But I knew that it was. *"Jessica."*

I had to call. When she answered I was going to feel ridiculous, but I had to call. I had to know.

With Aunt Sara on the bar stool next to me, her pale hands

wrapped around her jumbo *Café Du Monde* mug, I powered on my phone. The battery had been dead when Jessica returned it the day before. Now it was charged, and I made myself scroll through the call history for her number. Then I pushed the call button.

It was 6:30 in the morning. School started in a little over an hour. She should be awake . . . I knew that. Every morning, Jessica Morgenthal arrived at Enduring Grace absolutely perfect. Perfect hair, perfect makeup, perfect . . . everything. And there was no way she could achieve that in anything less than an hour. So she should be awake—

But her phone just rang.

I glanced at Aunt Sara. She had a day full of meetings planned, but hadn't even showered yet. She just sat there with tangled morning hair and no makeup, watching me as if this kind of thing happened every day.

I shook my head on the fifth ring. After the sixth, I got voice mail. "Hey, y'all . . . it's Jess. I didn't answer . . . get a clue. If it's important, leave a message. If not . . . you lose."

I hung up.

I got there early. Only by fifteen minutes, but it was crazy what a difference those minutes made. Cars of all sizes and makes crowded the staff parking lot, but only a pink convertible VW sat in the student lot. Not even the buses had shown up. Our Lady of Enduring Grace still slept.

It was one of those hazy mornings, the sky gray and cloudy, the breeze soft but steady. The lifting fog left a mist hovering just off the ground, making the oaks look more like shadowy specters.

Annoyed, I plopped down on a stone bench, pulled out my history notebook, and waited. I still had that test in a few hours and kept blanking on the generals.

By the time the bell rang twenty minutes later, everyone else had arrived.

Everyone except Jessica.

"So where is she?"

Amber looked up from her phone. If possible, she looked even skinnier than usual. "That's just it," she said, and her voice shook. "No one knows."

"What do you mean nobody knows?" Victoria asked. "She's sick, right?"

Amber's lips were dry. Her eyes, normally a pretty light brown, looked black. "She's not sick."

We'd just finished lunch. We had fifteen minutes until class resumed. For me, history was up next. We stood at the far side of the courtyard, near a climbing rose. At first, it had been only a few of us. Now a small crowd grew.

People were starting to find out. Rumors were starting to spread. Everyone wanted to know.

"Bethany texted me," Amber said. "The police are there right now."

"The police?" Again, that was Victoria, voicing all that I did not trust myself to say. "Why the police?"

Amber glanced at another text before answering. "Bethie says Jess went to bed early last night, said she had a headache. But this morning she didn't come down for breakfast, so their mom went to check on her."

I took an instinctive step back.

". . . but she wasn't there. Her purse was gone, her keys, her car."

"That doesn't mean anything," Madison, another of the cheerleaders, said. I didn't know her well, but she seemed more down-to-earth. "You know Jessica. She probably just needed to clear her head after yesterday. It's not like it would be the first time."

"Then why isn't she answering *me*?" Amber practically shrieked. "I'm her best friend!"

"Maybe the battery is dead—"

"Or she can't! Maybe that perv who killed those two girls last year saw Jessie and thought she was pretty . . ."

Around me, everything blurred, all the trees and benches and fountains and statues. I tried to latch onto what Victoria was saying, but I couldn't get past Amber's words: "*. . . that perv who killed those two girls last year . . .*"

Help me, please!

Jessica was in trouble. I knew that. I *knew* that, even if no one else did.

And I knew where she was.

Don't leave me here!

"I gotta go," I said, and then I was turning away and hurrying across the courtyard, trying not to run, or scream. I had to tell someone. I knew that, too. I had to tell the police, make them go to the house on Prytania. I had to—

"Trinity!"

I didn't see him until it was too late. I was so lost in my own panic that I barely knew where I was, much less that Chase Bonaventure had stepped into my path.

SEVEN

He reached for me as I stumbled, put his hands to my arms and held me that way until I looked up at him. Even then, I'm not sure what I saw . . . Chase, yes, the way he was looking at me, the threadbare remnants of something fragile and impossible in the blue of his eyes.

But she was there, too . . . Jessica. On that mattress.

Crying.

Begging.

"Hey—" His voice was strained. "You okay?"

I tried to bring him into focus. Tried to *breathe,* to think about anything other than the way his hands felt against my flesh. Warm. They were so warm. And I was so cold.

"Yeah. No—I . . ." Words and thoughts jumbled. "I gotta go—"

"No," he said quietly. So very, very quietly. "You don't."

I stilled, looked up at the glint of pure steel in his eyes.

"Pretending I don't exist doesn't make it true."

The quiet words wound through me, tightening like a strong, punishing cord. I wanted to deny them, deny that I'd been doing something as silly as turning left when he turned right, but the truth hovered in the shadows between us.

"Maybe I don't have anything to say—"

"Then listen," he said, and something cruel and ragged pierced deep. I'd listened before. That was the problem.

"I heard about Jessica—" I started, but he did not let me finish.

"I don't want to talk about her."

I swallowed hard, didn't understand. Their relationship highs and lows were legendary around school, but they'd been together a long time.

"It's okay," I said. "What happened Saturday doesn't matter anymore—whatever you want to say doesn't need to be said. I know you're worried—"

"About you." His words sliced through mine like a soft, gentle knife. "Because it does matter," he said. "*She* made it matter."

I stood there in the mist that had never fully lifted, trying to make sense of what he was saying. "I don't understand . . ."

The lines of his face tightened, bringing shadows that had not been there before. "Jessica doesn't know when to stop. She's *never* known when to stop. When one game fails, she tries another one."

"Game? What are you talking about? She's missing. She didn't come home last night—"

His eyes went flat cold. "But she did drive away. She drove away, Trinity. No one made her. She told her parents good night, then crawled out her window and drove away—just like she did the last time we broke up."

That stopped me. "You broke up?"

"Two weeks ago," he said. "That's what Saturday night was about, what all of this is about: her attempt to punish us—"

Us?

"No." I stepped back as the breeze slapped hair against my face. Just . . . no. I'd seen her. I'd seen her in the house on the bed. I'd heard her cry out. "*It's not a game!* She's in trouble."

Chase frowned. "Trinity—"

I took another step back, knew there was no point trying to make him understand. Because he wouldn't.

"I have go," I said again, and this time I didn't give him a chance to say anything else. I spun around and headed toward the water-soaked angel towering up against the gray sky. My history test would have to wait.

I had to talk to the police.

"When was the last time you saw Jessica Morgenthal?"

In the movies, you could tell a cop a mile away. They either had that hard-ass look that warned everyone to keep their distance, or they were all tough and edgy—and sexy as sin.

Detectives Aaron LaSalle and DeMarcus Jackson didn't fit into either of those camps, though neither was what my grandmother would have called hard on the eyes. They were younger than I'd been expecting, and they both looked like they could blend into any crowd, anywhere, and no one would think twice about it.

And it was strange, because even though I'd had Aunt Sara call them, the way they kept looking at me made me feel like they would have showed up at the condo sooner or later anyway.

"Yesterday at school," I said. We'd spent the first ten or fifteen minutes on casual chitchat, all phony getting-to-know-you kind of stuff. They'd asked me a lot of questions about Colorado—and what I thought about New Orleans. And the Saints. All this time after they'd broken an alleged curse to win the Super Bowl, people still talked like the game had been yesterday.

Aunt Sara was great. She sat right next to me on her shabby-chic sofa, not quite touching me, but definitely positioned between me and the detectives. LaSalle sat. Jackson didn't.

I had the distinct feeling he rarely did. There was an edginess about him, a raw energy like an animal constantly on guard.

"She gave me back my cell phone," I added. "I'd lost it Saturday night."

"When you were out together," LaSalle clarified.

"Yes."

"And how would you describe your relationship with Miss Morgenthal?"

It was a good thing I hadn't just taken a drink of the water Aunt Sara had handed me. I totally would have spewed. Miss Morgenthal . . . it sounded so prim and proper.

"We just met," I said, impatient. My nerves jittered. I'd had it with the small talk, but didn't know how to blurt out what I needed to tell them. "We go to the same school."

"So you're friends?" Detective Jackson asked.

"We have a few classes together. We talk."

"And play games?" Detective LaSalle's stare was hard. He sat a good four feet from me, but I felt like he'd pinned me against the sofa.

Aunt Sara sat straighter and leaned forward. "Detective." I wasn't sure how she did it, but she made the title sound like a sugar-coated slap. "I'm quite sure you have your reasons for your questions, but maybe we should listen to what my niece has to say."

It was an amazing transformation. Detective Steely Eyes almost seemed to melt right before me, morphing from all-business to good ole Southern boy charmer. When he spoke, even his voice was different, all soft, rounded edges and lazy drawl. "Of course, Ms. Monsour . . . or can I call you Sara?"

My aunt didn't smile, although the detective sure did. "Sara is fine."

I'm not sure why I wanted to smile, but the I'm-not-taking-any-bullshit tone to my aunt's voice sure got everyone's attention.

"Sara then," he agreed. "We appreciate your efforts to help us locate Miss Morgenthal, but you need to know we were headed here this afternoon, anyway."

Bingo.

My aunt, looking totally hot in skinny jeans and a tight-fitting black top, her hair artfully messy, frowned. "I don't understand—"

But I did. "Look, I don't know who told you what," I said, starting to feel sick to my stomach, "but you need to listen to me. Jessica is in trouble."

Detective Jackson, uncomfortably quiet through the majority of the exchange, stepped forward. With the diamond stud in his left ear and tidy cornrows covering his head, he didn't look a day over twenty, but I was guessing that he probably was. He was tall, lean, dressed GQ-like. "What kind of trouble?"

"I—" The words stuck in my throat. "I heard about those other two girls. The ones that vanished last year."

"What do you know about that?" LaSalle asked.

"Not much." Just that they'd been young and beautiful, and then they were gone. "It's just . . . Jessica is really scared. What if the same guy has her?"

"Scared," Detective Jackson repeated. "And how do you know that?"

Oh, crap. "I just do."

LaSalle stood. "Where is she, Trinity? Tell us where to find her."

I saw the way they were looking at me and knew what they thought. I thought about Chase and what he thought, that Jessica's disappearance was some big, attention-grabbing game. And man, did I want him to be right.

"There's a house on Prytania Street," I made myself say. "It's deserted—"

Aunt Sara swung toward me. Her eyes were huge, dark. *"Trinity!"*

The absolute dread in her voice made me feel about two inches tall. "It's not like that," I said, hating how my voice shook. "I-I had a dream. I saw her."

"A dream," Detective Jackson repeated. His eyes were narrow now. "And what were you doing in this dream? Playing another game? Getting a little revenge . . ."

Aunt Sara surged to her feet. "Don't be ridiculous!" she shouted. Truly, it was a shout. My chic, put-together aunt went after him like a furious mama bear. I'd never seen anything like it. "*We* called *you*," she reminded. "We called you because my niece is worried and wants to help, even though that girl has been nothing but a total bitch. Yet you stand here and accuse Trinity . . ."

Eyes on fire, she stepped toward Detective LaSalle, and I'd swear to God he took a step back. "Look at her," she said, sweeping an arm toward me. "She's a kid. A scared kid."

Detective LaSalle's features closed up, his face getting all stony and movie-cop like. "I've seen worse."

Jackson came around the dainty wingback chair. "Miss Monsour," he said—not Sara like his partner had been saying, "your niece claims knowledge of the victim's whereabouts."

"That doesn't mean she's involved."

The two cops exchanged a quick, skeptical glance.

"If she was involved, do you really think she would come forward?" Aunt Sara asked.

LaSalle frowned, focusing on Aunt Sara like he really hated what he had to say. "All due respect, ma'am, but what better way to play innocent, than to play hero?"

"You're wasting time." That was me. Finally I found my voice again, and my courage. I'd been raised to respect authority, but they were all missing the point.

"Doubt me if you want, but you need to go," I said, joining them in the center of the room. "Seriously. You need to go to that house."

Before it was too late.

LaSalle looked at me long and hard, as if I belonged in a mental hospital, then flipped open a small notebook and jotted something down. I could only imagine what.

"And did you . . . happen to dream *why* she was there? To meet someone maybe? To find something?"

They were good questions, ones I'd asked myself. But I had no answers. "No."

Soon after, they both left. They claimed they were headed to the house. Apparently they knew which one it was.

According to Aunt Sara, everyone did.

The afternoon crawled by. I asked my aunt about her meeting, but she was vague, simply saying that it went fine. For a while she fiddled. She rearranged picture frames, repositioned candles on the bar, even unfastened then refastened the tiebacks for the velvet drapes in the main room.

We went on that way, me trying to study, Aunt Sara fidgeting until she finally settled down at the table with her jewelry-making supplies. She made the most amazing necklaces, using crosses or fleur-de-lis, with vintage beads and buttons.

Normally I loved watching her, but as dusk brought shadows into the condo, the tension stretched tighter, as if we were waiting for . . . something. Every now and then I caught her staring at me, but she never said anything, and eventually she swept her supplies into their box and announced she was going to bed.

Neither of us ate.

She knew. That was all I could think. After the way she'd pulled me from that bad dream the night before, after the way I'd carried on about "being there" (really regretted saying that), my aunt knew there was something not right about me.

It was hard to go to sleep. I tried, but nothing happened. So I dragged my laptop into bed and got online, started to do a search about the girls who had gone missing last year, but wound up on Jessica's Facebook page instead.

Immediately I wished that I hadn't, but couldn't tear myself away, either.

During the day posts to her wall had piled up from her legions of "friends," all wishing her well and praying for her safety. There were offerings of candles and teddy bears and gris-gris, even an alleged voodoo chant, all turning the page into a bizarre memorial, as if she were already dead.

Help me . . . please!

The words blurred. Or maybe that was my eyes. I wasn't sure.

Love you so much, Jessie! Come home soon!

Can't sleep, my friend. Praying for your soul.

Her soul? Okay, that was a bit much.

Your beautiful smile will live forever in my heart.

That was from Amber. The sentiment was nice, but the drama of it all creeped me out.

I kept scrolling, though. I couldn't stop, but wasn't sure why. I scrolled through posts and pictures people had uploaded, a few inspired homage collages, until the very last post from that day, and only then did I look up from the screen, out toward the darkness beyond my window.

Over a hundred posts . . . but not one from Chase.

There was one on my page, though. Actually there were a couple of messages that hadn't been there the night before.

Missed you in history today!

That was from Victoria. A few other "friends" had posted comments. And Chase. His was at the very top, five simple words next to a small picture of him on a beach, making the peace sign with his right hand. His shirt was off, revealing how many hours he spent in the weight room—and a tattoo I'd never seen before. It was on his upper left chest, below his collarbone, a series of lines that reminded me of the Japanese I'd studied a few years before.

Oh, and his post?

I meant what I said.

The looks started the second I walked onto campus.

At first I told myself I was being paranoid. I was the new girl, while many of my classmates had been together since elementary school. It was only natural that they be a little standoffish.

But as the morning wore on, I realized this was different. Standing in groups of two and three, speaking in hushed voices, they watched as I approached. Stepped back as I passed. In home-room, Amber stared—and again, Chase was not there.

During lunch I made up my history test, finishing with a few minutes to spare. That left time to kill, so I headed for the shade of the courtyard as everyone else was spilling from the cafeteria.

And like earlier, everyone veered away as if I had some terrible disease.

Except Victoria. She broke from a group of cheerleaders and hurried over, grabbing me by the arm and dragging me to the edge of the cobblestone.

"Omigod!" I couldn't tell if she was excited or horrified. "Amber says you know, but that's ridiculous, right? Because if you knew, you wouldn't be here. The cops would be all over you, right?"

It took a second to work through all that. "Know what?"

She glanced back toward the group of girls, where Amber stood with her arms over her chest, watching. When Victoria looked back at me, I'd swear all the blood had drained from her face. *"Where Jessica's body is."*

She spoke quietly, but she might as well have slugged me in the gut.

"But you don't, do you? I mean, how could you?"

"Amber said that?"

"She said she overheard her parents talking, after they'd talked with Jessica's mother. Or maybe it was her father." Victoria paused to take a breath, grabbing at the blond hair that kept blowing in her face. "Trinity? Why aren't you saying anything?"

I looked away from her, toward the Gothic-like administration building, where several feet up along the stone you could still see the waterline from Katrina. It was hard to imagine this beautiful old campus completely immersed in dirty swamp water.

It was even harder to grasp that this was really happening. My grandmother had warned me. From the very first time, when I'd told her about seeing Sunshine die, she'd told me to never speak of what I saw in the shadows of my mind. She'd told me people would think I was different. That I would scare people.

And that in turn, they would turn away.

Victoria was my friend. She'd been sweet from the start, welcoming me when few others did. I'd been to her house. We'd gone shopping, to movies. If things had played out a little differently, she would have been with me Saturday at the vile old house. But Jessica and Lucas had one of those fuel on fire relationships, and she thought it would be a kick to give him the wrong place and time.

Now, after walking from Amber to stand with me, she was looking for confirmation that what Amber had said wasn't true.

That gave me a choice: (a) I could lie and tell her they were all crazy. Or (b) I could tell her the truth, and confirm that the crazy one was me.

Or maybe, (c) I could tiptoe down the middle.

"I never said anything about a body." Technically, true.

Victoria's eyes narrowed, as if she didn't understand what I'd said. "But you did talk to the police?"

"Amber told them about Saturday night."

"Omigod, they really think you might have—"

"They're cops. It's their job to investigate all possibilities. I'm sure they talked to everyone who was there."

But Victoria's eyes still burned with curiosity. "Amber said you had a dream, that you saw Jessica—"

She never got a chance to finish.

"It was just a game!" Amber said, closing in on us with her entourage. "It's not Jessica's fault you freaked out."

I swallowed, couldn't believe what I was hearing. Did she really think I was responsible for what had happened? "Look, I'm sorry about your friend—"

"You stupid bitch!" she spat, then oh-my-God, she lunged at me with her hands raised, like she was going to claw my eyes out. "I told the cops how you looked at her, all hateful like you wanted to make her go away and never come back."

I jerked back, but that wouldn't have stopped her if Drew hadn't come running around the gym. He practically long-jumped the last ten feet, reaching her inches before she plowed into me.

"Amber!" he said, but she didn't look at him, didn't slow down, just kept twisting to try and break free. "Come on, baby," he said, and this time there was something different to his voice, something intimate. "You don't want to do this."

She froze, her skinny body going completely stiff for a second or two before she went limp and he scooped her up and gathered her against him, holding her as she started to cry. "Omigod," she sobbed. "Omigod. *Jessie* . . ."

I stood there in complete shock, aware of little but the need to breathe. I think that's why I never saw him coming.

"You okay?" With the words came his touch, a gentle hand to my shoulder.

Numbly I looked up, realized how close he stood. And how badly I wanted to dive into his arms.

"Hey," he said, and then it all just kind of happened. I'm not sure who moved first, but I really think it was him. All I knew was that one moment I was alone, and the next Chase's arms were around me.

EIGHT

Beneath the shifting shade of the old oaks, he held me. Inside me a little voice screamed that I should pull away. This was wrong. We were at school, in a crowded, public courtyard. He'd been Jessica's boyfriend, she was missing, and some people actually thought I might have done something horrible to her.

But there was a louder voice, a stronger one, that wanted to drown in the feel of Chase's arms around me, his hands splayed and steady against my back. I'm not a small girl, but at five foot six, my head came right to Chase's chest, allowing me to hear the steady riff of his heart beating against the soft cotton of his shirt.

It was the most intimately we'd ever touched.

The day before I'd pushed him away, walked away. But here, now, I was tired of pushing. I wanted to stay that way, there in the sanctuary of his arms, forever.

I closed my eyes. Held on. Wished this was all some nightmare and that I could wake up. All except the Chase part. That part I wanted to last. But the rest . . . I wanted Jessica to magically reappear and for everyone else to forget all the stupid rumors.

The bell rang. It was time for English lit. But neither of us made any effort to move. Chase kept standing there, quiet and strong, holding me.

And I, hardly recognizing myself anymore, let him.

We walked in silence. He'd been waiting when I walked into the courtyard after last period. He'd reached for my backpack, and I'd given it to him. Just like that, I'd handed it to him as if I'd done so a thousand times before.

Then he took my hand. That was another first.

I made no move to pull away.

I didn't ask him where we were going, either. It didn't matter, as long as it was away. Quietly I walked with him to the seriously old Camaro he and his dad had found abandoned in a junkyard after Katrina. They'd restored it themselves.

Chase opened the door, and I climbed inside. Then he slid behind the steering wheel and we took off.

I knew people watched, but I didn't care. I just wanted to get as far away from Amber and Enduring Grace as I could.

And I wanted Chase to take me.

Eventually the press of once-beautiful old buildings gave way to trees, big, old trees that made the oaks at Enduring Grace seem young by comparison. We parked along a narrow street, climbing from the car to walk along a cracked sidewalk. He led. I let him. And for the first time I realized his limp was almost gone. Along with my fading bruises, there was virtually no reminder of Saturday night.

Except for the lingering residue of deception.

The sign said City Park, but the name sounded bland compared to the beauty around us. The park sprawled in all directions, all winding paths and fountains and statues. And birds. They were everywhere, herons and crows and even a few seagulls, swooping around us and perched in the moss-infested branches, some down on the ground.

I'd never seen—or heard—so many in one place.

"This way," Chase said, veering from a swarm of toddlers and babies and mothers. "I want to show you something."

I turned to follow, but stilled when I saw the bridge. Nestled among thick vegetation, it was old and stone and arched, linking one side of a lagoon to another.

"This place is so pretty." I'm not sure why I whispered, but using my full voice didn't seem right.

"You should have seen it before the storm."

At the edge of the greenish water, two huge herons stood amazingly still, as if they, too, listened.

"These trees have been here forever," he said, his voice even more quiet than mine. "Before my grandparents—their grand-parents. Before any of us."

I glanced at Chase, could tell that for a moment, he'd gone somewhere else.

"They've always been here," he murmured, "but the storm al-most took them."

Like it had taken so much else. And yet, despite the rain and battering wind, standing in saltwater for weeks on end, the old oaks had found a way to survive. They'd endured.

There was something to be said about that.

"Were you here?" I asked. "When the storm hit?"

He looked down toward a series of knobby roots jutting up from a blanket of leaves. "We got out in time."

"Thank God," I whispered, but the way his head jerked up told me I'd said something very wrong. "I mean—"

"No, don't." We stood in shade, but his eyes glinted. "People always say that, talking about God's grace and prayers answered, but it's hard to think about God and Katrina having much to do with each other."

Whoa. Heavy stuff—so not a path I'd meant to stumble down. I mean, what was I supposed to say to that? "I'm sorry."

The words rang totally insufficient.

"Don't be. We made it. The city is coming back. A house is just a house."

I swallowed. A house is just a house? The cryptic comment sent a new question jumping through me. Had Chase's family lost their house?

I had no idea, which, in turn, made me realize how little about Chase Bonaventure I knew. His mom was a lawyer, his dad a doctor. He had a younger brother and two dogs. And his smile was absolutely killer. That was about it.

"Did you guys lose much?"

Around him, shadows deepened. "Nothing that can't be replaced," he said, and then he was walking again, moving deeper into the seclusion of the trees.

I tried to take it all in, the stillness of the fading afternoon, the contrast of greens and browns—and the very real fact that Chase, the guy who by all appearances had everything, seemed as weary as the trees.

We walked quietly, and though the sun had burned off most of the cloud cover, the thick tree canopies made it seem more like dusk.

And then I saw the clearing.

There amid the play of shadows and light, trees gave way to columns. They rose up from a tangle of vegetation like forgotten guardians, standing in a perfect circle around a beautiful fountain. It was like walking into a nature preserve in New Orleans, and emerging in Ancient Greece.

Except for the tall iron fence surrounding the clearing. And the
DO NOT ENTER sign. Those served as stark reminders of where we
really were.

My breath caught anyway. "Wow," I whispered, pausing a few
feet from the locked gate. "That's so cool."

"I thought you'd like it." Chase closed in on the fence, taking
the iron in his hands and swinging a foot up to the crossbar.

"What are you doing?" The second the question left my mouth,
I wanted it back. It was pretty obvious what he was doing.

"No one cares," he said, climbing over and glancing back at
me. Those long bangs fell carelessly against his eyes. "Come on."

Maybe he didn't care, but I'd never been one to take warnings
lightly. I glanced around, saw nothing but trees—

Shadows slipped. I swung back toward a cluster of three oaks,
narrowed my eyes. I would have sworn something had moved.

"Trinity?"

My heart raced ridiculously—there was nothing there, just the
play of leaves and the sway of Spanish moss.

Swallowing, I turned back to Chase. The fence stood between
us, tall. Strong. Eyes on mine, he extended his hand—

And I could see him all over again, as he'd been Saturday night
when he'd run from the house, shouting my name. I'd been so
blinded by shock, I'd seen only what I'd let myself see: a joke. That
everyone had been in on.

"Trinity?"

But now I jerked the moment back into focus, the haunting
fountain and the shroud of weathered columns, and the tall slats of
wrought iron standing between me and Chase, and saw what I'd
not let myself see before, the quiet fire in his eyes. The . . . honesty.

"Are you okay—"

"You really didn't know, did you?"

He stilled. "Didn't know what?"

"About the game," I whispered. "What Jessica and Amber were going to do."

Behind him, the fountain danced. Above him, the sun shone brightly. But the shadows falling around him made the blue of his eyes look black. "No."

Inside me, something shifted.

"That's why I was there," he added, his voice noticeably rough against the wind. "To make sure you didn't get hurt."

Once, a long time ago when I was a little girl, my grandmother took me to Boulder, where we visited all sorts of shops and galleries. In one, an old man who looked a lot like a skinny Santa Claus was making glass figurines. It seemed like hours that I stood watching him with his torch, working the molten glass. I'm sure it wasn't really that long, but I'd been fascinated by the way he used a torch to make something so beautiful.

In the end, I'd fallen in love with a green dragonfly. I could still remember how gently I'd handled it, so scared that I would break it.

Odd that I would think of that while standing with Chase, but in that moment that's how I felt, like that fragile dragonfly of blown glass.

Not allowing myself to think or analyze, I stepped toward the iron rail and reached, held on while I lifted my leg and climbed for the top. There I jumped—and Chase caught me.

His eyes met mine, and my heart kicked hard. Slowly, he lowered my feet to the ground.

"She's jealous," he murmured. "You know that, don't you?"

Somehow I swallowed. "That's crazy." Jessica Morgenthal had everything. "She's one of the most popular girls in school."

"But she's also smart, and she has eyes," Chase said. "She can see."

The breeze blew hair into my face, but I made no effort to push it back, didn't trust myself to move. "See what?"

"You," he said. "How gorgeous you are. How different."

It was my turn to go very, very still.

"You scare her," he said. "You're everything she isn't—warm, sincere." As if in slow motion, he lifted a hand to slide the hair from my face. At the edge of my cheek, his fingers lingered. "Honest."

"I thought you two—"

"Not for a long time," he answered before I could finish. "But sometimes it's hard to let go—that's what the whole truth-or-dare thing was about."

"Letting go?"

"Payback," he said, stepping closer and bringing his thighs against my hips. "She knew it was over."

His eyes were warm, penetrating. And his hand was still touching me, those strong fingers that could crush a football stroking like a feather along my cheekbone.

And I was totally lost. Throat tight, I wanted to step even closer, to lift a hand and touch his face, put my fingers against the shadow of stubble beginning to show along his jaw.

And his mouth, that full lower lip . . .

"I never meant for you to get hurt," he said, and my heart sang a little more.

"It was no big deal," I found myself saying, and then because I couldn't breathe, I broke away from him, stepping to my right toward the lonely columns. Corinthian, I thought. Maybe Ionic. I didn't know.

It didn't matter.

"Why did you bring me here?" I turned, made myself confront the question that had been nudging me since we'd slipped into the Camaro. There'd been a sense of purpose to him from the moment he'd led me from the courtyard, and I, not wanting to think too much, had gone along for the ride.

But as we stood there with the shadows, I had to wonder why. I'd never been one to live in the moment, without trying to see through to the other side. Why, then, had I gotten into the car? Why, after the nightmare of the past several days, had I let him take me here?

"You really don't know?"

His voice was so quiet I had to concentrate on the words. "I wouldn't have asked, if I did."

The blue of his eyes shifted to something much darker—and much less discernable. "I brought you here to get you away from the poison at Enduring Grace." Slowly, dreamlike, he took a step toward me. "To get you alone."

I watched him close in on me, told myself to step back, turn away.

"I brought you here because if you try to walk away, there's nowhere to go."

At that moment I could no more have moved than I could have breathed.

"Because we need to talk. Two detectives came to see me last night," he added, and finally, finally I had something I could grab onto.

"LaSalle and Jackson?"

Chase picked a twig up from the ground between us. "They knew about Saturday night," he said. "And Monday."

I watched him roll the stick in his hands, wondering how he could be so rough and gentle at the same time. "Monday?"

He glanced up, held my eyes with his own. "You don't know?"

I shook my head.

He frowned. "Jess and I had it out. She followed me behind the gym, tried to tell me she didn't mean any harm Saturday night."

Not harm, not by her standards anyway. By her standards she sought only victory.

"I told her to save her breath," Chase said, and again something warm and elusive swelled through me. "That I knew the game she was playing and it wasn't going to work. That if she did anything else to you, she'd regret it."

My breath caught. I could feel it there in my throat, knotted up with doubt and longing, so strong I had to look away, toward the huge sprays shooting up from the fountain. The water rained back down around us, sliding like tears along the carved dedication: FOR THE PEOPLE OF NEW ORLEANS.

"She laughed," Chase said, but I didn't let myself look at him. "Told me I hadn't seen anything yet."

I stepped closer to the spray, felt the sting against my face. "That's what you think this is all about?"

He stood behind me, but the fall of his shadow told me that he moved. "Last summer," he said as his voice grew closer. "A few days before the Fourth of July, I told her things weren't working anymore. That we should take a break . . ."

His shadow merged with mine, stilled.

"She took off. For four days there was nothing—no texts, no calls. Not even to her parents."

Once, not that long ago, his quiet words would have surprised me. My world had been small in Colorado. My grandmother had been my center. Never would I have considered putting her through that kind of hell.

But after two months in New Orleans, I knew that one person's hell was another person's triumph.

"What about Amber?" I asked, turning without thinking.

He stood closer than I realized, so close I had to glance up to see his face.

"She said she had no idea."

And I could tell that he did not believe her. "Did you call the police?"

"Her parents did," he said, still rolling that stick in his hands. I wasn't sure he even realized it was there.

"But they weren't too worried. It was obvious she left on her own."

Exactly like this time. She'd told her parents good night, gone to her room. In the morning, they'd found her room empty. Her bed was unmade, her purse and car were gone. Those were the facts.

But all I had to do was close my eyes, and the dark silent movie of my mind would play all over again . . .

"She turned up a few days later," he said. "With a cousin in Pensacola."

I looked back toward the fountain, watching the glint of the setting sun play with the droplets of water. The facts lined up. The pattern was clear. Whatever I'd seen—

"Tell me about your dream."

Everything stopped. Around me, inside me. Everything just . . . stopped. *What?*

"Your dream," he said again, this time so gentle it hurt to hear. "Tell me what you saw."

I closed my eyes without thinking, tensed when I realized what I would see, what I'd been seeing continuously since Jessica disappeared.

But it was not Jessica that I saw there in the darkness, while afternoon slipped into dusk.

It was the glow of the green dragonfly.

"Don't," I heard Chase say, and then I felt his hand against my arm, warm, strong but oddly tender. He turned me toward him, brought his other hand to the side of my face. "Don't shut me out."

The dragonfly fluttered through the shadows in a slow, hypnotic dance. And then, from one heartbeat to the next, he was gone.

"Please—" Chase said, and I couldn't stand there one second longer without looking, seeing. I let my eyes open, let myself absorb the promise in his eyes, the one I'd seen from the very start, long before I'd known about Jessica.

"What did you see?" he asked, and there was something in his voice, something thick, persuasive, that seeped through my defenses, and touched me in a way I'd never anticipated. "Tell me," he said again. "Tell me about the dream."

I looked from him to the trees, to the sunlight slanting through the thick canopies and falling in stark streaks against the ground, and even as I reminded myself of all the reasons to hedge, the words were already forming.

"I saw her," I said, looking back at him, needing to see his eyes as I spoke, needing to see what was reflected there: acceptance . . . or scorn. "In that house, in the room upstairs where we all were. On the bed."

The angles of his face tightened. "Was she hurt?"

"I don't know," I said, making myself continue. I needed to—I had to. I had to know if he would take my hand again—or turn away like my grandmother had warned. "Her eyes were open and she was looking at me, like she was begging me to help her—"

He moved so fast I had no time to prepare.

NINE

He pulled me into his arms and wrapped me tight, held me like he had in my dreams. Through his shirt, I could hear the riff of his heart—I could *feel* it.

"Just a nightmare," he murmured against my hair. "Because of Saturday—"

I'm not sure why I struggled back, why I wrenched out of his arms. But in that moment I knew I had to, had to find a way to breathe. "It felt so real . . ."

Long bangs fell against his eyes, finally returning us to familiar ground. "Dreams usually do."

I held onto his words, knew that they were true. My grandmother hadn't liked to talk about dreams, but Victoria did. She'd told me hers, how wild they were. How real . . .

"Was I there?"

I blinked, refused to let the surprise touch my face. "No."

"Am I ever?" he asked. "In your dreams?"

The question blindsided me. For a moment everything faded,

the trees and the columns and the play of the fountain, leaving only me and Chase and the way he looked at me, touching without so much as lifting a hand.

The truth seemed every bit as dangerous as the lie.

"Please, Chase," I said, looking for a graceful way out. "I don't want to talk about my dreams." Especially not with him.

He didn't move, didn't back down. "Why not?"

In the distance, toward the south, cumulous clouds bubbled up from the Gulf of Mexico. Sometimes they would dump rain on the city, hard and fast.

And yet sometimes they only brought darkness.

"Because I don't want them," I said. "I just wish they would go away."

That stick was still in his hands. I wasn't sure how. "Everyone dreams," he said.

I knew that. Everyone dreamed. But not everyone's dreams came true. It sounded so nice, like what you'd read in a greeting card with a rainbow or sunshine, birds in trees: *May all your dreams come true.*

But not all dreams were good, and not all deserved to escape the shadowy theater of the mind.

"Even nightmares," Chase said. "We all have them."

When I was younger, my grandmother had said the same thing. Sometimes I'd woken up crying, and she'd always been there, holding me, running her hand along my back. She'd muttered soothing words and asked me to tell her what I saw.

After Sunshine, she never asked again.

"I dream about water," I whispered, watching the play of the fountain behind him, the spray up toward the sky, the streams sliding back along a bronze statue of leaping dolphins.

About running—and trying to breathe. "And fire."

A soft crack sounded between us, and I looked down to find the twig in his hands in two pieces.

"Sometimes it's nighttime." I made myself continue. "But sometimes there's sunshine. Lots of it. And blue skies and a breeze so warm you could wrap yourself in it, like a hug."

Around us that breeze blew, but somehow it didn't touch us.

"And then she's . . . there," I surprised myself by saying. Once I'd told Gran and she'd smiled. Then she'd cried. "She's there and she's beautiful and she's so real, smiling at me."

Chase stepped closer, slid a strand of hair from my face. "Who?"

I looked up as something inside of me started to tear. *"My mother,"* I said, and even though I'd become adept at hiding it, the emotion I'd bottled away so many years before leaked through. "And my father. He's there, too, all tall and strong and handsome; young, standing in the distance, watching us."

A rough breath broke from Chase's throat, but this time he made no move to touch me.

"Sometimes we're on a picnic," I said. "And sometimes we're at the beach. He smiles." And I could feel it, streaming through me as if he were really there. But he never touched me, not even in the fragile illusion of my dreams.

Only my mother did that.

"I used to love to go to sleep," I said. "When I was little. Because I'd see them and we were together . . . a family."

The oddest look came into Chase's eyes. "And now?"

"I hate it," I said without hesitating. "I hate going to sleep because I hate what it feels like when I wake up." That hollow, stark realization that of all possible dreams, all the events I see before they happen, the images of my parents would never come true . . . were in fact nothing more than fading fantasies of the future I'd lost before I'd even learned to remember.

"How old were you when they died?"

"Two."

His shoulders tensed. "What happened?"

It was an obvious question, a logical one, one I'd asked over, and over, and over.

But Gran had always been vague. "An accident," I said, because that's what she'd said: a horrible, horrible accident. But she'd never given details. "A car wreck, I think."

"You *think*?"

"My grandmother didn't like to talk about it." And neither did my aunt. She'd been in her freshman year at Tulane. "I think it was too painful, that she was trying to protect me from it."

"By keeping you in the dark?"

She hadn't looked at it that way.

But I did. "She said life was ahead of you, not behind."

"And you're cool with that?"

"No." Not in the least. It was my life and they were my parents, and I wanted to know. *Needed* to. "Being here . . . everything is more intense. It's like hitting play after being paused for the past fourteen years. I look around at the people and the streets and the buildings, the river and the trees, and I can't help but wonder what would have happened if they hadn't died. If I'd grown up here, with them."

Wordlessly Chase glanced toward the tree line, where a pink balloon bobbed in the breeze, its ribbon tangled against a high branch. I couldn't figure out why it hadn't popped.

"Saturday night I saw a picture of my mom for the first time," I surprised myself by saying. "And I recognized her—I have no memory of her at all, but she looked like she does in my dreams."

For so long I'd kept it all bottled up, the hopes and the dreams, the regrets. But standing there with Chase, age-old locks fell away, and all those fragments slipped out.

"But I want more than that, more than fading images of black and white. I want the stories that go with them. *The people.* I want to know who my parents were and what they were like, how they met and what they did. What made them laugh, cry. What was my mom's favorite color and what music my dad listened to . . ."

He looked back at me. "What were their names?"

For some reason I smiled. "John Mark and Rachelle." The names felt rusty on my tongue—I'm not sure I'd ever spoken them aloud. "Why?"

His eyes were still distant, but the blue had softened. "Because you deserve better than living in the dark," he said. "You deserve to know who you are—for those dreams to come true."

The wince was automatic. Fortunately, it was also inside.

There was no way those dreams, of my parents, the life we'd lost, could come true.

"And now I know," he said, stepping toward me.

"Know what?"

It was his turn to smile, a slow, lazy curl of his lips that made my chest tighten all over again. "What happens when the rest of the world goes away."

I lifted my eyes to his, and felt the scrape clear down to my bone.

"You let go," he said. "You relax."

I swallowed—hard.

He stepped closer, his eyes on mine. He didn't touch, though, not with his hands. But I could feel him. Really, really feel him. "Don't be scared."

I felt my mouth go dry. "I'm not—"

But we both recognized the lie.

He stopped only inches away, but still did not lift a hand. "Then what's that I see in your eyes?"

The urge to blink was automatic, to glance away like when you saw something shocking, something you were unprepared for. Instinct made you look away. Before curiosity brought you back.

But it was something even stronger that kept me from moving. I'm not even sure I breathed.

Until something shifted against the tree line beyond Chase's shoulder.

The moment broke, and my eyes narrowed before going wide the second I caught sight of the man not thirty yards away.

I must have made a noise because Chase swung around. "What is it?" Then he stilled. *"Mr. Bryce."*

The name meant nothing to me.

The man was tall, with wide shoulders and thick dark hair. He wore a gray suit with an unfastened red tie against his white shirt. There was something in his hands—a book? Stepping from the anonymity of the old oaks, he approached us slowly, his steps wary, as if *he* was the one who'd been caught off guard.

Chase slipped in front of me. "What are you doing here?" he asked, but there was no fear in his voice, none of the crazy adrenaline rushing through me.

The man stepped onto the concrete of the promenade, pausing by one of the columns. That's when I saw his eyes, and felt my breath catch. He was a total stranger, but the eyes I knew, the shape, the color—everything.

"I was waiting for you at the school," he said in a voice as flat as his expression was blank. It was as if every emotion had been completely smeared away. "I wanted to talk to you."

Maybe I should have stepped back, but instead I stepped closer to Chase.

"I already told the cops everything I know," he said. "The last time I saw her was after school—"

It all clicked then, the eyes, the dazed look on his face—the stack of white clenched in his hand.

Posters, I realized, focusing on the provocative picture in the center, the wide, mocking eyes and long dark hair, the knowing smile. And the words: MISSING centered along the top, REWARD along the bottom.

And I knew. Without another word, I knew the man wrapped so tightly inside himself was Jessica's father.

I'd heard about him, knew that once he'd played football for LSU and was now a successful doctor, that he doted on his oldest daughter.

That the word *no* was not part of his vocabulary.

"Mr. Morgenthal—" I started, but he didn't so much as glance my way, never looked from Chase. It was as if I wasn't even standing there.

"I know she treated you badly," he said, a hint of a parent's worst nightmare finally leaking into his voice. "I know she made bad choices. But that's Jessie," he said, and a trace of a smile touched his eyes, so dark and persuasive, exactly like hers. "You know that," he said. *"You know her."*

"Mr. Bryce, you know I would never hurt—"

"I know that, son, and I told the police that—but that doesn't mean you can't help."

"Help?"

"Bring her back," he muttered. "Tell her you're sorry."

Chase stiffened, but before he could say anything Bryce Morgenthal was stepping toward us and thrusting his phone at Chase. "Just call her. Tell her you didn't mean what you said."

I could only see Chase's profile, but it was enough to discern the wince. "Mr. Bryce—"

"Please," Jessica's father said. "If there's a chance . . . I've tried. I've called her. I've begged. But this isn't about me. It's about—"

"Her," Chase said. "It's about her."

From his voice, I could tell it was always about her. And from the way Jessica's father talked, even he seemed to think she'd left of her own free will.

The sound of twigs snapping came from behind me. Twisting,

I squinted against the whitewash of early evening—and saw my aunt hurrying toward me.

Behind her the once locked gate hung open.

By her side, Detective Aaron LaSalle matched her step for step.

"Trinity!" she called, and really, I glanced around, half expecting to find Amber or Victoria crouched behind a column or tree. So much for being alone.

"What are *you* doing here?" I asked, hating how freaked out the question sounded. "What's going on?"

She hurried up to me, lifting a hand to my shoulder as if seeing me wasn't enough. "Detective LaSalle called me, told me some man was seen following you—"

I stepped back, shaken by the realization of how many eyes had been trained on us. "He's watching us?"

The detective, looking all cool and casual in his khakis and black button-down, answered before she could.

"A beautiful young girl is missing," he said. "It's my job to bring her home." Then he glanced behind me. "You want to tell me what you're doing here, Mr. Morgenthal?"

I glanced back to see Jessica's father's eyes harden. "I want my girl home."

"That's what we all want—" Detective LaSalle started, but the ridiculousness of us all playing hide-and-seek in some remote park while Jessica was missing exploded through me.

"Didn't you go to the house?" I asked, twisting back toward the detective. He stood apart from us all, watching from behind dark sunglasses. "On Prytania? Like I told you?"

The detective's jaw tightened. That was the only clue I had that he looked at me. "We did."

"And?" I asked, shoving the hair back from my face and fisting it behind my neck.

"Nothing," he said. "There was nothing there."

That got me. That really, really got me. "But—" *I'd seen her. I'd seen her at the house, on the mattress.* "That's impossible. She was . . ." I broke off, tried again. "Are you sure?"

"I was there myself. I walked every room, every hall. We took fingerprints, collected trash. But there was nothing to indicate that Miss Morgenthal had been there."

"But—" I looked up, found Aunt Sara watching me very, very closely.

"I'm afraid your dream was nothing more than a fantasy, sweetheart," he said, and I felt myself sway, even as Chase slid a hand to my lower back.

"But we did find her car," LaSalle said.

Vaguely I was aware of Mr. Morgenthal surging forward, charging up to the detective, of questions and raised voices, words like Baton Rouge and a dorm parking lot, doors locked and sunglasses on the dash.

But I could not move, not while the world around me spun.

"LSU?" Jessica's father shouted. "How the hell did it get there?"

It was not the detective who answered. But Chase. *"Wesley."*

They all swung toward him. "Who's Wesley?" LaSalle asked.

Chase tried to play it cool, but I saw the way his arms tensed, even his jaw. "A guy she met in Pensacola last summer. They've been texting."

"Do you know a last name? How to find him?"

Chase shook his head.

The detective shifted his attention to Jessica's father. "Mr. Morgenthal?"

"No—I—she never mentioned—"

"Then we'll wait for the phone records," LaSalle said. "They've been subpoenaed."

"You think that's where she is?" Mr. Morgenthal asked, and

finally, finally desperation broke through the artificially blank veneer. "With this LSU boy—that he might have her?"

The detective pulled his iPhone from his belt and slid his fingers along the keys. "Anything is possible."

I wanted to believe him. I wanted to believe that was true, that what I'd seen in the darkness of my mind was as fictional as the picnic with my parents, a distorted manifestation of thoughts I had yet to reconcile. It was no secret Jessica was not my favorite person. I wasn't proud of it, but maybe it wasn't a stretch that bad things would happen to her in my dreams.

But as I looked from her father to Chase to the detective charged with figuring it all out, I couldn't suppress the feeling that they were clinging to wishful thinking.

"Please," Mr. Morgenthal said, once again offering his phone to Chase. "Call her." The man who looked so much like his daughter frowned. "I have to know," he said quietly. "If she's out there, she'll listen to you . . ."

Chase lifted his eyes to mine, the silent apology unmistakable. Then he reached for his own phone and thumbed out the number.

"Jessie," he said, and I didn't quite understand what I heard in his voice—or why it suddenly hurt to breathe. *"It's me."*

Aunt Sara opened the door. I walked inside. She followed, closing up behind her, standing with her back to me as she turned the key and slid the dead bolts. But she didn't turn around when she was done, just kept her back stiff and the palm of her right hand pressed to the thick wood.

That was my first warning that the silence from the car had merely been a prelude.

Her hair was loose, not straight like usual, but wavy from the humidity. She wore a long dress in swirls of brown and black that emphasized her awesome figure and gorgeous shoulders. I'd never really thought much about shoulders until I'd come to New Orleans and met my aunt—and Chase.

Only a single lamp illuminated the condo. Beyond the window, a thick blanket of clouds hid the stars, leaving the city warm and muggy and, despite the steady wind of earlier in the day, without even that reprieve.

Chase had wanted to bring me home, but my aunt had said no. The detective had offered to follow, but again, my aunt had said no. Only Mr. Morgenthal had said nothing, walking past me like I didn't exist.

The second warning came a heartbeat later, when my aunt turned toward me, exposing me to the most scorched eyes I'd ever seen.

Wordlessly she let her chic little purse slide from the bend of her arm. But she didn't set it on the table, as she normally did. She let it slip to the hard wood of the floor.

Then she broke more than the silence. "It was more than a dream, wasn't it?"

The question came at me like a swift punch to the gut. My first instinct was to deny, pretend. To lie. That's what my grandmother had taught me, to keep it all inside, to never let anyone know what I saw behind closed eyes.

But standing there in the glow of a single lamp, looking at harsh lines on my aunt's face, I realized I didn't want to pretend anymore. Not with her.

And even if I did, it wouldn't do any good. She already knew.

"Yes," I whispered, and her face twisted. I would have sworn it was pain. "But I swear to God I had nothing to do with what happened," I said, and I could feel myself starting to shake. "I . . . I don't know why. I don't know what happened. I just know what I told the cops was true—"

"Because you saw her," my aunt whispered.

Quietly I nodded.

The breath left her, like a beautifully resilient balloon visibly fading away. Closing her eyes she looked down, as if in prayer. All the while I stood there, frozen, wishing I was anywhere else. Anyone else.

Then she looked up. And started to move. Her eyes, no longer piercing, no longer horrified, were on mine. I saw her getting closer and knew that she moved, but rather than walking with her typical catwalk style, her movements were robotic.

I'm not sure why I wanted to run.

At the hall leading to my bedroom, she stopped. "There's something you need to see."

TEN

The trunk sat beneath the window in the room where I'd slept every night since arriving at Aunt Sara's. It was old, definitely antique. Pine, I thought. Nicked up, leather straps torn, hinges rusty, big clunky nail heads and a bulky lock.

I'd seen it countless times but never given it much thought. Aunt Sara used it as a table. A beautiful old hurricane lamp sat next to my glass dragonfly and a vacant-eyed nun doll, with my grandmother's Rosary draped over a black-and-white photo essay of New Orleans cemeteries. I'd looked inside a few times, found it beautifully haunting.

But I'd never looked inside the chest, never thought about it as anything more than a random piece of furniture.

Now my heart jackhammered like crazy as Aunt Sara cleared everything from the top. From underneath, she retrieved a skeleton key. A few seconds later she had the lock undone and was lifting the lid.

I swallowed. Twilight had given way to evening, leaving darkness beyond the window. Light glowed from the lamps on either side of the bed, but not overhead. Aunt Sara didn't like those, didn't even keep bulbs in any of the fixtures.

I watched her slow-motion movements, and as she lifted the top, I knew my life was about to change.

I wanted to look inside. I wanted to see, touch.

To know.

But something I did not understand would not let me move.

With the sweep of dark hair concealing her face, Aunt Sara kneeled beside the open trunk for what seemed like forever. When she finally twisted back toward me, her expression was completely unreadable.

"This belonged to your mother."

The words knocked the breath from me. My mother. The trunk belonged to my mother. It had been in my room all this time. All I'd ever had to do was look.

"It's time you knew the truth," she said, and instinctively I glanced toward the dragonfly on the rug, so beautifully yet infinitely fragile. One false move, one careless action, and it would shatter.

"Mama thought she was protecting you." *Gran*. "She thought if she could take you far enough away, keep you away, then you'd be safe."

That bad feeling got a whole lot worse. "Safe?"

"That's all she wanted for you, for you to be safe, to live a normal, happy life."

"I was happy." It was the normal part where things got complicated.

"But I always thought she was wrong," Aunt Sara said, "keeping you in the dark like that." She glanced inside the trunk, then back at me. "You have to be able to protect yourself, *cher,* and you can't do that unless you know who you are."

Who. I. Was. The thought made everything inside of me tingle. "Then tell me."

I'm not sure I'd ever wanted anything so badly.

Aunt Sara extended a hand. Numbly, I took it, barely registering how cold her skin was. Somehow I made it to the floor beside her, joined her on my knees in front of my mother's trunk.

"Your mom saw things, too," my aunt said. Her voice was low, strained. *Haunted*. "She knew things."

I felt myself go glass still, even as I stared at all the little boxes and jars and rocks neatly arranged inside.

"Her mama did, too," my aunt said as I kneeled there, and stared. Listened. "And so did her mama."

My mouth was dry, my throat tight. I almost didn't want to ask the question. "What kind of things?"

"All kinds of things—people, places . . ."

"Death?" That question came out before I could stop it.

Aunt Sara glanced toward me, and slowly she nodded. "Death."

It was a lot to take in.

"She was the most incredible person I'd ever met," my aunt said in a soft, faraway voice, as I worked up the courage to reach inside. I didn't know what to touch first. "They all were. I was just a kid, but sometimes your mama would take me with her to see her grandmother."

To the left, little white boxes sat in neat rows, each carefully labeled in block letters: Amethyst, Peridot, Rose Quartz, Black Opal, Turquoise, Larimar. "Was she . . . like my mom?"

Aunt Sara's eyes darkened. "The firstborn daughter, of the firstborn daughter, of the firstborn daughter," she said. "Your mom said it was in the blood."

Deep inside, something started to hum. For so many years I'd wondered. For so many years I'd lived in the dark. I'd never understood, had actually wondered whether I simply saw things before they happened—or if in seeing them, I *made* them happen. Now I knew.

I was my mother's daughter, her mother's granddaughter. *It was in my blood.*

"My mother wasn't happy when she found out about our trips. She'd been raised devoutly Catholic. She believed in miracles and the power of prayer and the Rapture, but had no use for dreams or psychic phenomenon. They scared her. Your mother scared her. For me to be with her, I had to create all kinds of excuses, like going shopping or to the park. Once I said we were going fishing."

Trancelike, I reached into the trunk and slid my fingers along a beautiful turquoise-blue stone. "Did she scare *you*?"

"Just the opposite," Aunt Sara said. "I always felt safe around her, her people. Really, really safe and peaceful. Whenever we got together there was this amazing energy."

I glanced up. "Energy?" I was familiar with the New Age term, but I'd never heard my aunt speak of it.

"Vibrations, your mom always said."

Pretty much summed up how I felt at the moment.

"You have it, too," my aunt said. "The strong vibration. The first time I touched you, if I'd had my eyes closed I would have thought I was touching your mother."

Breathing hurt. I concentrated on the blue of the larimar, the most pure and amazing blue I'd ever seen, like a tropical sea nestled against a bed of cotton.

"She called it the Atlantis stone," my aunt said as I picked up the oblong and cradled it in the palm of my hand. "Your mother used it when you were sick."

Running my finger along the smooth stone seemed like the most natural thing in the world.

"I'll never forget," Aunt Sara said through sudden laughter.

"One night you'd been running this high fever, so Mom and I stopped by to check on you. Rachelle was in the shower, so your dad told us we could slip into the nursery and peek at you, if we wanted. So we go in there . . ." She was really laughing now, almost too hard to talk. "And there's candles everywhere, all lit and flickering, giving off some amazingly intense smell, like they used down at the cathedral."

The image made me smile—until I remembered the candles at the house on Prytania.

"And then we see you"—Aunt Sara laughed—"all sprawled on your back in your crib, naked except for your little diaper, completely surrounded by rocks."

I felt my eyes go wide. "Rocks?"

"Larimar," she said, nodding toward the stone in my hand. "Turquoise and moonstone. Your mom had each stone placed about half an inch apart."

The visual made me laugh.

"So my mom goes totally nuts. She marches over and starts grabbing the rocks as your mom comes in wearing nothing but a towel, her hair dripping wet and hanging in her face."

"Uh-oh," I said. My grandmother had been a practical woman. We'd lived in the mountains, but she'd never allowed rocks into her home. Her insistence had seemed silly to me, but rather than try to change her mind, I learned to sneak them in and keep them in places she never looked.

"Yeah, big uh-oh," Aunt Sara said. "Your mother ran over and positioned herself between your grandmother and the crib, and my mother is all freaked out, going on about evil spirits and the devil and curses. I can still see her making the sign of the cross over and over."

The chill was immediate—and bone deep. My grandmother had quickly crossed herself the second I told her about Sunshine. At the time, I'd thought it was because of the dog.

"And then your dad comes running in," Aunt Sara was saying, "trying to calm everyone down."

With the image I could see him all over again, as he appeared in my dreams, standing in the distance, watching, the haunting mix of warmth and sorrow in his eyes.

"It was hard on him," she murmured. "The two women he loved most could never find any common ground other than you."

Throat tight, I looked back at the tranquil glow of the larimar, stunned by the warmth radiating like waves of sunshine from my palm, blazing up to my fingers and my arm.

"Tell me more," I whispered, closing my fingers around the stone. I squeezed it, not tightly, but more like the way a mother might hold a child.

"She took her gift seriously—" my aunt started, but I looked up abruptly.

"Gift?"

"My word," she said, and again, her voice was sad. "Not hers."

"What *did* my mom call it?" *Curse* was the word that came to *my* mind.

Aunt Sara smiled. "Responsibility."

Not so sure, I swallowed hard and looked back inside the trunk, found myself reaching for a worn composition book.

"She'd been taught that it was her duty to help people," she added. "Her grandmother said everyone was here for a purpose. We all have roles to play. And if she or her daughter or your mom could give insight or warning, then that was what they were here to do."

The firstborn daughter of the firstborn daughter . . .

"Was she open about it?" I asked. "Did she tell people about her dreams?"

"Not really. At least, not everyone. It was like she lived two lives. At work she readily shared her gift, but at home she was just a mom and a wife."

"At work? What kind of work?"

"In the French Quarter," Aunt Sara said. "In Jackson Square, where the psychics gather."

I'd seen them, the so-called spiritual advisers. I'd walked by them Saturday night before we'd headed for the house on Prytania. Tourists flocked around the tables, where mostly women sat with flashlights, tarot cards, and crystals.

Like the ones in my mother's trunk.

"She took people's money?" Not sure why the thought bothered me, I flipped open the notebook in search of . . . something. I had no idea what. "Like those 1-800 Dial-A-Wackos?"

Aunt Sara sighed. "Trinity Rose. That sounds like something your grandmother would say."

Probably because she had. Whenever one of those late-night infomercials came on, Gran had muttered under her breath and changed the channel. Sometimes after she'd gone to bed, I'd lowered the volume and watched—and cracked up at the absurdity.

I wasn't laughing now. Trying to take it all in, I thumbed through what turned out to be more of a scrapbook than a notebook, page after page where my mother had taped pictures of crystals and rocks, accompanied by handwritten notes.

About two-thirds of the way back, pictures gave way to charts and graphs.

My name jumped out at me.

TRINITY ROSE MONSOUR
NATAL CHART

Some of the information I recognized, such as the notation of my astrological sign, Aries. But the chart went on to map out my

Moon (Gemini) and something called my Ascendant (Scorpio), a list of all the planets, something called houses and a midheaven (Leo). Scrawled, handwritten notes filled the margins:

> Strong personality
> Self-willed
> Stubborn
> Restless/Cannot stand still
> Impulsive
> Violent

I blinked, but the words didn't change. Some of them . . . yes, they made sense. Even my completely by-the-books grandmother had called me stubborn, and it was no secret I had a hard time standing still. When I was younger, Gran had called me her little whirlwind. Later, I'd become Hurricane Trinity.

Impulsive . . . yes. Not one of my better traits. But violent? And then a bit further down, my mother had jotted another word, this one totally bizarre.

> Occult

I glanced up. "What is this? A map of my life?"

Aunt Sara frowned. "Your mother did them for all of us. I'm not sure it's really a map so much as a guide."

And what was the difference? I didn't ask that question, though, instead I flipped through the following pages, where I found charts for my father (sun sign Libra) and Sara (sun sign Scorpio), and a whole lot of people I didn't know, concluding with a man named Jim Fourcade (sun sign Libra). The writing in his margin seemed messier than the others, more hurried.

"Who's this?" I asked.

My aunt glanced over, her eyes flaring before returning to normal.

Yup. She was about to lie.

"A friend of hers, I think," she said. "Maybe a client."

Sure. That's why the last word my mother had written on that page was *Sacrifice*.

The rest of the notebook was blank.

For several minutes I sat with the blue larimar clenched in my hand, the journal open in my lap, and my aunt sitting quietly next to me. And all the while I couldn't help but wonder. My mom had known things. She'd seen things about people and tried to help them. Warn them.

And now I was seeing things . . .

"Did it ever make a difference?" I asked, looking up from the notebook. "The things my mother saw, the bad stuff. Was she ever able to stop anything?"

Aunt Sara's eyes met mine. "Sometimes."

Which meant not always.

"What about . . ." Horror and grief moved through me at the same time. "What happened to her?" I said. "Did she see that, too? Did she know she was going to die?"

I'm not sure I could imagine anything more devastating than seeing your own death, knowing it was coming and not being able to stop it.

Sure, terminally ill people probably realized what was going to happen, but my mother hadn't died of an illness. It had been an accident. What would she have seen? How much would she have known? I couldn't help but think how terrifying it would be waking up each morning, wondering if this was going to be the day . . .

Or maybe she'd known all along. Maybe she'd known the exact day and hour.

That thought was equally horrifying.

Aunt Sara looked at me, her expression so tender and sad my chest started to hurt. "She always said she'd never see you grow up."

I wasn't a crier. I don't know why, I just never cry. Not even when Gran died. It was like there was a tight lid somewhere inside of me, holding everything in.

But kneeling in that room lit only by lamps and memories, in front of my mother's trunk, my throat closed up, and my eyes filled. "What do you mean *always*?"

Had she known for that long?

"From the time you were itty bitty," Aunt Sara said. "One day I found your mama rocking you, holding you so close with the strangest look on her face. At first you were so still, I thought something terrible had happened."

The stinging in my eyes made me blink.

"Then I saw you were at her breast, but she was crying."

I didn't even try to stop my own tears. They spilled over my lashes and slid down my face.

I made no move to wipe.

Actually, I didn't move at all. I'm not even sure I breathed.

"I kneeled beside her and asked what was wrong. I remember it so clearly, because she wouldn't look at me. It was like I wasn't even there, and when she answered, it was to you and not me."

"To me?"

" '*My precious little baby,*' she said. '*How will you ever forgive me?*' "

Oh, crap. The larimar had been doing such a good job of keeping me warm. But my blood temperature dropped all over again. "Forgive her for what?"

Aunt Sara reached inside the trunk for a small pink blanket and wrapped it around her hands. "She never would say. All she said was, 'Mama's gonna miss you, *mon petite ange*. Mama's gonna miss you.' "

Swallowing hurt. "It sounds like she blamed herself."

"I think she did," my aunt said. "Can you even imagine?" She broke off, shook her head. "Knowing what she knew and knowing there was nothing she could do."

The silent tears became quiet sobs. I'm not sure who moved first, my aunt or myself, but before I could take a breath I was in her arms and she was holding me to her, rocking me. Rocking . . .

Like a mother rocks a child.

Like my mother had rocked me.

When she'd realized she was going to die.

It's called precognition.

Stories date back to ancient times, from the druids of Ireland to the Oracle of Delphi, mind-bending accounts of dreams and prophecy that foretold future events with uncanny accuracy. World Wars I and II showed up in sixteenth-century writings, as did the assassination of JFK. In the 1940s three young children in Portugal warned of the attempt on Pope John Paul II's life. Every major event was there, seen ahead of time, all the way up through 9/11. And beyond.

I sat at a small table at the back of the school library, staring at my laptop. Even the Bible, some scholars said, contained as much prophecy as history.

Sliding the hair from my face, I couldn't escape the irony of my grandmother discounting my mother's abilities, but accepting the Book of Revelation.

The only difference was the source.

Glancing away, toward the window overlooking the courtyard, I lifted a hand to my temple and rubbed. Aunt Sara and I had sat in front of my mother's trunk until after midnight. After that, sleep had been impossible.

Questions bombarded me. Questions about my mother and her family, the visions they'd had—the visions I had. Tomorrow night there would be a candlelight vigil at the school. Chase and the police and even Jessica's parents kept saying (hoping?) it was possible she'd left on her own. And would return on her own.

The vigil was designed to show her how much she was loved.

I wanted to believe that. I wanted to believe them. But I could not forget what I'd seen in the shadows of my dreams, the way she'd begged me to help.

Getting through the morning had been torture. I'd considered calling in sick, but knew that would only give Amber more ammunition against me. So I sat in class after class, trying to pay attention, while my mind raced to make sense of all that I'd learned the night before—and to learn more.

And then there was Chase.

All through chemistry I'd felt him watching me. I'd sat there at my small desk, as aware of him as if we'd been standing body-to-body.

I'd never meant to tell him so much. I still couldn't believe I'd unloaded on him about my parents and the fantasies that lingered after all this time, of being a family. I'd never spoken of that to anyone. That I would tell Chase, now, in the midst of what was going on with Jessica . . .

I might as well have stripped off every piece of clothing and stood before him naked.

Instead I'd given him even more. I'd opened the door, and let him inside.

"Don't be scared."

"I'm not—"

"Then what's that I see in your eyes?"

Hating the burn that lingered still, now, almost twenty-four hours later, I turned back to the computer and opened another window. Into the search engine, I typed six words: New Orleans Teenage Girl Goes Missing.

No one wanted to answer my questions, but I could do so on my own. Amber had mentioned two other girls who'd gone missing in the past year or so.

My search yielded over fifteen million results.

Apparently disappearing in New Orleans was not all that uncommon.

It took trial and error, but after a few minutes I hit pay dirt. Michelle DuPont and Addison Roubilet went missing six months apart, to the day. Quickly I did the math—nine months since Addison vanished.

Jessica's disappearance didn't fit the pattern.

But of course, you needed more than two data points to establish a trend.

Both girls had been eighteen. Jessica was sixteen. Both girls were blonds. Jessica had dark hair, like mine. Both girls had been out with friends, one never returning from going to the bathroom, the other disappearing in a massive New Year's Eve crowd in the Quarter. Jessica had been out with friends.

One week after each went missing, their parents received a brown box in the mail.

Nowhere did any article indicate what they contained.

Frowning, I jotted a few notes, ending with: *What was inside?*

"Shoes."

The word, the unnaturally quiet voice, went through me like a raw current. I twisted around to find him lounging behind me, those long bangs of his against his eyes but failing to hide the shadows.

I wasn't sure how he'd found me. I hadn't told a soul I planned to spend lunch in the library. *"What?"*

"What was returned to their parents," Chase said. "Their shoes."

ELEVEN

Their shoes?

The words hung between us, a sobering reminder of all that lay at stake. Only the drone of the overhead lights broke the silence, amplifying the stillness. I'd seen the librarian when I walked inside the dimly lit building, but not since I'd sat down twenty minutes before.

I wanted to look away, to tear my eyes from Chase's and glance toward the shelves of books and clusters of empty tables, but I could no more have moved than I could shove away the awful image of a parent receiving their child's shoes in the mail.

"That's so messed up," I whispered. "Who would do that?"

His mouth flattened into a hard line. "Like you said—someone seriously messed up."

The thought made my stomach twist.

"Psychopaths don't feel what we feel," he said, glancing beyond me, to the newspaper article on the screen of my laptop. "When my mom worked for the D.A., there was this case . . ." For a second, he seemed to go somewhere else. "It messed her up for a long time," he said. "For sickos like them it's all about the challenge. The game."

I cringed, hating that he was right. The box with the shoes had been the last either set of parents had heard or seen of their daughters.

"It's like taunting," I muttered.

"That's exactly what it is."

On the screen, the delineation of black against white blurred. I'd seen Jessica's shoes. In my dream. They'd been cast off in the corner of the room. *"Oh, God."* I barely recognized the sound that scraped from my throat. "Jessica's flip-flops . . ."

The cops had not found them at the house on Prytania.

Chase moved fast, twisting from the computer back to me.

"Stop," he said, and his voice was so low and soft I would have sworn he touched me. But one hand remained on the side of the table, while the other curved around the back of my chair. "You have to stop torturing yourself. Her parents haven't received anything—and they're not going to."

"But she didn't call you back, either," I said. "Victoria told me."

He edged closer, going down on one knee and bringing his face level with mine. "Is that why you're in here? Alone?"

I closed my eyes and pulled in a breath, came close to drowning on the musky smell of leather and some spice that was all Chase.

"Trinity."

The quiet command feathered through me, and once again I let myself see.

"It's okay," he said.

I watched his mouth form the words, slowly lifting my eyes to his, stunned by how badly I wanted him to touch me. Just touch me. "What's okay?"

"To let me see. Let me know." And then he did it, slid a hand from the sterile table to the side of my face, his fingers soft, but warm and strong and . . . there. *"Yesterday."*

I absorbed his touch, the warmth streaming through me. "Chase," I said, and again, my voice was quiet. But in the tomb-like expanse of the library, I would have sworn his name echoed.

Or maybe that was my heart.

"I don't know how to do this." The uncensored honesty surprised me. Emotion knotted my throat. "I don't know how to walk through every day like everything is normal—"

"Not normal." His thumb slipped to the side of my mouth. "But that doesn't mean you have to walk alone."

The words, so thick and quiet and devastating, scraped through me. I looked away from him, back toward the computer—

"But that's all you know, isn't it?"

I stilled.

"Living with your grandmother, in the mountains, so far from your home. The life you could have had." Gently he turned my face back to his—I hadn't even realized his hand was still against my cheek. "But it doesn't have to be that way. You're here now."

The backs of my eyelids stung.

"You're not alone anymore," he whispered, and when he said it like that, with his eyes on mine and his thumb skimming my cheekbone, it was so very, very tempting to believe.

His hand shifted, his index finger sliding beneath my eyes. "You didn't sleep last night, did you?"

I tried for a smile. I don't think it worked. "Not much."

"Neither did I." Something in his eyes softened, blue turning translucent. "I couldn't stop thinking about you."

My throat worked. My eyes stung a little more. I glanced down, to the silver chain he almost always wore, the blackened cross against the patch of wiry hair, the fleur-de-lis and dog tag on either side. All I had to do was lift my hand—

"I almost texted, but didn't want to wake you if you were sleeping."

I slid my hands to the skirt of my uniform, pressed my fingers against my thigh. "Why?" I asked before I could stop myself. "What were you thinking about?"

His eyes met mine. "Your dreams."

Two simple words, but they knocked the breath right out of me.

"Did you have another one?"

I glanced out the window, to the crowded courtyard. Soon the bell would ring.

Not soon enough.

"Nothing special," I said, choosing my words carefully. Just of a field. It was dusk. Clouds darkened the sky, shadows turning the overgrown grass from green to black.

Upon waking, I'd stabbed out the first five of LaSalle's numbers before stopping myself.

"What if I can make one come true?"

The bell rang. At least I thought it did because outside everyone started to move. But I didn't hear it, heard nothing but Chase's question—and the distorted haze of possibility.

"One of your dreams," he said when I looked away from the window. "What if I make it real?"

My eyes met his. My heart almost sliced free of my chest—my dreams were so not greeting-card material. "That's not a good idea."

For a frozen second he looked at me, and for the first time I realized the shadow about him had lifted.

"I don't know where Jessie is," he finally said. "And I can't make her come back. I can't . . . fix her. But I can do this." Never looking away from me, he pulled something from his pocket. "I found them."

The room tilted. It was fast and sudden, a fleeting moment of vertigo over as soon as it began. I'll never know why. But I think maybe, in that one fragile heartbeat before I asked the question, I sensed everything was about to change. "Found who?"

His hand touched mine, and I looked down to find a small square of paper pressed between his fingers and my palm, an address neatly printed in black.

Then I looked up.

"Your parents," he said. "I found your parents."

The house blew me away.

Tall and boxy and peach, with full-length windows, dark shutters, and tons of wrought iron, the late-nineteenth-century Italianate sat back from the street, shrouded by huge trees and overgrown shrubs, barely visible to the casual passerby. An iron fence cordoned off the yard from the sidewalk. A padlock glistened against the frail gate. A winding walkway led to the tall porch.

Through the branches of the countless live oaks, wind whispered, and Spanish moss swayed.

"This was Gran's house?" I asked, putting my hands to the iron, so warm from the afternoon sun.

Chase moved past me, toward the PRIVATE PROPERTY sign attached to the gate. "Been in her family since 1897."

It was hard to accept. In the mountains we'd lived in a one-story, four-room log cabin. There'd been the kitchen, the TV room, a bedroom for each of us. Here, in this moody old house where my grandmother had been born, and in turn had given birth to her children, there had to be no fewer than twenty rooms.

Darkness gaped from the windows, but I would have sworn curtains shimmied beyond the grimy glass. "She never said a word," I whispered. Neither had Aunt Sara. I'd been here for a couple of months, but never once had my aunt volunteered that our family had an ancestral home not ten minutes away.

"You're sure she didn't sell it?" I asked.

Chase looked beyond the fence, toward the flowering trees doing their best to hide the porch. "I'm sure."

So was I. He stood only a few feet away, but the set of his jaw and rigid stance of his body told me all that the dark sunglasses concealed. The closer we'd gotten to the Garden District, the quieter he'd become. Since getting out of his car, he'd spoken only in response to questions.

Understandable, I told myself. For the past few days he'd been a rock, standing strong in the face of questions and accusations and unthinkable possibilities. It was only natural the weight of all that would take its toll. That, and the fact that Coach had benched him for the week due to his bum ankle.

The urge to step closer, to reach out and touch, to promise him everything would be okay, made me look away.

That was so not a promise I could make.

My grandmother had lived here until the day she packed up and moved to Colorado. I tried to see them, to imagine them as they'd been, the yard manicured, the climbing rose and bougainvillea carefully tended, my father and my aunt playing hide-and-seek among the huge oaks while my grandparents watched.

But that was a fantasy, I knew. My grandfather had never even met his youngest child. He'd died of a massive heart attack two weeks before her birth. My grandmother had been left alone in this cavernous old house with two young children to raise.

Maybe that's why, ultimately, she'd walked away and never looked back.

Even the house looked sad. "Does anyone live here now?" I asked. I didn't think so, but it was hard to imagine a place like this sitting empty for fourteen years.

Still not looking at me, Chase fingered the padlock, which immediately fell open.

I didn't need precognition to know what was going to happen next. Chase Bonaventure and the status quo did not go hand in hand. He was not someone to stay out, stay away, no matter what signs or locks stood in his way. If he wanted in, he found a way.

"No." With the word he pulled open the gate. "Not since your grandmother."

Which meant that like the house on Prytania, my family home sat empty, as did so many other structures in New Orleans. You could barely travel a block without finding boarded-up shops or restaurants, houses big and small, a massive hospital in the heart of downtown. I'd even heard of an amusement park quietly rotting away.

It was like life just . . . moved on. But the buildings, silent placeholders, remained.

Standing in that swath of afternoon sunlight, I watched Chase move away from me, along the cracked concrete of the walkway.

At the porch, he took the three steps and veered right, vanishing behind a screen of hanging baskets, the fern oddly bushy and vibrant and . . . *alive*.

I'm not sure why it took me so long to move. But for a few minutes I was content to stand on the outside, watching the breeze play with the trees, the mix of sun flirt with shadows. Then I could see him again, at one of the tall windows framed by those black shutters, with his back to me, looking in. And all I could think was . . . *go to him*.

I eased through the gate and the shade of the beautiful trees, acutely aware of the scent of—

Gardenia, I realized as I slipped up the steps. There beside the railing, gardenia bloomed wildly, spilling and dripping, fragrant white against rich green. The smile was automatic.

My grandmother had loved gardenia. It had been one of her

few indulgences, a whimsy I'd never understood. But she'd almost always had a candle of gardenia burning in her bedroom.

Now I knew why—it brought her back here, even if only in her mind, her heart, to this place she'd felt compelled to abandon.

I wanted to know why.

Wood creaked beneath my feet when I reached the porch. I stilled, realizing the breeze had done the same. As had Chase. He remained where I'd last seen him, at the window with a hand lifted to the side of his face to shield his eyes from the sun.

"See anything?" I asked.

This time, he said nothing.

"Chase?" Moving closer, I saw the shimmer of gauzy white on the other side of the window. Inside, I would have sworn I saw the outline of sheet-draped furniture. "Is that what I think—"

I never got the chance to finish.

He turned, his eyes, no longer obscured by dark lenses, meeting mine. "When I was six, my mom's aunt from Phoenix came to visit."

It was such an out-of-left-field statement that I instinctively said nothing in response.

"They thought I was outside," he said. "Riding my bike. But it was hot and I was thirsty and I came back for some water. I was in the kitchen. They were in the living room."

I watched him, stunned that someone could stand so close, but be so very, very far away. "What happened?" I asked, because without doubt, something had. Something big.

He looked beyond me, but I knew he wasn't seeing the porch or the house, the trees. He was a kid again, standing in what should have been the safety of his mother's kitchen.

"They were looking at a photo album," he said, and my heart started to pound really, really fast. "And my great aunt was talking as if she'd received the most amazing news. 'It's all worked out so well,' she said. 'No one would guess they're not yours.'"

I felt my breath catch, my eyes widen, worked hard to shove the surprise away. *"Chase—"*

"I stood there," he said. "I stood there and listened to them talk about me like I was some stray dog they'd brought in from the rain."

"No," I said, and then I moved, stepping closer, lifting a hand to his arm. *"No."*

Something flashed in his eyes, the blue swirling like a marble. "I left. I turned around and left, walked out the door and ran."

The pain in his voice, that of the boy he'd been, the boy whose illusions had been shattered without warning or provocation, had my fingers pressing tighter.

"Where did you go?"

He looked beyond me, to that invisible spot beyond the shroud of the oaks. "Away," he said. "I ran from street to street, looking inside every house I passed, at every person . . ."

Wondering. He didn't say, but even without the words, I knew. I understood. It was the way I walked the streets of New Orleans, with each person I passed, wondering if they'd known my parents. If, once, they'd known me.

"A cop found me in Walmart," he said. "Took me home."

I made myself swallow. "I'm sure your parents were worried sick—"

"They lied," he said, and finally his eyes met mine. "Even after I told them what I'd heard, they tried to lie."

Nothing could have stopped me from stepping closer, bringing my other hand to his arm.

"She tried to tell me I'd misunderstood what I heard."

Desperation drove people to do stupid things. "I can't even imagine . . ."

"She kept telling me about the day I was born," he said, his voice harsher now, sharper, "as if she'd actually *been* there."

I really didn't know what to say.

"And then, when they finally admitted the truth, that I was adopted, they tried to say they'd never told me to protect me. That they hadn't wanted to burden me with the truth—"

"Like my grandmother," I whispered, as the pieces finally fell together. Chase's curiosity about my parents, his quick discovery of property records . . . it was as much about him and what he'd lost, as it was about me.

"But lies don't protect," he muttered, moving finally, lifting a hand to feather the hair from my face. "Lies destroy."

How well I knew that. "Did you ever find anything out about your birth parents?"

His mouth twisted. "No. They claimed the records were sealed, that even they didn't know. But I never stopped looking at people, houses, wondering if they were dead or alive, why they didn't want me—"

I grabbed his wrist, squeezed. "Chase," I said with absolute certainty. "They wanted you."

"They had a funny way of showing it."

"Maybe your mom was young, or they were poor. Maybe they had no way to care for you—"

He looked away, leaving me to stare at the barbed-wire tattoo peeking from beneath his shirtsleeve. He had two, I knew. The other, on his chest, was Japanese. I'd finally looked it up.

It was the symbol for honesty.

"There's so much good in you," I whispered. "It had to come from somewhere."

The breeze stirred through the roses climbing the iron of the columns.

"You're defined by what's inside you," I said. "Not by what's around you. That's all window dressing."

His eyes crinkled. It was the first hint of a smile. "Kind of like this house," he muttered. "Beautiful, but nothing compared to you."

The sigh came from somewhere deep.

"Speaking of," he said abruptly, shuttering the little boy away, like the sun burning through the clouds and chasing off the shadows. And then Chase was back, the Chase from before, from normal things like chemistry and late-night texting and even yesterday at the park, reaching for my hand and dragging me toward the walkway. "I've got some more window dressing for you."

"*John Mark's girl?* Well I'll be dayum-ed." The surprisingly tall woman with graying hair but baby-smooth skin looked me up and down. "Last time I seen you, you was just a little thang."

We stood on the narrow porch of the house my parents had lived in when they first married, a small lemon-yellow building on the periphery of the French Quarter, with green shutters and a pretty iron overhang. The owner, an elderly woman who'd introduced herself as Mrs. Vincent, had moved there after she lost her home in a neighboring parish to Katrina. She'd never heard of my parents.

But Emma Watson, her next-door neighbor, had.

"Cute as a bug, too," she said, and I didn't have to look at Chase to know that the guard he'd had wrapped around him all afternoon had finally lowered. "You grew'd up good, chile. Real good. A looker like your daddy."

"Thank you." It seemed the right thing to say.

"I always wondered what happened to you," she said. "After

your daddy . . ." Her face clouded over. "I know'd him his whole life," she said. "He was the cutest little thing. Once I fancied he'd marry my girl." Suddenly her eyes got a faraway sheen to them. "Just think, then she'd have been your ma instead of that witch."

Whoa. I mean . . . *whoa*. Witch? Before I could even process what was happening, Chase moved closer, positioning himself between me and Mrs. Watson exactly like he'd done the day before with Jessica's father.

"Emma! That's this girl's mother you're talking about!" Mrs. Vincent scolded, sounding and looking every bit the well-mannered Southern lady she appeared to be.

My dad's supposed friend frowned. "You're right. I surely am sorry," she surprised me by saying, then glanced from me to the street beyond, searching. "It's just . . . Your mama was different."

Chase reached for my hand. "Come on, we're out of here."

Warning bells went off all through me. Emma Watson knew something. She knew my mother saw things—I could see that in the older woman's eyes.

I could also see fear.

And I wasn't about to walk away.

TWELVE

I wasn't about to let her blow the lid on truths I myself had yet to understand, either. Not in front of Chase.

Whatever and whenever he found out had to come from me.

"So you knew my dad," I detoured, steering the conversation to safer ground. "What was he like?"

"Trinity—" Chase started, but I swung toward him, silencing him with a quick, pleading look.

The way he looked at me, the combination of concern with quiet understanding, made my heart stutter.

Maybe Emma Watson recognized my tactic. Maybe she didn't. I'll never know. But she did go along with it, escorting us to her house next door, where I counted seven rail-thin black cats sunning themselves and five small saucers beneath the front window. I would have sworn they were fine bone china.

She sat us down on a wide porch swing and offered us sweet raspberry tea. Chase answered before I could, turning down her offer. I have to say I was glad.

The photo album surprised me. After so many years of wondering, of wanting to know, to finally find pictures here, in the mementos of a stranger . . .

"Handsome as sin, he was," Emma Watson said as I flipped through the small, fading images. But they were enough to see my father for the first time in fourteen years.

Except it wasn't really the first time. Because the boy captured in the old Polaroid images, with the wavy, dark brown hair and wide-set teasing eyes, hamming it up with dogs and cats and an adorable little girl with dark ringlets, was the father who came to me in my dreams.

"He and Amelia used to love to catch crawdads," she said. "There was this canal not too far away, and they'd go there for hours, coming home with a big box full for us to boil up."

"I've never had a crawfish," I whispered.

Chase's hand found mine, squeezed.

"Never? Well, I'll be," Mrs. Watson said, shooing away one of the flies that had strayed from the remains of the moist cat food. There must have been over twenty-five of them swarming the dishes. "Your granny had a real way with them, especially in étouffée or a gumbo."

I'd never had those dishes, either.

"She was a good woman," my dad's friend went on as I flipped the pages, the colors intensifying as the boy grew into a gangly teenager. "That there is their prom picture," she said.

Against the cracked plastic my finger traced the outline of my father, standing in a ridiculous baby-blue tuxedo with a white bow tie and a big smile, while next to him Emma Watson's daughter, in some light pink antebellum concoction, beamed.

"They were always so good together," she sighed.

I kept flipping, drinking in image after image. "That was his dog?" I asked, pointing to the black Lab that had been aging right along with my father.

"Archibald," Mrs. Watson said. "He was the most amazing hunting dog . . ."

I looked up. "Hunting what?"

"Duck mostly."

I frowned, instinctively glancing at Chase. I could only imagine what his thoughts were. "Thank you," I whispered, unable to stop the smile. "For giving me this."

His eyes warmed, but he said nothing.

I returned to the album, hesitating on a picture of my dad and Amelia in front of a barbecue grill. They each wore T-shirts saying New Orleans Saints. In the distance, a pudgy little girl with dark pigtails was running from a boy with a hose.

I must have made some kind of noise, because Emma Watson leaned closer. "You were such a pretty thing," she said. "Right from the start."

The band of emotion pulled tighter, making it hard to so much as breathe.

"And little James," she said, the big hoops in her ears swinging despite how still she sat. "You two were so cute."

Something I couldn't read shone in her eyes, something that made me want to look deeper, even as I returned to the album. I flipped the page, found more shots of my father and Amelia. Had I not known, I would have thought they had married, just like Emma Watson had wanted.

"What about my mom?" I asked, looking up from the last page. "I didn't see—"

"Didn't like the camera," Mrs. Watson said.

Beside me, Chase barely suppressed a cough.

"I surely am sorry that I can't tell you more," she went on, as I handed the collection of photos back to her. "Maybe you should check with her cousin . . ."

The bleached-out blue of late afternoon gave way to the gunmetal gray of dusk. With the two- and three-story buildings obscuring the remains of the sun, Chase fiddled with his iPhone, as he'd been doing nonstop for the fifteen minutes since we'd left Emma Watson's house.

"Find anything?" I asked.

He stopped walking and looked up. "Something's not right," he muttered, glancing around the mostly residential street. "Property records point to a man named Marcel Arceneaux."

"Is he my mom's cousin?" Mrs. Watson had given us an address, but no name.

"He died three years ago."

"Then who lives there now?"

"I can't tell," Chase said, once again returning to the Web page on his iPhone. "Maybe no one."

We were so close. That's all I could think. So. Close. "Then let's go find out," I said, moving again, heading for the intersection two buildings away.

The irony was not lost on me: twenty-four hours before I'd been uneasy about climbing a fence. Now, drunk on all Emma Watson had disclosed, I was the one pressing.

Chase's hand caught me before I veered out of reach. "I don't like walking in blind."

My heart squeezed, and I could see him all over again, the little boy running from his house, the lie—the only life he'd ever known.

"Neither do I," I said, lifting my eyes to his. "But sometimes we don't have a choice. Isn't that what this afternoon has been about?"

He edged closer, putting himself between me and a man with gray hair and dirty clothes a few sizes too big, a face like leather. During the transition from day to night, the streets of the Quarter became a dangerous no-man's land.

"*I knew,*" he said when the man finally vanished around the corner. "About the house in the Garden District, that it was empty. I knew about your parents' house, who lived in it."

Because while everyone else in my life had thrown up stop signs, Chase had pulled back the barricades and taken me by the hand. "But not Emma Watson," I realized. She was the wildcard.

"She could be anyone," he said, watching a long black limo glide to a stop in the intersection. "With any agenda."

No traffic came from either direction, but the long Humvee with dark windows did not move.

Only a few hours before, I would have thought Chase's internship at his mother's law office had left him paranoid, unable to accept anything at face value. Now I understood.

"Chase," I said as the limo finally glided away. "*We* showed up on *her* doorstep. I asked the questions. She just answered. The agenda is mine."

He glanced from the now empty intersection, to the recessed doorway behind me. "She called your mom a witch."

Somehow I didn't wince. "And Amber calls me that at least once a day," I pointed out, knowing I'd made the right decision to steer the conversation away from my mother. Still, though, the memory of what I'd seen in the other woman's eyes lingered. It was the same awareness I'd seen in my grandmother's when she'd moved her hand over her body in a shaky sign of the cross.

"It doesn't mean anything," I insisted.

"This is New Orleans."

I crooked a smile. "I noticed."

His frown deepened. "Everything means something."

Uncomfortable, I looked beyond him, saw the poster duct-taped to a NO PARKING sign.

Jessica's smile was model perfect, with her big sultry eyes glittering in that way that was all her own. Normally she preferred skinny jeans and tank tops, but her parents had chosen a shot featuring a boxy T-shirt, thigh-length cutoffs, and a goofy Labradoodle I'd never seen or heard of.

At the bottom, someone had taken a marker, replacing the word REWARD with FRIDAY NIGHT PRAYER VIGIL, OUR LADY OF ENDURING GRACE.

Chase turned toward the sign, stilled. The worry in his eyes . . .

I looked away, knew I couldn't turn back now. I'd filled in some of the blanks about my father, but my mother remained a big unknown. And the images I saw, the things I knew, came from her. If Jessica was in trouble, if I'd connected with her as my research into precognition suggested, then I had to find out how to sharpen the focus—and bring her home.

If Chase wouldn't take me, I'd have to double back and go by myself.

"Just a look. We walk by, stay on the sidewalk." What could it hurt? "Then we can go. Promise."

He turned back to me, lifting a hand to slip a sweep of hair behind my ear.

The way he looked at me made me feel as though he'd slipped away my clothes instead. "What?" I asked.

His hand fell away. "Jessie would have lied." A passing taxi almost absorbed the words. "She would have pretended to go along with me, then the second I turned my back, run off and done exactly what she'd wanted to."

I suddenly felt about two inches tall.

"Come on," he said, still so uncomfortably quiet, tender. Then, taking my hand, he led me deeper into the Quarter.

From bars and restaurants a few blocks away, the scent of sin and dinner drifted. At the one-way street we turned on, there was no sign to give away the name. The whole Quarter was a maze of them, laid out on a perfect grid. Tall narrow buildings, most in pastels with steps and shutters and dark windows, crowded both sides of the street. Not too far away stood the beautiful old cathedral.

Chase stopped, shifting his attention to the faded lime building behind me. Three crumbling steps led to a small porch, where a skinny tabby lay in the shadows, bathing itself.

"It should be right here," he said.

There was something weird in his voice. "What do you mean *should* be?" Either it was or it wasn't.

"I don't see a B," he said.

I glanced at him, then at the A on the peeling orange door. "Maybe," I started, but stopped when I saw the blood. A splotchy trail of it, leading from the sidewalk to the cat.

The tabby wasn't bathing itself. It was cleaning a wound.

"Oh, my God, he's hurt," I said, hurrying toward the steps. At the rail, I started up. "Chase," I called, glancing over my shoulder. "Come help—"

I froze.

Chase was gone.

THIRTEEN

"Chase!"

I vaulted down the steps and hit the concrete running. "Chase!" He'd been no more than five feet behind me when I turned around. No more than twenty seconds could have passed. "Chase!"

He was gone.

Heart racing, I spun around. "Chase!" I called again, but this time it was more of a scream. *"Chase!"*

People didn't just disappear. I knew that. Except—

Some people did. Especially in a city like New Orleans.

I started to run, the street stretching longer with each step I took. "Chase, please!" I cried. He'd wandered around the corner. That was all. Looking for the B. He didn't mean to scare me. He was going to be right back.

Except when I reached the end of the block, I saw only strangers.

"Have you seen a guy?" I asked a young woman in a black suit.

She had on high heels and carried a briefcase. "Tall," I said, "dark hair, navy slacks, and a white shirt?"

She shook her head.

"But he was just here!" I darted from her to the next people I saw, an older couple. "I'm looking for my friend," I said, rushing to describe him.

But they only smiled and pointed me in the direction of the police station.

I didn't want the police station. I didn't want the police. I wanted Chase.

"Oh, please," I whispered, remembering my phone. I grabbed it and punched his number, running back to the street with the skinny green house and the bleeding cat. That was the last place I'd seen him. Maybe he'd . . .

I don't know what I thought, but my grandmother had always told me if we got separated to go back to the last place I'd seen her.

I crammed the phone against my ear, listening as it rang. "Come on, come on!" I said, closing in on the little staircase.

The cat was gone, and Chase did not answer his phone. "Where are you?" I asked his voice mail. "I'm here, Chase, right where you left me . . ."

I made myself slow down as I ended the call. I made myself breathe. I was overreacting. I was being silly, letting my imagination and the fact that I was alone in a city I did not know get the better of me. There had to be a logical explanation. Chase would not go off and leave me.

"Chase!" I shouted as another taxi eased by. I'm not sure why I watched it reach the end of the street—maybe because that's what Chase had been doing. But I waited until it turned the corner before spinning back around—

—and saw him.

Relief sang through me. A narrow alley ran between the green building and its peach neighbor, and as I turned and looked, I saw Chase slip behind the building.

I wanted to smack him.

"Chase!" I called, darting after him. He probably hadn't meant to completely freak me out like that, but who goes off and leaves someone standing there, without saying a word?

"That was so not nice!" I said, turning behind the building at the same spot he had. "Are you out of your—"

The courtyard stopped me. There tucked behind the narrow green house with dark green shutters, a tropical oasis awaited. Dirty cracked concrete gave way to a cobblestone patio. Bougainvillea and roses in full, tangled bloom climbed brick walls. A pretty little iron table and chairs sat off to the side, beneath hanging baskets dripping with ferns and begonias.

And in the center of it all, through the lengthening shadows of dusk, petunias in little clay pots surrounded a gorgeous three-tiered fountain, in front of which the skinny tabby lay, repeatedly licking a paw then rubbing it behind her ear.

"Oh, my God," I whispered, trying to make sense of it all.

Then I saw the red door, and the letter B.

And behind me, hinges creaked.

I spun around, saw the gate I'd come through now stood closed. "Chase?" I called, reminding myself to be calm, that everything was okay. Chase didn't know I'd followed him.

But where was he?

Swallowing against the tightness in my throat, as if someone had curled invisible hands around my neck, I made my way to the gate, squeezed the handle, and pushed.

Nothing happened.

The wind, I told myself. It was only the wind.

But even as I tried to grab onto the thought, I realized the truth.

There was no wind. Not even a flutter.

And my legs were starting to shake.

"Chase!" On a deep breath I stared at the door with the B, realizing he must have gone inside.

In a movie, that would be when the teenage girl would sashay into a dark room or building, as if nothing bad could possibly happen to her.

I hated movies like that.

Of course, movies also had ominous music to cue the viewer something bad was about to happen, but I didn't need music. I had stillness and the echo of trickling water from the fountain, and a chill that sliced straight to the bone. And I did not want to go into that building, B or not.

Fumbling with my BlackBerry, it took me several tries to stab out the words.

Chase . . . where r u?

I hit send, waited.

No answer came.

I mean it. WHERE R U?

I counted to ten, stared at the cat.

She lay stretched on her side and perfectly contented, in a sliver of fading sunshine, watching me. Through eyes of gold.

That did not blink.

There was not a trace of blood in sight.

"Chase," I whispered, and my hands started to shake. "Come on, come on, *come on*!"

Please

 I hit send.

Come back.

 With each word, my fingers found it increasingly difficult to find the right keys.

Dom'r Irsve ne hwew

 The second I sent the message, I caught movement out of the corner of my eye—and almost fell to my knees. "Chase."

 An old woman emerged from the shadows. Her long, flowing robe was as white as her hair. Her eyes were as dark as her skin.

 "Put down the phone, chile."

 I took an instinctive step back. "W-who are you?" And why was she watching me like that, as if *I* was the freaky one? "Where's my friend?"

 Her face remained without expression. "*Chile.* You cannot bring that phone inside."

 I swallowed hard. Inside? I was not going inside. "Are you . . . are you my mother's cousin?"

 A soft breeze whispered around her, tinkling wind chimes I had not seen before, but not moving a hair on her head. "Come," she said.

 The walls of the courtyard started to push closer. I spun around and fought the urge to lift my arms to shove everything back. Away. *"Where's my friend?"*

 Her eyes glowed like black diamonds heated from the inside out. "You waste my time," she said, and then she was turning, float-ing back toward the door.

"Wait!" I practically screamed after her.

The second I realized what I was doing, I froze. "Is . . . Is he okay?"

She turned back to me. "I did not see your friend."

The disembodied words came at me through the shadows, settling against me, oozing through me like a horrible cold mist.

"I am afraid you have a choice to make, Trinity Rose. You, chile, and you alone."

Trinity Rose.

She knew my name.

Her eyes met mine, and I would have sworn I felt the impact clear down to my soul. "Do you want to know about your mother, or do you want to find this so-called friend?"

In my hand I still held the phone. I glanced down at my bloodless fingers curled around the pink case, and wished like crazy that I'd saved Detective LaSalle's phone number as Aunt Sara had suggested.

"You must come alone," the woman said. "Your friend cannot see what you can."

I started to shiver from the inside out. The gate was locked. I could not get out. There was nowhere to go—no one to hear me scream.

Chase. Where was he? What had happened to him?

My fault, I knew. *My fault.* He'd wanted to wait. He'd told me something didn't feel right.

But I hadn't listened. I'd begged him, and now he was gone.

"Come," the woman said, and with the single, hypnotic word, she shifted, a frail hand emerging from the folds of her robe—and extended a knife.

Somehow I didn't scream. At least not out loud. Inside I screamed over and over.

Wake up! Wake up, wake up, wake up!

But you can't wake up when you're not asleep.

"When you are ready," she said, laying the knife on the little iron table.

"What's that for?"

Again her eyes met mine, but this time she looked more maternal than demonic. "It is for you."

And then she was gone.

My phone fell from my fingers, and as if my legs had a mind of their own, they started to move. Toward the door with the B, where the woman with the long white hair had vanished.

Stop, I told myself. *Stop!*

But something greater pulled me toward the darkness, as if the house was a magnet and I was a scrap of metal.

At the table I picked up the knife, my hand curving around the cool, smooth handle of carved bone.

I didn't want to think what kind.

At the door I extended my arms in front of me, both hands secure around the handle of the knife as if it could protect me.

Then I stepped inside.

FOURTEEN

The cat slipped by me, and the magnetic pull stopped.

I staggered at the unexpected release, reaching out to steady myself against the closest thing I could find. A soft, buttery light bathed the room, making me blink to focus. That's when I saw the grandfather clock.

It was tall and beautiful, intricately carved with a traditional face and columns running along the sides, an astrological dial along the top, and Roman numerals for numbers.

Six thirty-five, it read, and through the quiet, I could hear the steady heartbeat of the pendulum.

Slowly I turned, and felt what was left of reality shift from beneath me.

I'd walked into an old darkened building, and emerged into a nineteenth-century parlor.

I'd seen the movies. My grandmother loved them. Old classics where a man and woman sit on some dainty sofa, with a silver tea setting on the table in front of them, heavy drapes against the tall windows and a grand piano in the corner, walls covered by a heavy floral fabric or simply painted pink or peach.

The room with the clock was dusty rose. And beautiful.

Everything was there, the sofa covered in rose velvet and the formal chairs, the tables and the glass lamps, the artwork on the walls. The piano.

No, no, no . . . that was not music I heard. At least not in the room. Only in my mind.

French doors dominated the wall in front of me, tall and white. Closed. I could think of a thousand reasons to leave them that way, but found myself moving toward them anyway. Until I saw the china cabinet. Beautiful and wide, with shimmering glass and dark, polished wood, it sat in the far corner like a child being punished.

Unable to look away, I crossed the thick Persian rug until I stood close enough to lift my hand to the cool, perfectly clear glass, and totally forgot to breathe.

It was all there, everything that had been in my mother's trunk, the crystals and rocks in all colors, red and blue and topaz. Black. The feathers and the seashells. The small jars of ash. The misshapen stick and the vials of liquids.

Trancelike I shifted the knife to my left hand and used my right to ease open one of the doors and pick up a jar. I pried off the lid and slid the small, perfume-looking bottle beneath my nose, smelled roses. And something else. Something stronger.

Closing my eyes I inhaled again, and the room shimmied around me, as if a huge droplet of water separated me from everything else. I fumbled to return the vial to the dust-free shelf and ran my hands along the curious assortment of seashells.

I'm not sure what made me turn, but the second I saw the mirror to my left, I started to move. A square of black framed an intricate pattern of silver swirls and circles and birds, which gave way to a coppery circle in a Celtic pattern. The mirror itself glowed from the center, as perfectly round as it was black.

I'd never seen a black mirror before, but knew without hesitation that's what it was.

I crossed to it, didn't think twice about stepping onto the wooden footstool waiting beneath. The slight elevation brought me to the height of the mirror, and with a slam of my heart, I lifted my eyes, and looked.

It was like looking into the deadest hour of night. Through the pool of cool obsidian, I saw nothing, not even my reflection.

Not sure what I was expecting, or why disappointment slipped through me, I started to pull away. And saw her.

She was beautiful, with long dark hair and gentle, smiling eyes, gazing with uplifted hands at an older woman. In her open palms a baby bird sat very still. And the older woman frowned.

"Mama," I whispered, but then the image dissolved and the black flashed, and another image came of the woman with the long hair, older now, rocking a babe of her own. Tears ran down her cheeks as the infant lifted a chubby hand to wipe them away . . .

"No, no, no . . ." I whispered, backing away.

But the room held me, and I could not move.

"Stop!" I cried, not sure who I was talking to, but knowing that I needed it to stop, all of it, the images swirling in the black and the crazy way the room rocked around me.

Then I saw the girl running through the darkness, falling, rolling. And then she was underwater and I couldn't breathe, couldn't move, couldn't do anything as the oxygen squeezed from my lungs.

The room kept spinning, faster, harder, like an out-of-control carnival ride. And the house flashed with tiny insidious earthquakes of lightning. Over and over again.

Then I saw the body, pale and still, laid out on a marble slab.

Nearby a woman was crying—Aunt Sara? And through the fading heartbeat of the room I could hear another voice, this one male, shouting *no* over and over again. But I saw no face and felt—

Absolutely nothing. I felt nothing at all, as if I was watching the scene play out while drifting away, floating, leaving my body behind.

My body, I realized. It was my body stretched out on the cold slab, with wet hair plastered against my face.

My dead body.

"*No . . .*" I managed, frozen at first, then fighting, twisting, clawing at the nothingness until finally I thrust my hands toward the mirror.

And saw the blood.

It dripped along the glistening silver blade and ran down my arms.

I screamed, and everything just stopped. The flashing. The spinning.

The lightning.

It was like being thrown from a speeding car, one second you're racing along and then you slam into something hard, bouncing on impact, rolling . . .

I lay there in the stillness for a frozen eternity, until the breath hit my lungs. Then I was scrambling to my feet and running, across the room and to the door, yanking it open and staggering into the night.

"Oh, God!" I cried, going down on my knees. But I wouldn't let myself stay there, couldn't curl up like a baby no matter how incapable of thought I was.

My phone, I remembered. I'd dropped it by the fountain—

The gate crashed open, giving way to a man running through the darkness, his arms extended in front of him, a gun in his hands. On the ground, I stilled.

Until I saw the figure behind him.

"Chase!" I'm not sure who moved first, who moved faster. I only knew that before I could so much as breathe, I was by the fountain and in Chase's arms, and he was holding me, holding me so tight, as if he would never let me go.

"I've got you, baby," he murmured against my hair. *"I've got you."*

"Where were you?" I cried, pulling back to see his face. That's when I saw the blood at his temple, and everything tilted all over again. "My God," I whispered. "What happened to you?"

His eyes darkened, flashed, shifted to the other man, the one I'd completely forgotten in my rush to get to Chase.

Detective Aaron LaSalle stood between me and the old house, his gun drawn and ready. "Are you okay?" he asked.

Somehow I nodded.

"Trinity," Chase said. "What the hell is going on?"

I swallowed hard, scrambled for words.

There were none.

"I d-don't know," I whispered. "I turned around and you were gone . . ."

He shook off my explanation, as if the words weren't the ones he wanted. "You were screaming," he said. "Just now when we were coming down the alley. Why were you screaming?"

Numbly I turned back toward the darkened house.

"Holy shit," Chase muttered, and the alarm in his voice super-charged my heart all over again. I glanced up at him, saw him staring at my hands.

"W-what?" I started—then saw the blood seeping between my closed fingers.

"Trinity," Chase whispered, helping me uncurl my hands to reveal my palms.

Somewhere along the line night had fallen, leaving a thick web of darkness. It was enough, though, enough to see the deep cuts across the center of my palms and the ooze of blood.

"What the hell happened to you?" The words were from Chase. I knew that because I saw his mouth move. But the strangled voice was one I'd never heard before. Nor had I ever seen his eyes go wild like they did as he ripped his T-shirt from his body and used it to bandage my hands.

All this was happening, but like the image in the mirror, it was as if I watched, rather than lived. Saw, rather than felt.

"The knife . . ." I said, spinning around.

LaSalle's cop-on-the-hunt gaze scanned the shadows of the courtyard. "What knife?"

It wasn't there. "I-I . . ." Didn't know. Didn't understand. "There was an old woman . . . she gave it to me . . ."

"Baby, what are you talking about?" Chase asked, and I blinked again, turned back toward the door with the B.

"She was here." My mind raced, struggled to put the pieces together. "I . . . I saw you. After you left, I—"

Against my arms, his fingers tightened. "I didn't leave."

I tried not to sway, wasn't sure that I succeeded. *"W-what?"*

"You stopped," he said. "You stopped and started walking back to the steps."

I shoved at the tangled hair falling against my face, but the T-shirt bandage made me clumsy. "The cat," I said. "It was hurt. I was trying to—"

"Trinity." It was Chase's voice that made my heart slow to a horrible crawl, the gentleness. The concern. "There was no cat."

And just like that the spinning accelerated, and I felt Chase move closer, his hands grip my biceps, holding me firmer. "Yes, there was. It was on the steps and it was bleeding and . . ."

Chase looked beyond me to where Detective LaSalle stood.

I hated the look that passed between them.

"Forget the cat," LaSalle said. "I need to know what happened inside that house."

I wanted to dive back into Chase's arms and feel them close around me again, to hear his voice whisper to me, through me, to promise that this would all be okay.

Except I knew that was impossible.

"I-I thought I saw Chase come back here. So I followed. There was this woman, it was like she was waiting for me." God, that sounded crazy, even to me. "Like she knew I was coming."

But that was also impossible. How could she have known, unless Emma Watson had told her?

"She said if I wanted to know the truth about my mother, then I had to go inside."

"Ah, *baby*," Chase murmured, and I died a little all over again. "I should never have brought you here."

But Detective LaSalle was already striding toward the door with the B. I hurried along behind him, Chase by my side.

The door stood closed. I was sure I'd left it open. None of that mattered, though, because LaSalle didn't slow down, just lifted a leg at full speed and kicked the door down.

Not open.

Down.

Rotting wood disintegrated at the blow, revealing the gape of darkness beyond.

I practically slammed into his back, stood there staring, shaking. "No . . ." I whispered, and then I was moving again, stepping away from Chase and around the detective, into the big, empty, rancid-smelling room.

"No, no, no!" I cried, spinning. "There was a clock . . ."

But now the wall stood vacant, peeling.

"And a sofa," I said, blinking hard, thinking that maybe—

I didn't know what I was thinking, but realized that I'd better shut up fast.

It was all gone, everything: the sofa, the tables, the rug, the lamp. The French doors—the china cabinet.

The mirror.

All . . . gone.

"Trinity?" Chase said, again beside me. "What are you talking about? What's going on?"

I twisted toward him. "W-what time is it?"

Frowning, he pulled out his iPhone and checked. "A little after seven thirty—why?"

An hour. In the blink of an eye, I'd lost a full hour. And a whole lot more of my sanity.

"You kids wait here," LaSalle said, moving past me, deeper into the suffocating darkness. From his belt he withdrew a flashlight and clicked it on, bathing the room in a brilliant white light.

The walls were a faded, barf-looking green, not dusty rose. No artwork adorned them, at least not the framed kind you bought in galleries, only the spray-paint kind, weird tattoolike drawings similar to what I'd seen at the house on Prytania.

LaSalle crossed to the far side, where his feet crunched on what sounded like broken glass.

Chase kept me against his side, and I didn't know whether to scream or cry. Or run. That's what I wanted to do. Get out of there, away from that place. To breathe—and think.

"I want to go home," I whispered as LaSalle squatted to run his fingers along the floorboard. I glanced up at Chase . . . saw the blood at his temple. "What happened?" I asked. "What happened to *you*?"

He'd always been bigger than life to me, the drop-dead gorgeous football player with the amazing body and killer smile, the dimples that could melt your heart, the unexpected kindness that made me dream. But in that moment, with his bangs falling against his face and unease drenching his eyes, he looked like he'd looked into the gates of hell.

"Chase, I'm sorry," I whispered. And I was. So very, very sorry. "I should have listened to you. I should have let you take me home."

He pulled me closer, tangling a hand in my hair as he pressed a kiss to my temple. The protective—*possessive*—way he held me was enough to make me cry. His chest was so warm.

"You were gone," he muttered, and it was almost as if he blamed himself. "I turned around and you were just gone."

"Chase—"

"And then . . ." He let out a rough breath. "I don't know. Everything went black."

Swallowing, I was torn between watching the detective and watching Chase. "Black?"

"I don't know how long I was out. I woke up to a man and woman leaning over me, asking me if I was okay."

"Chase," I murmured, lifting a hand to brush the bangs from his temple.

The sight of my blood staining the T-shirt wrapped around my palms stopped me.

That odd glitter still in his eyes, he looked beyond me, toward LaSalle. "My wallet was gone, my phone still in my pocket. That's how they reached my dad."

A few more pieces drifted into place. "And he called LaSalle," I realized.

Chase nodded. "No one had seen you. You were just *gone*. He was calling for backup when we heard you scream."

I looked down toward the dirty, dust-covered floor. A floor that had been clean a few moments before, gleaming hardwood covered by a gorgeous rug.

"I'm sorry," I said again, this time as Detective LaSalle returned. His eyes were hard, guarded. His mouth was set and grim.

"This is the room you were in?" he asked.

I nodded.

"There's nothing here," he said, and I could already tell what he was thinking: that I was either totally out of my mind or a bald-faced liar. "No knife," he said. "No woman."

Just like there'd been no trace of Jessica at the house on Prytania.

Chase still held me pressed against the warmth of his body, but I couldn't stop shaking. She was here! I wanted to scream, but realized there was no point. The more I said, the crazier they'd all think I was.

"I want to go home," I whispered.

Detective LaSalle kept eyeing me, as if through the sheer force of his will he could make me confess. "I'm sure you do."

"Come on," Chase said. "She's been through enough."

The detective's eyebrows bunched together. "Has she?"

He didn't believe us. That was so obvious. "I must have fallen," I murmured. "Hit my head—"

"Ah," LaSalle said. "Let me guess. Another dream?"

FIFTEEN

I wanted to scream. More, I wanted to grab a can of spray paint and erase everything. Not only this day, but the past few weeks and this entire city. To be back in Colorado in the mountains, with Gran . . .

"She didn't dream her hands," Chase pointed out.

"Obviously not." Suspicion remained sharp in LaSalle's eyes—he was so not buying our story about vanishing cats and women and rooms. "I'll take you home," he said, but the second the words left his mouth, Chase pulled me tighter.

"I can," he started, but stopped when a different voice broke through the silence.

"Chase!"

"Dad," he said as the detective swung his flashlight to reveal a tall man in scrubs running through the courtyard.

The very dark courtyard.

The man raced in and smothered Chase into his arms. "Ah,

Christ, I've been worried sick," he said as Chase hugged him back, assuring his father he was okay.

I didn't hear what either of them said after that, because I couldn't stop looking beyond the door, to the crumbling cobblestone and empty hanging baskets, the broken clay pots—and old dried-up fountain.

And the skinny cat with the glowing yellow eyes, slinking through the shadows and into the night beyond.

"Tell me what you know about Chase Bonaventure."

Fresh out of the shower, I hovered in the hallway with my back to the wall, listening. Chase's father had insisted on taking him to the hospital to have his temple looked at, leaving LaSalle to drive me to my aunt's.

I'd really hoped he'd be gone by the time I came out. Instead, he was grilling my aunt.

"Chase?" she said, and though I couldn't see her, I knew she was looking at the cop like he was crazy. "You can't think—"

"Trust me, Sara, I can think just about anything. Because I've seen just about everything," he said, and it was bizarre, because his voice was different than before. It was lower, gentler.

I slipped closer, saw them standing near the breakfast bar. Not much space separated them. Aunt Sara was tall, but Detective La-Salle dwarfed her. She'd been doing a yoga video when we arrived. Still in her tight workout clothes with her hair knotted up on her head, she stood in a fighter's stance, glaring up at him.

"I don't get paid to see the best in everyone," he added in that oddly compassionate voice. "Even when I want to. My job is to see the worst. To consider it, explore it. And here's what I'm seeing right now: a beautiful girl is missing. The day before she vanished, she and her ex-boyfriend were seen arguing. Maybe things got out of hand. Maybe—"

No way could I keep standing there, listening.

"No," I said, crossing toward them. "Chase isn't like that."

They both swung to look at me. Detective LaSalle spoke first. "They never are, sweetheart."

"He's a good guy—"

"Who made threats." LaSalle turned all cop again, his voice as point-blank as his eyes. "I've got witnesses saying that he warned Jessica Morgenthal she'd be sorry—"

He'd admitted the same to me. But not like *that*.

"You can't believe what Amber Lane says," I said, wincing when I forgot about my palms and clenched my hands into fists. Quickly I uncurled my fingers. "She's a drama queen, and Jessica's best friend. All she wants to do is make Chase look as bad as possible."

LaSalle lifted a single brow.

I really hated that.

"From all accounts," he said, "Chase Bonaventure has done that by himself."

"That's not fair!"

"No," he said, "it's not. But it's not about fair, either. It's about finding the truth, no matter how ugly or shocking it is. Violence is rarely random. A huge portion of the time, the victim knows the perp. Sometimes it's anger or revenge, sometimes just passion—"

"Aaron," my aunt said. "We're talking about kids."

Aaron?

He shot her a quick, apologetic look. "No," he said. "We're not."

Her eyes narrowed, but he jumped in before she could say anything.

"I wish being sixteen meant nothing bad ever happened. I wish being sixteen meant you weren't capable of anger or hate—or violence. But it doesn't," he said, and I couldn't help but notice the change in him from the night he'd first come to take my statement. Then he'd been stony.

Tonight he seemed rattled. "My job is to think about everything. I can't rule out someone because his mother might run for D.A. The bottom line is a girl is missing. Maybe she drove off on her own. Maybe she's playing a game, trying to get attention or prove a point. Or maybe some sick bastard hurt her. Maybe someone she trusted—"

"Not Chase," I whispered, but he kept right on going.

"Maybe she wasn't the nicest person in the world. Maybe she pushed someone too hard. Maybe Chase got mad, or you wanted revenge. Amber was jealous, or Pitre wanted to teach her a lesson. Her sister had had enough, or the guy from LSU got jealous. Things went too far. Accidents happen. Someone got scared. Now it's my job to bring her home, one way or another."

It was "the other" that worried me.

His gaze locked on mine. "If you can help me do that, Trinity, great. But if you're hiding something . . . I will find out."

Long after Detective LaSalle left, the chill of his words lingered. After my shower I'd put on my favorite flannel pajamas (light blue with panda bears scattered all over), but I couldn't have been colder if I'd been standing naked in a Colorado blizzard. My whole body shook from it.

I watched my aunt fill a glass measuring cup with water then slide it into the microwave, pull it out a few minutes later and pour it into two mugs. She'd been oddly quiet since LaSalle left, mechanical almost, as if she was running through some kind of mental checklist.

"Thank you," I said.

Still in her yoga clothes, she looked up from the mugs where green tea steeped. "For what?"

I sucked in a sharp breath, then took a huge leap of faith. "Sticking up for me," I whispered. "Believing me."

Her face fell.

"It was real," I said, needing for someone to believe me. For her to believe. "I saw her, I really did."

"Oh, *cher*," she whispered, not asking who, or when, or how. Not asking anything.

"I'm not crazy," I said, shaking my head. Because I could see them still—LaSalle, Chase's father—looking at me like I had a serious mental problem. And Chase . . . Omigod, the memory of the confusion in his eyes ripped me up. "I don't care what anyone says," I muttered. "I'm not crazy."

"No," she said quietly. "You're not."

I picked up one of the unlit votives and rolled it in my hands. "It was all there . . ." In the room—or some dark corner of my mind. I no longer knew which. The line between dream and reality—*vision and reality*—was increasingly obscured.

"The woman and the mirror—the knife . . ." Woodenly I replaced the candle and turned my hands palm up. I'd wrapped the gauze as tightly as possible, but blood still leaked through.

That was real.

"I didn't do this to myself," I said, but that wasn't true, was it? "At least, I didn't do it on purpose." But the knife *had* been in *my* hands. I had no memory of cutting myself, but obviously I had. "I-I don't know how it happened."

Aunt Sara's eyes darkened. "Was the mirror black?"

It took a second for me to latch onto the fact I'd just mentioned a mirror. I nodded then, and she frowned.

"Your mother had one," she whispered. "It was her mother's, and her mother's before her."

The firstborn daughter of the firstborn daughter . . . "But—"

"She saw things in it," my aunt said. "She saw—"

By the way she broke off, I could tell she didn't like what she'd remembered. "What?" I came around the counter, to where she stood near the island in the center of the kitchen. "What did she see?"

Aunt Sara looked down, into the greenish-brown tea in the two mugs.

"Things," she said, looking up several seconds later. "Things she would never tell me about."

I felt my eyes widen, but even open like that I could see the body again—pale, laid out like a sacrifice. I saw the woman, heard the shout of a guy, and once again felt myself start to float.

"She saw herself die, didn't she?" I whispered. And again, without waiting for an answer, I knew. "My mother saw herself die."

My aunt's eyes clouded over. "I have something for you," she said, lifting a thin bronze chain from the counter next to her mug. I'd barely noticed it sitting there—Aunt Sara always had some kind of charm, pendant, or beads lying around.

Curious, I lifted my hand as she reached toward me, watching as what looked like a medallion settled against the bloodstained gauze.

"It's from your mother," she said, as the most phenomenal warmth moved through me. "She treasured it."

The edges of my vision blurred, but not enough to distort the ornate curve of a tarnished dragonfly, or the warm glow of the orangish-gold crystal in the center.

"I should have given it to you when you first got here . . . but I was hoping you wouldn't need it."

I looked up. "Wouldn't need it?"

It was crazy how pale her face was. "Her grandmother gave it to her—for protection."

"A lot of good that did her," I murmured, but even as the cynicism moved through me, I unfastened the clasp and drew the chain around my neck.

"Not her," my aunt whispered, and my fingers froze. *"You."*

"Me?"

Her eyes went as dark as her skin was pale. "Mama Collette promised it would protect *you*—and it did."

I didn't sleep. Everything kept playing in my mind like a movie on repeat: Emma Watson and the bizarre courtyard, the mirror and the glowing dragonfly that had been in my mother's family for generations—and Chase.

I hated how badly I needed him to call.

He didn't. I told myself he was still at the hospital, but that only made me worry more. What if the gash on his head was more serious than we'd realized?

Victoria put that fear to rest. She'd talked to Lucas, who'd talked to Pitre, who'd talked to Chase. Chase who was home and completely fine.

I don't know why I kept checking my BlackBerry. It beeped when a new message arrived, and there was no beeping. But every few minutes I grabbed it and fumbled with my laptop, dreaming up excuses. He was busy with his parents—or he'd fallen asleep. Pain pills could do that. But as the hours stacked up, another possibility needled deeper.

Chase had not called or texted, because he'd seen the blood on my hands. He'd heard me babbling about nonexistent old ladies and clocks and meticulously preserved rooms.

A story that had absolutely no substantiation.

After being lied to by virtually everyone he'd ever trusted, Chase Bonaventure needed substantiation.

God. I should never have told him anything, not about my parents, or my dreams.

Especially my dreams.

It hit without warning, sometime during the darkest depths of the night. I had no awareness of closing my eyes. I had no awareness of falling off. But then I was there . . .

Trees rose up around me. They were tall and old and frail, little more than skeletons against the sun-bleached sky. Some had green to them—most did not.

Squinting against the glare, I turned around, and saw the field.

Memory trickled through me. I'd been here before . . .

"Where am I?" I called.

But only the cry of a lone bird answered. I looked for him, that lone bird perched somewhere high out of sight, but the edges of the branches blurred, and I could make out nothing.

"Trinity . . ."

The sound of my name sliced through the silence with deafening softness. I spun again as the low roar started, soft, like purring on the horizon.

"Help me," she whispered, and even as I started to run, I knew.

"Jessica!" I called, but the roaring grew louder, no longer a puff but an assault. The overgrown weeds slapped my legs—the mud tried to hold me in place. "Where are you?"

"Hurry . . ."

I twisted, using my hand to shield my eyes from the unnatural brightness. Against the absence of color, silver streaked high into the sky, until finally the roar of jet engines fell into silence.

Then I saw the truck.

"Wait!" I shouted, running again, harder. "Wait! Come back!"

But the old white pickup never even slowed. It came straight for me—

"Trinity!"

I felt my whole body jerk, recoil—

"Wake up, *cher*—please!"

A soft glow replaced the terrible blinding white, and I sat there, frozen, trying to breathe.

Aunt Sara had her hands on my upper arms, her mascara-smeared eyes steady on mine. "You're okay," she promised. But her voice gave away the lie. "Just give yourself a minute."

My throat burned. My body trembled. I'd been there . . . been somewhere. Just like the night before, I'd seen the field and heard her. But tonight there'd been more.

"I need to talk to Detective LaSalle," I whispered, closing my bandaged hand around the warm glow of my mother's amulet. *"Please,"* I said.

Even if he thought I was crazy.

"This isn't much to go on," he said shortly before six, standing with a cup of coffee near the breakfast bar. Clearly we'd pulled him from sleep. He hadn't taken time to shave or formally dress, had just come over in jeans and a white T-shirt.

Under almost any other circumstances, the ratty flip-flops would have made me smile.

Aunt Sara nursed her own cup of coffee. She'd pulled her hair off her face and scrubbed away the mascara, pulled on her own pair of jeans and a T-shirt promoting the wetlands.

"She was white as a ghost," she whispered. "Whatever she saw—"

"I got it," he said quietly, cutting her off. "A field, an airplane, and a white truck."

Even I had to admit it was like looking for a needle in a haystack.

"Maybe by the airport," Aunt Sara suggested.

He put down the mug and flipped his small notebook shut. "I'll let you know," he said, turning toward me. "I'd like you to keep quiet about this," he said. "The fewer people who know, the fewer we have to worry about."

I stilled. So did my aunt. "You don't really think," she started, but the regret in his eyes silenced her question. He did think. He'd made that clear the night before. He thought about everything.

"Just get some rest," he said, a few minutes later, before he left. "Keep a low profile today—"

My mind raced through everything I'd had planned. No tests or anything . . . "But the vigil—"

"I'll go with you," Aunt Sara promised, and that seemed to satisfy him. Shortly after he left, she insisted I go back to bed. "I have a few appointments I can't reschedule," she said, standing outside the door to her room. She'd had a lot of those this week. "I'll feel better knowing you're resting."

With a tight smile I slipped back into my room and tried to go to sleep. But like that was even possible. For a while I lay watching the ceiling fan, then I crossed to the trunk and once again sorted through all the little vials and boxes.

It was after I got dressed that I fired up my laptop and reached for my phone, and felt my heart stop.

Seven messages. All from Chase.

U OK?

That first message was from 1:07. I must have been asleep by then. The next text came two minutes later.

U there?

I swallowed, my throat so tight it hurt. Chase *had* texted me. The third came ten minutes after the first.

Need 2 talk 2 u.

Now my palms started to throb.

WANT 2 talk 2 u.

They were just cold words on my phone, but I would have sworn he'd reached out and touched me.

COME ON, BABY. T2M

Baby. He'd called me that the evening before, in the courtyard when he'd held me and promised me everything would be okay. Just the memory brought a rush of warmth.

T2M. Talk to me.

If only I knew what to say, how to explain everything he'd seen go down.

WHAT'S GOIN ON?

My hands shook. It took three times to pull up the last message, sent at 4:42.

I WAS THERE. I KNOW WHAT HAPPENED. U DON'T HAVE TO HIDE.

That one I stared at a long time. Maybe the words were supposed to be reassuring, but the quick stab of cold made them feel ominous.

I dropped the BlackBerry, shoved it to the edge of my bed. Then I opened the browser and did a quick search on amulets.

What I read both fascinated and chilled me. The pictures were beautiful, the explanations intricate. I'd heard about rabbits' feet, but I'd thought that was a bunch of superstitious baloney. But according to the author, amulets dated back to the beginning of time and crossed all religious and ethnic lines. Some called them magic. Others called them divine.

The result was the same, a connection with a higher being, manifested through a stone or crystal or metal.

I didn't realize how tightly I was clenching the medallion until my palm started bleeding again.

Some kind of protection, I thought, hurrying to the bathroom. With a fresh wad of gauze, I was almost back to my bed when I heard the beep of an incoming message.

I didn't want to look. For a long time, I didn't. At least four minutes *seemed* like a long time. I told myself it was probably Aunt Sara checking on me.

But I knew that wasn't true.

On a deep breath, I reached for the phone—and saw four messages had arrived while I was cleaning up my palm.

One from Victoria . . . three from Chase.

SIXTEEN

I told myself to read Victoria's first. But of course, I didn't.

WHERE R U?

That was Chase. Glancing at the time, I realized it was lunch break at school.

R U OK?

Then:

COME ON. T2M.

I swallowed against the knot in my throat, and pulled up to Victoria's.

HEY! WHERE R U? MISS U! IT'S CRAZY HERE 2DAY. AMBER IS SUCH A BITCH. WAIT TIL I TELL U! U R STILL COMING 2NITE, RN'T U? IT'S GONNA BE NUTS.

The courtyard looked like a shrine.

With late afternoon giving way to dusk, I followed the paved walkway past the graceful oaks and eerily tranquil fountain, to the multimedia circus unfolding at Our Lady of Enduring Grace.

Up the six steps leading to the Administration building, a Gothic-like oil portrait of Jessica, with her dark hair flowing around her face, her lipstick bloodred, stood in greeting. A collection of teddy bears and flowers spread out along the concrete, with balloons bobbing in the breeze. Candles flickered. Music drifted through the trees, something haunting and New Age.

Jessica, with her near-desperate need to be the center of attention, would have *loved* it.

And yet it made me want to cry. No matter what had gone down between us, no matter how hateful she'd been, she was a person. People loved her. Everywhere I looked, they gathered: the staff, a large portion of the student body, hoards of teens I'd never seen before, some standing in small groups, some staring up at the huge screen in front of the library, where images of Jessica flickered like slow-motion lightning.

There she was last year, on the homecoming court. And along the sideline of a football game, cheering. At the Christmas dance . . . draped all over Chase.

He was laughing, his arms so very, very tight around her.

The image stopped me, long after the slide show had flitted on, sharing pics of spring break and track meets, random shots of Jessica and Amber and Chase and Drew, of Pitre and Victoria, all from the year—

Before.

All from before.

Before I'd come to Enduring Grace.

Before I'd walked into their lives . . . into the house on Prytania.

Soon they would all disperse for the football game. But for now, it was all about Jessica.

"Hey," came a soft, quiet voice, and I blinked before looking to my right, where my aunt stood close to my side. Beyond her, at the far edge of the courtyard, no fewer than three news crews prepared to go live. "You okay, *cher*?"

My lips pressed tight. I'm pretty sure my smile looked as fake as it felt. "Fine."

"You don't have to do this, you know. No one is making you be here."

But that wasn't true. "I need to be here," I said, as Victoria broke from a group of three others and waved, heading my way. "If I stay away, everybody will only think the worst."

Her hand found mine and squeezed. "What they think doesn't matter. You know that, don't you?"

I did. But I also knew I needed to be there, not just because of what people would or wouldn't think, but because of Jessica. It was as if she was reaching out to me . . .

"Trinity!" Victoria called, closing in on me and wrapping me in a quick hug. "I was beginning to wonder if you'd be here."

I pulled back, struck by the sprinkle of what looked to be glitter beneath her eyes. In her skinny jeans and simple black shirt, she looked somewhere between ready for a hot date, and ready for a funeral.

"I have so much to tell you," she said, rushing, flashing my aunt a quick smile, before tugging me deeper into the drama. "You are so not going to believe how crazy everything's getting."

Against the giant screen, Jessica's life kept playing. But as Victoria dragged me toward a long table draped in white, other things began to register, like the uniformed cops standing on the perimeter, watching. And the small crowd near a podium, where an older woman and the man I recognized as Jessica's father stood with their arms wrapped around Bethany. And Chase . . . He was there, too.

With Jessica's family.

I ripped away, looked away, didn't want to risk him glancing over . . .

"Have you *seen* this?" Victoria asked, wedging her way between several well-dressed older folks to close in on the table. There, a line of young and old led to a large book open against the cloth, where a little girl with pigtails was writing in a guest book, and the principal was standing in greeting.

But that's not what Victoria wanted me to see.

A computer sat off to the side, the fading light bleaching out the image on the computer monitor. It wasn't until we stood right in front of it that the picture of Jessica came into focus—and the words in all caps across the top of the Facebook page: SEARCH-ING FOR JESSICA MORGENTHAL.

"It's crazy," Victoria said. "Amber created it yesterday and it already has over eight hundred fans."

Fans. It was a sick word considering the subject.

"Look at this," she said, pointing to a text box on the upper left side of the page.

> **We search for our dear friend Jessica Morgenthal,
> last seen Monday night,
> and pray our fears do not come true.**

But from the tone of the most recent comments—and the so-called candlelight vigil—it sounded like most people did not expect Jessica to come home.

> Prayers and hugs to the Morgenthal family! I remember
> Jess from elementary school. She always had such a
> sweet smile!

Around me, shadows slipped closer. I closed my eyes, concentrating on the small whitewashed room of my dreams, and the field, the airplane, and the white truck. Something. There had to be something else . . .

Nothing came.

Except the cold. The cold circled around me, seeping deep. Hating it, hating all of this, *wishing I could be anywhere else,* I made myself look back—and saw the man.

He stood toward the podium, next to the Morgenthals. Fairly young, I realized, but in that timeless way that could have placed him at twenty as easily as thirty. His reddish brown hair was long, fastened behind his neck. That's what made him look young. His suit was tailored and dark. That's what made him look older.

But it was his eyes that got me, narrow and piercing and . . . trained directly at me.

The shiver just happened. "Who is that?"

Victoria brushed up against me. "Who?"

"That guy," I said.

But already he was gone. "He was just there, by her parents."

"Oh," Victoria said, already turning back to the screen. "Probably that Wesley guy she hooked up with from LSU. Can you believe he actually showed up?"

I kept looking—but saw only Chase.

"This is just so bizarre," Victoria said, and despite the fact I would have sworn I still felt those eyes, watching me, I turned back to the computer, and started to read.

How can we go on without Jessie? The world is now a darker place.

I always wished I knew Jessica better. Even though she would never talk to me, I'm sure she was a great person.

And this, from Amber:

Once in our lives God gives us a gift. My gift was my best
friend. I wasn't ready to give her back and will now be left
to wonder WHY for the rest of my life . . .

The entries blurred by, a virtual who's who of Enduring Grace.
Except Chase. His name was not there.

But when I glanced up, he still stood with Jessica's family, holding a crying Bethany in his arms.

"Check this one out," Victoria said, and the second I saw the
user name at the bottom of the page, my stomach knotted.

IWUZTHERE

Then I read the entry.

You got what you deserved.

I stared. "Oh, my *God*—why hasn't someone deleted that?"

Victoria double-clicked on the user name. "Amber did, but as
soon as she did, another one appeared."

On the screen, a profile page appeared, blank except for a black-
and-white picture of the house on Prytania.

"The cops told her not to delete anything else."

I stared so hard my eyes got dry. "Detective LaSalle?"

"IDK," she said, and while under other circumstances her
speaking in text might have made me smile, I was no longer sure
I knew how.

"You don't get to be here."

I barely had a chance to look up, much less prepare, before

Amber, dressed in total goth black, was closing in on me like an anorexic avenging angel. "You've got some kind of crazy nerve—"

"*Amby*—" Victoria gasped, but I cut her off before she could say anything else.

"I know this must be hard on you," I said, much as a parent might say to a child in the midst of a temper tantrum. "You two have been friends for so long . . ."

Amber wrenched past Victoria, her face twisted with so much emotion I couldn't even begin to identify it all. Anger, sorrow, fear. "You'll never replace her," she spat. "You might think you can, but they've been together forever—"

I stiffened, felt the edge of the table cutting into the backs of my legs. "I don't want to replace her," I said, as unemotionally as I could.

But Amber just kept glaring at me, her eyes dark and wild. Vaguely I was aware of the crowd around us jostling, a low murmur running through the courtyard.

"All boys like new toys," she said, "but he loves *her*." Twisting, she got right up in my face. "Has he told *you* that?"

"*Amber*," came a low firm voice, and then Drew was there, and Pitre and Lucas, all muscling their way through the press of bodies.

"Of course not," Amber said, when I said nothing, "because he doesn't."

I swallowed hard, knew better than to say anything. Because there was nothing. Absolutely nothing to say to that.

But when I glanced beyond her, through the haze I saw the giant screen where the slide show still played, and Jessica, in an absolutely killer dress, stood wrapped in Chase's arms.

"This isn't helping anything," Drew said, and then he was at Amber's side, pulling her back from me and into his arms, pressing her face to his chest as he looked over her head toward me, mouthing two simple words, but giving them no voice. *I'm sorry.*

Pitre and Lucas cleared space around us. "You okay?" Pitre asked.

"I will be."

But the look in his eyes said he didn't believe me. "You weren't at school today."

"I-I'm . . . okay," I detoured as Drew dragged a hysterical Amber toward the back of the courtyard.

"You can't let her get to you," he pressed. "Everyone knows she's spewing lies. Dreams are just dreams."

"Or are they?" Lucas smirked. "Seeing anything else . . . *interesting,* Trin-Trin?"

I hated when he called me that. And I wasn't about to give him anything to use against me. I just didn't get what Victoria saw in him. Annoyed, I glanced toward the screen just as Chase looked up.

The moment crystallized around us, the fall of shadows and the whisper of a flute, more than a hundred people separating us. But I felt him.

I felt him.

Even as to my right, images of his relationship with Jessica continued to shine through the growing darkness.

And then someone was grabbing my hand, squeezing and urging me back, away.

Disoriented, I swung around, found my aunt. Her face was ashen—her eyes were wide, dark.

I followed her without speaking, weaving away from the table toward the edge of the steps of the Administration building, where one of the news crews was reporting live, while a second was packing up.

"We have to go," she said, tugging me to keep moving.

"No—I—"

She stopped. "Aaron called."

That made me stop.

"There was a hit-and-run," she said quietly. "A white truck," she added. "A few miles from the airport."

I wanted to wake up. I wanted to wake up and stretch against the warm cotton sheets, to roll over and look out the window, see the snow-capped mountains in the distance. I wanted to sit and reach to the foot of the bed, to bury my hands in soft fur and feel the kiss of Sunshine . . .

But Sunshine was dead, and there were no mountains in New Orleans, only the sticky heat of a fading day, interrupted occasionally by an equally sticky breeze—and the roar of a jet soaring into the reddish swirls of twilight.

In the distance, men moved in a straight line, close to fifty of them, walking slowly, flashlights aimed in front of them. Dogs raced along ahead. Overhead, a helicopter circled.

Near a skeletal bald cypress several car lengths away, Jessica's parents and sister huddled close. By my side, Aunt Sara stood with my hand in hers. She had not let go since we'd arrived.

She'd barely spoken, either. "Is this it?" she'd asked. "The field from your dreams?"

The question had sounded so nice, innocent, but rather than conjuring images of waving grass and sunshine and butterflies, it had chilled me to the core. Because yes. This was the field of my dreams.

And I didn't know what was worse, for them to find something—*find her*—or for them to find nothing at all. The former meant I'd seen a glimpse of Jessica's future, or her past.

The latter meant I was out of my mind.

Both meant I was walking a thin, dark line.

"This is seriously messed up," Victoria whispered from my other side. She'd caught up with me as I'd slipped into my car at Enduring Grace, insisting on coming with me. Aunt Sara had driven separately, meeting me for the vigil after a long afternoon of meetings.

"I wish they'd tell us what was going on," she said, continuing the mostly one-way dialogue she'd initiated the second she'd climbed into my car an hour and a half before.

"I'm sure they will," I murmured, choosing my words carefully. What else was I supposed to say? This wasn't what I signed up for, to be a voyeur of my own life. And so many others.

Gradually, as minutes became hours, the crowd grew. By the time we'd arrived, the local news stations had already been set up. Jessica's family arrived shortly after we did. Countless other police and search personnel joined the group combing the field. I could only imagine what would happen after the football game ended and word of the search leaked to the student body.

"They must have found something," she speculated yet again. "Do you think—"

I cut her off with my eyes. "I don't know."

And I didn't. I only knew that Detective LaSalle had taken me more seriously than he'd let on, alerting precincts around local airports to be on the lookout for anything strange involving a white truck.

Late in the day, shortly before the vigil, the call came in. An officer in Kenner had gotten a report from an older man about a white truck driving recklessly away from a field north of Louis Armstrong Airport. The truck had swerved, sideswiping the older man's car . . .

But I did not know how to draw the connections for Victoria. Because without my dream, the dots were just dots, random and without consequence.

And I wasn't ready to talk about my dream.

"Omigod, I swear I'm getting eaten alive," she said, swatting at her neck and then her arm, as she'd been doing ever since we arrived. Situated between the Mississippi and Lake Pontchartrain, the field was essentially a marsh. "If I get West Nile—"

I glanced at her, struck by how beautiful she looked despite the heat and humidity and near-complete darkness. Her hair was loose, sticking to the sides of her face. Her eyes were agitated.

"*I know,*" she whispered before I could say anything, then glanced back to where men both in and out of uniform searched for Jessica. "I'm sure Jess would much rather be standing here with the mosquitoes then out there . . ."

I felt something sharp and desperate flash through my eyes. "We don't know that she's out there."

"No," Victoria agreed. But her voice betrayed her doubt.

The red-orange glow faded, turning trees into specters. Shadows deepened until even they slipped into darkness. The crowd grew.

"I'll be back," Aunt Sara said, while on my other side, Victoria texted like crazy. "I'm going to see if I can find anything out."

I looked up into her eyes, and felt the jolt of her conviction. "I'm okay," I said, but she hesitated before taking off toward a few uniformed officers standing near the Morgenthals. We'd seen Detectives Jackson and LaSalle only once, right when we'd arrived. Since then, they'd been out with everyone else.

"Omigod," Victoria said, continuing only when I turned to look at her. "He says it's all over the news."

My body ached from standing in one place. "Who says?"

"Zach," she said as her fingers flew across her phone. "The guy from the mall I was telling you about."

I almost smiled. It was completely inappropriate, but for just that one fraction in time, having something else to think about, something other than Jessica and the heat and the mosquitoes, how badly I wanted a sip of water, was kind of like stepping into a nice cool blast of air-conditioning. "*That's* who you're texting?"

"He's watching right now," she muttered, distracted. "But he says he hasn't seen us or anything."

I'd noticed the news lights and cameras off to my right, hadn't realized it was already after ten.

"He says the detectives got a lead, but no one knows what or from whom."

Swallowing, I glanced back toward the edge of the horizon, where searchlights were little more than a glow. Somehow, even the barking of the dogs seemed innocent and benign.

"Lucas doesn't mind you two talking?" I asked, needing to focus on something, anything other than the endless drag of second to second.

"Are you kidding?" Victoria said. "Lucas doesn't know."

I shot her a look. "You need to just break up with him, you know that, don't you?"

She frowned. "I'm trying."

"Try harder."

Earlier in the evening her hair had been silky straight. Now it curled into damp ringlets against her face and neck. She shoved at them, went back to texting Zach. I didn't know much about him, other than that she'd met him while at the mall last weekend and had not only walked away with four new pairs of jeans, including the totally awesome Miss Me pair she'd worn tonight, with the fleurs-de-lis on the back pocket, but also the sales guy's phone number. And he had hers. And he'd been texting ever since.

And she was still technically with Lucas.

I'm not sure how much time passed before a fresh wave of lights cut in from behind us, followed by the sound of car engines. I turned as they went silent, stiffened as the doors opened and the guys poured out.

Apparently the football game was over.

"*Victoria!*" I tried to keep my voice soft. "Lucas is here!"

She made a faint muffled sound, and I could only hope she had the sense to tell Zach she had to go, because one by one Lucas and Pitre and Drew slid from the 1970s T-bird belonging to Chase's cousin. And then he was there, too, not in the same car, but emerging from his Camaro.

My heart kicked all on its own.

Instinctively I took a step back as he scanned the clearing. I would have sworn his limp was more pronounced.

"Chase!" I heard Bethany call, and then he was closing in on the Morgenthals and the breath was rushing out of me.

Until Lucas spotted us and started over.

"I missed you tonight," he said the second he reached us, and while the words were sweet, the quick whiff of beer was anything but. He caught Victoria around the waist and hauled her against him, and while she didn't exactly go willingly, she didn't hold her ground, either. It was crazy how fast she went from gushing about Zach to making out with Lucas.

I didn't get how tight a hold he had on her, just because whenever she tried to break up with him, he cried.

Not wanting to stare, I stepped away and tried not to listen. My options were limited. Aunt Sara was nowhere in sight. I could continue to stand and wait, or I could slip away and give Victoria and Lucas some privacy.

I hated how tight my chest got. I hated how hard it was for me to walk away, because walking away meant walking toward, and the thought of that, of seeing Chase—

It made no sense. I'd never been one to run. But the thought of walking toward Chase turned me to blown glass all over again.

I'd taken five steps when Lucas's voice stopped me.

"Aren't you going to answer that?"

I'm not sure what made me twist around. The edge to his voice, maybe, or just instinct, the kind that came from knowing too many secrets. Turning, two things struck me first: the fear in Victoria's eyes.

And the accusation in Lucas's.

"It's nothing," she said.

But he so did not believe her. He tracked her, taking a step forward for every one she took back. "Then answer it."

"I don't want to."

"Then let me."

"Lucas—"

"Give me your fucking phone!" he roared.

"No, it's not—"

"It's that Zach guy, isn't it?"

"W-what? I don't know anyone—"

"You think I'm dumb?" he snarled. "You think I didn't see your Facebook page?"

I moved the second he did, racing toward them as he snagged her wrist like it was one of Chase's passes. His hand closed around her flesh and jerked her toward him, slamming her body against his chest.

"Stop it!" I shouted as her head snapped back and I saw the terror in her eyes. "Let go of her!"

As if in slow motion, he looked up, and his eyes met mine.

I felt the splinter of poison clear to my soul. "This is none of your business, bitch."

So much for keeping a low profile.

My heart pounded like crazy. He was so much bigger than me, but Victoria was even smaller than I was. "Just let go of her," I said as calmly as I could. "I'm sure we—"

With a horrible sound somewhere between a laugh and a snarl, he yanked her closer, sliding his free hand down to press her up against him.

My last two steps went by in a blur. I didn't take time to think or plan, just closed in on him and reached for his arm. To stop him—pull him away. Something. To make him leave her alone.

He struck out hard, fast, the back of his hand catching me in the chest and sending me flying backward.

SEVENTEEN

Everything went white. I felt the impact before the pain registered, before the breath rushed out of me and my head snapped back against the tree. Then I was sinking, crumbling like a rag doll.

Maybe I screamed—or maybe that was Victoria. It all happened so fast I don't know. I just knew that I crumpled into myself and tried to breathe, felt myself gasping instead. And then there was this low roar and Lucas charging me like some kind of crazy person. I tried to roll away, crawl away, but it was happening too fast.

Then it all just stopped, like someone hit pause. But just as quickly the moment ran forward and Lucas was flying back, Victoria was crying, and someone was there, crouching down on the ground in front of me, and everything else just fell away.

"Trinity."

I blinked, focused on the voice.

"Trinity." This time firmer, stronger, and then I felt the hands

on my body—strong, tender, firm, gentle—and blinked again and finally focus settled back into place, and I saw him. Maybe for the first time ever—I saw him. Really, really saw him. His face . . .

There was no way to describe his face, or the crazy rush that went through me. His eyes were dark and ravaged, his mouth a hard line. He looked like he wanted to scoop me into his arms and crush something with his bare hands all at the same time.

The roar had been his.

"Chase," I whispered, and even that, just his name, hurt.

Slowly other things began to register, and beyond Chase's shoulder I saw Pitre slam Lucas to the ground and Victoria huddled with Drew, shaking.

"Get. Him. Away," she said.

Pitre flashed a tight look, then one back at me. "Is she okay?"

Sprawled beside me, Chase nudged me between his legs and against his body. "I got her," he said.

That was all Pitre needed to hear. He yanked Lucas's hands behind his back much like his brother the cop probably did when making an arrest, and shoved him toward the parking area.

And then it was Chase and me—*again*—sprawled in the damp grass. He held me tight, so tight that I could hear the insane riff of his heart, and for the craziest of moments, I wanted to stay that way, safe in his arms, forever.

His arms were strong, solid, his hands gentle as he ran them along my body, inspecting inch by inch. When at last he pulled back and tilted my face to his, when I saw the way he looked at me, I wanted to cry. It was tender and possessive and protective, all those things I'd dreamed of my whole life.

"You okay?" he asked.

Throat tight, I nodded.

He looked down and took my hands, turned them palms up. There was no way to hide the renewed surge of the blood.

"Son of a bitch," he snarled, but already I was shaking my head and trying to scoot away.

He wouldn't let me.

"Chase," I said, driven by something I didn't understand. Something dark, and unsure.

I was starting to think about him too much. I was starting to turn to him, reach for him. Depend on him.

Trust him.

And I knew, *I knew,* it was wrong. He wasn't the one. He couldn't be. There were too many dark corners in my mind, corners I did not know how to share. One day he'd realize that. One day he'd be gone, and I'd be left with this huge gaping hole in my heart, and then what?

Then *what?*

"What's going on?" he said through clenched teeth, and the remains of that crazy beautiful moment shattered, and it was still us, but the us of before, the us of the courtyard. "Why are you avoiding me?"

An unwanted sense of hopelessness clawed at me. "Chase—"

"What?" he said before I could finish. *"What aren't you telling me?"*

The suspicion in his voice, the sharp glitter of blue in his eyes, froze me. I didn't know how to make him understand. Actually I was pretty sure that was impossible. *Look, Chase . . . I . . . um, see things. Know things. I know you saw an empty room last night, but I saw an old lady and a clock, and this supernatural mirror . . .*

Against my chest, my mother's amulet throbbed.

"You should go," I whispered.

His eyes met mine, burned even hotter. "You should tell me the truth."

I swallowed, said nothing.

"Did you get my texts?"

I nodded, and his face fell. "And before?" he said. "At the vigil?"

And I could see him retreating, more than just his body, but him. Pulling back. Away. Like a tide returning to sea. "You didn't want to see me."

Again, through the tangle of dark hair, I nodded.

That look he'd had a few minutes before, the one that made him appear as if he wanted to punch something, twisted his face all over again.

"Please," I said as I saw my aunt finally, finally hurrying toward us. I made myself stand, even though the field around me tilted and my body rebelled. "Don't make this harder than it has to be."

He stood, forcing me to lift my face to see him. And it was all I could do to keep from reaching up to brush the bangs from his forehead—and diving right back into his arms.

In that moment it was all I wanted.

"Just go," I whispered, because that moment didn't matter, couldn't matter. Only the moments yet to come. The moments that I saw and knew and felt.

The moments nobody else could even imagine.

Without another word, he did. Chase did exactly what I asked him to do, turned and walked away, toward the parking area where Pitre held Lucas shoved up against the old T-bird.

It wasn't until Aunt Sara convinced me there was no point just standing around and that I should go, when I pulled off the road a few miles away and sat alone in my car while the radio softly played, that I closed my eyes, and cried.

For a long time I just drove, turning down streets with neither names nor lights, staring at the ramshackle structures on either side of me. Cars occupied some driveways. Most houses sat dark. Every now and then soft white glowed through windows. In those houses there would be people, a home.

The word lodged like a horrible knot in my throat.

I wanted to go there, go home. But I no longer knew where home was. Wasn't sure I had one. The only home I'd ever known was among the pine and aspen in the mountains of Colorado. In New Orleans I was a guest, a visitor, someone unknown drifting through lives that had not asked for the interruption.

So I just drove.

Close to midnight, my phone buzzed. The little jolt was immediate, and completely unwanted. I didn't want to anticipate. I didn't want to . . . want.

The more you wanted, the further you had to fall.

"Hey," came my aunt's voice, quiet, tired, and all the air pretty much whooshed out of me. I was the one who'd told him to leave me alone. It made no sense for me to be disappointed when he did just that.

"Wanted to let you know they're calling it a night," she said.

"Did they find anything? Are they done?"

"Not sure. Aaron—*Detective LaSalle*—said they'd done enough for tonight and they'd get back at it in the morning."

"So no . . ." It was hard to force the word out. "Body?"

"No body."

I wanted to feel relief at that, and I think that I did. But fissures of unease continued to ripple through me.

"Are you home?"

"Not yet."

"Oh, *cher*—"

"But I'm on my way," I said before she could lecture or lament. "I'll meet you there." And then we said good-bye and I turned off the sad street with as many vacant lots as houses and headed toward the Warehouse District.

On the outskirts of the Quarter, along Canal Street, the night showed few signs of winding down. Groups of people moved along the sidewalks on both sides of the street, shop lights blurring with those of the big hotels. But I saw no sign of Cemeteries, one of the streetcars that ran the main drag.

The pace slowed as I reached the Warehouse District, where most of the bistros and galleries had closed for the night. At our parking garage, I rolled down the window and slid my access card through the scanner, pulled inside, and parked next to Aunt Sara's spot. Relieved it was empty, I slipped from the car and hurried toward the metal door. If I was lucky, I could get upstairs and into the shower before—

To my right, a shadow shifted.

Picking up my pace, I glanced over my shoulder, saw no one. Annoyed with myself for being so jumpy, I turned back toward the door—and froze.

The towel had not been there before. I was sure of that, knew there was no way I could have missed a dirty, wadded-up pink beach towel not two feet in front of me. Frowning, I started to veer around it, and heard her.

The whisper was soft, the voice more like a breath. *"Trinity."*

Something warm and paralyzing flashed through me. I told myself to move, knew that I *had* to move. But the voice would not let me.

"Trinity . . . please."

My chest locked up. My lungs wouldn't work. I could feel my heart slamming, but nothing else worked.

"No, no, no," I said as a horrible roar swept in from all directions, swirling and pulsing. Distorting.

"Trinity . . ."

The towel glowed. "No," I whispered again. It wasn't possible. But the only way my body would move was toward that towel. I went down on a knee and reached for it, could no more have stopped my hands from closing around the damp terry cloth than I could have made myself breathe.

And then I saw her.

"Jessica . . ." I drifted, floating, no longer in the shadowy garage but in a room small and dark, and she was there, huddled in the corner in a gown of white, looking at me through eyes that did not blink. Calling out. Begging . . .

"Help me."

"Jessica," I said again, but she gave no indication that she heard me, saw me, just sat there with her knees gathered to her chest, rocking.

"Where are you?" I screamed. "Tell me where you are!"

"Waiting for you."

The voice was not hers. It was low and thready, that of a man. With a quickness that had not been possible only moments before I twisted around and saw him, saw the man behind me, his shoulder-length hair pulled behind his neck and his suit of black, the eyes that pierced. And the knife in his hand.

"You," I whispered. Or maybe I screamed. Or maybe there was nothing at all, just the soundless agony of a dream. But on a rush of adrenaline I scrambled to my feet, and started to run.

EIGHTEEN

Darkness absorbed me. The roar took everything else. I tore for the street, knew it was my only chance. It wasn't that late. There could still be a car.

Something hard caught me from behind. An arm. Around my chest. Wrenching me back. "No!" I screamed. But another arm joined the first, a hand sliding to my mouth.

"Trinity!"

The scream ripped through the silence, and everything just stopped. Froze. Went blank. The hands fell away and I was falling, going down to the punishing concrete and rolling into myself, and then the hands came back, but not hard like before. Soft. Gentle. Tentative.

"Trinity—oh, my God! Oh, my *God*!"

Vaguely I was aware of being tugged, of rolling, of my body being shifted, and when I blinked, when I finally hacked through the shadows of my mind, it was my aunt I saw, crouched over me, her hair wild and stringy against the twist of horror on her face.

"Oh, my God," she said again, and finally other things slipped into the haze of awareness, and I could feel how badly she shook. "What happened—are you okay?"

"There was a man," I whispered, but even as I said the words, I knew that he was gone. "He was here . . ."

She gathered me closer, clinging to me as she twisted toward the back of the garage. "I just got here," she whispered as I tried to breathe. "I didn't see—"

"Sara?"

Through the fog I made out the older woman from the third floor, who lived directly below us and waited tables in the Quarter. She was running toward us, her face contorted. "My God! Are you okay? What happened?"

Methodically Aunt Sara started to rock, just rock, back and forth. "Call the police," she whispered. "Ask for Aaron . . . LaSalle."

"I saw her—she was in a small room. It was dark and she was huddled in a corner . . ."

"You saw her," Detective DeMarcus Jackson repeated, very slowly. "And were you in this room, too?"

"No, I—" Words shifted around inside me, none of them adequate. I could see the disbelief in Jackson's and LaSalle's eyes, even as they pretended to take me seriously. "Maybe," I said. "I don't know. One minute I was in the garage, reaching for the towel, then I was . . . with Jessica."

"Floating," Jackson said, throwing back at me a word I'd already used.

Frustration made me want to scream. The two had shown up at the condo with lightning speed. I hadn't even had a chance to shower—my aunt had barely let go of me long enough to get me a glass of water.

Now, every second dragged, and the more I talked, the crazier I knew I sounded.

"I know you don't understand," I said, changing approaches. "And I know you think I'm crazy or making all this up—"

"Trinity!" Sitting next to me, Aunt Sara squeezed my hand really tight. "That's not true."

"But I'm not," I said, despising the way my voice cracked on the words. "*It was real.* The second I touched the towel, everything just flashed and then it was like I was seeing through someone else's eyes . . ."

Jackson wasn't even subtle the way he half-coughed, half-cleared his throat. "So you were seeing through the towel's eyes?"

He might as well have laughed. I sat there staring at him, refusing to look away, even as something sharp and hot flashed through me, obliterating every molecule of respect I'd tried to have for him. I knew his job was to ask questions. I knew his job was to investigate, be skeptical.

But I hadn't realized it was to belittle.

"I was there," my aunt bit out. "I found her. She was terrified!"

"*Sara.*" Up until that moment, Detective LaSalle had been quiet, standing off to the side while his partner questioned. Now he crossed toward us, bracing a hip against the edge of the sofa. "I'm sure she was. No one is disputing that." He looked exclusively at her, his eyes so solid and convincing, until finally she lifted her face to his. Then he swept in with the killing blow. "There was no towel."

I felt my aunt stiffen.

"We looked," he said. "Everywhere."

"Found a few soda cans," Jackson put in. "Some gum wrappers, a fast-food bag, a crushed Mardi Gras mask."

"Then he took it with him," I blurted without thinking.

"Or maybe it's like the knife from last night." It was bizarre to hear how scraped clean Jackson's voice could get. He looked like such a cool, hip guy, with his cornrows and pierced ear. But pure ice ran through his veins. "And the woman," he said. "Maybe she and this man and the towel are all—"

"Stop it!" I jumped up, glared at him. "I'm not crazy!" I said. "*I'm not.* Don't you get it? I saw him! A man—at the vigil, then in the parking garage! He said my name—"

Aunt Sara stood and reached for me, pulled me against her. It stunned me how something as simple as a touch, an arm around my waist, could settle through me like a deep, forever breath.

"Why is it so hard for you to believe her?" Her voice was strong and calm, yet forceful. "She's young, she's pretty, she was alone. If he saw her at the vigil, he could have followed—"

LaSalle and Jackson exchanged a quick look. Then LaSalle stepped closer. "Does anyone else know about your . . . dreams?"

For twenty minutes there'd been nothing but doubt and sarcasm. Now, the quick slice of concern in his voice chilled. *"Everyone,"* I whispered.

His brows went alarmingly tight.

"Amber found out," I explained before he could ask. "She's had a field day with it."

Again LaSalle glanced toward Jackson. "We need the footage from the school." Then, to me: "Do you think you'd recognize him if you saw him again?"

Mouth dry, I nodded.

"Good girl," he said.

"My God." Aunt Sara's movement was subtle, a slight step toward Detective LaSalle, a hand to his forearm. "You think it could be him, don't you? Whoever has Jessica."

His expression gentled. "I get paid to think, Sara. To consider every option. And at this point, they're all on the table—a random mugging, some sick perv trying to copycat."

LaSalle's voice trailed off, but through the ensuing silence I heard what he didn't say, what he did not need to say—or a perp trying to cover his tracks.

Or absolutely nothing at all.

At some point I would have to sleep. I knew that. But long after La-Salle told me he didn't want me leaving the condo alone, long after they checked the windows and tested the locks, after they left, I finally showered. I stood there until the warm ran cold. Then I stood there a little longer.

By the time I slipped into a huge Saints T-shirt and stepped from the bathroom, it was close to two A.M.

The sight of Aunt Sara, sitting on the sofa with her arms wrapped around her middle, her eyes dark and trained straight ahead, threw me right back to the parking garage.

For a moment I just watched, stunned by the difference. Normally my aunt was Miss Put Together. Yes, she had the scattered soul of an artist, but she hid that well, pouring herself into whatever she was doing, whether it be evaluating commercial real estate, decorating her condo or preparing a gourmet meal, making an awesome new necklace.

She had friends. Or at least, she'd had them before I came along. She didn't talk much about what her life had been like before I showed up, but I knew there'd been girlfriends and a boyfriend. Her best friend, Naomi, had followed her fiancé to Austin, Texas the month before I arrived.

But Aunt Sara did not like to talk about any of that. Much like Gran, she almost never talked about herself—or the past.

Seeing her sitting on the sofa, so still and shaken—I'd never seen her like that. I told myself to turn around and walk away, give her the privacy she so religiously clung to.

But walking away seemed lame. Whatever she was thinking, whatever she was feeling, was because of me.

"I'm sorry." The words shot out of me. *"I'm so sorry."*

She twisted toward me, the fully controlled mask sliding down on the rare, naked moment with lightning speed. "Trinity."

My throat worked. "This is all my fault," I said. "You had this great, perfect life going, and then I showed up and now you're spending your nights—"

"Stop." The force of that one word flashed in her eyes. She stood, crossed to me. "I don't want to hear you saying things like that ever again."

"But it's true."

"No, it's not." She closed in on me, lifting her hands to the sides of my face. "Actually, nothing could be *further* from the truth." It was weird how intense but soft her expression was. "You've brightened my life, *cher*. You've given me something I didn't even know was missing."

Slowly, I shook my head. "Drama," I whispered.

Her smile was somewhere between amused and heartbreaking. "My brother," she whispered. "You've given me back my brother and your mother—all swirled together in the wonderful young lady you've become."

The sting at the backs of my eyes was automatic. I blinked furiously, hated all the little fissures of emotion springing up inside of me.

"You are such an amazing person," she said with a ferocity that made me long to believe. *"They would have been so proud of you."*

I'd been trying. I'd been trying really hard to hold myself together, but there in the shadows of my aunt's condo, sometime after two in the morning, everything caught up with me, and the cracks split wide open.

"Hey," she said, moving fast, pulling me into her arms and hugging me tight. "I mean it. You're everything they ever dreamed of—warm, loyal, compassionate. Bright—"

Whacked out of my mind, I added silently.

"Funny," she whispered, and I would have sworn somehow she'd known exactly what I was thinking. But that ability came from my mother's side of the family, not hers. "Loving." She hesitated a long moment before continuing, as if for a brief heartbeat, she'd gone somewhere else. "I still remember you when you were a baby. Sometimes when your parents went out, you'd come stay with us at . . ."

The way her voice trailed off gave me the opening I'd been seeking. "The house?" I asked. "The one in the Garden District, where you grew up?"

She pulled back, her eyes meeting mine. "You know about that?"

I didn't blink. "Chase showed me."

Her sigh was barely audible. "You loved it there," she whispered, and I could tell that she had, too. "There were so many places to hide . . . You'd come over and I'd laugh the whole time, because you were so cute the way you ran around from one secret hideaway to another . . .

"You always had a doctor kit with you," she said with a laugh, and my heart squeezed. "No one escaped you, not even your cat. He'd lay there forever, just letting you jam that stethoscope all over his body."

I swallowed. "I had a cat?"

"You loved him so," she whispered. "After the fire—"

The words just stopped. Everything did.

"Fire?" Despite the chill, the word burned the back of my throat. "What fire?"

It was like a body blow. Never once had anyone mentioned a fire.

Aunt Sara didn't move, gave no indication that she'd heard my question. But I knew that she had.

"Please." My stomach churned as I pulled back and looked up at her whitewashed face. "Don't shut me out."

Slowly she blinked, and I could see then, see the bottomless brown of her eyes, the dark twist of pain and love and regret. Of fear.

And before I even asked the question, I knew.

"My parents," I whispered. "The accident." The one everyone refused to speak about. All along, I'd assumed it was a car wreck. "It was a fire, wasn't it?"

She closed her eyes, and I had my answer.

So much hit me at once, all the emotions I'd seen reflected in her eyes, but more. Worse. Because screaming in the middle of it all was the undeniable assault of betrayal. I'd been lied to. By everyone.

"No," I whispered, pulling back, stepping away. I wanted to turn and run to my room, slam the door behind me and hit the rewind button. The do-over. Wake up again and make different choices, ignore the dream, steer clear of the candlelight vigil—

But we didn't get different choices. At least, like my grandmother said, not in the past. The only thing we could do over was the future.

"You lied," I muttered, and Aunt Sara winced, the color flooding back to her face. "You lied about *everything*."

She had the good grace—or flat-out intelligence—not to come after me. "Not everything."

"You knew," I pressed. "You *knew* I thought it was a car crash!"

"And how is this better?" she asked. "How is this better for you to have to imagine a fire destroying the house, what their last moments must have—"

She broke off with a quick hand to her mouth.

I stood there, trying to process, to understand. *To breathe*. But it all collapsed around me, the truth—the lie—that had been perpetrated on me for the past fourteen years.

My parents had been killed in a fire.

"Was I there?" The horrific band tightening around my chest told me that I was.

Finally, someone chose not to sugarcoat. "Yes."

"Was it day or night?"

"Night."

"Were we . . . sleeping?"

"Yes."

Like a weary sprinter, I ran backward through my mind, tripping over all the inconsequential things like hikes through the mountains and trips to the store, blizzards and the summer I'd come down with chicken pox, looking for . . . anything. Any remnant of what Aunt Sara was saying—smoke, flames, heat.

Screams.

Terror.

If nothing else, the terror should still be there. The fire.

It should *be there*.

"But I saw their house," I said, speaking with no real awareness of doing so. "Gran's house. They're still there."

"They were staying down south, at a friend's house."

And I would have sworn I saw the embers of those long-forgotten flames still burning in her eyes. "Then . . . where was I? How did I get out and they—"

Died.

They died.

While I lived.

"A neighbor saw the flames, got you out. By the time he ran back . . ."

It was too late.

Numbly I lifted my hand to the amulet dangling around my

neck, the one that had once belonged to my mother, and closed my fingers around the smooth, timeless edges of the brass dragon-fly. Even when all else was cold, decimated, it warmed.

It lived.

"Trinity, I'm so sorry," my aunt whispered, echoing my words of only a few minutes before, when I'd thought she was the one in need of comfort. *"I am so horribly sorry."*

The sun rose. The clouds burned off. The sky turned bright blue. Aunt Sara fixed coffee and set out some grapes. I took another shower, fiddled with my laptop.

Nothing seemed real.

The more I tried to understand, the less anything made sense.

Aunt Sara had a meeting. She tried to cancel, but I urged her to go, told her I needed to be alone. I think she felt guilty; either that, or she needed to get away as badly as I did.

I promised to stay put, keep the doors locked. Open for no one. And finally, shortly before eleven, she left.

Shortly after eleven, Victoria texted.

I am so sorry. Lucas is such an ass.

Sitting on the floor stretching, I welcomed the distraction and thumbed out a quick reply.

Don't worry about it. r u ok?

Our messages flew back and forth.

I'm good. Great! R U OK?

I'm OK.

What about Chase? Did he call you?

No.

Oh.

I don't want him 2.

Really?

Really.

Oh. Guess what? Zach called. He asked me out.

R U sure that's a good idea?

Best. Idea. Ever.

What about Lucas?

History.

I wanted to believe her. I did. But I also knew better. Victoria and Lucas had one of *those* relationships. I started to warn her, but she texted again before I could. Absently, I clicked over.

The message was not from Victoria.

NINETEEN

Chase.

I stared at the bright pink of the silicone case against the white gauze circling my palm, the way the letters of his name glowed against the screen. My chest rose and fell. Part of me wanted to hurl the phone across the room, watch it smash against the window.

But the memory of how he'd looked at me in that one shattered moment when I'd told him to go but before he'd yet to move, of how badly I'd needed him just a short breath later, when I'd run through the garage and the detectives had mocked me, when my aunt had blown the lid off the lie of my life, made me want to pull up the message as fast as I could, drink it all in.

It's no surprise which part won.

NEED 2 C U.

My eyes watered.

ITS IMPORTANT

My heart got into the game, slamming against my ribs. Breathing hurt. Wondering . . . remembering . . . wanting.

Those didn't help.

EMMA WATSON LIED

The messages kept coming, one after the other. And with them came my own questions. WHAT DO YOU MEAN? LIES ABOUT WHAT? HOW DO YOU KNOW? WHERE ARE YOU?

WHY WON'T YOU LEAVE ME ALONE?

But as fast as my thumbs formed the questions, I deleted them.

I JUST LEFT HER HOUSE.

Shock brought a dull blade of unease. I'd been working so hard to manage everything, keep certain truths from getting out. It had never occurred to me Chase would go back, *without me*.

What in God's name had that woman told him?

I NO Y SHE HATES UR MOTHER.

I froze.

NOT BECUZ OF HER DAUGHTER, BUT HER SON IN LAW.

I tried to swallow, but my throat wouldn't work.

A COP

Then:

AM GOIN 2 C HIM NOW.

And finally my fingers started to move. *Fly.*

This time I had no choice but to hit send.

The second I read his reply, I realized I had no choice but to break a promise, either.

LOOK OUT YOUR WINDOW. I'M ALREADY HERE.

Aunt Sara wasn't happy. Via a rapid exchange of texts she reminded me of all the reasons I wasn't supposed to go anywhere. But I, in turn, pointed out that LaSalle had said *alone*. And while Detective I-Can't-Trust-Anyone didn't trust Chase, I did.

Even if he had backed me into a corner.

"He grew up in the Garden District. She lives on the outskirts of the Quarter. Those aren't parallel circles."

In the passenger seat of the restored Camaro, I stared straight ahead. I'd asked him to leave me alone. I'd *begged* him to. But he'd turned around and played the one card he knew there'd be no way I could resist. I wanted to be angry about that. Really, really angry.

But even more, I wanted to reach out and put my hand to his arm, look into his eyes and ask him to hold me the way he had when he'd found me running from the French Quarter courtyard. I'd felt safe then. For that one, fragile, fleeting moment, *I'd felt safe.*

I wanted to feel safe again.

But Chase didn't know. He didn't know about the man in the parking garage—or the fire.

I wasn't ready to talk about either.

"According to the deed, your dad was twenty-one when he purchased it. Five years later he married your mother."

Woodenly, I kept my eyes on the window, where the remains of the Ninth Ward zipped by. It was hard to imagine this barren stretch of weeds and garbage had once been a thriving community. Only a few houses had sprung back up, the Brad Pitt houses as they were called, a handful of brightly colored structures that looked more like modern art than homes.

I counted three separate tour buses in the area.

"I didn't see how Emma Watson could possibly have known him his whole life."

I'd been so focused on keeping her from talking about my mother, I'd never made that connection.

"But she was telling the truth," Chase said, and I twisted toward him so fast, my hair slapped my face.

I hated being played. *You said she lied.*

Slowing for a red light, he shot me a quick glance. "She did."

I felt my eyes narrow, telling him without words he'd better keep talking.

Instead he stopped the car and reached over, took my hand in his.

I winced.

He frowned. "I'm on your side, T. Why is that so hard for you to believe?"

Looking at him hurt, because looking at him made me want. Made me long. "I just want everyone to stop."

"Stop what?"

Deciding what I did and did not need to know. Where I could and could not live. What I should and should not do.

"Playing God," I whispered. I just wanted to wake up in the morning like everyone else, walk through the day without worrying about what I was going to see—or imagine.

"It's *my* life," I said, wrenching away and looking back to the street. "The light's green."

He laughed. It was so not what I'd expected.

Not looking like he gave a damn whether the light was red,

green, or purple, he took his time returning his attention to the road.

"Welcome to mine," he muttered. But it was five minutes until I understood what he meant.

We zoomed along Judge Perez Drive, the main drag cutting through St. Bernard Parish, where a succession of abandoned strip malls and gas stations lined the road. The parish had been hit hard by Katrina. Virtually every building had been completely under water. Less than half the population had returned. Like a scene from some bad sci-fi, entire neighborhoods, once crowded and middle class, sat empty and rotting.

After a few miles Chase turned onto what looked like a boulevard—but other than a few dead trees, there was nothing on either side. I frowned, oddly uneasy. Then he turned again, onto a street with a sidewalk but no houses, and stopped.

"I thought we were going to see my mom's friend—"

He pushed open the door and stepped into the late-morning sunshine, staring at a long strip of badly cracked concrete leading away from the road. It almost looked like . . . a driveway.

But it led nowhere.

"Chase?" I asked, following him from the car. "Where are we?"

"My life," he murmured. And then he walked away.

I stood there on the remains of what had once been a sidewalk, watching him walk toward a tangle of weeds and bushes in the outline of a house. And from one breath to the next I knew where we were.

I watched him approach what must have been a carport, moving through a back door that no longer stood. He would be in the kitchen, I imagined as he took a few steps and lifted his hand to a refrigerator that was no longer there.

Orange juice or milk, I thought inanely, and then I didn't think at all, I just crossed through the knee-high weeds and went to him, lifted a hand without thinking, and laid it against his back. I felt him stiffen, felt the lingering ache of loss clear down to my soul.

It was so easy to get lost in your own life and your own grief, your own . . . drama. It was so easy to see only your own darkness.

But standing there in the glare of a sun not shielded by even the thinnest of clouds, I realized I had no exclusive rights to heartache.

"I'm sorry."

They should have been my words. I was the one fumbling for the right thing to say.

But it was Chase who spoke first.

"You have nothing to be sorry for," I whispered.

He didn't look at me, barely even moved. Were it not for the rise and fall of his shoulders, I would not have even known that he breathed. "I heard what Amber said to you," he said. "About me and Jessie."

I stiffened, did not want the memory. "She can't hurt me."

He moved without warning, twisting toward me so fast I had no time to step back. And then when his eyes found mine, I didn't want to.

"But you're afraid I will," he murmured. "That's why you told me to leave you alone."

Around us a warm breeze swirled through walls that no longer stood, but that I, somehow, felt.

"I'm sorry," he said again. "Sorry for dragging you into all this."

Only a few inches separated us, but I quickly did away with them, stepping into him and tilting my face to his, making sure he saw me—*really saw me*—before speaking.

"You haven't dragged me anywhere I haven't chosen to be."

His eyes flashed. "I've never known anyone like you," he

muttered as my throat burned. "You don't run," he said. "Even when everybody else is sprinting. You don't run."

If the wind had blown only a whisper harder, I was quite sure it would have taken me with it.

"If things had been different . . ." he started, but his voice trailed off without finishing.

"What?"

Sunlight glinted off the silver chain around his neck, the dog tag that hid the cross. "Just thinking about you," he surprised me by saying. "And Jessie . . . how different her life could have been if she'd had you for a friend instead of Amber."

It was an odd thought. "Don't use the past tense," I whispered.

Sliding his arms around my waist, he pulled me and held me, resting his chin against the top of my head. We stood that way for what seemed like forever, just letting the sun soak in and the breeze swirl.

My homes still stood. My grandmother's in the Garden District and my parents' in the French Quarter, the small cabinlike house where I'd grown up. They were all still there for me to go back to, walk through, remember and imagine.

It was hard to imagine something as fundamental as a house being just . . . gone.

"Show me your room," I whispered, and when I felt his body tense against mine, I reached for his hand. "Show me where you grew up."

He pulled back and looked down at me, the blue of his eyes a dark glitter. Then he threaded his fingers through mine and took me on the tour.

"There was a pool table here," he said as we passed through what had once been a game room. "Out back was the Ping-Pong table."

I smiled, rocked by the magnitude of the gift he was giving me. "Where was the sofa?"

He glanced to his left, his gaze somewhere far, far away.

I could only imagine what he saw, remembered—*or who.*

Quietly he tugged me deeper into the past, drawing me down what he said was a hall, past his brother's room to a spot bordered by a line of riotously blooming irises. I didn't even know how that was possible that they could thrive, while so much else had been washed away.

"It wasn't anything special," he said.

"But it was yours."

He looked back at me, and smiled. *"It still is."*

I don't know how long we stayed there among the invisible walls of his childhood, but for one of the few times of my life, I was content to be in the moment, without looking to the other side. Words seemed inadequate, so I let the silence do the talking, right up to the moment Chase stood and announced it was time to go.

"Emma Watson was your grandmother's housekeeper," he said after we'd been driving several minutes. "Worked for her for twenty-five years, right up to the—"

"End," I whispered.

Slowing for another intersection, he frowned as he turned onto a two-lane highway. "She was like a second mother to your father, her little girl a sister. When he got older, it was Emma Watson who told him about the house for sale next to hers. Her daughter—Amelia—had a serious thing for your dad. According to Ms. Watson it was mutual."

"Until he met my mom." And took the first step down the road that had, ultimately, led to his death.

"And Amelia married someone else."

Around us, the remains of the broken community gave way to huge trees crowding the narrow road. "The cop?"

"Jim Fourcade."

Within minutes the bumpy road emptied into a clearing, a big open rectangle ringed by huge trees that looked as tired as they were old. The house sat toward the back, wide and brick and clearly new, one story with a big wraparound porch. The gravel road led straight to a parking area in front of a closed garage, before winding around behind the house to another structure farther back.

Chase shifted the car into park. "Ready?"

I had the door open before he killed the engine.

Stepping into the dappled sunshine, I couldn't help but notice how peaceful it was here in the middle of nowhere, where there was only the trees and the song of the birds, the tinkle of unseen chimes, and the river somewhere beyond. I would have sworn I could *feel* it.

We started toward the house, where at the bottom step a dream catcher dangled from the railing. Having spent so much time in Colorado, I'd seen my share of the Native American talisman, but I'd never seen one dangling above a statue of the Virgin Mary, and I'd never seen one like this, carved of a pale driftwood, with amazingly uniform feathers seemingly crawling up strands of red and black beads, toward the web in the center, like fish swimming toward bait.

Catching up with me, Chase reached for my hand and I instinctively took his. I winced, too late remembering the gashes on my palms.

He pulled open the screen door, and I knocked. And knocked. And knocked.

No one answered.

Frustrated, I glanced around, keying back on the new motorcycle and old pickup next to where we'd parked. "Maybe he's around back," I said, already pulling away.

Chase tugged me against him, moving a step or two ahead of me as we left the porch and edged around the house.

"Wonder how long he's been back," Chase said, and I didn't even have to ask. I knew. This close to the river, Jim Fourcade had surely lost everything.

"What I don't understand is why he'd *come* back," I said. "If it happened once, it can happen again, right? Just because you've had one big hurricane doesn't mean there can't be others, and if what they say about global warming is true . . ."

Chase shot me a quick look. "It's his home," he said, and I could tell that to Chase, it was as simple as that.

The dogs came out of nowhere. The second we stepped into what I would have called a backyard even though there was no fence, I heard the barking. By the time I swung right, they were halfway toward us, three of them, big and fast and growling as if they'd been waiting their whole lives to tear into us.

"Shit!" Chase yanked me behind him, going very still as he jutted out a hand. "Easy, guys." His voice was steady, commanding. *"Easy."*

The dogs—I think they were rottweilers—kept running.

"Easy!" he shouted again, this time a little more desperate, and a whole lot louder.

The huge dogs didn't care. They closed in on us, running hard, and sickly I realized what Chase had known all along. We would never outrun them.

"Allez!"

The rots went absolutely, insanely still, like some invisible cage had dropped around them. They stayed on all fours, staring straight at us with slobber oozing from their mouths and hunger in their eyes, but they didn't move a single muscle.

Heart slamming, I pivoted right and my breath caught. Adjacent to a separate but identical dream catcher, someone stood in the shadows of the back porch, tall, dark, as absolutely deadly still as the dogs. Like a predator, I thought a little insanely, watching. Waiting.

I should have felt relief. I knew that. But the echo quickening through me was anything but. Instinctively I stepped closer to the safety of Chase, felt his hand again reach for mine, felt my fingers slide in against his.

"What the hell—"

The agitated voice from behind us broke the strange silence. We swung around just as a man erupted from the smaller garage, where through the shadows I made out what looked to be a boat.

He strode toward us, working some kind of white rag in his hands. When he got close enough for me to see the grease—he stopped. Cold. Like . . . death. The wind kept whispering—I was sure that it did—but everything else slowed, allowing me to see the lean lines of his leathery face, and the dread in his eyes.

"Mary Mother of God," he muttered. "You're the girl."

TWENTY

Silver. I'd never seen anything like it. Everything about the man was silver, from the shoulder-length hair slicked back into a tight ponytail behind his neck, to the whiskers crowding his jaw, his brows—and his eyes. From between narrowed lids they glowed, as if he'd come face-to-face with something of great beauty—or even greater ugliness.

"What girl?" My question was barely more than a choked whisper.

"The girl with the dreams," he breathed, and my knees wobbled.

Chase edged closer, held on a whole lot tighter. I could feel the strength of his hand and his body, and for that I was grateful.

He knew. This man, this complete stranger, knew about me—and my dreams.

"How do *you* know that?" That was from Chase, and the words were as uneasy as they were accusatory.

"You're on my property, son. The way I figure, that puts questions in my mouth, not yours."

Chase stiffened, making the Gothic cross on his T-shirt tighten against his chest.

The man shifted his attention back to me, and I would have sworn the silver in his eyes . . . tarnished. "My God you look like your mama."

The words sounded ripped from a throat too accustomed to cigarettes and whiskey, and in response, my own throat tightened. "So it's true . . . you *did* know her."

"What's true is you shouldn't be here," he said as his hands fisted against the grease-stained rag. "What in sweet God's name is Rosemary thinking—"

"She's not thinking anything," I whispered, so tired of all the lies. *"She's dead."*

Expressionless, Jim Fourcade looked away, off toward the wall of trees, where somewhere beyond the river flowed, and even though we stood in a clearing and the sun lashed down from high overhead, I would have sworn a shadow fell around him. That, combined with the way his sweat-stained T-shirt and baggy jeans hung on his lean body, made him look as weary as the frail cypress trees in the distance. "I'm sorry to hear that."

His words were barely more than a mutter.

Once I would have accepted his sympathy and said something all nicey-nice, like "that's okay," or "thank you," following the rules of etiquette and respect my grandmother had drilled into me. But that was before. Before she died and before I came to this strange place, before everything changed. Now something deep inside me gave way, allowing questions to spill like flood waters.

"What I want to know is why," I said, not giving a flip at how rattled he looked. "Why shouldn't I be here? Why did my grandmother keep me a virtual prisoner in the mountains? Why does everyone look at me like I'm some sort of psycho?"

Curled around mine, Chase's hand tightened.

"What is everyone so afraid of?" I asked. "Why does everyone think it's better to leave me in the dark? If it's something bad, *shouldn't I know*?" How else could I protect myself? "I'm not a little kid. I'm sixteen years old! *I have the right to know.*"

Jim Fourcade's eyes returned to mine, and yeah, they still glowed. I was starting to think that's just the way his eyes looked, like embers lit by an internal fire.

"You're right," he said, and my heart just about stopped. "You're right."

So not the answer I was expecting. But the thrill of anticipation kept me from lingering on my surprise.

"How did you know it was me?" I asked, this time quieter, calmer. "How did you know about my dreams?"

Jim Fourcade let out a deep, full-body breath, looking beyond me and Chase, toward the back porch, where the guy in the shadows—

I swung around.

He was gone. So were the dogs.

"Come on," Mr. Fourcade said, heading toward the house. "It's hot as Hades out here."

It was, that was true. But at the thought of going inside that house, something sharp and visceral twined through me. Because of *him,* I knew. The guy who'd stood so weirdly still . . .

I tugged at Chase's hand, shooting him an *I-don't-want-to-go-in-there* look the second he glanced back at me. He nodded, his hand firm around mine as he led me to the edge of the patio.

"We'll stay out here," Chase said, and at the screen door, Mr. Fourcade swung around, and laughed.

"There's nothing that can happen inside, son, that can't happen outside."

I felt my eyes widen, hated the spurt of panic. This man was supposed to be my mother's friend.

Or was he? Had Chase said that? I scrambled through all that he'd told me in the car, realized that I'd filled in gaps with my own stupid little fantasies.

Chase had never once said Jim Fourcade was my mother's friend.

I'd just assumed.

This man was Emma Watson's son-in-law. Emma Watson who hated my mother. We were in the middle of nowhere. No one knew we were here.

No one would come looking.

No one would suspect . . .

"Suit yourself, though," Fourcade said, glancing toward a rusted wrought-iron table in the far corner. Nearby sat a shiny new gas grill big enough to cook for my entire chemistry class all at one time.

"I was on the force almost twenty years," he said, picking up a tin watering can and moving toward a cluster of droopy red flowers in clay pots.

"That's longer than you've been alive," he pointed out. "My resignation doesn't mean I don't still have friends there."

I swallowed, watching the curiously gentle way he went down on one knee and fussed over the faded flowers.

"Folks talk," he went on. "Especially when a pretty girl goes missing and another girl claims to have dreams."

Chase stayed close to me, shifting his hand from holding mine to secured around my waist. "How'd you know that girl was Trinity?"

Fourcade looked up at Chase—then me. "Because she's got her mama written all over her. Those eyes . . ." He had to be somewhere in his forties, but in that moment, he looked ancient. "I would know Marguerite's girl anywhere."

I stiffened. So did Chase. *"Marguerite?"* The scrape of disappointment almost overwhelmed me. "My mother was Rachelle."

Fourcade let out a heavy breath. "Rosemary did good," he said, but his smile was weary.

"At what?" I asked, because seriously, I was starting to think my grandmother had spent her whole life keeping secrets from me. "Lying?"

"Protecting."

There it was again. One man's lies . . . another man's virtue. "From *what*?"

Fourcade pushed back to his feet, the way he crossed the patio reminding me, for some crazy reason, of an ancient wolf, once powerful but now worn out from all that he'd seen. *Done.*

"From the truth," he said, and all I could think was here we go again. More circles. "About your mama," he added before I could call him out on the doublespeak. "And yourself."

It wasn't until I felt the sting that I realized I'd curled my hands into fists. Wincing, I glanced down at the ooze of blood once again staining the gauze.

"Sweet Mary." Fourcade was by my side before I could manage even a breath, going down on his knee and taking my hands in his with the same unexpected gentleness he'd bestowed upon the plants. "What happened?"

"Just an accident," I said, stunned by the way his big bony fingers could move so tenderly, slowly unwrapping the bandage.

"Hey, what are you doing—" Chase started, but this man, this former cop who'd known my parents, silenced him with a quick, lethal glance.

"Get me Mama Faye's salve!" he shouted, and I looked from him to Chase, wondering who in the world he was talking to.

Within seconds, I had my answer.

The dog-silencer emerged from the darkness of the house, moving with the same sleek, predatorlike grace as when he'd stood in the shadows of the patio. He was taller up close, a hint of a goatee at his jaw, his hawklike eyes as silver as the man kneeling before me.

The two exchanged a quick look I didn't understand. Then Fourcade was turning my hands palm up and the younger version of him was joining him on his knees, bringing the shiny silver tube over my palms.

"What the—" Chase started—but Fourcade blasted him with another of those slicing looks.

This time Chase refused to be silenced. He lunged closer, reaching for me. "Ever heard of asking?"

Fourcade stood and stopped him. Vaguely I was aware of the way the cop took Chase by his arms and backed him away, of the terse exchange of voices. But only vaguely. I couldn't have looked at them if I'd tried, not with the way the younger version of Fourcade kneeled in front of me, squeezing the tube over my palms. With a single finger he spread the amber salve along each of the cuts, leaving a tingle of warmth everywhere he touched.

"This will help," he said, and it was all I could do to swallow. Because I saw him then, saw that he was no man, but much younger, probably not much older than me. Unlike all the silver of his father, he was dark, with closely cropped hair the color of night, his complexion that of olives, his jaw clean-shaven. His cheekbones were razor sharp, his eyes deep-set.

Wolf and hawk, I thought a little maniacally, but with a whole new sympathy for Alice and the rabbit hole.

"You need to be more careful," he said, those silver eyes lingering on mine for a heartbeat longer than was comfortable. And then, he was gone.

"What the hell," Chase was saying, shoving against Fourcade. But there was no longer a need. The cop released him, stepped back while Chase dropped down in front of me, taking my palm-up hands in his. "Are you okay?"

I nodded, staring at the angry red wounds. But that was a lie. I was not okay, not even close, not when I could still feel a slow burn seeping through flesh and muscle, deeper, closer, clear to the bone.

"What is this stuff?" Chase asked, glancing toward Fourcade.

I couldn't help but wonder what Chase was the most upset about—the mystery salve, or the way the Silent One had touched me.

Fourcade joined us, offering Chase a roll of gauze. "It will help," was all he said.

Chase muttered his doubt under his breath as he started to wrap my left hand. Then he looked up at me. "You can wash it off, later."

Peripherally I saw Fourcade stiffen, and realized I'd arrived at a crossroads, whether I wanted to be there, or not. I could wash the reddish, sulfur-smelling stuff off. That was true. And maybe I should. That would have been the smart, rational, logical thing to do. I didn't know Jim Fourcade from an axe murderer. I only knew that he'd known my parents—and that he recognized me.

That did not mean he didn't want to hurt me.

But some inner awareness stopped the tug-of-war before it really got started.

"No," I whispered, and really, only a few days before the flicker of dismay in Chase's eyes would have changed my mind.

But standing beneath the twirling dream catcher on Jim Fourcade's back porch, I realized if I wanted answers, this was a path I had to take.

"Why did you call my mother Marguerite?" I asked, lifting my chin to stare Fourcade straight in the eyes.

His smile was oddly satisfied. "To see what you knew."

"A test," I realized as Chase carefully rebandaged my right hand.

"Only if you choose to think of it that way," Fourcade said. "You have to realize . . ." He hesitated, glancing beyond me before again meeting my eyes. "I always knew this day would come," he said. "I . . ." He swore under his breath. "I just knew. But I didn't know it would be today. You caught me flat-footed, Trinity Rose—it took me a minute to catch up with where we are."

I wasn't totally sure I got all that, but was willing to go with it. "And where are we?"

"You said you wanted the truth," he said, spinning around one of four rickety-looking wrought-iron chairs. He sat backward in the chair, his legs straddled. "And if that's my role in all this, so be it."

His role?

Chase secured the last bandage, holding my hands gently as he looked down at me. "Let's go."

"No." The weirdness of it all wasn't lost on me, the fact that I was in the middle of nowhere with a potentially mentally unbalanced stranger—and Chase.

And that I felt safe. Totally, absolutely, without a shred of doubt safe.

Lifting my eyes to his, I smiled. "I'm good," I said. Because I was. I was so, so good.

Because of Chase.

He'd done this for me.

I'd done everything I could to push him away, but like a rock in hurricane-force winds, he'd held firm, and found Jim Fourcade.

I reached for his hand and squeezed without thinking, realizing only after, that nothing happened. There was no quick sting, no burn. No pain in my palms whatsoever.

"Let's see what he knows," I said quietly, then made myself look away and focus on Jim Fourcade. "Why Marguerite?"

Much to my shock, he didn't pretend to misunderstand me. "That was her professional name."

"Professional name?" Chase asked.

"The name she used in the Quarter," Fourcade said.

"Her psychic name," I realized.

Fourcade nodded.

No wonder. No wonder my research on Rachelle Monsour kept turning up absolutely nothing. "Which was her real name?"

"They both were."

I frowned.

"Her mama named her Rachelle. Her mama's mama chose Marguerite."

"Like a middle name?"

"It's complicated," Fourcade said. "Most people are content to go by one name for everyone. But some people . . . need a buffer."

Chase drew me back against him, using one arm to anchor me against his body. "A buffer?"

Fourcade rocked forward, bringing the chair onto two legs. "To protect."

That little tidbit went through me like a jackhammer. "To protect? From what?"

His mouth tightened, but he said nothing, and I knew, I knew he was testing me again, gauging how much I knew before deciding what to tell me next.

"You mean from her visions?" I asked, and pretty much automatically, I lifted my hand to my chest, where the tarnished dragonfly dangled from the old bronze chain.

Fourcade smiled. "Her visions," he said. "And her work."

We were getting closer. "You mean as a psychic?"

"No," he said, and his eyes were doing it again, getting all glowy-glowy. "With me."

"With you?" Chase and I spoke in unison.

Fourcade sat only a foot or two away, but between us, the miles and years lengthened. "There was a little girl," he said. "Six years old. She got on her bike one afternoon to go see her grandma. One block away, only one turn. Her grandma was outside waiting. But Meggie never showed up."

Around us the wind teased an odd collection of spoons-turned-chimes dangling from a nearby tree, providing relief to the stifling humidity. But I could find no sign of relief for Fourcade, not from the heat, or the past.

"We looked. We looked and looked and looked. Everywhere. Five minutes. That's all it should have taken—what the hell can go wrong in five minutes?"

A lot, I knew. A whole lot.

Everything.

"There was no trace," Fourcade went on as Chase rubbed his hands up and down along my arms. It was only then that I realized I'd started to shiver.

Yes, the temperature was somewhere in the nineties.

"There was a canal running behind her house. That's where we found her bike."

The image formed, as vivid as it was sickening.

"But not the girl," I whispered, not sure how I knew, just knowing that I did.

"No. Not Meggie." The breeze rustled a long strand of silver hair that had worked free of his ponytail, but he made no move to brush it back. No move to indicate that he'd even noticed. "And then one day I'm in my office, and in walks—"

"My mother."

Fourcade's eyes met mine. "I can still see her," he said, and from the way he looked at me, I had to wonder who he was seeing at that very moment. Me? Or a ghost?

My money was on the ghost.

"Her eyes," he said. "It was like someone had punched me in the gut."

My breath caught. Behind me, I felt Chase's do the same.

"Told me she'd had a dream," he said, still looking at me—but clearly seeing her. "I thought she was nuts."

Instinctively my fingers again found my mother's dragonfly, and rubbed.

"Then she led me straight to Meggie."

I closed my eyes, but immediately wished I hadn't, because I saw her there, not my mother or the missing child, but Jessica, alone in the darkness of the house on Prytania.

Or *was* it the house?

I no longer knew—it made no sense that she would return to that place two nights after we'd all been there. Had she lost something? Seen something she wanted to see again? Had she arranged for someone to meet her there?

I'm afraid your dream was nothing more than a fantasy . . .

"Gone. That beautiful little child had been tossed in a marsh south of town, like nothing more than a piece of trash."

And my mother had known. My mother had . . . seen.

Swallowing hard, I opened my eyes to see Fourcade press a leathery hand to his face. "My partner thought she did it."

"Holy shit." That was Chase.

"Omigod." That was me.

"But I knew better," Fourcade was saying. "I knew how bad it looked. And I knew how crazy it sounded, that she'd had a *dream* . . . But I also knew Rachelle," he said. "She and your daddy lived next door to my mother-in-law. That's why she chose me. That's why she felt comfortable coming to me. She'd tried to hold quiet, to live with what she knew . . ."

But she hadn't been able to.

"I stood up for her," he said. "There was an investigation. It got real bad. But in the end there was no evidence . . . not even when the second child went missing."

Chase held me tighter. "Did she help find that one, too?"

Fourcade nodded. "People started calling her a witch."

Like his mother-in-law, Emma Watson.

"After the fifth child—"

I gasped. "Five?" And she'd kept on. My mother had kept trying to help, even when doing so amounted to burning herself at the stake.

"Five," Fourcade repeated. "But that little girl we got to in time. We found her before that monster could do anything to her, because by then, your mama was seeing as clearly as he was."

I wanted to cry. For those little girls, for my mother, even for Jim Fourcade. Because even after all this time, and really, it had to be over fifteen years, I could see the weight of all that had gone down in the burnished glow of his eyes.

"That's when the game started," he said, and I felt myself go ice still.

"What game?"

"It was in the papers," he said, still in that faraway, faded voice, the one that hurt to hear, because in it the past still lived. "Some idiot found out about your mama's role in the investigation, and printed it. They freakin' printed it in the paper for every crack-job in the world to see."

I looked away, toward the back of the yard, where I finally found the dogs from before, two sleeping, one alert, watching.

And a whole new picture started to form, of this former cop who lived so far out of the mainstream. At first I'd equated the trees and the birds, the isolation, with serenity. Maybe even escape. Now I had to wonder.

Had Jim Fourcade turned his back on society, or had society turned its back on him?

Did he live in the middle of nowhere for peace . . . or protection?

It chilled me to realize the same could be asked of my grandmother.

"What happened?" Chase asked, and I glanced up at him, realizing for the first time that I'd forgotten. Only a few days before, I'd done a major league tap dance to keep Emma Watson from revealing anything about my mother in front of Chase. But that was all gone now. Somewhere along the line, I'd let my defenses drop, and started to ask questions. In front of Chase.

And he wasn't running in disgust.

He was standing with his arms around me, holding on.

And despite the shock of all I'd learned, my heart did a long slow free fall through my chest.

"Someone started to play with us," Fourcade said. *"With her."*

I didn't like the way that sounded. "What do you mean, play?"

"Games," he said. "New Orleans is a world unto itself, and your mama was by no stretch the only one with abilities. There are others—there always have been. Some people turn away from the unexpected, the unexplained. But others embrace it. The more bizarre, the better. They seek it, hone it. *Crave it.*"

I'd been naive, I realized. Naive to think that if only I could find answers to my questions, everything would be better. Everything would make sense. I'd never let myself believe—I'd never even considered—that everything could get worse.

"He turned it into a contest," Fourcade said. "A game . . . like chess. He would make a move specifically and explicitly to find out if your mother could match him. If she could beat him."

Against my back, I could feel the rise and fall of Chase's chest. "That's messed up," I muttered.

Fourcade's mouth flattened into a tight line. "And she could," he said. "She could match him. She could see through his eyes, know what he knew. Feel what he felt . . ."

I couldn't even imagine. It was bad enough catching glimpses of Jessica. I couldn't imagine what it would be like to actually feel what she was feeling. Or worse, to feel what her abductor was feeling. See what he was seeing.

Want . . . what he wanted.

"Who would do that?" I asked. "What kind of sick, twisted . . ."

Very slowly, Jim Fourcade lifted his eyes to mine. "The man who killed her," he said. "The man who murdered your parents."

TWENTY-ONE

Nothing prepared me. Nothing could have. How could anyone be prepared to hear that the parents you thought died in an accident had actually been murdered?

Murder. It was such an ugly word.

An even uglier image.

So much twisted through me all at once. It was hard to explain. Shock made me cold. Fury made me shake. And sorrow . . . The slow bleed made me feel as fragile as the glass dragonfly in my bedroom, as if the wind blew hard enough, I would simply shatter.

Some sicko had murdered my parents.

Some sicko had killed them while they slept.

As part of some sick psychic game of chess.

All because she'd tried to help. Because she'd come forward with what she saw, and tried to make a difference.

They'd never even had a chance.

"Hey," Chase said, and then he was turning me toward him, lifting a hand to the side of my face and looking down at me, frowning, maybe shaking a little himself. His touch was so gentle I wanted to cry. Instead I sunk into him, exhaling slowly as his arms slid around me. "I'm sorry," he said.

And I had to wonder for what. For what Fourcade had told us—or for unearthing this stone in the first place, for digging when I'd asked him to stop . . . for bringing me to this crossroads?

I wanted to lose myself there, in his arms, in all that warmth. But I knew I couldn't. I couldn't allow myself to crumble—and I couldn't turn my back on the truth.

It took effort, but I grabbed onto the determination that had brought me this far to begin with and twisted back toward my mother's cop. I made myself step away from Chase.

"What happened to him?" The question came from me; I knew it did because I felt my mouth move. But the voice I heard, all raw and thick and scraped, was one I'd never heard before. "Is he in jail?"

"Some say he was killed," Fourcade said. "Some say he died on his own. Others say that after your mama was gone, after the game was done, he just . . . went away."

"And you?" I asked. "What do you say?"

Fourcade rocked back, returning the chair to all four legs. But his eyes, timeless and silver and unspeakably tortured, remained on mine.

"I say that your mama knew," he said. "I say that she saw and she knew and she moved every mountain to make sure the ugliness of her life never touched yours."

A feather could have knocked me over.

"I say your grandmother was a saint, giving up everything she'd ever loved, ever known . . . to protect you."

Chase stepped into me, his arms once again drawing me back against him.

I didn't feel a thing.

"I say you should pray," Fourcade said, but really, his voice was barely more than a murmur. "I say you should pray it's not too late."

Dusk fell in a gauzy veil. Earlier, on the drive down into St. Bernard Parish, I'd made out buildings and houses, even one of the hauntingly beautiful aboveground cemeteries. But on the drive back there was only the gathering darkness. Not that it mattered. I doubted I would have seen anything to begin with.

We drove in silence. I'm not sure how we could have done anything else. It's not like we could talk about football or next week's chem test, not with the weight of Fourcade's revelations pressing down on us. We couldn't even talk about that.

Wow, so some psychic pervert killed your parents. But you know what I don't get? If your mom was so powerful, why didn't she realize what he was going to do?

No, Chase was not going to ask that. I could tell by the way he stared straight ahead, his jaw hard as stone, his hands clenched too tightly around the steering wheel. I was pretty sure we'd blown way through any and all familiar territory.

Swallowing, I looked away from him, out the passenger window. He wasn't going to ask, but I was. I already had. And I was pretty sure I knew.

My mother *had* seen. She'd known. The pieces were all there, the story my aunt told about finding my mother rocking me, crying. That my mother had known she would not see me grow up. *She'd known.*

But why hadn't she done anything to stop it? Why hadn't she done anything to protect herself? My father? Had he known?

It was weird, but I had the feeling they hadn't necessarily been on the same page.

The car slowed and I blinked, realizing Chase had not been driving toward the Warehouse District, but to a neighborhood with wide, tree-lined streets and huge, gorgeous houses.

"Where are we?" I asked.

He veered right, easing the Camaro down a long driveway next to a big two-story house. Night had completed its fall, but through the scatter of security lights, I could see the brick was painted white, and the style looked Spanish.

A garage door lifted, and Chase pulled inside, slowed to a stop, and killed the engine.

I had my answer.

The Bonaventure's house was amazing. It was everything I'd imagined a home belonging to a successful lawyer and respected surgeon would be, all high ceilings and dark hardwood floors, lots of crown molding and bold antique furniture, marble and granite and state-of-the-art electronics.

It was also quiet, and still.

Chase led me across the marble floor of the foyer, with its amazing chandelier hanging two stories above, to the sprawling family room, where a wall of windows and French doors looked out onto a cabana. Shadows hid detail, but I could tell there was a pool. And from the sound of barking, I knew the dogs must be out there, too.

"Hungry?" he asked from behind me. "We can order a pizza or sushi—"

I turned toward him. "No, thanks."

He watched me carefully, as if he half expected me to bolt.

I more than half wanted to.

"A drink then? A soda . . . beer?"

My mouth was dry, my heart thrumming hard. This was all so

very real. I was at Chase's house. We were alone. He was looking at me in that way I'd always dreamed, when I'd lay awake in
my bed, wondering what it would be like if he kissed me. And
more.

I'd wondered, but I'd never believed.

But there he was, looking at me as if he could see right through
me—and very much liked what he saw. *Wanted* what he saw.

"No, I'm good," I said, wrapping my arms around myself. It
wasn't cold, not even cool. But I needed to hold on as tightly as I
could. "I just want to go home."

But that was so a lie. *Leaving* was not what I wanted.

Chase's shoulders fell with a rough breath. "Not an option."

I concentrated on the Gothic cross on his shirt, anything to
avoid looking at his eyes. "Chase, please—"

"You shouldn't be alone," he said, and then he was moving toward me, erasing the distance between us.

My instinct was to back away. But the open space behind me
was only an illusion of the windows.

"Not tonight, Trinity," he said, and the way his voice rough-
ened on my name made me everything inside of me quicken. "Not
after today." He stopped close enough to touch. But he didn't.

At least not with his hands or his body.

"Because we both know what will happen."

I'm not sure how I stood there without moving, given the deceptively small earthquakes tearing through my body.

"You'll run," he said quietly. "And you'll hide."

Like I'd done before.

Everything closed in on me then, everything I wanted, and
everything I feared. I was safe. I knew that. For that moment, in
Chase's house, with its security system and neighborhood patrol,
with *him,* there was absolutely no reason to be afraid. I'd faced so
much more: the house on Prytania and the horrible dreams, the

abandoned courtyard and the field by the airport, the man in the parking garage . . .

"You don't have to be afraid," he said, lifting a hand to my chin and easing my face toward his. "Not of me."

The rush swirled deeper. I could lose myself there, I knew. I wanted to.

That's why I looked away. Because no matter how badly I wanted to let go and trust, to believe, I wasn't sure I knew how.

"Did you say something about pizza?" I asked, and Chase's eyes went even smokier.

He so knew what I was doing.

The slow rhythm of drums and chants washed over me the second I stepped from the small bathroom adjacent to the kitchen. Not too far away Chase sat in the family room, sprawled on the huge sectional sofa in front of the TV.

The glazed look in his eyes, so like that afternoon at the scrap of land that had once been his home, told me he had no idea how long I'd been gone.

A rocky field gleamed on the wide screen of the TV, with a big concrete tower on either end, and a bunch of dead things. Never blinking, never even moving, Chase just kept mowing them down, one after the other.

I could only imagine what he saw in the edges of his mind.

Quietly, I tossed my purse onto a formal chair and crossed to the sofa.

It was just a game, a game I myself had played numerous times. But games were supposed to be fun, and there was nothing fun in the way Chase kept destroying everything that so much as looked his way. Watching him should not have hurt. Watching him should not have made that big aching chasm inside of me fracture even more.

But it did.

"You're good," I murmured, driven by something I didn't understand. "You must play a lot."

He stared straight ahead. "When I need to."

"*Need* to?"

The haunting music kept drifting, gradually louder, gradually lending an unexpected beauty to the savagery of his actions. "To get away," he muttered, and finally his eyes flickered, just a trace, a small little flash that told me he was much more aware than I'd realized. "To forget."

The music still played. I was sure that it did. But the chant faded to more of a low hum. And when I looked at Chase, the bangs falling into his eyes and his T-shirt loose, casual, his jean-clad legs spread wide, I knew his relaxed stance was a complete and total sham.

Only a few days before, I'd thought he had the perfect life. Now I realized it was also the perfect lie.

"Forget what?" I whispered without thinking.

Someday I would have to stop doing that.

"Everything," he said quietly. "The lies, the secrets . . . Jessica." He turned, obliterating me with his eyes—and one simple word. "*You*."

I went to step back, but my legs wouldn't move. "Me?"

Something about him changed, softened. "This wasn't how things were supposed to be," he said in that same quiet, almost robotic voice. "I would change it all if I could."

My throat burned. *My whole body burned.* "What would you change?"

The shadows about him deepened. "Jessica," he said. "Your parents . . . the fear I see in your eyes."

Instinctively I glanced away.

"I want to make it go away for you, too," he said as my heart drummed so hard I could feel it in every pulse point. "If you'll let me."

Slowly, I looked back toward him and felt the promise in his eyes slip into my blood.

He extended a hand. "Come here."

And I did. Just like that, against better judgment and every remnant of uncertainty, I took his hand, and went to him. "You make it sound so easy."

"Not easy," he said as I sunk down beside him. "But worth it."

And somehow, I believed him.

"The world as we know it no longer exists," he murmured as around us the apocalyptic music crested. "Humanity has been forced to flee. Space travel is the norm. Genetic engineering has created a whole new race."

Called Spartans. I actually knew that. Growing up in the mountains was not like growing up in a cave. I'd had a friend, Jeffery. His grandmother and mine played bridge. While they did, Jeffery and I hung out. He, too, had been killer at *Halo*.

"There are these aliens," Chase explained. "The Covenant. They're the bad guys."

They looked like giant toy Transformers.

He reached for the second controller and handed it to me. I would have sworn my fingers tingled. "It's up to us to stop them."

Us. And in doing so . . . find a way to forget everything else. "What happens then?"

His eyes took on a smoky gleam. "Let's find out," he said, resetting the game so that two survivors stood on the rocky field.

He scooted closer, ran me through the basics of my controller. "And this," he said, sliding his arm around me to hover his finger against a trigger, "throws a grenade."

"What about this one?" I asked, joining my clumsily bandaged hand with his as I slid both to the right.

He glanced at me. His bangs fell into his face. "That one shoots."

Somehow he'd ended up so spooned against my back that I could feel his heart, his breath. "Okay."

"It seems like a lot to remember," he said, "but once you get started . . ." His heavy-lidded eyes met mine. "Instinct takes over."

Before, I'd shivered. Now, despite the slow swirl of the ceiling fan, my whole body burned.

"Just go with it," he murmured. "See where it takes you."

His bottom lip was fuller than his top. Had I ever really noticed that before?

"Ready?" he asked.

I nodded, lifting my free hand to slide the hair from my face. It was all I could do not to do the same to Chase.

"I like when you do that."

I tried to swallow. My throat was too tight. "Do what?"

"Move the hair from your eyes."

I stilled.

"They're pretty."

No one had ever told me that before.

Just when I was sure my heart was going to slam out of my chest, he broke the moment, glancing from me to the big TV screen. "See those nooks in the rock?"

I did. I saw it all, all that he showed me, and all that he worked so hard to keep hidden.

"The weapons are there," he said, and somewhere inside, I smiled. Weapons were hidden—but so were cracks. "All you gotta do is—"

"Chase?"

He glanced over, his arm still around me. "Yeah?"

"Shut up."

He smiled, and from one heartbeat to the next everything exploded around us, the music blasted, and shots started flying. With his left hand he guided his player to the cliffs before I'd barely moved mine two steps.

"Watch out!" he called, but my player went down before I'd fired my first shot.

"Sniper got you," he muttered, mowing down cyborgs left and right. "If you'd just followed my lead—"

I'm not sure why I shoved him. But I did. Reflex made him swing to look at me—and his player went down.

"Oops," I said, and then the laughter took over.

Chase went still, watched me, and then like he'd promised, instinct took over.

All that tension and uncertainty, the dreaming and imagining and the crazy urge to run and hide . . . it all fell away, and Chase was leaning into me, and I wasn't pulling back, wasn't looking away, was instead reaching for him.

His hand found the side of my face, settling against my cheek with amazing tenderness. For the faintest of heartbeats our eyes met, held, and then his mouth lowered toward mine, and my mind went blank.

The kiss was soft, slow. Endless. My arms lifted, first to his shoulders, then to slide around his back—and pull him closer. With one arm to the sofa, he eased me backward, leaning over me so that the chain around his neck dangled, his jaw scraping mine as our mouths moved together. It was crazy. It was wonderful. It was everything I'd ever imagined and more, and all I could think was that I never wanted it to end.

And yeah, Chase Bonaventure was good at that, too.

And then he was gone, not really gone, but pulling back, his hand still cradling my face. I could see his eyes, the blue, blue glow, and it was all I could do to breathe.

"You have no idea how long I've wanted to do that," he whispered.

For so long I'd waited. And for so long I'd wanted. *"Chase,"* I whispered, lifting *my* hand to *his* face. This time I let my thumb skim along his bottom lip. "Quit talking."

His smile was devastating. "Okay," he said as his mouth came down to mine once again, not as gentle as before, but crushing almost. Demanding.

Our bodies slipped and slid, tangled. Sensations swirled, creating a wave of emotion I'd never imagined. I felt myself sink against the sofa, the heaviness of his body pressing against me. All the while my hands ran along all those hard lines of his body—as his roamed along mine. Everywhere he touched, I burned. And everywhere I burned, I wanted more.

Thought shut down, and feeling took over. The moment consumed. *Owned.* I felt him push closer, felt my body welcome. His hand skimmed down my side, fingers splaying around my rib cage toward my chest, where I suddenly realized how flimsy my bra was, because the sensation of his thumb and forefinger closing around me nearly sent me into meltdown.

There was a noise. It was low and mewling and I was pretty sure it came from somewhere deep within me.

"Chase." That was definitely from me. But I'm not sure if it was a word or a breath.

"So beautiful," he muttered, and vaguely I was aware of the music still swelling, the strings and drums and the growing tempo as his mouth slid from mine and pressed little kisses along my jawbone, his whiskers scraping as he eased lower, along my neck, and I found myself arching, lifting into him, needing to give even as I wanted him to take.

And then I saw her. In the darkness of my mind, where all those protective barriers of thought and consciousness had totally fallen away, came the image, as stark as it was horrible, and everything else stopped. My hands and my mouth and my breath, even the rhythm of my body against his. It all stopped as I hung there mindlessly, lost between what was real—and what was not.

"Trinity?" Chase's voice was soft and confused as I felt him ease back from my collarbone. But I couldn't see him, couldn't see beyond the blur of shadows. "What's wrong?"

She lay on a dirty blanket spread across a concrete floor, as still as death. But her eyes were dark and open. Pleading.

"Jesus," Chase whispered, and then he was gone and in the place of all that drugging heat came a blast of cold so sharp it knifed straight through me. "What the hell—"

No, I told myself. *No, no, no.* "No." And then I wanted to run again, to run as far as I could and to hide, but I knew it wouldn't make a difference, because no matter where I went, it would never go away, not when the one thing I most wanted to get away from was as much a right of my birth as the color of my eyes and the curve of my mouth.

Birthright . . .

I made myself blink. I made myself pull back the focus. Made myself see.

And as soon as I did, I wished I hadn't. Because the way Chase was looking at me, with his bangs falling into his face and his mouth moist and swollen from the way he'd been kissing me even as confusion glittered in his eyes, absolutely ripped my heart from my chest.

"Jesus," he whispered, and only when his hands fell away did I realize he'd still been holding my arms. "You see things, too."

TWENTY-TWO

No. Just . . . no. I wanted to scream it as loud as I could. I wanted to make it all go away, to pretend my mother's blood didn't run through my body. To make Chase stop looking at me like I was one of the Covenant he was so good at slaughtering.

"Yes," I said, because I knew, *I knew* nothing that I wanted mattered. And worse, that he already knew. He'd seen it all, from the house on Prytania to the courtyard in the Quarter to Four-cade's. He'd heard everything the cop had said. And I'd let him. Like a love-struck fool, I'd let him. All because I'd wanted so badly to believe. "I see things, too."

He absorbed the words like a physical blow. *"Jesus,"* he muttered and everything I was holding onto so tightly, all those bits and parts and fragments started to shift again. To slice. I jerked away from him, rolled toward my feet.

But he stopped me. His hands found my shoulders, and he just . . . stopped me. Not physically. I could have twisted away. But the way he looked at me, the sudden shift from shock to something warm and protective.

I couldn't have moved if I'd tried.

"I wish you'd told me," was all he said.

And I lost it. The bits and pieces broke free, and my eyes filled. I tried to stop it, I really did. I didn't want to cry in front of him. But when a dam breaks, sandbags hardly do the trick, and there was no way I could blink it all away.

"I'm sorry," I whispered, glancing away, toward the carnage on the rocky field of *Halo*.

Nothing prepared me for Chase to scoop me back against him. Nothing prepared me for the way he held me. Only minutes before it had been all hot and hungry, but this gentleness, this quiet, unexpected understanding, was so much more devastating.

"You saw her, didn't you?" he asked all quiet and sad, as his hands moved against my tangled hair. "You saw Jessica."

I nodded.

"And it wasn't a dream."

Again, I nodded.

He let out a rough breath. "She's really . . ." His voice fell away, but the word hung there anyway. *Missing.*

"Yes," I whispered, and the horror of it all registered deep in his eyes, the safe buffer of illusion stripped away to reveal the cold, hard edges of reality.

"Just now," he managed. "Did you see her again? Is that what . . . is that why you—"

"It was like she knew," I said. "As if she could see us, like we were betraying her."

He swore under his breath, far more crassly than I'd ever heard from him. "Are you saying . . . So are you like . . ."

I could see him struggle for the right words.

". . . connected to her, like your mom was to the psycho who—"

He stopped himself from saying the words, but we both knew, because we'd both heard.

Killed them. The guy who'd killed my parents.

"I don't know." And I didn't. "Has Jessica ever said anything about . . . seeing stuff?"

He shook his head, sending his bangs back against his eyes. "No." Then he frowned. "But she's got a Ouija board. She says she talks to her cousin who died of leukemia a few years ago."

That was an interesting little bomb. Me and Jessica? Psychically connected?

It was hard to imagine.

"It's possible," I said. "I don't know why it happens." Only that since I'd arrived in New Orleans, the visions had been happening with increasing frequency. "When I walked into that room Saturday night, I thought—"

"Saturday night?"

I wanted to look away, knew that I couldn't. "Yeah."

"You saw something then?"

I nodded.

His breath was rough, choppy. "You knew—"

"No." I stopped him before he could go too far down that path. "I was confused. I saw a girl on the mattress." The memory chilled. "I thought it was me," I said. "At first. I didn't know what was happening."

"Has it happened before? Have you always . . . seen things?"

Talking about it felt strange. "Sometimes," I admitted. "Mostly when I was a little girl." Back when I'd seen Sunshine dead two days before she'd died. "My grandmother warned me not to talk about it, that people wouldn't understand."

Against my waist, his hands stilled.

"It only happened a few times," I said, "so I pretty much forgot all about it, until—" At the memory, I looked away, stared off into the darkness beyond the French doors.

"Until what?"

I didn't want to go back. I didn't want to remember. But I knew that I had to. "Until I saw my grandmother," I whispered. "Dead."

Chase swore under his breath.

"It was last summer," I said. "I was up in the mountains, hiking. I'd made it through this rocky pass and was looking at these alpine flowers when I saw her. She was in the kitchen, at the sink washing sweet potatoes. The sun was coming in through the windows when she went all still. Her eyes . . ." God, I could still see her eyes, the way they'd gone all frozen and dark. "Then she just fell."

"Trinity."

There was something in his voice, so warm and amazing that I looked back toward him, and felt myself die a little more. He looked like he wanted to cry. Chase Bonaventure looked like he wanted to cry.

Because I'd seen my grandmother die.

"I ran," I whispered. "All the way down the mountain. I ran so hard it hurt and then I got home and burst through the door into the kitchen and . . . there she was."

He closed his eyes.

"Alive," I said. "Sitting at the table working a puzzle."

Slowly, his eyes opened.

"She smiled. She smiled and said my name, asked me to join her."

"She was okay—"

"I didn't know what to do. I didn't know if I should tell her, because she'd told me to never talk about what I saw. But it felt wrong not saying anything. Not warning her."

Chase's hands reached for mine.

"So I tried," I said. "I tried to tell her, but it was like she knew, because she wouldn't let me. Every time I tried, she changed the subject or asked me to go do something for her. I remember that night, after she went to bed, I tore through the kitchen, looking for sweet potatoes."

His smile was so tender it made my heart hurt. "Did you find any?"

"No. None. So the next day I didn't think twice about running into town for her. She said she was going to her friend Marian's for the afternoon, and that she had a craving for pizza for dinner. So I went. I took her Buick and drove to the store. I remember walking through the produce section and seeing the bin of sweet potatoes, frowning at them like it was their fault I'd seen what I'd seen."

Against mine, Chase's hands squeezed.

"I found her when I got home." The memory still had the power to steal my breath.

"I'm sorry," he muttered, and I could tell that he was.

"In the kitchen," I said. "On the floor in the sunshine . . . with a peeled sweet potato in her hand."

When his eyes got all dark and intense, I realized how badly I wanted to dive back into his arms. I'd never had that before. My grandmother had been warm and kind, but not the huggy-feely type. She'd been more about bucking up and enduring than hugging and cuddling.

"Marian gave them to her," I whispered. "Marian gave her the potatoes." And there on Chase's sofa, with his hands holding mine, the tears started again.

"Trinity."

His voice was strong, solid, an anchor. Blinking, I made myself look at him through the watery veil. Let myself see.

Him, this moment . . . it was everything I'd ever wanted.

"It's not your fault," he said. "You couldn't have stopped it."

I swallowed against the thickness in my throat. My grandmother had told me the same thing after Sunshine died. "When I saw Jessica—"

He shook his head, sending the bangs back against his eyes. "You had no way of knowing."

"I tried," I said. "I tried to tell the police."

Chase let out a rough breath, drawing back slightly, but still holding on. Tightly. "That's why you keep pushing me away."

The moment just kind of stopped. I looked at him in the dim lighting of his gorgeous family room, with our legs still tangled and our hands still joined. My body still burned.

"This is so wrong," I said. "Jessica's out there somewhere, but here we are—"

"No," Chase said before I could finish. "*This* has nothing to do with Jessica."

"But it does! It has *everything* to do with her. You were her boyfriend—and I can't just pretend I didn't see her staring at me through the darkness."

Again, his hands squeezed mine.

"*That's* why I pushed you away," I said, this time quieter. "Because of Jessica. Because of me, what I see . . ."

"Trinity—"

"Because *I was scared,*" I whispered, and Chase frowned.

"Of me?"

I swallowed, made myself continue. "Of what you'd do when you found out." Each word felt a little like walking on broken glass. I'd never been so absolutely honest with anyone, not my grandmother or aunt, not even Victoria. "The way you'd look at me."

Methodically, his thumb skimmed along the edge of my hand. "What do you see now?"

I didn't want to look. Because I didn't want to see. Doing so hurt in ways I'd never even imagined. Because when I looked at him, at the vortex of strength and tenderness in his eyes, I saw a lifetime of dreams. The kind I wanted—not the ones that made me wake up with a scream burning in my throat.

"You want to know what *I see*?"

His question was so hoarse I'm not sure how I managed to breathe, much less nod.

"I see someone who's beautiful," he said, and deep inside, I started to shake. "And amazing, and perfect exactly the way she is."

The melting started slow, gathering force with every breath I managed.

"I'm not going anywhere," he murmured, again tightening his fingers around my hand. "I'm not—" Then he stilled. "I'm sorry—are you okay?"

I blinked. "Why wouldn't I be?"

"Your hands . . ." Gently he turned them over. Only a few hours before they'd bled, and I'd winced in pain. But even before we saw the bandages, I knew there'd be no blood.

Because I felt no pain.

"Thank God," he muttered, but I was already pulling back, trying not to yank as I tore at the strips of gauze.

"Trinity—what the—"

I wasn't sure what came over me, what drove me. But I knew what stopped me.

The sight of my flesh, absolutely and completely perfect.

Chase took my hands the second the bandages fell away. "That's impossible."

I stared. I couldn't do anything else. And even still, with my eyes wide open, belief did not come.

The wounds were gone.

With excruciating gentleness Chase skimmed his index finger along the pinkish flesh, where only hours before cuts had criss-crossed and bled. Now his finger traced the curve of my lifeline, and I felt nothing but the faintest echo of a tingle.

"The salve," I whispered. The one Jim Fourcade's son had applied. "It must have worked."

Chase's eyes, totally flat, met mine. "Nothing works that fast."

The darkness came as it always did, like sunset at warp speed. One minute the sun boiled low against the horizon, turning the tall trees into skeletons. In the next, shadows danced.

I spun around. He was there. I knew he was. I could feel him.

But I didn't know where—or who.

"Chase!" I called. It had to be him. Hadn't he been there only minutes before?

But my memory blurred, and I couldn't be sure.

"Chase!" He'd been looking at me in that warm, melting way of his, his hand holding mine. I'd felt safe—or at least, that's what I'd told myself.

But even as he'd held me, I felt the presence of another.

"Chase! Come back!" And then I started to run.

But I didn't know which way to go.

Someone was out there, watching. Waiting. I could feel them, knew that they followed me. Everywhere I turned—

The sudden wash of light blinded me. I froze, squinted against the intrusion. "Chase?"

I jerked, pivoting toward the deep voice.

"Dad . . . Mom . . ."

Chase. I twisted toward him, felt him pulling away. "Trinity."

I opened my eyes to a wash of brightness, saw Chase hovering over me.

"This is a . . . surprise."

The voice came from across the room, and with it the last vestiges of sleep crumbled away.

"Mom . . . Dad?" he said, pulling away as other things began to register, like his parents standing absolutely motionless in the shadow of the foyer, his father in a dark gray suit, standing rigid with his arm around Chase's mother, almost as if . . . holding her up. She was a beautiful woman with beautiful dark hair in a beautiful dress, with beautiful jewelry. Even her makeup had no doubt been beautiful earlier in the evening. Now the mascara smeared beneath her eyes created a stark contrast between the black of her lashes and her ashen complexion.

Chase was across the room in a heartbeat. "What's wrong?"

Alone there on the sofa, I sat very, very still.

"*Oh, Chase,*" his mother said, reaching for him and drawing him into her arms, holding on tight.

And I would have sworn every drop of blood in my body crystallized into something hard and sharp.

Chase held onto his mother, looking over her head to where his father stood. "*Dad?* What's going on?"

Jessica.

Only two days had passed since I'd last seen Richard Bonaventure, but during them it looked like he'd lived another decade. "Bryce called a little while ago."

Bryce. Jessica's father.

Now I was on my feet, not joining them, because they stood in a closed circle. But standing with a hand to my mouth.

"They found her purse," Chase's mom whispered. "*In that field by the airport.*"

The room started to spin. I swayed, fumbled for the edge of the sofa.

"*Jesus,*" Chase whispered, and I could tell the difference, see the difference. Up until an hour ago, he'd been operating under the blind belief that this was all a game. That Jessica would magically return, waltz back in with the pleasure of having taught everyone a lesson.

Now he knew that was not going to happen.

"Was there . . . did they find—"

"I don't know much," his father said. "Bryce didn't say much besides something about a note."

I saw Chase stiffen. "A note?"

Around New Orleans, Susan Bonaventure had the reputation of a barracuda. But in that moment, she just looked like a horrified mother. "In the purse," she said. "Typed on plain white paper . . . daring Jessie to go to that awful house."

Daring . . .

"That's why she was there," Chase muttered.

"She was lured there." With the words, the lines of his mother's face tightened. "This wasn't random," she said. "She wasn't there by accident. Whoever did this targeted her very carefully."

"But . . . how did her car end up in Baton Rouge?" I asked without thinking.

Even had I not been watching, I would have felt it the second Susan Bonaventure's icy stare found me. "You must be Trinity," she said. No warmth, no welcome. Just cold hard facts, presented in perfect lawyer style.

"Hi," I said, so totally lamely. I didn't want to, but I made myself move toward Chase's outstretched arm.

"Really?" his mother asked, no longer looking at me, but at her son. "With everything that's going on, you really think this is appropriate?" He was five inches taller than she was, but the way her face pinched up made it seem as if she looked down at him.

"Mom." He took my hand and tugged me against him. "Trinity's been trying to help."

Now that pinched look found me. "So I've heard."

I swallowed, searched for words. "I know how hard this must be for you."

"Does your aunt know where you are?" she asked.

I nodded. "I texted her."

That did not seem to make Susan Bonaventure feel better.

"Chase," his father said. "We'll talk later. But for now, you need to get this girl home."

This girl.

Chase stepped toward his father. "She has a name, Dad."

"I'm well aware of that. I'm also well aware that every time the two of you get together—"

"Richard." Susan's voice was as severe as her black dress. "That's enough." Then to Chase. "It's late, honey," she said. "I'm sure Trinity's aunt is ready for her to be home."

The abrupt shift from aggressor to conciliator left me a little breathless. No wonder some said she was a shoe-in as the next D.A.

"Come on," I said, and this time it was me who tugged at him. "I didn't mean to stay this late."

Chase, still locked in a staring match with his father, lingered a few seconds longer before leading me into the foyer.

"There and back," his dad called as Chase pulled open the door. "Keep your phone with you."

The cool swirl of night air could not have come soon enough. I stepped into it, exhaled for what felt like the first time in hours.

Behind me the door slammed, and then Chase was turning me around and pulling me into his arms, bracing his forehead against mine. "They had no right to talk to you like that."

"They found her purse," I said, holding on tight. *In the field I'd told them about.*

Chase pulled back, and I saw his throat work. "We have to go back," he said, and suddenly everything about him went hard, determined. "To the beginning," he said. "If there's any chance that she's still out there . . ."

"Go back?" I whispered, but even before his annihilated eyes met mine, even before he spoke, I knew.

"To the house," he said. "The house on Prytania."

TWENTY-THREE

"Avoiding me doesn't make it go away."

I looked up from my BlackBerry to find my aunt watching me from across the table. It was barely nine in the morning, and even though she was still in her big Saints sleep shirt, she already had beads and charms and chains strewn everywhere.

It was the first time we'd really talked since Friday night.

"I know you're mad at me, *cher*," she said. "And I know you're disillusioned. But running off with Chase again isn't going to make any of that go away."

Like I didn't know that. But I had to try. He was convinced going back to the house was the key, that if I went inside, I might . . . pick something up. Because now he believed. And now, like me, he knew time was running out.

"I'm not mad at you," I tried to tell her.

"No?"

"No."

But she so didn't believe me. She sighed, grabbing a fistful of uncombed hair from behind her neck and dragging it forward. "Trin, I saw the look in your eyes Friday night. I can imagine how you must feel—"

"Can you?" I'd barely slept. I'd already downed a full pot of coffee. Both combined to make the words sharper than I'd intended. "Can you really?"

She winced. "I'm *trying,*" she whispered, but I looked away, didn't want to see the raw emotion in her eyes.

She *was* trying. I knew that. But she was on the outside looking in. She didn't see what I did. She didn't . . . *feel* it.

From the huge windows, midmorning sunshine poured in, but everywhere I looked, shadows slipped closer. Blinking, I tried to focus on a stack of papers at the edge of the table. Most looked official, typed with a few signatures and a seal. On top sat a light pink page torn from Aunt Sara's to-do tablet.

Leaning closer, I squinted at the unfamiliar handwriting. Fleuriffic, Fleurever . . . "What's this?"

She looked up with a handful of crosses, and stilled.

"Fleur de Chic," I read on, "Fleurleans . . ."

Her expression went strangely blank, as if I'd asked her another question about my parents, rather than simply reading a list. "I-I wasn't going to say anything until all of this . . ."

I felt my eyes flare. They must have darkened, too, because again, she winced.

". . . but yesterday I signed papers for a property on Royal Street."

My phone buzzed—or maybe that was the room. But I made no move to find out. *"We're moving?"*

"No, no, no," she rushed on. "Not to live in, but to work in. A shop," she said, as I tried to shift my mind from where we'd been to where she was going. "It's something I've dreamed about forever . . ."

But never spoken a word of.

"To sell my things," she said with a surprisingly unsure smile, gesturing toward the necklaces and bracelets and rings scattered across the table. "Mom thought I was crazy, but everything just finally fell together . . ."

Gran pouring oil on dreams . . . the irony made me smile. But it wasn't a happy one. All this time I thought Aunt Sara had simply been crafting, but in reality, she'd been amassing an inventory.

Intrigued, I glanced back at the list. *"Fleur-ever?"*

She made a funny face as she picked up a mass of tangled chains. "No?"

The glimmer of normalcy, of the way things had been before the game of truth or dare, when things had been simple and easy and not littered by lies and dreams, felt really, really good. *"This Fleur's For You?"*

She didn't look up, kept working the necklaces. "That was Aaron's."

And then the glimmer was over, and reality came crashing back down. *"Aaron?"*

Her fingers stilled as, through a sweep of long bangs, she looked back up to meet my eyes. "He stopped by last night," she said in the oddly quiet voice I was growing to dread. ". . . to tell us about the purse."

I watched her, hated the hesitation in her voice. It wasn't the first time she'd called Detective LaSalle by his first name. Nor was it the first time he'd stopped by to handle what could easily have been settled through a phone call.

"He likes you . . ." I said, letting the comment dangle as other things came back to me, like the way he looked at her and how he sometimes touched her arm. The first time she'd pulled away, but Friday night . . .

She'd asked for him. When she'd found me in the parking garage, she'd asked the woman from the third floor to call . . . Aaron.

"Trinity," she said, and I could tell from her voice she knew I wasn't going to like what she said. "He's not the monster you make him out to be."

Everything inside me tightened. "He thinks I could be involved with what happened to Jessica."

"That's not true."

"Did he say that?"

"No."

"Then—"

She pushed the hair back from her face. "Sweetie, I know this is hard, but he's just doing his job—you have to give him a chance."

"A chance for what?" I almost screamed. It was all closing in on me, the walls and the lies and the secrets, the *truth,* boxing me in so tight I couldn't even breathe. "To decide the only way I could know about that field is if I'd been there—"

Her eyes flashed. "Don't even say that," she said. "That's not going to—"

I shoved back from the table. "But it could," I said, standing. "It's what happened to her, isn't it? My mom?"

Every drop of color drained from my aunt's face. "Trinity—"

"No, don't," I said, backing away. "Don't try to tell me he's on my side."

Slowly she came to her feet, but made no move to come after me. "Where are you going?"

The threadbare edges of her voice made me want to cry. "With Chase."

But I did not say where.

The yellow crime-scene tape was new. It stretched around the property like ribbon around a package, except there was no bow, and this was one gift I didn't want to open.

Not wanting to draw attention to what we were doing, Chase parked a few streets away. We approached the old house through the persistent drizzle, full of stops and starts, slipping behind cars and trees every time we thought someone might see us.

In the end, no one much cared. Sundays in New Orleans weren't necessarily lazy, but rainy days were. It was like the city just went inside and held its breath. Only three vehicles passed us as we made our way to the old house. Once I thought I saw someone looking out a window, but by the time I did a double take, the gauzy curtains were closed again.

Two houses away, we hesitated beside one of those massive oaks. And already my heart slammed stupidly. It was just a house. I knew that. It was broad daylight. And Chase was with me. He totally believed if I walked back into that house, something miraculous would happen.

I wasn't so sure.

"Come on," he said, taking my hand as we took off. I ran with him, through the rain, until manicured grass gave way to knee-high weeds. There we veered right, toward the obscurity of the overgrown backyard.

Darkness had a way of making everything look sinister, much as the rain made everything look dreary. Vines still climbed the sides of the house, but with daylight they were green not black, and every now and then a splash of color leaked through the tangle. Flowers, I realized. Bougainvillea and trumpet vine climbed the house, splashes of red and orange making the peeling paint and gaping windows look even more forsaken.

But not sinister, like before.

Just old. And empty.

"You okay?" Chase said, twisting back toward me.

It was only then that I realized I'd stopped just off the back porch in the pouring rain. "Yeah."

With his Tulane T-shirt plastered to his chest, he shoved the rain-soaked hair from his forehead and extended a hand. "Let's go in."

Everything was . . . gone. The fast-food bags and cigarette butts, the dust and the tattoolike graffiti, the piles of bones in the corner. The blood. All gone, replaced by the smell of Lysol and dark smears against the walls.

"What the hell—" Chase said, and finally I exhaled. Because whatever I'd been expecting, whatever I'd been fearing for the past twelve hours, fell away like shadows when the lights came on. On a weird little rush I stepped away from him and glanced around the big room that had looked so sinister only a week before.

"This is bullshit," he said. "Crime scenes are supposed to be preserved."

"Maybe it's not a crime scene," I murmured, crossing to the far side. There I lifted my hand to one of the smears along the wall— and went straight to my knees.

"Trinity!"

I hung there, trying to breathe, understand. But not really doing either. Vaguely I was aware of Chase reaching for me, touching me, saying something. But detail wouldn't form. Words wouldn't come. There was only this lingering residue of something buzzing through every nerve ending of my body.

"Talk to me."

I blinked, tried to swallow, gradually brought him into focus, the way he kneeled beside me with his hair all wet and falling into his eyes. *"Chase."*

His eyes were dark—totally spooked. But he wasn't turning from me. Running from me. He was right there, on the floor with me, holding on like he never intended to let go. "What happened? Did you see something?"

Shakily, I shoved my hand into the front pocket of my jeans and closed my fingers around the smooth blue stone that had once belonged to my mother. I'd grabbed it before leaving. I'm not sure why, but the larimar made me feel connected. Like she was with me.

"No," I managed. Not really. There'd been no image, no snapshot. Just a zap. "It was like I got shocked."

"Jesus," he muttered. "You're cold as hell." Then he pulled me against the damp warmth of his chest.

And someone started to clap.

We both twisted around, saw them standing in the shadows inside the window, Pitre and Drew and Amber.

"And the nominees for best actress are . . ." she said, slowing the cadence of her clap, until each smack of her hands echoed through the cavernous room.

I stilled, even as I felt Chase gather me closer. His arms were like tight bands around me, as if he could make a barrier between me and Jessica's snarling best friend.

"You suck," he said, and I saw Drew wince.

"*Really?*" Chase's cousin said, standing a little straighter. The way his hair was slicked back from his face emphasized how freakishly green his eyes were. "You tell me you're coming here to see if . . . what? *She has another dream?* And you think I'm gonna stay at home? Really?"

Chase stiffened. "It's not a freak show."

"But if you're trying to reenact the crime, shouldn't we all be here?" Drew asked as Bethany appeared at the window behind them. Soaking wet, she looked ready to cry.

Actually I was pretty sure she had been.

"Chill," Pitre said, moving away from the other two. He

reached out for Jessica's little sister and helped her inside. "My brother said the cops have been all over this place."

"*They* cleaned it," I whispered.

"There was nothing here," he said. "By the time they got here, the place was already spotless."

"It's called destroying the evidence," Amber snarked in. With her stringy long hair and wet clothes plastered to her body, she looked even more emaciated. But her mascara was perfect. "God, you're pathetic," she muttered.

The words came at me like the daggers they were meant to be, but I refused to let them touch me. Refused to let any of them touch me.

Even Chase.

I pushed away from him and stood, stepped back from them all. "You've got a real problem, you know that, Amber? You want it to be me, don't you? You actually want me to be involved."

Her chin came up. Her eyes narrowed. "You couldn't even wait for them to find her body before you let him in your pants, could you?"

"You think I'd hurt someone just to get a guy? That's sick."

Amber said nothing, just smirked as if I'd confessed, and inside, the chill oozed deeper, first through my flesh, then blood and muscle, finally reaching the bone. But I refused to lift my arms to hug them around myself, refused to give her—or any of them—any sign that they could get to me.

I was trying to help. The words were right there, but I held them back, knowing they would do no good.

"Just get the hell out of here," Chase said, once again inserting himself between me and his friends.

"And miss the little slut's show?" Amber shot back. "No way."

Chase pivoted toward his cousin. "You've got five seconds to get her out of here—"

"No." The word broke from my mouth before I even realized it was there. It was as if some other force came over me, guiding me when moments before I'd been at a loss. Amber and Drew and Pitre . . . they didn't matter. If they wanted to make fun of me, let them. I'd felt something when I touched the house, a muted current running through the wall, like the pulse of a human body. I didn't know what it was, but it had been real and it had been powerful, and if there was any chance, *any chance at all,* that something of Jessica remained here, some strange psychic residue, I had to find it. I had to know.

It's what my mother would have done.

It's what she *had* done.

"I don't care what you think about me," I said. And in that moment, I realized how amazingly liberating that discovery was. From the day I'd arrived in New Orleans, I'd wanted to fit in. To be like everyone else. To be liked.

But standing there in the shadows of that big gaping room, with Amber crucifying me with her eyes while Drew looked on like it was a spectator sport and no one seemed to give a damn that Jessica's little sister was falling apart behind them, I realized how wrong I'd been. I didn't want to be like *them,* standing in judgment and casting stones, so small-minded and hateful.

And it was probably better if they *didn't* like me.

Because I sure didn't like them.

Finding Jessica. That was all that mattered. And while I didn't necessarily want an audience, I wasn't going to let them stop me from doing what had to be done.

Once, the curved staircase had been beautiful. Even now, crumbling and in disrepair, a faded grandeur remained, like the wedding dress I'd found stashed in a box under my grandmother's bed, all yellowed and threadbare. The second I'd put my hands to the fabric, the years had fallen away and I'd seen her as she'd been so long ago, smiling and young and elegant.

Maybe that's why my chest tightened as I made my way up the staircase we'd not used the week before. With each step my movements dragged, but I kept going, refused to look back. Doing so was no longer an option.

At the top, a narrow passage stretched in both directions, four rooms to the left, four rooms to the right. I remembered that from before. But unlike that horrible night, all the doors stood open.

Hand fisted around my mother's dragonfly, I stepped into the coolness of the shadows—and one by one, all the doors closed.

My heart slammed hard, but I made myself keep moving. Until I heard the footsteps, and relief surged. *"Chase—"*

But when I turned, only shadows spilled across the hall.

"Please," I whispered, though I wasn't sure to whom. Myself, God. My mother. Breathing hurt. Walking felt insane. But only a few feet away, the room waited. All I had to do was turn the glass knob. All I had to do was step inside. Then I would have my answer. Then I would know if anything of Jessica remained.

The second I lifted my hand, something cold shoved me back.

I staggered, cradling my arm as—

The amber glow stopped me. Through the shadows at the end of the hall, light radiated like the sun through clouds, and drawn, I moved like the flow of water down the river. Behind me, darkness bled. In front of me, silence echoed. No one had followed, not even Chase.

I didn't allow myself to wonder why.

I didn't allow myself to hesitate, either. I lifted my miraculously healed hands to the glowing wall—and remembered why you should never use a blow dryer while standing in a shower. I expected heat. I got ice. The shock jolted me, even as I made my hands run along the punishing chill until my fingers stumbled against the small knob, and the heavy door creaked open.

I stepped inside, and forgot to breathe. I spun around. Or maybe that was the room. I wasn't sure. Just of the spinning, the shadows. The cold. The stench of whiskey and smoke and something else, something stale and rancid and primal.

"Jessica," I whispered, and my knees buckled. I went down hard. Shoved. By something I could not see. I flailed out to brace myself, but the second my hands slapped the icy floor, my whole body sang, and everything went black.

"Trinity."

The voice came at me through a long tunnel, faint, fractured. I tried to twist toward it, reach for it, but the darkness kept spinning. Flashes of light. Vortexes of sound. Then shadows, silence. There was my body kneeling without moving on the floor of the small room, but I was not in it. Didn't know how *to be* in it. Where it was. How to get back.

"Trinity!"

The release came so fast it jolted through me, a hard cruel zap like slamming into a frozen wall, and I felt myself jerk, recoil, felt my eyes open and then I could see him, see Chase squatting beside me. His hand was on my body. I could *see* it.

But through the frigid veil I felt nothing.

"This was a mistake," he muttered, reaching for me, dragging me to him. But the numbness insulated me from the warmth I craved.

"*Je*-sus." His hands. To my face. One on either side. Cradling. Gentle. I knew they would be gentle, because Chase was always gentle. And I wanted that. I wanted to feel that . . .

"Chase." Finally my mouth worked. Voice came, followed by

the shallow rasp of my breath, the struggle of warmth against cold making my arms and legs tingle as if they'd been sleeping, starved of blood, oxygen.

"I'm here," Chase muttered and I used his voice to pull myself back into my body. The moment.

The room.

"I shouldn't have let you come up here alone."

I blinked, stared down at my thighs, where jeans that had once been damp from the rain were now dry. I wanted to look up. At Chase. Into his eyes. I wanted to see the dark blue light there, the one that always promised me everything was okay. I *needed* to see that.

But I did not trust myself to move.

Did not trust myself to do anything.

Chase had questions. That's why we were here. But I had no idea what to tell him. No idea what was real or what was some kind of weird distorted memory—or unspeakable fear.

No idea what I'd seen.

Felt.

"Hold me," I whispered, and he did, he moved with a gentleness that made my heart ache, taking me into his arms and pulling me against his body—his still-wet body.

My clothes were dry. But his remained cool and damp.

I wanted to cry. I didn't know why, didn't understand, but knew that I wanted to cry.

"Baby," he murmured against the top of my head. "Baby."

I made my arms lift, made them wrap around his middle, even though they felt about a hundred times heavier than before. And I held on. Held on so, so tight.

"What the hell happened—did you see something?"

I made myself breathe. That's what I concentrated on. That's what I needed to do.

"You can tell me," he said quietly—so unbelievably gentle that something inside of me hurt. *"You can tell me."*

"I c–can't." Didn't know how. Didn't understand.

"Yes, you can."

"No. I . . ." Breathe. Slowly. Make the hard thrumming of my pulse fall quiet. Make my body stop shaking. Then I could think.

Then I could allow myself to remember.

"Take me home," I whispered, because that's what I needed, to go home, where it was bright and safe and the walls didn't throb. And the silence did not scream.

"Trinity." Chase's voice was oddly quiet as he pulled back and tilted my face toward his, and even as I tried to turn away, he kept his finger under my chin and his eyes staring on mine. Any other time, I would have sensed what was coming. Any other time, I would have braced myself. But even though Chase held me, everything I felt, heard—*knew*—kept shifting.

"Detective Jackson is here."

I blinked. The rolling continued, all those pieces I'd worked so hard to keep together, rolling, like marbles. Scattering. "W–what?"

Chase's hands were on my shoulders, holding firm—when had that happened? "Detective Jackson is downstairs," he said, and even as I told myself it was Chase's voice—*I knew it was Chase's voice*—I couldn't make everything connect.

"Detective Jackson?"

He pushed to his feet, bringing me with him. I was aware of all that, aware of the blood pouring back into the numbness of my feet and the violent tingle in my soles and toes, but the connections weren't there.

"He wants to talk to you."

I blinked, swallowed, flexed my fingers. Exhaled.

"Baby, you gotta help me out here," he said so steady and calm, so normal, as if I wasn't zoning in and out right in front of his eyes. "If I don't get you downstairs, he's going to come up . . ."

I looked past him, down the hall where all the doors again stood open, allowing light to spill in and kill the shadows.

"Okay." And then I slipped past him, past the room where Jessica had been trapped like an animal in a cage, where I'd heard her scream, beg, cry.

"Wait! Come back! You can't leave me here!"

"Watch me."

"No—you'll be sorry!!"

That voice? I knew that voice. But I no longer knew if the ugliness was left over from the game I'd unwittingly played the week before—or if the terror stemmed from something far more unspeakable.

"Well, well, here she is, patron saint of the Lost Souls Club."

The staircase sprawled out in front of me, wide and curved and rotting, leading down to the spacious foyer, where there'd once been marble and crystal and flowers.

I don't know how I knew that. I just did. Places had memories, my grandmother had once told me. Long after everything else is gone, the people and the things, something of them remains.

"Won't you join us?" LaSalle's partner asked, as if inviting me for beignets and café au lait. He stood at the base of the stairs, his foot propped on the bottom step. With his dark collarless shirt and pressed pants, the big diamond stud in his left ear and those neat little cornrows, he looked all *GQ* again, like a man waiting for his date to join him, not . . .

I wasn't sure what I was at that moment. A witness? Person of interest? Suspect?

"I've got you," Chase said, yanking my awareness back to him. I felt him take my hand, loved the warmth of his flesh, the strength of his fingers threading between mine. Through the push-pull of vertigo, I was aware of him leading me down the stairs.

"Holy shit," I heard someone mutter, but it was a second before I linked the voice to its owner.

"*Pitre,*" I whispered.

He stood off to the side, near the arched doorway that led to the room that had once been used for dining. "She's like an eff'in ghost again."

"I told you to get the hell out of here," Chase said.

But Pitre just stood there in the arched doorway. Only darkness gaped behind him, but I would have sworn he had his back to a wall. "I . . . c-couldn't," he murmured. "Not after . . . not after last time. Not until I knew if . . . she was okay."

In his eyes that same bottomless confusion glittered, just like the night in the closet. "So scared," I murmured, driven by the voices I'd heard, the images I'd seen. None of which made sense. "It was so dark, and she was alone. So many closed doors . . ."

Pitre shook his head from side to side, staring at me as if I had a bloody weapon in my hand. "What the fuck happened—"

"She thought it was just a game," I said, unable to look away from him. "Until she saw the knife."

Pitre shook his head, as if he didn't understand. "There wasn't a knife," he said. "That was Saturday night—"

Chase didn't let him finish. "*Now,*" he seethed, and with the single word Pitre faded away. Or maybe he backed away. I wasn't sure. I only knew that by the time I reached the marble of the entryway, he was gone.

"I'm going to need you to come with me, Miss Monsour."

The front door hung open. Outside, through the haze of late afternoon rain, I saw a black SUV parked in the street.

"You didn't say anything about going anywhere with you." That was Chase. His voice was hard.

"Look, we can do this the easy way," Detective Jackson said, "or we can do it the hard way. But trust me, either way, your girl-friend is coming with me."

Sometimes I dreamed. Actually, I dreamed a lot. I'd fall deep, deep into sleep and see things. Do things. Things that seemed real. And then I would wake up, and it was like the two worlds, the dream world and the real world, would crash into each other and it would take me a few minutes to tell one from the other. To know where I was. And what was happening. What was real.

Disoriented, I stared up at Detective Jackson, at the handcuffs dangling from his fingers, and prayed for that moment to come, the one where pieces fell into place.

"I'm calling my mom," Chase said.

"That's a good idea," Detective Jackson fired back, so totally casual.

I'll never know if lightning really streaked down from the sky somewhere beyond the front door—or whether it was only a trick of my imagination. But the line was that stark, that severe, and from one heartbeat to another the veil between the two worlds shattered and the numbness fell away.

Holy dear God. Detective Jackson was looking at me like he knew something bad. Something really, really bad.

"Where's Detective LaSalle?" The question tore out of me, chased by a sharp blade of panic. "He—"

"Looking for your aunt."

I stilled. My heart slammed hard. "My aunt? Why?"

Detective Jackson's smile was the kind that said I was either a total moron—or a world-class liar. "Really, Trinity? You want to do this here?"

I tried to swallow. Couldn't. "Do what?"

Never looking away from me, he slid a hand into the pocket of his sports coat and pulled out a small plastic bag. "Recognize this?"

Shadows slipped and fell, but not deeply enough to conceal the small silver hoop dangling in midair. *My earring.* One of a pair I'd purchased my first week in New Orleans, when I'd finally been free to pierce my ears.

"Where did you get that?" I breathed.

Jackson's smile cut straight through me. "I think the better question is, where did *you* lose it?"

Curled around my hand, Chase's fingers tightened.

"It is yours, isn't it?" Jackson asked.

My mind raced. I tried to remember, but even as my fingers found the empty spot at my ear, I could find no memory of taking the earrings out.

Slowly I looked up, to the knowing in Jackson's eyes—and the confusion in Chase's. "I . . . don't know."

"Oh, but the look on your face says otherwise," Jackson said, slipping the bag back into his pocket.

Chase stilled. "What are you talking about?"

Jackson smiled. "Do you want to tell him, sweetheart . . . or shall I?"

Everything around me—inside of me—started to vibrate. *"No,"* I whispered.

"It's called the missing link," Jackson said, and his voice was empty, cold, completely stripped of emotion—or reprieve. "And it was found yesterday, about ten feet from Jessica Morgenthal's purse."

The walls pushed closer, but I could not move. Could not even breathe. It was happening. Just like I'd said earlier, to my aunt, when she'd promised me I was wrong.

"In the field," Jackson went on in that same whitewashed way. "Exactly where *you* told us to look."

The roaring started deep inside, a horrible grinding that drowned out everything . . . everything except the feel of Chase's hand, so warm and strong, simply falling away.

TWENTY-FOUR

He backed away, one step, two, until no part of our bodies touched.

Jackson almost looked bored. "*A dream,* you said, but I don't see how that's possible. After all, when earrings fall out while you're sleeping, they don't usually show up fifteen miles away."

"Trinity?" Chase said, the desperation in his voice so very, very clear. "*You* told them where to look?"

In my dreams, in my fantasies, there was no desperation. No doubt.

No hand that fell away.

"But maybe the whole thing with the parking garage *was* a dream," he offered. "That would explain why the surveillance video shows no one but you."

Chase stilled. *"Surveillance video?"*

I looked at him, saw the dark void in his eyes. I tried to make my throat work, to explain, but something inside of me was slowly and methodically shutting down, taking my capacity for speech with it.

"Gosh, she didn't tell you about *that,* either?"

This time I was the one who took a step back. But words wouldn't form. Someone had been there. The same someone from the vigil. He'd followed me . . .

Or had he simply been like the knife and the old lady?

"Or maybe . . ." Jackson said, drawing out the word. "You were just trying to cover your tracks, like with the Facebook posts."

The walls, so dirty and old and forsaken, edged closer. *You have the right to remain silent,* was all I could think. *Anything you say can and will be used against you . . .*

"Facebook posts?" Chase asked.

Jackson shifted. "Every computer has signatures," he said. "Footprints. Everything leaves a trail, and all trails can be followed. It's all there on the hard drive—the Facebook postings from IWUZ-THERE, the research into the DuPont and Roubilet cases, the ins and outs of how psychics operate."

Chase turned toward me. The look in his eyes—*God*. The scorched look in his eyes destroyed me. "Trinity . . . what the *fuck* is he talking about?"

"Maybe it was an accident," Jackson rolled on, before I could force a single word past my throat. Before I could *think* of a single word. "That happens. Things spin out of control. No one is saying you meant to hurt anyone." His mouth twisted. "She goaded you. Tricked you. Locked you in that small room. You were mad. You wanted to give her a taste of her own medicine. But things went too far. You panicked . . ."

God, he made it sound so cut and dried.

"You didn't mean for it to happen," he said as the ringing in my ears tried to drown him out. "You felt bad. That's why you came to us with the story about your dreams, like the bystander who helps put out the fires he starts."

Chase still looked at me, but I could tell he was beyond the point of seeing. "*Trinity*. Tell him he doesn't know what he's talking about."

Why? The word, the question—*the truth*—almost made me double over. But I didn't ask, because I already knew.

Chase needed to hear.

Chase needed to hear me refute what Jackson was saying.

Chase. He was the one who needed the words. The denial.

"I can't," I heard myself mutter, even as everything else faded. "I did research all of that. I pulled up those stories. I told them about the field . . ."

All true. All could be proven. And all were completely circumstantial. Even the IWUZTHERE account. If it was there, it didn't mean I created it. My computer was a laptop. I had it at school. It wouldn't take long for someone to "borrow" it.

But Chase took another step back.

When I was thirteen, a family from Boston built a place a few miles up the mountain from us. The woman had a daughter from a previous marriage. Her real father was dead, like mine. Her name was Cynthia. She was a year younger than me, and she'd been devastated about leaving the only home she'd known and moving to the wilderness of Colorado. But her stepfather had grown up near Denver, and he'd wanted to come home. The fact that that meant ripping Cynthia from hers hadn't mattered.

We'd become friends. That summer we did a lot of hiking. She liked to take pictures, so we'd spent a lot of time photographing trees and wildlife.

One night she stayed at my house. We were going hiking in the morning. But she forgot her camera. So after breakfast we went over to her place to pick it up.

Instead we found her stepfather gutting an elk. Blood had been splattered everywhere, on the table by the shed, across the ground, on his face and his clothes, the big knife in his hands.

All color—*all life*—drained from Cynthia's face. Her eyes went insanely dark. And she'd just stood there, frozen, looking without seeing.

The elk had been one we'd seen before. It was young, probably not a year old. She'd taken countless photographs of it. She'd even trained it to eat from her hand. For weeks she'd worked to earn the little doe's trust.

And her stepfather had slaughtered it.

Even in that moment, when I'd stood helplessly by her side, as sickened as she was, I knew I'd never forget the clash of confusion and horror in her eyes.

I'd never imagined to see that same look from *Chase*.

But I'd feared. I'd feared it so bad. Gran had warned me. She'd known. That's why she'd kept me hidden from the rest of the world.

The detective kept talking. Every now and then a word broke through the buzz roaring through me, the one that screamed louder with every second Chase stared, to the point where it was all I could do not to slap my hands over my ears and start screaming for everything to stop.

I never saw Detective Jackson move. I had no idea he'd approached me until his hand closed around mine.

I looked down, saw the darkness of his flesh against the paleness of mine. My fingers were curled tight, bloodless. Even my nail beds were without color.

Slowly, his fingers uncurled mine—again I could see it happening, though I felt absolutely nothing—revealing the shiny tube concealed within.

Behind me, I heard Chase mutter something but couldn't make out anything beyond the shiny tube of Too Faced lip gloss in the palm of my hand. "It must have been in that room . . ."

"That's Jessica's." This time I did make out the words—and the shock in Chase's voice.

"It must have fallen out of her pocket," I said, but I had no idea how it had gotten into my hand.

"Sorry, sweetheart," Jackson said. "I was here. I searched this house. There was nothing left to find."

Through the numbness came a slow burn, as if the cool tube of the lip gloss was searing into my flesh. I jerked, watched the tube fall to the marble . . . saw the faint glow of red against my blood-less palm.

"I'm sorry you had to find out like this," I heard Jackson saying to Chase. "As we told your parents, we had our suspicions, but it wasn't until we found her earring that we had anything concrete. When the shoes showed up—"

"Shoes?" Chase sounded like he was going to throw up.

"Yeah," Jackson said. "I guess you wouldn't know that, would you?"

My blood ran cold. Because I knew. Even before Jackson said a word, I knew what was coming.

"What shoes?" Chase asked.

"Jessica's."

With her name everything else stopped. The rain, the cold, the buzz. All stopped. Even the moment stopped. Fractured.

"They showed up yesterday, postmarked the day after Trinity trolled on the Net for info about the DuPont and Roubilet cases. That's where the bait was."

"Bait?" Chase's voice was no more than a breath.

"The shoes didn't come in a plain brown box, like the press claimed. And they didn't come via the U.S. Mail."

All my life I'd had nightmares. Sometimes they were violent, insidious, images of death and blood and desecration. Sometimes they'd simply been frightening, the reality of being followed or chased, the awareness that someone tracked my every move. And I'd learned how to wake up. I'd learned how to jerk myself to at

the very last moment, to spare myself. To put an end to the
terror.

But standing in the damp shadows of that long-neglected
house, the one left to stand in silent witness to evil and ugliness
and depravity, to watch and know and remember, I couldn't make
myself wake up. Because I wasn't asleep. This nightmare was real.

Wordlessly, eyes dark and unfocused, Chase backed away from
me, breaking my heart a little more with each step he took.

By the time he slipped into the darkness, there was nothing
left.

"Trinity."

My aunt's voice destroyed the drone of silence the second the
door shot open. Numb, I looked up from the larimar stone in my
oddly healed palm and saw her rush into the small, sterile room
with only a table and two chairs. I'd been sitting there for what
seemed like hours.

"Omigod," she said, swirling in like an exotic, gale-force wind.
Her hair was loose and tangled. Her face was flushed, her lips pale.
Her dress was short and black, with odd smears across the front.
"I've been so worried."

My throat hurt. Maybe crying would have helped. But there
weren't any tears.

"Trin?" she said, and then she was down on her knees in front
of the metal chair, taking my hands in hers for the briefest of seconds before her eyes filled and she pulled me into her arms. "Omigod," she said again, and again. "I got here as fast as I could."

I felt the breath leave me. I felt my shoulders fall, and my head
bow toward her.

"What have they done to you? What happened? Aaron said
he'd told DeMarcus to wait until I—"

I pulled back. Looked into her eyes. And started to shake. "They think I did it."

"No." Her face got all hard, furious. "No, they do not."

"Jackson said they have proof—"

"No," she said again. "He was trying to break you, that's all. They're desperate, reaching for straws."

"Her shoes—"

"Aaron told me, but that doesn't mean anything. Any sicko could have sent those shoes—her parents aren't even sure they *are* hers, and they sure don't mean *you're* involved."

"But her purse," I said. "I told them where to find it . . ."

"Because you *found* it for them, in your dream."

The cold pale walls of the century-old building pushed closer, even as my aunt was doing her best to push them back. "My earring—"

"—fell out at the house Saturday night," she insisted. "That's all."

She believed me. No matter how bad it looked, my aunt believed me. "I was just trying to help . . ."

"I know you, *cher*," she muttered, and then she was pulling me into her arms and holding me, just holding me, and like a child I sank against her, craving the warmth.

It was all I wanted, to be held.

Chase.

"There was a woman," I told her, closing my eyes but unable to escape the memory. "Mrs. Aberdeen. She was some kind of attorney. Detective Jackson kept saying all these horrible things—" Like he'd said earlier, in front of Chase. "And she kept telling me not to say anything."

Aunt Sara held me so tight I could feel her heart slamming against my chest. "I'm sorry, sweetie . . . so sorry . . ."

"He told me that accidents happen, that they understand that, if

I'd tell them where the body was, they'd work with me. That I'm still a juvenile—"

"No." Aunt Sara jerked back again, her fingers digging into my biceps. "You are not going to confess."

I shook my head slowly, feeling my stringy hair slip against the sides of my face. "But some of it's true," I whispered. "I *was* mad at Jessica. And I did pull up those news stories . . ."

Aunt Sara frowned.

"But I didn't make those Facebook postings," I said. "And I never went to that field. I swear to God, I didn't—"

"I know you didn't."

The absolute unwavering faith in her eyes, her voice, fed some place deep inside of me. No matter how hard I'd pushed earlier, how hateful I'd been, Aunt Sara was standing by me. *"I want to go home."*

"And I'm going to take you there," she promised. "Aaron's taking care of it. They have nothing to hold you on."

I blinked. "W-what?"

"You didn't break," she said through a sad, proud smile. "They have nothing to warrant an arrest."

I sat back, tried to bring everything into focus.

"Oh, *cher,* I'm so sorry," she said again. "None of this should have happened. DeMarcus went too far. If Aaron had been here . . ." She pursed her lips. "You're going to be okay, you understand me? You're going to be okay."

Maybe it was the way she looked at me, the love and promise in her eyes. Or maybe it was the way she was touching me, and wouldn't let go. All I knew was that finally, finally my eyes filled. "He walked away."

Aunt Sara blinked, absently shoving a tangle of dark hair from her mouth. "Who walked away?"

"Chase," I whispered, and the tears fell. "Chase walked away."

She rocked back, sliding her hands to take mine. There was warmth there. Strength.

"He was with you?"

"At the house," I said, seeing him all over again, letting go. Backing away. "I trusted him," I said. Like a fool. "I—God, I was so wrong!" I'd known all along. I'd known better than to let down my guard. But somehow I'd forgotten all that. I'd started to believe.

"I told him," I whispered, and the regret practically tore me in half. "I told him everything."

Aunt Sara's beautiful face fell. "About your dreams?"

"And Mom."

She let out another rough breath, flicking her tongue against her front teeth.

"I—He—We . . . I thought I could trust him," I muttered. "He said he wanted to help. I tried to keep him away, but he kept after me, telling me he was going to find out the truth whether I wanted him to or not."

"Oh, sweetie . . ."

"And I trusted him," I said again, because really, it all kept coming back to that. *"I trusted him."*

Aunt Sara squeezed my hands.

"You should have seen the way he looked at me." I sniffed past the tears, shutting them away—*ordering* them away. I was not going to let myself cry another lame tear over anything.

Aunt Sara's smile was sad, but full of strength and promise and what I'd always imagined maternal love would look like. "Give him time," she said in a strangely quiet voice. "He'll figure it out. He'll be back."

I looked down, back toward my mother's oceanlike stone. "It won't matter." Because no matter what Chase figured out, it would never erase what had already happened. *"He walked away."*

Nothing could change that.

Aunt Sara pushed open a door. Beyond sprawled the brightly lit reception area of the 8th District police station in the heart of the French Quarter. Once a beautiful old bank, the historic building with its high ceilings and boxy rooms seemed far too majestic for its current purpose.

"What time is it?" Normally I would have checked my phone, but I had no idea where it was.

"A little after eight," Aunt Sara said, following me through the door. Her gold pumps echoed against the hard tile.

I'd gone to the house on Prytania shortly after lunch. At the most, Detective Jackson had shown up late afternoon. Two or three hours, I realized. I'd been in that claustrophobic little windowless room for two or three hours.

I looked around. My heart beat erratically. My breath was a little choppy. There were chairs. Most of them were full. There was a sign-in desk with a line of six people, four guys and two women. A guy that looked somewhere in his twenties was complaining to anyone who would listen about his pickpocketed wallet. One of the women had blood on the side of her face.

"Hey, hang on—"

The rough voice came from behind me. My heart stopped as I swung around—but it was not Chase who called to us. It was Detective LaSalle. Dressed in a sports coat and khakis, he pushed through the door, his face a collection of hard, worried lines—and something so real and sincere it made everything inside of me twist.

"You okay?" he asked, putting a hand to my aunt's wrist.

She looked up at him. "We will be."

Then he glanced at me. "I heard DeMarcus was pretty rough in there," he said, and for a fleeting moment, I had to wonder if this was some kind of good cop/bad cop routine.

My eyes met his. I refused to blink. "I had nothing to do with what happened to Jessica Morgenthal."

LaSalle's mouth flattened. "Then you have nothing to worry about." We stood that way a long moment before he returned his attention to my aunt. "Got a sec?" he asked.

She glanced back at me.

"Go ahead," I said. "I can wait."

She didn't look thrilled, but let him lead her back to the door we'd just used. "I'll be right back," she said, then slipped away, leaving me alone in the crazy rush of nighttime in a police station.

And I lost it.

I'll never know what made me turn. I'll never know what made me head for the door, the darkness. What made me walk outside. Run.

But I did. I did all of that. Without stopping to think. Without stopping to care. I knew that I needed to get out of there. To get away.

To breathe.

Beyond the big white door that separated those who watched from those who did not, I hurried past the massive columns that had once welcomed patrons to a grand old bank, down the few stairs, through the iron gate, to the rain-cooled night beyond.

And just ran.

No one knew. No one cared. I'm not sure anyone even noticed. People filled the streets and sidewalks. Walking. Lingering. Laughing. Dancing. Drinking. Some were old, some were young. Some looked like they belonged. Others looked like they'd fallen down the rabbit hole.

Bourbon Street had that effect on people.

Several blocks from the police station, I slipped into the throng of partygoers, and vanished.

I don't know how long I walked, how many blocks I passed. I just knew that I never wanted it to stop. I wanted to be anonymous forever, to walk without being seen, look without seeing. To close my eyes without . . . remembering.

I moved with the crowd, let it guide me, direct me. I didn't want to think. I didn't want to consider. I only wanted . . .

To go back.

That's what I wanted, I realized. To go back. To before. Not the night before, when Chase had looked into my eyes and promised to help me forget.

No, before that, before I'd even imagined or considered. I wanted to erase all that. Forget all that. Forget Chase, New Orleans. All that I'd learned about my mother and my birthright. *Myself.* I wanted to go back to Colorado, before my grandmother died. I wanted to stay home that day, to keep her from getting those ridiculous sweet potatoes. I wanted to go back and—

I didn't know. I didn't know what the "and" was. I just wanted it to be different. Everywhere I'd turned right I wanted to turn left. Every time I'd said yes, I wanted to say no.

And to all that I'd said no, I wanted to scream YES!

Different. That was all I could think. If I could do it all differently, take different roads, the end would be different, too. I wouldn't be here. I wouldn't know and I wouldn't feel, and the screaming— that horrible silent screaming that reverberated through me like shards of broken glass—would stop.

I kept walking. I let the crowd absorb me, carry me. I stopped fighting and just went. Down the street, past bars and clubs and strip joints, shops that sold souvenirs and sex toys and voodoo gris-gris. Finally I stopped and turned, stared in the smudged window of a shop that promised anything my heart desired. There were dolls and feathers and potions—and oddly smooth black rocks.

It was like looking inside my mother's chest all over again, all save for the doll part.

"You lost, little girl?"

The voice startled me. It was low and quiet, filled with warmth and intimacy and the promise of something forbidden. Yeah, all that from a voice.

I twisted toward it and saw him, all tall and olive-skinned, a black-feathered Mardi Gras mask framing crazy-dark eyes, cheek-bones wide and flat—

But then someone bumped into me from behind and I staggered, twisted around as strong arms caught me.

The guy with the mask was gone.

Instead someone else held me, with blond hair not black, light eyes not dark, his mouth warm, easy. "Hey, sorry!" he said. "Didn't mean to bump you like that."

I spun around, searched the crowd.

"You with somebody?" the guy asked. His burnt-orange T-shirt read UNIVERSITY OF TEXAS. He looked about twenty, *maybe* twenty-one.

"There was this guy . . ." I said.

"Sorry, didn't see anybody," he said. *"Just you."*

Something about the way he said "just you" had me pivoting back toward him. His smile was wider, all warm and carefree and so completely totally unaffected that all those hard, tight, twisted-up places inside me started to loosen.

"Buy you a drink?" he asked, and before I knew it we were inside one of the endless stream of smoky nightclubs on Bourbon Street, with a sticky floor and a live band blaring from a small stage while we stood pressed against the bar with shots of tequila in our hands.

"To chance meetings," he said, then lifted his hand to his mouth and threw back the yellowy liquid.

Different, I reminded myself. *Different*.

Then I smiled, and did the same.

TWENTY-FIVE

My eyes watered. My throat burned.

"First time?"

I nodded.

His smile warmed. "Second time's usually better," he said, motioning to the bartender. "I'm Cody by the way," he said. "Grew up south of Dallas, but a lifelong Saints fan. Flew in for the game today."

Eyes still watery, I managed a smile. "I'm Trinity."

"You're awesome is what you are," he said, reaching for the shot glasses the bartender slid our way. Neither had even asked about my age.

"To good times," Cody said this time, then all but inhaled the tequila. I had a feeling these were not his first of the night.

More than a little awed by his absolute lack of reaction, I lifted my glass—and went very still. I hung there, frozen, stunned, wanting to move but unable to, until the moment released me as quickly as it had seized me, and I spun around, toward the far end of the bar where—

Nothing. No one was there. Well, not as in *no one* because the club was packed, but no one with a feather Mardi Gras mask. No one watched. Not me, anyway.

"Hey, you okay?" Cody asked.

"Yeah, I thought . . ." Crazy, I told myself. Residue from the day. No one had followed me.

No one watched.

"Thought what?"

"Doesn't matter." Trying not to shake, I brought the little glass to my mouth and downed the tequila in one big gulp, fighting the burn with everything I had.

"There you go," Cody said, laughing as he slid his arms around me and pulled me against his body. "Want another?"

I gazed up at him, at the shaggy blond hair falling against his face and his wholesome clean-cut looks, and made myself smile in return. "Give me a minute."

"No prob," he said, steering me away from the bar to the sweaty press of bodies on the crowded dance floor. His hands found my hips, and his started to sway. Against mine. Real close.

I could feel him. All of him. He was definitely well built, and he definitely lifted. His whole body was rock hard.

Yeah, his whole body.

Drawing me against him, I felt the bulge in his jeans pressed up against my abdomen, and something inside me stuttered. He kept moving, gyrating, rubbing against me as his hands slid down to cup my butt. My head swam. Everything got a little fuzzy, and then his mouth was coming toward mine, and I was tilting my head toward his—

Around us everyone pulsed and swayed, but the blur of movement caught my eyes, and I twisted again, twisted hard, spun around as I saw him vanish into the crowd.

I didn't stop to think. I didn't stop to plan or analyze—or apologize. I tore away and pushed through the throng of drunken dancers.

"Hey! Trinity!"

I kept going, didn't look back. Faster. Kept going, worming my way through groups of people that had suddenly become some kind of distorted carnival ride, all blending and blurring together, until I couldn't tell where anything started—and where anything ended.

At the back of the club, I stopped and reached for the wall, tried to breathe. To see.

But there was no one there.

Again, not *no one*. Just not him.

"Hey!" Cody caught up with me. He was breathing a little hard. "Are you okay? Is it the tequila? Do you want me to—"

"No!" The word ripped out of me. I twisted away from his reach and lunged for the door, started to run the second I hit the moist night air. Maybe I should have felt bad. And maybe I did in a small way. Cody hadn't done anything wrong—and he had bought me two drinks. I'd given him green lights from the start.

But this had nothing to do with Cody.

I wove through the crowds, ignored the grumbling and catcalls as I pushed and shoved and darted in front of people. I wasn't sure where I was going, whether I was chasing something—or being chased. And none of that mattered, either. That was detail, and details only got in the way. Something far more powerful drove me.

He'd been there. Someone had been on Bourbon Street—following me. Someone had touched me, talked to me: *You lost, little girl?*

That voice. That's what drove me. He'd been in the club. I knew he had. I hadn't seen him, but I'd . . . felt him.

Now I ran. Off Bourbon Street, down one of the one-way streets that ran toward the river. Fleetingly I caught a glimpse of a sign for Royal Street—where the police station was.

And I ran even faster.

The rain had passed, but puddles lingered along the crowded sidewalks. Everyone moved slowly, ambling like they didn't have a care in the world. Some looked at me. Most did not.

Restaurants and shops blurred, the sound of laughter and jazz and blues morphing into a warped soundtrack for the craziness swirling through me. My breath chopped in and out of me. Still I ran. Even when the déjà vu hit. Even when it closed around me.

Even when it wouldn't let go.

I'd run before. I'd seen these buildings before. But I didn't know when—or even if the buildings were the same. They all looked alike, old and brick and dark.

Until I heard the cry of a tugboat call from the river.

Then I stopped and braced my palms against my thighs, tried to catch my breath.

Earlier, I realized. I'd seen the buildings earlier, in that awful room in the house on Prytania. But first I'd seen Jessica, lying on the mattress with her hair tangled and her eyes terrified, then huddled in a dirty gown in a corner with her arms wrapped around her knees.

But between those two flashes, between the bed and the corner, I'd seen Pitre.

"No," I whispered. Just . . . no.

I squeezed my eyes shut, but the images I'd seen there in the darkness kept oozing through me, Pitre sneering, Pitre laughing. Pitre closing the door and shoving a chair up under the knob so the door to the room with the mattress could not be opened.

"Wait! Come back! You can't leave me here!"

"No." The word was little more than a whisper. Not Pitre. That had to be residue. A remnant from the game of truth or dare we'd all played, when Jessica had crossed so many lines. They'd had words that night. She'd insulted him. He'd insulted her back. He'd been the one who found me. And he'd been the one to help me. He'd been kind. He'd texted me the next day. He'd found me at school and asked if I was okay. He'd been with Chase at the field by the airport. And he'd been at the house that afternoon. He'd been there when I came downstairs and—

The memory of the look on his face made me double over yet again.

He'd looked horrified.

The perp always returns to the scene of the crime.

Oh, dear God, no. I shook my head, making myself stand straight and gather my bearings, even as more thoughts sliced through me. Pitre wouldn't have framed me like that. Pitre wouldn't have—

Or would he? At the end of the day, I really knew him no more than I knew Chase, and look how that had turned out.

And where was Jessica now? *Where was she?* I'd seen her at the house, seen Pitre . . . then I'd seen her again, bunched up in a dark corner, rocking.

Then I'd seen the buildings, tall, brick, and dark. Abandoned.

And I'd started to run.

She'd been alive . . .

I spun around and took it all in, the buildings on either side of St. Louis Cathedral, the Cabildo and the Presbytere. The old apartment buildings that flanked Jackson Square. All brick.

But none abandoned.

Other things started to register, dotting in from the haze like pinpricks of light. I'd made it all the way to the edge of the Quarter, where the pedestrian mall gave way to the riverfront. Tourists and locals mingled along the parade of shops and bars. The scent of fried food and stale alcohol filled the air, while two street performers did gymnastics as a third, spray painted in all silver, stood like a statue. And in the center of it all, the wrought-iron fence surrounded the park, where the life-size statue of Andrew Jackson balanced on the back legs of a bronze horse.

And the psychics. Table after table of them. They surrounded the square, each with their own collections of cards and mirrors and flashlights.

I started to move. Slowly at first, drawn. Unable to stop.

My mother had been here. Not recently, but she'd been here. She'd done this. She'd had a table. She'd sat where so many had sat after her. She'd watched and waited. She'd put herself on the line.

And in the end, she'd been murdered.

I picked a table at random. It was farther down, toward Decatur, where by day artists captured life that went by. Even now, one or two remained, along with the horse-drawn carriages waiting alongside the wet street to give outsiders an inside look at the haunted city of my birth.

A black cloth draped a small square table. A young woman sat facing me, with long, snow-white hair and eyes lined in black. She watched me approach, neither smiling nor frowning. Just . . . watching. On her table sat three decks of cards and two flashlights. A small sign advertised tarot and palm readings.

My hands found my pockets, and slid inside.

I stopped a few inches from the table. She looked up at me, waiting.

I looked down at her, waiting.

She was really quite beautiful in a striking, poignant kind of way. There was something in her eyes, something haunted and wise and . . . wary. Her dress was as black as her eyes, all drapey and flowing. A silver chain hung around her neck, with a small oval dangling in the middle. In the center was one engraved word: Grace.

"Hello, Trinity," she said, and I almost jumped out of my skin. The step backward was automatic, but still she neither smiled nor frowned. Just watched.

"Why did you say that?" I asked, and wow, even I could tell how freaked out my voice sounded.

"What would you have liked me to say?" she asked.

"Why . . . *Trinity*?"

"Isn't that your name?"

I made myself swallow. Made myself breathe.

The breathing was harder.

"Why would you think that?" I asked, neither confirming or denying.

She smiled, her extreme, bloodred lips curving ever so slightly. "I think we both know the answer to that," she said.

My heart slammed so hard it hurt. "I . . ." Questions jerked around for voice. "Is someone following me?"

"Now?" Her eyes never left mine. ". . . or all your life?"

I backed away. Slowly at first, not letting myself look away. Not trusting myself *to* look away. Then something in her eyes, something sad and . . . scared, had me twisting around so hard that I smashed straight into something warm, and soft.

"Oh, excuse me!" came a voice, and I blinked, swallowed hard as I made myself focus, see.

The woman was unusually tall, with short silver hair and a nice, concerned smile. "N-no," I stammered. "That was me."

Around her seven other older folks moved toward the river, and I let myself get swept up with them, walking with them, like I belonged.

Anything to get away from Grace.

"Are you okay?" the woman who looked like your average all-American grandmother asked. She even wore polyester bright blue pants and a turquoise shirt, with all sorts of tacky Mardi Gras beads draped around her neck. One read Harrah's, and immediately I knew where she'd been—and the grandmother image took on a whole new dimension.

"Dear?" she asked, and then I remembered she'd asked me a question, and as the pedestrian walk light came on and we moved to cross Decatur, I answered.

"Fine," I said. "Just . . ." What? Spooked? Freaked?

"Lost?" she asked, and my throat got totally tight on me.

Was I lost?

Oh, yeah.

I had been for a long, long time.

"No," I said. "I was . . . looking for someone."

We reached the other side and most of her group moved toward the left, in the direction of Café du Monde. But along the Moonwalk that separated the Quarter from the river, the woman with the heartbreakingly kind smile hesitated. "Would you like to join us while you wait?"

She was worried about me. I could tell from the way she looked at me. I could only imagine what I looked like with my hair tangled and stringy, having dried naturally after getting rained on. And my jeans and T-shirt—I'd been in the rain, in that disgusting room, in the police station, and on Bourbon Street.

"No," I said forcing a smile—*making* a smile. All the while I looked around, watching groups and couples and loners coming and going on both sides of the street. "I'm fine."

She so did not believe me. "Okay, well if you change your mind, we'll be over there getting beignets," she said. Then she flashed a deck of cards.

Not tarot. The playing kind.

"And we'll probably be a while," she said.

I swallowed, nodded. "Thank you," I said, and then I had the stupidest urge to hug her.

But I didn't. Instead I edged closer to the old Civil War cannon in the heart of Artillery Park, which afforded the absolute best view of Jackson Square. There I again lost myself in a group of tourists busy with cameras and cell phones, while I watched.

I don't know how long I stood on the platform, while a barge inched its way upriver and cars zoomed past on Decatur. But eventually the ship vanished around the bend and my breath evened out and I started to move again. No one followed me. No one paid much attention. I'm not even sure anyone noticed. I kicked a rock across the railroad tracks and made my way to the brick walkway toward the park frequented by national reporters shooting in New Orleans, with its benches and statues and picture-perfect view of the river. I wanted to sit. And think. To let myself go back to that room on Prytania, if not in body then in mind, and remember.

From somewhere unseen, the wail of a saxophone infiltrated the serenity of the riverfront. Up above high thin clouds skittered across a nearly full moon. I walked along the levee, soaking it all in, the rhythm of the river and the call of the tugboat, the wharf and the glow of the riverboat *Natchez* up ahead, the couple making out in the shadow of a monument. I probably watched them longer than I should have.

Chase.

Thinking about him hurt.

I looked away, toward sharp gray rocks sloping and crowding down to the moon-dappled river. I kicked a small one, watched it bump down to the edge, then vanish beneath the murky water.

Closing my eyes, I invited the memories to come to me here, where no one else would see or witness or judge. To give me detail—answers. To show me the truth. It was the only way I'd ever find out what really happened to Jessica.

But even as the thought formed, another truth cut in. I could let myself see. I could find Jessica, lead the police straight to her. But in the process, I'd only succeed in making myself look even more guilty.

Frustrated, I looked downriver, toward the massive Crescent City Connection bridge twinkling like fallen stars. My mother had known the risks, and she'd taken them. And look where it had gotten her.

I went to kick another rock, but stilled, knowing—*knowing*—that I was no longer alone. I hung there frozen, absolutely unable to move, even as the panic choked off my breath. I could feel him behind me. Feel him . . . watching.

No, I told myself. *No! Not like this.*

Abruptly the moment released me and I twisted around, saw the shadowed figure not ten yards behind me. It was a public place, frequented by locals and tourists. But I would have recognized the distinctive mask covering his eyes anywhere, the tilted edges and deceptively beautiful black feathers fanning up from the center.

The knife in his hand was new.

On a silent scream I turned and took off. The truth chased closed behind. On Bourbon Street he'd been just one among many. There, alcohol flowed, inhibitions crumbled, and anonymity ruled. Strangers came on to strangers every hour of every day.

The fact he'd followed when I'd been so deliberately careful shattered the illusion of insignificance.

Music from the *Natchez* grew louder. The boat wasn't far. There would be people there, security guards. If I could just reach the wharf—

A jerky glance over my shoulder told me I'd never make it. He was gaining on me, only a few steps behind. With another hard burst of adrenaline I lunged forward, but against the uneven bricks, my ankle went out from under me, and my feet tangled. I staggered, trying to catch myself. But momentum was stronger, and I went down. My hands and knees hit first. The sharp edges of rocks placed to protect sliced. My elbow buckled, and my head smashed against granite.

My vision blurred. Stars danced. Shock muted the feel of the foot to my back. But even as darkness came, there was no mistaking the terrifying sensation of rolling.

TWENTY-SIX

The cold shocked me. It was like a thousand splinters hitting all at once, then nothing. Just nothing. No pinpricks. No pain. No anything.

I tried to open my eyes, but they wouldn't work.

I tried to use my arms, my legs, but they were heavy, motionless.

There was only the sensation of sinking, of breath leaving, and tightness.

I told myself to fight—begged myself to fight.

But there was no fight in me, only a sweet lethargy, a numbness that made everything else go away.

Except Jessica. Through a swirl of shimmering blue and white light I saw her as she'd been before, when I'd kneeled in that disgusting closet. She'd had her arms around her knees, and she'd been rocking. Now she sat cross-legged, twirling ratty hair around her index finger. Over and over again. There was something dark smeared around her mouth. Blood, I thought at first. But then she lifted her left hand, and I saw the chocolate bar. She took a small bite and again started to rock, staring off into nothingness.

And through the silence, a tugboat cried.

Where are you, I thought, but she just looked at me, and cried.

The cold came again, sharper, endless needles of it. I felt myself reach for her, felt my arm stretch out—and touch. She grabbed my hand and pulled, drew me to her—and held on.

I don't know why I fought. I'll never know why I fought. But I did. I jerked back and tried to pull her with me, away from the darkness. But then the heaviness seeped back into my limbs, and I stopped moving altogether.

Warmth then. Cozy, secure. Complete. Instead of sinking I drifted, as if carried. Cradled. Safe, was all I could think. Finally, at last, safe. There I lingered, like an infant nestled in a blanket, letting go totally and completely.

Time lost meaning. Fear lost substance. Secure there, I floated in the unexpectedly warm embrace for a long time. It was all I'd wanted. All I'd wanted when I was a little girl and I'd seen Sunshine dead days before she'd died, when years later I'd found my grandmother on the kitchen floor. All I'd wanted only a few hours before, when Detective DeMarcus Jackson had confronted me—and Chase had backed away.

Arms around me. Holding on. Cradling.

It was all I'd wanted.

That's why I didn't try to open my eyes. Because I didn't want the dream to end, or the warmth to fade away.

But even that fear faded, replaced by a growing curiosity to explore the promise of what came next. Already, I could feel it spreading through me like sunshine.

Would Heaven be sparkling and shimmering white? Would there be angels flying around? Would I hear harps?

Would I see my parents?

My eyes opened, slowly at first, tentatively, bracing against the rush of air.

Nothing prepared me for the darkness—or the feel of flesh, of strong arms around my body. Soft lips against the top of my head.

"Chase . . ." I whispered, and abruptly he pulled back, scorched me with the burning glow of silver. *"You."*

Jim Fourcade's son stared down at me, his face a sharp collection of lines and angles, his hair damp and slicked back to reveal his eyes, narrow, concentrated, as if he didn't trust himself to so much as blink, much less look away.

It all came back on a violent rush, the guy on Bourbon Street, with the mask and the voice like liquid sin, the feeling in the bar, the awareness only a few minutes before, on the river's edge, when I'd spun around to see the knife.

"You were following me," I whispered, as awareness zipped like an overdose of adrenaline. I surged against him, pushed and shoved and—

He held me steady, tight. *"Easy there,"* he said, much as he had before when he'd asked if I was lost, all low and warm and hypnotic. I felt myself still, felt myself force a breath.

And that's when I noticed the blood. It was on his hands, his T-shirt, a thin streak vanishing at the whiskers along his jaw. "You're bleeding—"

He stayed steady, unaffected. Nonblinking. Just holding me. Watching. "Rocks are sharp."

"Omigod, the knife . . ." My mind raced. Questions splintered. Answers refused to form. Jim Fourcade was my mother's friend. She'd trusted him with her life. This guy was his son . . . "That was you."

"No."

"Yes, it was! I saw—" Or had I? Had I seen? Had I seen anything? Anything real? Or had it all been something else altogether, like the nonexistent Victorian room off the courtyard in the Quarter, something with neither form nor shape, left over from the images of Jessica in the darkness?

"Easy . . . don't try to talk."

But that was impossible. "Did you see anyone? A man? With a knife?"

His hand lifted to my face and eased a strand of wet hair from my eyes. "There was no man."

"W-what?"

"No knife."

Just like there'd been no cat that evening in the Quarter, when I'd turned and Chase had vanished.

But there had been. I knew that. Maybe not for Chase, and maybe not for Jim Fourcade's son, but the cat had been as real as the man with the knife.

But only for me.

A wave of cold swept through me, bringing a shiver. Instinctively I turned toward the warmth, and he held me tighter, cradling me against his body. And finally little things began to register, like the way he held me sprawled in his lap, our legs tangled, his arms anchored around me. Before, at his father's house, he'd seemed lanky, maybe even thin. But the proximity of my body to his told a different story.

"What happened?" Fragments of memory drifted, but none of them fit together. "Why are you holding me?"

"You asked me to."

We were both wet. The night air was cool, the breeze slipping against my damp clothes. But I didn't feel . . . any of it. Only heat, as if, like his father, his body burned from the inside out. "When?"

"After you started breathing again. You were cold."

I stilled. "Started breathing again?" And then it all came back to me, hard and fast and without mercy, the fall, rolling over the

rocks toward the river, the startling slap of cold. Sinking. The lead-
enness of my body. The weight dragging at me—like it had less than
a week before, in the dream Aunt Sara had pulled me from. I'd woken before finding out what came next.

Him, I now realized. This guy I'd seen for the first time only
the day before had gone into the river after me, pulled me back.

Given me breath.

His breath.

". . . I don't even know your name," I whispered.

His eyes met mine. "Dylan," he said, shifting me away from
him as he stood and extended a hand. "Come on . . . you need to
get out of those clothes."

Dylan. I stared at his hand, the wide square palm and blunt-
tipped fingers. Open. Waiting. Then at the rocky slope on which we
sat, the river beyond, with the play of moonlight and stars against the
dark blanket of water. Everything looked exactly as it had before I'd
fallen.

But that was the thing about one moment to the next. No two
were ever the same. With every exhale life shifted, moved forward.

You could never go back.

Slowly, I put my palm to his, and stood. "I don't want to go
home."

In the river, the water had claimed me. Now the cascade cleansed.
In the small white bathtub I stood with my eyes closed and my
head tilted, letting warmth stream against me. All the while memories taunted, and thoughts teased. I tried to separate reality from
fantasy from . . . nightmare.

But clarity evaded me.

I'd seen Jessica. That was real. I'd returned to the house on

Prytania and invited the images to return. That had happened. I'd seen her—and Pitre.

That's where the uncertainty began.

Someone had spoken to me on Bourbon Street—*You lost, little girl?*

Jim Fourcade's son?

Or my imagination.

Someone had followed me—or had they?

Now, the young psychic, Grace, had asked, *or all your life?*

With the cooling of the water, I tried to make sense of the jumbled images. There'd been a long dark corridor and some kind of horn—or siren.

Vision—or memory?

And the man, the one with the mask and the knife. The one I'd run from. Had he been there? Had he been real? Or had he simply been part of the same vision . . . the same memory?

Dylan Fourcade *had* been there. He was real. And he was in the next room, doing God only knew what, while I stood in his shower. Naked. Separated only by a closed door—without a lock.

It was an odd feeling. I probably should have been frightened. But he, this complete stranger, had gone into the murky waters of the river after me. He'd dragged me out, brought me back.

When I looked into the silver of his eyes . . .

I don't know how long I stood there before the water cooled—*before I even noticed that it had gone from hot to cold*—but finally I stepped out and toweled off. I pulled on the huge black T-shirt he'd given me, hesitating at the scent of soap and leather and something else, something vague and spicy.

Stepping into a pair of his gym shorts, I realized that even wrenched as tight as they would go, they wouldn't stay up. Fortunately I didn't really need them, not when the shirt was longer than most of my dresses. So after running my fingers through my hair and slicking it back from my face, I turned toward the door leading to the main room—and caught myself in the mirror.

Twenty-four hours. That's all that had elapsed since I'd been with Chase on his sofa. We'd played *Halo*. He'd kissed me. I'd kissed him back. We'd—

I silenced the thought, didn't want to go back.

The girl in the mirror was a stranger, the one with the finger-combed hair and shower-smeared makeup, wearing the shirt of a guy she didn't know and the necklace of a mother she didn't remember, legs bare.

Bare. It was the perfect word. Everything I'd ever believed in had been stripped away, leaving me here, now, like this. Alone with a stranger—who looked at me like he'd known me forever, but wished that he hadn't.

His apartment was small, three boxy rooms connected by a narrow hallway along one side. The front room had a couch and a television, a bunch of milk crates stacked to form a desk. On top sat a very new-looking laptop. A collection of black-and-white photographs hung on two of the four walls. There was a door to the bathroom, and a small hall which led first to the bedroom, then to the kitchen. I found it odd that the kitchen was in the back, but a lot of the older buildings in New Orleans had a similar layout. The apartment was on the second floor. From the bar below leaked the strains of a saxophone.

After a few minutes and deep breaths, I found him kicked back on the ratty sofa watching a football game on a surprisingly small TV, and something inside of me shifted. I had so many questions and couldn't help but think he had the answers.

Nothing prepared me for him to glance my way. He didn't smile, not with his mouth, but the silver of his eyes gleamed. "Better?"

"Much. Thank you."

He rolled to his feet and headed toward me. He'd changed out of his wet, dirty clothes from the river, but he'd let me clean up first. "There's some roast beef in the fridge if you're hungry," he said, and then he was gone, slipping by me and vanishing into the bathroom.

I heard the door close, the water come on, and knew that he, too, had taken off his clothes.

Uncomfortable, I hurried to the kitchen, where a TV tray and bar stool served as table and chair, and a wood door led to a small balcony. In the white fridge that looked straight out of the fifties, I found myself smiling at the collection of fruit and yogurt and sandwich fixings, orange juice, milk, and beer.

The old Trinity would have reached for the juice. But the memory of the tequila came rushing back, those few sweet moments when I'd been with the guy from Texas and everything else had fallen away.

That's what I wanted. For all the craziness to fall away, go away. To not think about any of it. For me to just . . . be. The new Trinity was tired of sitting in that tight little box, with everyone watching and judging.

I reached for the beer, found a bottle opener and flipped the top, took a long, deep swallow, let the cool, bitter liquid slide like an elixir down my throat.

"You sure about that?"

I spun around and found Dylan in the doorway, a white towel around his shoulders, unfastened jeans low on his hips—and his chest absolutely bare.

"You're fast," I whispered . . . yeah, like an idiot.

"Only when it's called for," he said, closing in on me.

I stepped back. It was automatic. My legs bumped the cabinets. And he kept right on coming.

Mouth dry, I gulped another big swallow of beer.

He took the bottle from my hands. "Come on. Get your stuff."

My chin went up. An odd little panic spurted through me. "No."

He stopped inches from me, standing so close he had to look down to see me. I'd never really realized how tall he was, not until that moment, when I had to tilt my chin to see him.

Less than an hour before, we'd been sprawled together on the slope of the river. Our legs had tangled. Our mouths had—

You asked me to, he'd said. *After you started breathing again.*

Shock did weird, weird things to my sense of . . . everything.

"Hiding doesn't get you anywhere," he said in that soft, oddly hypnotic voice of his, the one that sounded like it should come from a magician or shaman, someone wise and knowing—not an eighteen- or nineteen-year-old guy with dark, edgy eyes and an apartment above a bar in the French Quarter.

I shifted, worked hard to keep my breath steady. "Who says I'm hiding?"

"You're here, aren't you?"

He knew. God help me, he knew. Everything. He knew why I'd been alone by the river—and he knew why I didn't want to go home.

Feeling reckless, I took the bottle from his hands and indulged in another long, slow sip. "Maybe this is where I want to be."

In his eyes, the faintest flicker registered. Surprise, maybe. Curiosity.

Compassion.

Whatever it was, it was enough. Enough to draw me closer, to make me want . . . more. He hadn't turned away. He hadn't stepped back. He'd pulled me from the river. He was here. He was now. I wanted to feel that again, that safety. That sense that everything was okay, that everything was going to be okay. I wanted what I'd lost.

"Maybe . . ." Something dark and reckless whispered through me, and for the first time in my life I went with it. I stepped into Jim Fourcade's son and pushed up on my toes, lifted my face—and brushed my lips against his.

At first he did nothing, just stood there removed somehow, even though my body was pressed to his. Then I slid a hand to the back of his neck and shifted my mouth, sprinkling small kisses against the corner of his.

His hand caught mine. Hard. He dragged it away from him, physically stepped back. Even before he spoke, I saw the warning in the lines of his face.

"Careful, little girl. You don't want to start a game without knowing who you're playing with."

"Don't tell me what I don't want," I practically hissed. "That's all anyone has done my whole life. Don't let anyone know. Don't let anyone see. Don't ask questions. Don't make waves. Don't take chances—" I'd tried. I'd tried so damn hard to be good. Be perfect. To do and not do as I was told. To please my grandmother. "And look where that's gotten me."

He had the good grace to wince. "You're not thinking straight."

"How do you know that? Maybe that's exactly what I'm doing, for the first time in my life."

"Trinity—"

"What? You don't like what you see?"

His eyes darkened. He flicked a glance down along my body, slowly back up. "Do I look like someone who doesn't like what he sees?"

I swallowed, not sure why his rejection stung so badly. "Then what?"

The second the answer to my question hit me, I stepped back, broke all contact. "Omigod." Humiliation made me want to run. *"You think I'm a freak."* The words were raw, hoarse. In my desperation to find my way back to safety and warmth, I'd jumped to conclusions. I'd been wrong. As with Chase, Dylan knew. And as with Chase, he was stepping back. "You saw me running, didn't you? You saw me run from something that wasn't there. You saw me—"

He moved so fast I didn't have time to breathe. His hands came down on my upper arms, and he pulled me back to him. "I don't think you're a freak."

His voice was as raw, as hoarse, as mine. "Then—"

"Goddamnit." That was the only warning I got.

TWENTY-SEVEN

He dragged me toward him, his hand finding the side of my face for a fractured second before his mouth came down against mine, and all the pieces from before, the jagged slivers that hadn't fit together, settled wordlessly into place.

Before, on the riverbank, when I'd drifted through the darkness, it had been him pulling me back, him suffusing me with warmth and light. He'd put his mouth to mine and given me his breath. He'd brought me back.

I felt it all over again, this time with the fragile awareness of a hazy dream. I felt his mouth slant over mine. I felt his arms gather me close, his body against mine. I felt his recklessness—and utter restraint.

I felt little parts of me breaking away, even as new parts of me bloomed, and fused.

I felt him walking me backward, toward the wall.

Or maybe that was the hall to his bedroom.

I didn't know, didn't care, couldn't think. Just knew that—

He pulled back so abruptly I staggered, swayed against him. His breath was as hard as his body, his eyes dark and drenched with something I didn't come close to understanding. Even his voice was . . . obliterated. *"This isn't what you want."*

I hung there, in his arms but a world away, not moving even as the space between us stretched and morphed into something ugly and unrecognizable. "Dylan—"

"You're lashing out," he said, his voice all quiet and dangerous. "Using me like that kid in the bar."

I felt myself go absolutely, horribly still.

"But it's not going to change anything," he said, and again his eyes glowed like burnished silver. "It's not going to make what happened earlier today go away."

Somehow I made myself move. Somehow I made myself back away from him, sever every sliver of contact. He knew. *Everything.* "You were there," I whispered again.

His nostrils flared.

"Your father . . ."

"Still has friends," he said.

Which meant that Dylan knew about Detective Jackson and the evidence against me, that I'd been hauled in for questioning, and that Chase had walked away.

"So you took it upon yourself to follow me?" It took every ounce of control I had not to slap my hands against his chest, and shove him as hard as I could. "That was you on Bourbon Street, wasn't it?" It was what I should have asked all along, if not for the fog of tequila. "In the bar! My God—you idiot! You scared me half to death!" That's why I'd twisted around and started to run, tripped and rolled into the river. "If you hadn't been sneaking around—"

The sudden glitter to his eyes stopped me cold.

"Then your fun and games would be all over." Reaching

around me, he plucked the beer bottle from my hand—I hadn't even realized I was still holding it—and brought it over the sink, turned it upside down. "If I hadn't been there, you'd be dead."

I wanted to hate him for that, for yanking that veil of safety from me, for making everything real again. And maybe I did. He was right. If he had not been following me, I could have died. Right there in that river, I could have sunk, and no one would have known I was gone, until it was too late.

"Maybe it wouldn't have happened at all," I said, as much to myself as to him. "Maybe if you hadn't been following me in the first place, I would have stayed in that bar—"

"With the guy that was all over you? Did you even get his name?"

I shot him a look that so said *go to hell.* "Does it matter?"

He stepped closer, shrinking the pale green walls of the kitchen around us. "You have no idea, do you?" His voice was quiet, rough. "No idea how . . . special you are."

I tensed, felt the whisper of that one word, *special,* clear down to my soul.

"Or how dangerous the game can be," he went on, boxing me in between his half-dressed body and the counter. His arm was inked. I couldn't make it all out, just something round and webbed. "But my father knows. He's seen it before. And he's not about to let what happened to your mother happen to you."

I stood frozen, struggling to so much as breathe, staring up at this guy I'd known less than a day, but who seemed to be a walking encyclopedia of my life.

"So what?" I asked, using sass to mask the quick lash of vulnerability. "He appointed you my bodyguard?"

His eyes met mine. "I wish it was just your body."

The words, the absolute lack of any emotion in his voice, chilled me.

But then he was turning from me, dragging the towel from around his shoulders as he headed back toward his bedroom. "Now get your things, little girl. It's time to go home."

I'm not sure which punched harder—little girl, or *home*.

Charging after him, I caught up with him as he was grabbing a T-shirt from an old dresser. "What's the matter?" I asked. "Tired of the job already?"

"This isn't about me," he said, pulling the dark gray cotton over his head and hiding all traces of the ink on his bicep. "I would have thought you'd realized that by now."

I lifted my chin, squared my shoulders, did everything I could to pretend this was perfectly normal. But the truth of the matter was, I'd never been alone with a guy in his bedroom before. "Why do you call me little girl?"

Slowly he turned toward me. "What would you rather I call you?"

"My name is Trinity."

He reached for his wallet and shoved it into his back pocket. "Trinity Rose."

The shiver was automatic. "How do you know that?"

He pushed past me, toward the hall leading to the front room. But he stopped two steps away from me, and turned. "You were the one sent away. You were the one scrubbed of your memories— not me."

I had to make myself breathe. "Then don't send me away now," I whispered as more pieces slipped together. *Dylan knew. Dylan, this veritable stranger who'd gone into the river after me, who'd pulled me back and kept me safe, knew. So much more than anyone had told me.*

He hesitated, one foot in his surprisingly tidy bedroom, one foot in the narrow little hall. "They're looking for you. Your aunt—"

"Please," I said before he could finish. "Let me stay. Just for a little while. I'm tired." Confused. "You won't even know I'm here."

"Tea?"

"Tea. It'll help you sleep."

Standing next to the stark bed that looked more like a cot, I took the smooth white mug and glanced at the brown liquid inside. "I don't think I need any help."

Dylan stepped back, lifted a shoulder. "Your mother liked it. Thought you might want some, too."

He so played dirty. After shooting him a quick look to let him know that I was on to his game, I brought the mug to my lips and drew in a slow sip. The liquid was hot, bitter. "What's even in this?" I asked with a scrunched-up face.

He laughed. "Herbs . . . chamomile mostly, buchu leaf, I think. Lemongrass. White oak."

Fatigue pulled at me. It felt like the day had lasted forever, and in a way, it had. The clock beside the bed read 10:26. Only twelve hours before—

I blocked the thought, sipping again, more eagerly this time. The initial bitterness gave way to smoothness as I took a third sip while Jim Fourcade's son flicked off the lamp and slipped from the room.

It never occurred to me that he was drugging me.

Still wearing only his boxy T-shirt, I slipped between the sheets and released a slow breath, my thoughts drifting from the awareness of sleeping in a stranger's bed, to the veiled anticipation of—

The thought never finished. Sleep came hard and fast. Consciousness dissolved. And then the long corridor opened before me, wider than the hallway in Dylan's apartment, grimy but oddly sterile. Abandoned but not empty. Doors lined either side, all closed. Except one.

Yellowy light pooled outside a room on the right, and I felt myself start to walk, even as I told myself to turn away. Go back. But my legs kept moving toward the light, drawn like a magnet, until I stood outside. There I tried to breathe, gagged instead.

"Trinity."

The voice jolted through me and I turned, saw her. Saw Jessica. Sitting against the wall with her knees to her chest, a stained white gown covering her body. She rocked. Her eyes were wide, dark. Vacant. Her hair was stringy, so far from cheerleader perfect that my chest automatically tightened.

"Please," *she whispered, but it didn't sound like her. The voice was too thin.* "Help me . . ."

Frozen, I watched her lift an arm and reach for me, tried to make myself step back. But movement would not come. Only Jessica's frail, pale arm, reaching out with some kind of weird band wrapped around her bicep.

"Please . . ." *she whispered, but then the light went out and darkness bled in, pulsing, throbbing, all except for the glow of a flashlight that appeared on the other side of the room . . . where a Mardi Gras mask lay discarded.*

I screamed. Or at least I tried. I broke the hold of paralysis and backed away, started to run. Tried to breathe. But the darkness kept closing around me.

"Trinity . . ."

I spun around as the lights flashed and bright white bathed the corridor. Toward the right, two double doors. To the left, some kind of circular—

The flash killed it all, brought instead a glowing, fragmented window. Hands grabbed me, dragged me. Something heavy pushed against my chest. Gasping, I swung my elbows—and froze.

"Hey . . . I'm here. You're okay." *The words were low, strong, as drugging as—*

I made my eyes open, felt the scream stall in my throat. The eyes were electric blue, tilted, and absolutely totally unblinking.

"There you go," came a quiet, mesmerizing voice, and I turned to find Dylan by my side. "You're okay."

I blinked, blinked again. But the weight on my chest remained, the sleek, Siamese cat with its penetrating gaze and sable body. Its ears were black, perfectly pointy.

Through the hazy light I saw Dylan lift a hand to run it along the animal's muscular back. "It's okay—he won't hurt you."

I tried to breathe, coughed instead. It seemed I'd been doing a lot of that all day, trying to breathe. My whole body burned, as if I'd been running and running—

"Tell me," Dylan said. "Tell me what you saw."

Everything swirled. The long corridor and the small room, Jessica on the floor, the mask . . .

"Hurts so bad," I whispered, pressing my hands to the throbbing at my temples.

Dylan lifted his hand from the eerily still cat and brought it to rest against the back of mine. "The man with the knife . . . did you see him again?"

Soft light spilling in from the hallway cast his face in an array of shadows. I watched them play against the faint goatee at his jaw, the hollow of his cheek. "You said there was no one there," I reminded. Just him. And me.

His expression tightened. "That doesn't mean you didn't see him."

I glanced at the clock, saw the hour approaching midnight. Had I really been asleep for over an hour?

Before, in his kitchen, I'd asked him if his father had sent him to guard my body.

I wish it was just your body.

Questions surged. Answers pierced. Dylan knew that I saw things. And he knew they were real.

Suddenly the cat nudged my chin with his mouth—and nipped. I pulled back, couldn't stop looking at those unblinking blue eyes. "I . . . didn't see him before."

"He saw you," Dylan said. "Bakta likes to watch before he comes out."

I'm not sure what made me lift my hand, and touch the cat's wiry fur. "Bakta?"

Dylan . . . grinned. "Black Tail—that's what happens when you get named by a two-year-old." He gave the cat a good hard scratch between its pointy black ears, then nudged the weight from my chest. "Here," he said, slipping the mug back into my hands. "This will help."

I stared at the tea, the bitterness that had given way to something smooth and inviting . . . then sleep.

"I'm scared," I admitted for the first time, and God help me, the dark glow in Dylan's eyes touched me as surely as if he'd returned his hand to mine.

"I know you are."

"I didn't ask for this."

"No one does," he said, and there was a very real sadness to his voice. "Doesn't change anything."

For a long moment I watched him, perched there on the edge of his bed, looking as angry as he did . . . regretful. Then I drew the mug back to my mouth, and sipped.

"Try to get some rest," he said, standing and backing away, even as I sipped again. "I'm one room away."

I watched him leave, wanted to feel glad and grateful that he was gone and I was alone. But then the edges of memory slipped closer, and I saw her again. Saw Jessica.

Earlier, I'd fallen off immediately. But this time sleep hovered just out of reach. I don't know how long I sat there, cross-legged with Dylan's sheets tangled around my legs, staring at the tea but seeing a kaleidoscope of images. But I do know when I got up: when the phone rang. It was a faint sound, a muted song clip from the front room. If there'd been any other sound, I probably wouldn't have heard it. And then I would never have known.

Maybe I should have stayed in his bed. That would have been the right thing to do. Dylan was a stranger. I had no right to his phone conversations. And yet something drew me toward the edge of the hall, where I pressed my back to the wall, and listened.

"Didn't you get my text?"

Slowly, I let out a breath.

"Yeah," Dylan went on, and with a quick glance I saw that he sat at the far side of the room, at the dark blue milk crates that doubled as a computer desk. The laptop glowed. "She's still here," he said, and the words—simple, direct—went straight through me.

"I got her to drink some more," he said, and immediately my hand found my mouth, and my stomach churned. "No. Not a thing."

I wanted to gag. I wanted to run. But I couldn't. I couldn't move.

"Shit," he muttered. "That's messed up." A moment of silence, then: "I'll call the aunt."

The sense of disappointment, of betrayal, cut in hard and fast—and released me from my inability to move. I staggered back to his bedroom, looked around wildly. Blindly. I'd trusted him. I'd believed him. Yet there he was, about to call my aunt, despite the fact I'd asked him not to.

I swallowed, made my thoughts clear. I didn't have much time. I couldn't stay there, couldn't let Aunt Sara take me back to her apartment—to Detective Aaron LaSalle—not after what I'd done.

ELLIE JAMES

Not after I'd run. She might not let me out again. Detective Bad Ass would no doubt be with her. He would be even more suspicious—

I made it up as I went along. From Dylan's dresser I grabbed his keys. Then I eased back to the hall and listened for his voice:

". . . this is Detective Jim Fourcade's son . . ."

I moved quickly, slipping to the cool linoleum floor of the kitchen, to the back door. Quietly I turned the knob and pulled, let myself into the whisper of night air. The patio was small, the iron railing not very high. I wasn't thrilled about jumping, but I was even less thrilled about my aunt coming to get me. Climbing over, I first lowered myself to crouch on the edge, then jumped. The ground came up hard, sang through my bones.

I didn't let that stop me.

Adrenaline surging, I hurried along the cobblestone path, toward the gate at the far side. There, I burst into a narrow alley as a voice ripped into the saxophone-infused night. "Trinity—no!"

I ran faster, straight for the car Dylan had parked in a small lot one street over. He was stronger, faster, but I had the advantage of knowing where I was going. And I had his keys.

I drove. My hands clenched the wheel. My gaze darted between the front window and rearview mirror. Lights glared. I refused to slow down, though. Refused to turn back. Dylan couldn't follow me, but others could.

I didn't have a map or a GPS, but I did have a memory for detail, and I knew how to read signs. By the time I cruised past the Brad Pitt homes of the Ninth Ward, I knew I was okay.

The night made everything look different, darkness replacing the fast-food restaurants and strip malls I'd noticed the day before, but I watched closely, until I saw the turnoff.

Off Judge Perez, streetlights gave way to trees, leaving only the steady beam of headlights to cut through the darkness. I slowed, remembered the road was narrow, with no shoulder and an abundance of potholes. If I were to run off—

I refused to let my mind go there. All I could think was Fourcade. Dylan's dad. He was the only one. My mother had trusted him. He would understand. He would know. Him I could tell. I could tell him what I saw when I closed my eyes.

With one last curve, the headlights hit the clearing, then the house in the middle of nowhere. I slowed as I neared, acutely conscious of the fact that no light shone from any of the windows.

I parked where Chase had the day before, in the gravel drive next to the old pickup and the motorcycle. My heart slamming, I pushed open the door and stood, hesitating a second to make sure I didn't hear the dogs.

The wind slapped from all directions, cooler here away from the concrete of the city. Damper. Pushing against it, I headed toward the house, where the statue of the Virgin Mary waited with her arms outstretched, and the dream catcher gyrated.

Then I heard the voice.

"You didn't say good-bye."

TWENTY-EIGHT

The silhouette emerged from the camouflage of the porch columns, and stepped into a sliver of moonlight. "Why so shocked, little girl? I told you hiding wasn't going to work."

"You . . ." I backed away, tried to understand. "How—"

Through the darkness, the silver of his eyes glowed. "I followed you."

"But that's not possible. I left you—"

"And I took a shortcut," Jim Fourcade's son said, coming down the three steps from the elevated porch.

I twisted around, saw the motorcycle beside the car I'd borrowed. My throat burned. Disappointment churned through me. I thought about running, but knew he'd catch me before I could get away.

"You lied to me," I seethed, spinning back toward him. "You made me think I was safe!" The words tore out of me. "But I heard you! I heard you say you were going to call my aunt—"

Beside the violently twirling dream catcher, he stilled. "I wasn't going to tell her anything, except that you were safe." His gaze raked over me. "Because you were."

Something in his voice—regret, maybe—scraped through me, casting everything I thought, everything I'd believed, into question. "You drugged me."

"I didn't drug you."

"The tea—"

"—was my idea," came a different voice, quieter, raspier, and from the direction of the front door, pale yellow light broke the darkness as Jim Fourcade stepped from the shadows.

"If you want to be mad, Trinity Rose, be mad at me."

Shock speared through me. This man, my mother's friend . . . he was the one who'd wanted me drugged?

"No," I whispered, backing away. Maybe I couldn't run. Maybe I couldn't hide. But I couldn't just stand there, either, not when every time I blinked, my whole world shifted. "I trusted you . . ."

"And you still can," Fourcade said, joining his son at the base of the steps. "I'm on your side."

I took another step back, as somewhere in the distance, the dogs barked. "How can you say that? How can you expect me to believe—"

"Because it's true," he said. "You're seeing things, aren't you? Just like your mother. You're seeing things and they're tearing you apart."

My mouth moved, but no words came out.

"That's the way it was for her, too," he went on, his voice so threadbare it hurt to hear him. "A gift that tortured. Every time she closed her eyes, seeing without knowing, knowing without being able to help."

The wind blew against my eyes, drying them like sandpaper.

"The tea always helped," he said. "The herbs cleared the clutter, let her see."

His son stepped toward me. "And you did, didn't you?"

I looked at him standing in the shadows of the night, this virtual stranger who I'd thrown myself at only hours before, while high clouds smeared away what little light the stars provided. I was still wearing his T-shirt. My legs were bare. I hadn't even taken time to grab my clothes—or my shoes.

"I saw it in your eyes," he said with another step toward me, and deep inside, something uncomfortable shifted. "I heard it in your voice."

Maybe I should have turned away. It's what I wanted to do, what the old Trinity, the one who preferred the cautious route, would have done.

But the old Trinity didn't exist anymore. She'd died with my grandmother. Maybe long before that, with Sunshine. It had taken this, coming to New Orleans and breathing the thick, muggy air that my mother had, walking the centuries-old streets that she'd called home, to convince the new Trinity that she didn't need to hide anymore. Didn't need to be scared or ashamed. That it was safe.

Except I *was* scared. How could I not be? I saw things. I knew things no one should know.

"A room," I whispered, and my voice thinned on the word. "It's dark, abandoned." Staring straight ahead, I saw the two Fourcades, one with silver hair, one with black. With a slow blink they merged and moved toward me.

"She's against a wall," I said with what little voice I could find. My arms hung against my body. My hands opened. "In a gown."

He stopped before me, took my hand. "What kind of gown?"

"Dirty," I said, closing my eyes and opening myself, inviting the images to return. "Stained." Against me, the wind whipped. "There's something on her arm . . . like a . . . bracelet."

Against mine, his fingers tightened. "What else?"

"She's scared." My whole body started to shake, and then I was there again, in the suffocating darkness, turning in slow circles.

"There's boxes, lots of junk. Trash." I wasn't sure what made me look up. "A light," I murmured. "Leaking through some cracks. And a sound . . . a wail . . . like a horn . . . I—"

"My God."

Like a fist to the gut, the hard edge to the voice made me sag.

"Hey." Gentle now. Soft. Arms around me, easing me to the ground. I sat but barely felt the gravel against my knees, swallowed, made myself look. Made myself see.

Jim Fourcade held me, watching me through eyes the same silver as his son's. "You're okay," he said. "You're perfect."

"I don't understand."

Nothing prepared me for his smile, as warm as it was heartbroken. "You found her," he whispered. *"You found her."*

The wharf hulked against the night, a stamp of pure darkness against the glow of lights from a complex downriver. While the rain-slicked French Quarter partied and the Central Business District slept, along the Mississippi barges slipped like shadowy ghosts, silent save for the occasional cry of a horn.

With a shiver, I pressed my hands to my temple, trying to merge reality with the distorted slide show flashing through my mind. Every time I tried to hold on, the image shifted—and the invisible vise around my head tightened.

Fighting it, I sucked in a slow breath, counting to five as I let it out.

"He should be out by now," I murmured, resisting the urge to hug my arms around my body. The afternoon storms had moved on, leaving behind the first breath of fall. The breeze off the water swirled against my bare legs, making me grateful for the fuzzy pink slippers Jim Fourcade had mysteriously produced. They were a little big, but so much better than being barefoot.

Almost an hour had passed since he'd vanished inside the falling-down structure that had once served the Port of New Orleans. I didn't want to think about what was inside now.

A few feet away, his son turned toward me. I'd never met anyone who could be so still, even when he moved. "Give him time."

The ironclad calm to his voice made me want to scream.

"He's had time—" I started, but a wave of pure ice cold doubled me over. I caught myself, hung there while the fuzzy images flickered faster: Jessica, rocking, crying. Fading. Even when I blinked, focus would not come, just the distorted sight of Fourcade's son lunging toward me.

"No." I darted past him, toward the metal door hanging open. "Something's wrong—"

He caught me from behind. *"Trinity."*

"No!" I thrashed against him, my heart pounding so violently I couldn't even breathe. "Let me go!"

"You know I can't do that." His voice was quiet, hypnotic. "You can barely stand up."

I hated that he was right. But somehow I made myself twist from his arms before he could stop me, even as a swirl of bluish white danced before my eyes. Staggering, I was three steps from the door when my knees went out from under me.

Darkness swam. Light flirted against it. Shaking, I brought my hands to the sides of my face and pressed.

But the low buzz would not stop.

"Hey."

The voice broke through the static, and I opened my eyes, made myself focus. He crouched with his hands on my shoulders, steadying me. But nowhere near as much as his eyes. They were dark and glowing, safe . . .

"What do you see?"

My mouth opened, but no words came out. I swallowed, tried again. "Jessica . . . she's . . ." *Not here.* I didn't know where the words came from, so I pushed them aside. "Hurt," I said. I could feel it, the sharp sting of pain radiating from the wrist I'd unknowingly wrapped my hand around. "Bleeding." I barely recognized my own voice. "There's not much time."

A few feet away, the wind sent an empty plastic bottle skittering along the damp concrete, but Fourcade's son didn't move. "If she's in there, my father will find her."

"But I have to—"

"No, you don't."

I looked away from him, watched the bottle rolling toward a puddle at the edge of the building. Dyl—

I broke the thought, refused to let his name form. His name threw me back. His name returned me to those first few distorted moments by the river, when he'd held me . . .

His name took me back to his apartment—his kitchen.

Jim Fourcade's son. That's all he was. For all intents and purposes, a stranger.

"You can let go of me now," I whispered.

Surprisingly he moved, shifting so the shadows slipped from his face. "Can I?"

"Yes."

His hands fell away. I swayed, but caught myself, pushing to my feet and putting a few steps between us. My whole body hummed. I wasn't a waiting kind of person. So close, was all I could think. We were so close. I wanted—

I didn't know what I wanted. To be inside, yes, but even as the thought formed, I realized how absurd it was. I was a sixteen-year-old who'd been in the city less than two months. What could I—

Movement to my right drew my attention to an old pylon with

a fraying rope hanging from rotting wood—and a skinny white cat watching me through unblinking eyes.

The quickening was immediate. I tensed, wanted to step forward with an outstretched hand, even as I wanted to step back, and make it all go away.

"Do you see a cat?"

Out of the corner of my eye, I saw Fourcade's son edge closer. "What do you want me to say?"

It made absolutely no sense, but I would have sworn he sounded . . . amused.

"The truth," I said, watching the motionless animal. "Is there a cat—or am I staring at thin air?" *Again*.

"There's a cat."

The quick flutter in my gut was ridiculous. "You can see it?"

"I can see it."

I glanced back at him, with his low-slung jeans and his T-shirt, the faint goatee and military-short dark hair, and the smile just happened. "Really?"

His eyes met mine, for the briefest of heartbeats, before shifting toward the pylon.

The cat was gone. "That's not funny . . ."

"I'm not laughing," he said as tires screeched and headlights cut in from behind us.

I spun, recognized the Lexus immediately, and before I could process what was happening, the car stopped and the driver's door flew open, and Aunt Sara was racing toward me.

"Oh, thank God!" she cried, pulling me into her arms as a siren screamed somewhere nearby. "Thank God, thank God, thank God!" She squeezed me tight. "I've been so worried."

The twist of guilt and relief paralyzed me. I'd done this to her. I'd run. I'd vanished. I'd left her to worry . . .

"I'm okay," I whispered, and then my arms were moving, lifting to wrap around her. *"I'm sorry."*

"I know," she said, still holding me, not letting go. "I know how hard all of this is—"

"I was scared," I said. "I didn't know what to—"

And then I saw him, and everything else fell away.

Chase.

In the same torn jeans and Tulane T-shirt he'd worn that afternoon, he stood beside the car, watching.

My throat knotted. My heart forgot to beat.

Looking at him hurt. Seeing his eyes, normally warm and bright and such a vibrant shade of blue, shadowed now, ravaged.

Aunt Sara pulled away, stepped away, leaving nothing between me and Chase but a few puddles, and the memory of the last time I'd seen him.

Around us the cool breeze of that no-man's-land between night and morning whispered, sending an empty fast-food bag ambling across the gravel of the parking lot. From somewhere behind us a siren wailed. Chase started to move.

"Trinity."

My chest tightened. So much emotion there, all hot and boiling. I wanted to move toward him. I wanted to run. I wanted to feel his arms close around me, feel him hold me, make it all go away.

But . . . I couldn't move.

He walked slowly, like I might disintegrate if he moved too fast. All the while he kept his eyes on mine, until he stood so close all I had to do was lift an arm, and I could have touched.

"I'm sorry."

The words came at me through a vortex of hurt and regret, of shock and denial and relief, and I felt my eyes sting, felt the flood of moisture even as I tried to lock it all away. And then he was moving again, moving when I couldn't, eliminating the last breath between us and reaching for me, taking me into his arms and holding me.

Even as I stood glass still.

"I'm sorry," he said again, this time with a hand against the back of my head, holding me tight, so tight, just like I'd wanted before, at the house on Prytania, when he'd . . .

Walked away.

"I shut down," he said in a voice so raw I knew exactly where the surprise of Jackson's words had thrown him, back to the day he'd raced into his kitchen for water, and walked out with no idea who he was anymore.

"I was wrong," he said. "I just . . . Shit," he muttered. "I lost it."

My throat hurt. I made myself swallow. I knew I needed to say something, but the words wouldn't form.

"I walked," he said, and now he pulled back enough for his eyes to meet mine. "For a long time I just walked. And I kept thinking, I kept thinking about everything, about what Jackson said and what you said, but more than that about the way you'd looked at me, what I'd seen in your eyes, and I realized . . ." His expression twisted. "I tried to call you."

But I did not have my phone, didn't even know where it was.

"When your aunt told me what happened . . ." His hand came to the side of my face, gentle, so very, very gentle. "We've been looking for you all night."

I'd been trying to be brave. I'd been trying to be strong and do the right thing, to take charge instead of following directions, to be the person my mother had been. But standing there with the breeze slapping my hair against my face, I no longer knew what was a lie, and what was real. Maybe the new Trinity was the illusion, an ironclad façade to shield myself from the hurt that came from letting anyone close. The old Trinity was still there, wanting more than anything to just let go.

And I did. Blinking against the hot, salty sting, I felt the warmth shimmy all the way to my toes. "It's okay," I whispered.

"No, it's not." Long bangs fell against his eyes, but did nothing to conceal the blue. "I should have known—"

I stepped back into his arms, closing mine around him. I held on tight, squeezing my eyes shut as I drank in the unexpected wonder of the moment, the amazing way he held me, the happiness flowing through me. I absorbed it all, never wanted it to end.

Then I opened my eyes—and saw Jim Fourcade's son.

He stood in the shadow of the forgotten wharf with the glow of the port behind him, and the emaciated white cat in his arms. His eyes gleamed of burnished silver. And the moment froze, locked around me like Chase's arms, stripping me of my ability to move.

Until Detectives Aaron LaSalle and DeMarcus Jackson stepped from inside the darkness, and shattered the illusion of sanctuary.

Chase still held me. I knew that he did. I could feel his arms, his body. But the way the cops looked at me brought the cold pouring back, and I knew. I knew.

Before they said a word, *I knew.*

"No," I whispered, trying to back away even as Chase held me. "No . . ."

"How nice of you to join us," Detective Jackson said as Jim Fourcade staggered through the doorway.

"I don't understand . . ." I whispered, staring at the silver hair falling against the older cop's leathery face, his clothes . . . torn. Shock ripped through me. "You . . . you called them?"

His eyes, oddly flat, met mine. "Trinity, I had to."

Had to? What did that mean? "Why?" The question was somewhere between a gasp and a shout. "I trusted you! I thought—"

"That he'd play your game?" Jackson asked as Aunt Sara rushed over to Detective LaSalle and put her hands to his chest. My heart slammed crazily against my own. "Like he played your mama's?"

I took the words like a physical blow, unable to look away from my mother's friend. His son had moved to join him. "You're making a big mistake."

"Am I?" Jackson asked. "Really? Because it doesn't look that way to me. Your mama's friend may have swallowed your story, but evidence doesn't lie. I knew sooner or later guilt would get the better of you and you'd slip—"

"*No.*" Everything shifted, tilted. I lunged toward him anyway, had to make him go back inside.

Chase wouldn't let me take so much as a step.

"You have to go back!" I could see her . . . I could see her! "Look again. She's in there!"

"Is she?" Jackson's smile was horribly mild. Despite it being the dead of night, he looked ready to go out on a date, with a sports coat and pressed slacks, dark boots.

"And why would you think that?" The question was soft, deceptively gentle. "Is this where you left her?"

Chase's arms tightened around my waist. "That's bullshit and you know it!"

"Back off, Jackson—" That was Dylan's father.

Jackson started toward me, but before he took two steps Aaron LaSalle pulled away from my aunt.

"Everyone take a deep breath," he said, heading toward his partner. "We'll take this to the station and sort it all out—"

"No!" The word ripped out of me, and with it came a new strength. I scrambled from Chase, edged away from them all. "You can't do that."

LaSalle tracked my every move. "Why not?"

"*Aaron.*" Aunt Sara was at his side again, taking his arm as if to hold him back. Of course, that still left Detective Jackson—

and the relentless parade of warped images: *Jessica rocking. Jessica bleeding.*

Jessica . . . fading.

"Jessica—" I started, but Jackson finished for me.

"—doesn't need you."

My mind raced. My options were limited. "Let me go in—" The door was only a few feet away. "Let *me* look."

"Why? Because you know right where to look—or so you can slip away again?"

The web of dampness pushed closer. Vaguely I was aware of Fourcade moving toward the detective. "Give her a chance—"

I didn't wait for a verdict. I spun around—and ran for the door. Darkness swallowed me the second I crossed inside, thick and stale, penetrating. Maybe it would have been smart to pause and orient myself. Let my eyes adjust. But I heard the shouting behind me, and knew there was no time.

"Jessica!" I called as a glass bottle rolled from beneath my foot, and my ankle twisted. I staggered, flung out an arm to brace myself, trying not to think about the sticky substance beneath my fingers.

"Answer me!" I cried. "It's okay! You're safe!"

Too late it occurred to me that I may not be alone.

I went very still, frozen in the vat of darkness, praying that what I couldn't see, couldn't see me, either. I didn't know what had possessed me to do something so reckless, but hoped that if anyone else had been inside the rotting building, the cops had scared them—

I felt it before I saw it, a low hum, like that of a generator.

I didn't want to turn. I didn't want to see. But I knew I couldn't stand there like some terrified animal—

Slowly I lifted my hand to the bronze chain around my neck and turned . . . felt everything inside of me go into instant and total lockdown.

Fuzzy at the edges, sharper in the center, a glimmer of light broke the nothingness, as if someone had dropped a flashlight, leaving the beam to—

He stood beside a stack of old crates, tall, motionless, his eyes more chilling than the nothingness. *Pitre*.

TWENTY-NINE

Everything drained. My breath, my blood, everything I'd been trying to believe about what was and was not possible. *"No."*

I tried to back away—knew I *had* to back away. Get away. Get out. *Run.* But shock gripped me, trapping me in that one horrible moment. *Pitre.*

My friend.

"No," I murmured again. That was all. All I could think. All I could say. No. Not Pitre.

Even as the pieces slid together.

"Trinity." And just like the weekend before, he lunged for me. Except this time he was not here to rescue.

This time he was in pursuit.

Shock splintered into adrenaline, and I twisted with a strength born of purpose, and ran. It was like sprinting through a nightmare, stumbling, clawing, trying to make sense as everything shifted, fractured, as foe became friend, and friend became foe. Knowing you had to get out . . .

"Trinity—shit!"

But slamming into one dead-end after another. Disoriented, I veered right. I'd been so wrong, blind. I'd refused to let myself see, even though I *had* seen. And heard. The ugly truth had been there in the darkness of my mind: the old house, Jessica and Pitre. Arguing.

"Wait! Come back! You can't leave me here!"

"Watch me."

"No—wait— Why are you doing this?"

"Doesn't feel so good when the tables turn, does it, Jessie?"

The door had to be close. I hadn't been inside that long. All I had to do was—

I never saw the crate. I slammed into it, staggered, made myself keep going, knew I couldn't go down. The door. The cops—

He caught me from behind, tackling me at full speed. We flew forward and went down hard, my hands and knees no match for the weight of his body.

The sharp rush of pain stunned me. "No!" I panted, trying to crawl from beneath him—but he was bigger, stronger, dragging me back like I was no more than the emaciated cat I'd seen outside. "Don't," I cried. "Pitre . . . please . . . *don't hurt me!*"

"Jesus," he muttered, his hot, sweaty body smothering me against the sticky concrete. His voice was no more than a breath, but it was desperate. "Stop fighting me."

I twisted, tried to push up on my elbows. Couldn't. He was too big, too strong. "Oh, my God," I whispered, tasting blood in my mouth. I swallowed, tried again. "Please don't—"

He crammed a hand between my face and the ground, pressing his sweaty palm to my mouth. "Sh-h-h!"

I stilled, all those awful, disparate pieces grinding together. *I'd trusted him.* Even when I'd see him in the shadows of my mind, I'd trusted him. Believed him. I'd allowed myself to see only the best.

Now the enormity of my mistake threatened everything. If he so much as suspected how much I knew . . .

"Fuck," he muttered, more to himself than to me. *"Fuck, fuck, fuck."*

Wincing, I tried to breathe, shifted the weight from my stomach to my hip and lifted a hand to tug at his wrist. *"Please,"* I mouthed.

He closed in on me, scraping his face along mine. "I'm not going to hurt you," he muttered, and it was all I could do not to gag on his hot, stale-beer breath. "Just be still and let me think."

Swirls of blue slipped closer. I fought them, fought the press of his body crushing the breath from mine. "Can't . . . breathe . . ."

I felt him stiffen, felt his heart slamming a frantic riff against my back. Then the heaviness of his body miraculously lessened, and his hand relaxed.

Sucking in all the oxygen I could, I dragged it deep and let it swirl around inside. All the while I strained against the darkness, listening. LaSalle, Jackson . . . Fourcade. Chase.

They should have been right behind me.

"I-I didn't mean to hurt . . ." he said, the words oddly broken. "I swear to God I didn't mean to hurt . . . her."

Her. Not me.

I didn't want a confession, was already a liability enough. "W-what are you doing here?" I asked instead, my eyes fixing on a flashlight on the ground a few feet away. It must have been his. "Did . . . Chase call you?"

"Jessica," he panted. "My brother . . . heard she might be here."

His brother the cop. But I still didn't understand why he was *here*. If he'd taken Jessica, wouldn't he know where she was? And if he'd left her here, wouldn't he want to be as far away as possible when she was found?

"But she's not, is she?" I whispered, staring at the flashlight. If I could reach it . . .

"Fuck," he muttered. "Where the fuck is she?"

I swallowed, tried to scrape the fear from my voice. "Pitre . . . *what's going on?"*

And why did he sound so terrified?

"Just a game," he half-said, half-breathed, much as Jessica had the week before. From the way he straddled me, I could feel the jerky breaths saw in and out of his body. "An eff'in game."

Stall, was all I could think. Drag the moment out as long as I could.

"Ah, Jesus. I never meant to hurt her. I just wanted . . . to show her what it felt like to be out of control, to be messed with—"

I moaned, shifting to curl into myself.

He stiffened, easing up so that I could roll into a fetal position. "She was supposed to be there!" he went on almost incoherently. "You believe me, don't you? I was only gone an hour—she was supposed to be there when I got back . . ."

I rolled onto all fours and scrambled back.

Pitre made no move to come after me. I'm not even sure he remembered I was there. "But she was gone," he mumbled, and I could tell that he, too, had gone somewhere else. "I-I thought she got out, that she was just laying low, to make me sweat—"

"Trinity!"

He froze. I froze.

"Trinity—*where are you?"*

Something soft and fragile swelled through me. I felt myself rise to it, felt the words rise *through* me. All I had to do was call out and—

I swung back toward Pitre, saw the vague stillness of his body crouched a few feet away. If I screamed—

"Tri—ni—ty!"

With a sharp twist of my ankle, I scrambled to my feet and staggered into the darkness. "Chase!" Before I could say anything else he was dragging me into his arms and holding on, tangling his hand in my hair.

"Chase." I closed my eyes to the silence, listening for breath from somewhere beyond. All I had to do was tell him . . . "I was so scared."

"I've got you," he said, pulling back enough to smooth a damp strand of hair from my face. "Everything's okay."

"But . . ." I followed the faint beam of the abandoned flashlight to where Pitre no longer stood. "Jackson and LaSalle—"

"Waiting outside," Chase said. "They gave me five minutes to bring you back . . ."

I struggled back enough to put my hands to his chest. *"No."*

"T, there's nowhere else to go," he said, his frown so sad and tender that something inside of me bled. "I'll go with you," he said. "I'll call my mom. She'll come. Everything will be okay."

But I couldn't do it. I couldn't go back outside, to the station. "I have to help her," I whispered. "I'm the only one."

Through the glow of his flashlight, I saw his eyes darken. "T," he said, and his voice wrapped around my heart, and squeezed. "She's not here."

"I know." Had known since the fragile moments before LaSalle and Jackson had materialized from inside the wharf, when the realization had drifted through my mind.

She's not here.

But Pitre was . . .

My body burned. I could feel the perspiration gathering, dampening the big T-shirt hanging from my shoulders. I closed my eyes against it all, wished I could have another cup of my mother's tea.

And then I started to rock.

"She's hurt," I whispered, making myself go back to that sad old house, where she and Pitre had played along the edge of a blade.

Wanted . . . to show her what it felt like to be out of control . . .

"She's . . ." I let my mind wander, could still see the room in which she sat. "Wearing a gown," I whispered. "And there's . . ." Blood? Smeared against her face.

"A horn," I said as the images took over. "Maybe a siren. There's a hall. It's long and narrow." I made myself stay there, in that dark, rancid corridor, turning, taking it all in. "Double doors at one end, some kind of big desk or station at the other." Drawn, I looked up. "There's light," I said, much as I had to Fourcade a few hours before. But standing in the penetrating darkness of the wharf, I found detail I had not seen before—or maybe the tequila had finally worn off, allowing my thoughts to sharpen.

"Broken. Shining through and against some kind of . . ." I didn't know. I'd never seen anything like it. It looked like art—or a window. "There's a man in the center, like . . . a tree trunk." He had his arms lifted. "There's other men around him . . . like branches. I—"

"Holy shit."

I opened my eyes, saw the bleed of shock in Chase's eyes.

"We're at the wrong place," he muttered. "She's at the eff'in hospital."

I blinked, didn't understand. "No," I said, shaking my head. "She's alone . . . by herself."

"Big Charity," he said, and now his eyes glittered. "It's been closed since Katrina."

I rocked back, felt the surge move through me. "Then we have to go!"

He reached for my hand and tugged me toward the door. "It's not that far—"

"Not that way," I said, pulling back. *"They'll take me."*

The glow of his flashlight made the blue of his eyes look black. "It's the only way."

But I couldn't do it, despite the gentleness in his voice. "They won't listen to me—you heard them! *Please,*" I said. "We'll find another way out of here." There had to be one. The place was falling down around us.

Chase frowned, but he was no longer urging me toward the door. I could see his mind working. "I don't have a car—"

With a set of keys dangling from his left hand, Dylan stepped from the shadows. "But I do."

We ran. We had a head start, but knew it was only a matter of time before Jackson and LaSalle caught up with us. The second Chase's five minutes expired, the cops had started shouting, running with their flashlights and their guns into the wharf. That's when we darted from the other side to make our getaway in Jim Fourcade's car.

I'm pretty sure he knew.

Just as I was pretty sure he had our backs.

It was okay. LaSalle and Jackson could follow. They could find us. It's what I wanted, actually, to draw them to the abandoned hospital. Because once they were there, they'd have to go inside. And once they got inside, they would find her.

We left the car in plain sight beneath a streetlight across from the facility that once served the city's underprivileged. The art deco building dominated an entire city block, big and dark and surrounded by a chain-link fence. It was hard to imagine a facility so massive could simply be abandoned.

But that was the way of it in New Orleans, where despite rebuilding, much of the city lay in ruins. Some structures had been torn down. Others simply sat and waited, frozen in a time-warp as if someday something magical would happen and the life from before would just . . . resume.

The decay told the truth. Life was not frozen. It had simply moved on.

"This way," Dylan said, tromping through a puddle beside a sign that warned of K9 patrols inside the building. Beyond the fence, a crumbling walkway led to the main entrance.

Heart pounding, I hurried toward him.

"Omigod," I whispered, staring at the display over the entrance. Below the words CHARITY HOSPITAL, the image of a man dominated the center of a large, decorative screen, much as I'd seen in the darkness of my mind.

"You sure about this?" Chase asked.

I nodded.

"Then let's go." Effortlessly he vaulted over the fence, much as he had at City Park. How was it even possible that afternoon had been less than a week before? It seemed like a different lifetime.

Fourcade's son edged closer. I didn't know much about him. I was pretty sure he wasn't yet twenty. But with a gun in his hand and a glint in his eye, he reminded me of what his father must have been like all those years before, when my mother was still alive.

"You okay?" His voice was quiet, understanding. "You can always wait—"

I moved before he could finish, for the second time in a matter of days climbing a fence designed to keep people out.

We made it to the front door as a siren kicked in from somewhere in the distance. An ambulance, I told myself, but secretly I hoped it was LaSalle.

Getting in was stupidly easy. The landscaping was overgrown, big rambling bushes and trees concealing a series of windows. The first one Fourcade's son checked was unlocked, almost as if—

Nothing prepared me for the wall of ice. I slammed into it the second I scrambled inside, staggering, doubling over as an invisible fist caught me in the gut.

"Trinity!" I must have cried out because Chase spun around and was by my side in a heartbeat. "What's wrong? Are you okay?"

I didn't know how to explain it. "C-can't . . . breathe . . ." I managed. God knew I was trying.

"Yes, you can," Dylan said. He went down on a knee to the other side of me—and everything just kind of wobbled.

I didn't want him to be there. I didn't want to look into the hard silver of his eyes and remember how out of control I'd let myself—

I didn't want Chase to know I'd kissed someone else.

I didn't want to know it, either.

"What do you mean you can't breathe?" As if to demonstrate how, Chase sucked in a breath, let it out slowly.

"No." My chest constricted. Still hunched over, I braced myself with palms to my thighs. "I can't—"

"Don't fight it," Fourcade's son said, watching me, but thankfully, not touching. "Just let it go," he said. "Just—"

Another wave swirled through me, stronger than before.

"Come on, baby . . . sit down," Chase said. "You don't have to do this."

I shook my head. Rest wouldn't help. "No . . . it's this place," I whispered. "It's like . . . every emotion I've ever had is pressing in on me at the same time—"

Light flooded the darkness. "They are." Dylan aimed the huge Maglite he'd grabbed from his father's car at me. His eyes were dark, steady. "This is an intense place. A lot of people won't even turn down Tulane."

I wanted to grab the light, bathe myself in it, *hold* it deep, deep inside of me.

"She's here," I whispered. "I can feel her." Around me the walls breathed, and the stillness thrummed with every beat of her heart. "We have to—" I reached for Chase, held on to him as I stood. "Come on."

He didn't look convinced, but he didn't fight me on it. He took my hand as the chorus of sirens outside grew louder, and led the way to the stairwell. "Which way?"

The vibration from within intensified. "I don't know," I said, rubbing a hand to my wrist. "Just . . . hurry."

I'd seen darkness. In Colorado, when the sun slipped behind the mountains and night covered the land, so far removed from city lights. Most nights stars winked and twinkled. But some nights they did not. Some nights clouds took over, settling down like a thick wool blanket.

I'd lived darkness. In the mountains . . . in my mind. My dreams. Sometimes I would find a flicker or flame to lead the way. But sometimes there was nothing but pure blind instinct—and pure blind fear.

None of that, not what I'd seen or what I'd lived, what I'd dreamed, compared to the basement of the old hospital. During Katrina it had flooded, water reaching the ceiling. Early on, when they'd hoped to reopen the hospital, they'd made efforts to clean everything up, but all these years later, the stench of decay hit us the second we emerged from the stairwell into the utter and complete darkness.

"Dylan—" My voice broke on his name, but before I could say anything else, the beam of his Maglite cut through the corridor. Stacks of chairs lined one side, while soiled sheets and blankets

were crammed up against the opposite wall. Empty fast-food bags, soda bottles, syringes, and a thousand other kinds of trash and filth lay everywhere.

Someone had been down there recently.

Pressed so close against Chase that I could feel his heart pounding against my back, I held myself very still, waiting. I'm not sure for what. Just . . . waiting.

"Trin?" He still held my hand. I couldn't have let go if my life depended on it. "Do you feel anything? Can you tell if she's here?"

I closed my eyes and opened myself, immediately wished I hadn't. "No!" I shouted, but the buzz wouldn't stop, the jumble of voices as if everyone in the world was talking to me at one time. Scratch that. Shouting. Begging.

Pleading.

"Stop," I said, and then did what I'd sworn I wouldn't do only a few minutes before. I jerked away from Chase and brought my hands to the sides of my face, blocking my ears. "Stop, stop, stop . . ."

The glow of Dylan's Maglite found me, and the voices stopped.

He edged in front of me, sandwiching me between the two of them. "You ever been down here before?" he asked Chase.

"A bunch," he said. "My dad used to teach here."

"You lead then."

Chase frowned.

"What?" Dylan asked.

"I just . . ." The beam of the Maglite made him look unnaturally pale. Frowning, he shoved the bangs from his eyes. "I don't think Trin should be down here."

The protective rasp to his voice washed through me like the most amazing sedative. He was here. *He was here.*

He'd come back.

Squinting, my eyes adjusting to the shadowy darkness, I sucked in a sour breath and let myself look around, saw the sign on the wall. Dark letters directed visitors to the cafeteria. Another sign—

"Oh God," I whispered, my hand instinctively lifting to close around the tarnished dragonfly at my chest. My stomach churned. "You think he put her in the morgue."

In a gross way, it made sense. No one would find her here in the bowels of the hospital. No one would even look.

"You're not going in there," Dylan said in a voice so horribly quiet my throat tightened.

"No, I . . ." Did have to. If that's where she was. I had to. "I can do it."

His eyes narrowed. That was the only warning I got. Without another word he pivoted and took off down the narrow hall, taking every molecule of light with him.

"No!" I shouted as Chase let loose the most imaginative stream of cussing I'd ever heard from him. Lunging into the primal darkness, we followed.

At the door to the morgue, Chase stopped. "Wait here."

I stared at him, felt myself start to shake. "No! I can—"

The second he kicked open the door, I gagged. The smell of death and antiseptic hung heavy in the air, seeping into my body with the breath I tried not to draw. In the center of the cavernous room stood Jim Fourcade's son, absolutely still, the beam of the big Maglite trained on the freezer drawers hanging open.

"*Jesus* . . ." That was Chase. I think. Or maybe it was me. I didn't really know, couldn't really tell thought from nightmare.

"Get her out of here!" Dylan shouted, pivoting and closing in on us. At the door he shoved the Maglite into my hands as his eyes met Chase's. "You got a phone?"

Chase nodded, pulling his iPhone from his pocket. The faint glow joined with Fourcade's, and together the two of them stepped into the cold room once habitated by the living and the dead. I

stood there, my fingers in a death grip around the big light. All I
had to do was step inside. All I had to do was—

The bang from somewhere behind me shattered the awful silence. I spun toward the stairwell, lifted the big Maglite as a man
staggered into the corridor. Stunned, I pivoted back toward the
morgue, but he was on me in a heartbeat, yanking me against his
sweaty body.

"Trinity!" Chase shouted, and through the soft glow of his
phone, I saw him freeze several feet away, his eyes dark and—

The cool metal of a blade touched my neck.

THIRTY

"Easy, darlin', and no one gets hurt."

I stood in the stale, putrid shadows, eyes locked with Chase's. He stood so motionless, I wasn't even sure that he breathed.

But I knew that I did not.

Beside him, Dylan edged closer, equally still, even when he moved. Carefully I glanced down at his hand, saw the gun.

"Please." The word came out weak, broken, so I forced a swallow and tried again. "Let me go."

The tall man dragged me back from the morgue. He'd seen the guys. I had no idea if he'd noticed the gun.

"'Fraid I can't do that," he muttered, shifting me in front of him, like a shield. "I said a prayer, darlin', and here you are."

"No." The gun was off the table. A clean shot was impossible. "Let me go," I said again. "We won't follow—"

"But he will," the man muttered, and I gagged on the stale smell that washed over me.

My fingers tightened around the flashlight. I didn't lift it, though, didn't want to prematurely draw his attention to the only chance I had. "Who?"

The man tightened his arm around my middle. "He's coming," he said as I tried to dig in my feet.

But he kept dragging.

"Drop it!" With the words a new light flooded the corridor, and a quick glance revealed Jim Fourcade emerging from the stairwell. His eyes were unyielding steel, in his hand, a gun. "Back away from the girl."

My heart thudded violently. My throat, separated from the blade by only the thinnest stretch of skin, totally closed up.

"I didn't hurt her," the man snarled as I stared at the threadbare remains of what had once been a cotton dress shirt. His gray slacks were dirty, too, his loafers covered in . . . blood.

But it was the Mardi Gras mask, partially concealed by a torn front pocket, that made my heart stagger.

Fourcade's eyes gave away nothing. "I mean it. Let go of the girl. *Now.*"

The man didn't even slow. With a strength born in that thin expanse between life and death, desperation and insanity, he wrestled me deeper into the darkness of the corridor. I couldn't see Chase anymore. I couldn't see the morgue. I moved without thinking, going limp in his arms. He staggered from the unexpected weight, the knife scraping up to my chin as he yanked me back against his body. Heart slamming, I slid a leg behind his. We tangled. He tripped, staggered, his arms flailing out.

That was the only opening I needed. I twisted, vaguely aware of shouting as I swung the Maglite and smashed it against the side of his head.

A horrible sound broke from his throat. He flew back and recoiled into himself. I fell. Rolled.

Everything after that—

It all happened so fast. "Get her out of there!" I heard someone yell, and then arms were closing around me, dragging me across the sticky floor. I thrashed, opened my mouth to bite down—

Then I heard the voice.

"I've got you, baby," Chase muttered, cradling me against his chest. "I've got you."

I sagged against him, held on tight. Refused to fall apart. Around us shouting erupted, footsteps and swearing and—gunshots. Five of them, the horrible echo ping-ponging through the concrete of the basement.

"Get a medic down here!" I heard someone shout.

Four uniformed cops pounded by, guns drawn. Twisting, I followed them. I saw the heap and heard my aunt scream. She ran past us as we scrambled to our feet, dropped to her knees next to Detective DeMarcus Jackson.

Both kneeled in blood.

Chase tried to hold me back, but I staggered forward as one of the uniformed cops rolled the man who'd held a knife to my throat onto his back.

I stopped.

Looks could be so deceiving. He'd looked timeless the first time I'd seen him, with his reddish brown hair pulled behind his neck and his tailored gray suit slightly big, his eyes sharp and piercing. Then, in the parking garage, he'd looked threatening. "It's him," I whispered. "The guy who followed me."

Moments before he'd seemed powerful. Now I saw a body that looked gaunt and malnourished, his hair filthy and tangled, his face heavily whiskered. And he lay so very still . . .

I'd seen death before, even murder. But that had been an animal. Seeing the blood drain from a body that had been alive and desperate only a few minutes before, as he now lay lifeless—

"Don't look," Chase said, trying to turn my head into his chest, but I was so done with being protected.

Alone, I thought. Broken. The man in the baggy designer suit looked as cast aside in death as he'd obviously been in life.

Open door number one; open door number two. Take a different path—dream a different dream. Even the road not taken led somewhere.

It took a moment for my aunt's voice to register. Numbly, I glanced over to see her rock back with a hand to her mouth. *"Aaron."*

And suddenly I realized who had been shouting moments before. Who had made the kill.

Jackson crouched over his bloodied partner. Their faces were close. I could see LaSalle's mouth moving.

"Easy," Jackson said. "Try again."

"Fffffif ffffffflr."

Aunt Sara reached for his hand.

LaSalle's eyes fluttered open. His mouth was so swollen his lips were indistinguishable. "Jjjjjjeeeeesss . . ."

Jackson stiffened. "The girl," he said.

LaSalle closed his eyes, opened them again. "Ffffifff floooo—"

We were running before he finished.

Fluorescent light washed through the corridor, revealing closed doors along each side. All except one. Uniformed cops swarmed, and paramedics rushed. Vaguely I was aware of urgent voices and shouting—and the muffled sound of masculine sobs.

"Pitre?" Chase murmured, but his All-State receiver did not look up, just sat slumped with his back to the wall and his knees to his chest, his head lowered, rocking. He must have followed us, too. His clothes were wet, filthy, his shoes covered in mud. In front of him kneeled an older version of himself, in the uniform of the N.O.P.D., but with the ravaged eyes of a brother.

Emotion clogged my throat. Sometimes games were fun, I remembered thinking the week before, and sometimes they were not. Pitre's game, no matter how pseudo-noble it had started, was going to leave the kind of scars no amount of penance could erase.

I'm not sure what made him look up, but slowly his head lifted, and his shell-shocked eyes met mine. Something flared there— sorrow? Gratitude? Respect? I'll never know. But as my own eyes filled, he looked back down.

And then Jim Fourcade stepped from the open doorway, and everything else fell away. Leaner, I thought. Somehow from one day to the next he looked leaner, stripped bare, like a tree in the aftermath of a violent storm. He was still standing, still there, but there was something in the stark silver of his eyes, and without even a word, I knew what was inside that room.

And started to pray.

My mother's friend lifted an arm and extended a hand. I stared at it, at his palm and scraped fingers, the solidarity he was offering. And something inside of me tightened. He'd done this before. He'd lived moments like this one. With my mother. He'd been by her side. He'd taken her hand, given her his strength.

By stepping toward him, by putting my palm to his and curving my fingers around his hand, it was like I was joining them. Joining her.

Then I saw Jessica.

She sat on the far side of the dirty hospital room, on the floor with her bloody arms wrapped around her knees. Rocking. Just rocking. Discarded candy bar wrappers surrounded her. Chocolate stained her face. Bruises and blood, some new, some old, covered her arms. Her hair was stringy. And I knew, I knew I would never forget the look in her sunken eyes, dark and vacant and staring.

And like the dead guy in the basement, I was pretty sure she didn't see anything. Until she spoke.

"Chase," she whispered, looking beyond me to where Chase stood at my side. Somewhere along the line his hand had fallen from mine. "Chase . . ." she said again. *"You're here."*

Amber couldn't stop crying. For a while she paced, but the second Drew arrived, she dived into his arms and totally lost it. I'd always thought she looked stupid skinny. But at six in the morning, in the Tulane Hospital waiting room, with no makeup and uncombed hair, swollen eyes and sweats instead of designer clothes, she looked like a girl overcome by the news that her BFF had been found . . . alive.

Bethany fidgeted. I tried to see Jessica's younger sister as she'd been a little more than a week before, when she'd climbed through the broken window in a fragile attempt to impress her older sister and her sister's boyfriend. She'd seemed like a little girl then, with a serious case of hero worship. Now the sterile glow of fluorescent lights revealed an awareness to her, a wisdom beyond her years, and I couldn't help but think that I'd had it wrong. She was the sister with the strength, the confidence. She was the sister who was going to take her sibling by the hand, and lead.

Throat tight, I glanced away, to where Chase stood with his parents. Susan and Richard had been so elegant and reserved a few nights before, but like the rest of us, now they looked like people roused from bed during the predawn darkness by a phone call. They had their arms around their son, as if comforting him. But I was pretty sure he was doing most of the comforting. The Bonaventures and Morgenthals had been friends a long time.

We were all there. All waiting. All except Aunt Sara, who'd gone to check on Detective LaSalle. He'd been the first to stumble across the room where Jessica was being held. There'd been a fight. Detective LaSalle had been bludgeoned with something. The junkie had run, ending up in the basement after discovering cops swarming the hospital lobby.

We would never know. We would never know why that man with a spotless record but track mark–littered body had taken Jessica—and possibly the other girls. We would never know if he'd been watching her, or if she'd simply been at the wrong place at the wrong time. If Pitre had never lured her—

Pitre. He was the only one from that night who wasn't with us at the hospital. Because he was at the 8th District police station, in serious trouble. He'd lured Jessica to the house to teach her a lesson. He'd locked her in the room, gone to get a burger. He'd wanted her to feel the fear I had when she and Amber had played their joke. He'd never seen the man hiding in the shadows.

When he returned an hour later, the room had been empty, and hell had begun.

Across the room, the morning news played across a muted television. I watched a reporter standing outside Big Charity, no doubt conveying all that had gone down.

Relieved there were no pictures of me, I glanced toward the sterile room that pretended to be cheerful, with its collection of plastic plants and sofas and magazines, where Amber and Drew held each other and Bethany stood stoically—but Chase no longer stood with his parents.

I turned as he came up behind me with a Styrofoam cup in his hand. "Hey," he said. "You okay?"

I'm not sure why my throat got all tight, probably because of the word "okay." I knew what he meant and I knew what the right answer was. And technically, I was okay. Jessica was safe and her abductor was dead, but . . .

In the course of one week, my life had changed forever. If Jim Fourcade had not asked his son to follow me . . .

I looked away.

"Just tired," I said, taking the coffee Chase offered. I sipped, welcoming the warmth despite the bitter taste. A little sugar could go a long way.

"Then why don't you go home—" he said, reaching for my free hand. But he never finished. Instead he stilled, his eyes going dark. "Whose shirt is that?"

I looked down at the huge black T-shirt hanging from my shoulders. "Oh," I whispered, not sure how much to tell him. "I . . ." Fell in the river? ". . . had an accident."

"What kind of accident?"

"Just . . . I fell," I hedged. "Dylan—"

"Dylan?"

There was a hard edge to Chase's voice, one I'd never heard before. "Jim Fourcade's son. He was there," I downplayed. "His dad asked him to keep an eye on me."

"You're wearing his shirt?"

I'm not sure why I smiled, maybe because Chase sounded so totally bothered by the fact I was wearing another guy's shirt. Or maybe because for the first time since we'd been together on his sofa, the little kick in my heart was a happy one.

I didn't want to think about Jim Fourcade's son—or why I hadn't seen him since the morgue.

"It's just a shirt," I said.

But Chase looked like he did during football games when the other team intercepted one of his passes . . . which did not happen often. Actually, I'd only seen it happen once.

"It doesn't mean anything," I said, setting the small cup on a table and stepping into him, wrapping my arms around him. He was all rigid and tight, like he wasn't about to let down his guard.

I'll never know what would have happened next, because Jessica's parents emerged from around a corner, stepping into the waiting room. Marian and Bryce Morgenthal were both tall, beautiful people, but in that moment they were just tired, haggard parents. Bethany flew to them, and they hugged. The Bonaventures moved closer. Amber and Drew held hands. Chase and I separated.

"She's going to be okay," Jessica's mother said. When they met mine, her eyes filled. "Thanks to you."

I stiffened, tried to back away. That was instinct. But Chase wouldn't let me.

Through her tears, Marian Morgenthal smiled. "She's awake now . . . and asking for you."

I'm not sure what I expected. Jessica had looked gaunt and frail when I'd seen her huddled in the corner of the hospital room. And it's not like we were friends. That she would want to see me before her sister or BFF . . .

For a long time I stood outside her door, trying to figure out what to say. How to act. What I really wanted to do was walk away.

But that was the coward's way out, and I was so done with that.

Telling myself the only way to get it over with was to do it, I took a deep breath and for the second time that day, stepped into a hospital room where Jessica waited.

Before, at Big Charity, she'd been on the floor, her gown stained, her hair tangled and matted with blood. Her eyes vacant. Now she lay propped up in a bed, the sheets clean and tucked around her. Machines beeped. Tubes and cords ran to and from her body. Oxygen ran to her swollen nose. A half-eaten bowl of ice cream sat on a tray, next to a huge plastic cup with a handle and a straw.

She'd showered. She'd washed her hair. Her face was scrubbed clean. The blood and chocolate and grime were gone, but the cuts and bruises remained. As did the fear. Dark smudges still ringed her swollen eyes, but they were no longer as vacant.

"Hey," she whispered, and I made myself swallow, even though my throat felt like someone had a cord wrapped around it, pulling tighter and tighter.

"Hey," I said back, sifting for the right words. *You look better? I'm glad you're okay? I bet that ice cream tasted good . . .*

In the end, I didn't need to say anything.

"Thank you," Jessica said as I neared her bed, and I just stopped. That was not what I was expecting.

Her mouth was swollen, her lips cracked, but the faint smile was obvious, and somehow with that one simple gesture, we were just two girls, one in a hospital gown, the other in a T-shirt, neither of us with makeup, both of us with stringy, air-dried hair.

"For what you did," she said, and her eyes—wow, I'd never noticed how pretty they were, even bruised with shadows of blood and fatigue, rather than powder and glitter. "I don't think I could have done that."

I think I shrugged. "It was no big deal."

"It was everything," she said. "After what I did to you . . . you could have just walked away."

I looked away.

"But you were there," she whispered. "I don't know how . . . but I could . . . feel you."

My eyes whipped back to hers.

"My parents . . . told me how you put it all on the line . . . for me."

The way she said "for me" tugged at me. It was as if she considered herself synonymous with the filth in which we'd found her.

Eyes on mine, never looking away, she stretched out an arm— thin, pale, and bruised—and extended her hand. And when she spoke again, her voice was so quiet it barely registered over the beeping of the machines. "You were . . . amazing."

Amazing. It was not a word I'd associated with myself. I'd come to this city of my birth, frightened and alone, looking for answers, connections. To finally belong. There was still much I didn't know, but in that moment I realized that sometimes what brought people together wasn't that which made us the same.

But that which made us different.

With the morning sunshine filtering through the blinds, I stood there a long moment, watching the way the light played with the shadows between us.

Then I stepped closer, and took her hand.

THIRTY-ONE

They call them Cities of the Dead. Row after row of weathered white houses stretch in all directions. Angels guard them. Crosses and rusty ironwork adorn them. Shadows dance, and the silence whispers.

I'd heard about the odd, aboveground tombs. I'd read about them. I knew the water table was too high for in-ground burials. I'd been horrified after the hurricane at reports of floating caskets and lost coffins . . .

But nothing prepared me for actually seeing.

"I can go with you," Aunt Sara said.

Squinting against the blinding afternoon sun, I glanced back at her and felt the warmth clear down to my toes. She'd insisted on coming with me, even though she was totally wiped out. She'd showered and nibbled on a shrimp po-boy, but fatigue still dulled her eyes. Dark circles ringed them. Without makeup, her skin was smooth, but pale. Even her hair, normally thick and glossy and perfect, hung there.

But the second I'd mentioned where I wanted to go, she'd reached for her purse and offered to drive.

"Thank you," I said, and meant on so many more levels than she could possibly realize. She'd taken me in. She'd put her life on hold and welcomed a homeless teenager. She'd stood by me and held my hand. She'd shared her home and given me the two most amazing gifts I'd ever received: herself . . . and my mother.

I didn't know how I'd ever be able to pay her back.

"But if it's okay . . ." I swallowed, frowning as a tour group tromped along on an adjacent row. The force of the breeze stole the guide's words, but I didn't need to hear them. I knew what he was saying, the legends he was telling, the spectacle he was trying to build.

In New Orleans, cemeteries were practically museums.

But for me, St. Louis Cemetery was a sacred place.

I'd been wanting to come since I'd arrived back in August, but for some reason had been putting it off. Now, after all that had gone down over the past week, the time seemed right.

"You want to go alone, don't you?" Aunt Sara asked, sliding the hair back from her face.

I watched the tangled mass fly right back in and was grateful I'd opted for a ponytail. "If you don't mind—" I said, shifting the backpack over my shoulder.

Her smile, even with her lips dry and cracked, made me want to throw my arms around her and hold on tight.

But this was something I needed to do alone.

"They'd be so proud of you," she whispered, and my chest tightened. "Just like I am."

I turned before she could see my eyes well up and made my way through the shifting shadows cast by crosses and some of the most haunting statues I'd ever seen.

Two rows over, across from a crumbling depiction of the Virgin Mary, I stopped. Automatically my hand lifted to my chest, my fingers once again closing around my mother's dragonfly. Such a small thing really, a necklace. And yet to me . . . it was everything.

Because it was hers.

The aboveground tomb looked like all the others, with a crumbling Celtic cross on top and an intricate iron fence around it. But the marker made it different.

The marker made it mine.

> *John Mark and Rachelle Monsour*
> *Beloved parents*
> *United Forever*

"Hi," I said, going down on my knees and placing the backpack on the ground next to me. From inside, I removed a handful of daisies and put four in the little stone vase to the right, five to the left. Then I retrieved a thermos of water and gave each a drink.

My eyes stung. Fighting back the tears, I fumbled around in the bag, then placed five white votives in a neat line in front of the tomb.

God, how I wish I . . . remembered. Something.

Anything.

"I'm here," I whispered, lighting the candles one by one. *"I'm here."*

Home. Finally.

Where I belonged.

EPILOGUE

Six days after we found Jessica, the package arrived.

I was texting with Victoria when the intercom buzzed. Not thinking much of it, I answered, but no one responded. Only static. Puzzled, I went to the window, saw the box. It sat on the porch, small and cardboard, with absolutely nobody around.

That's when the hated tightness started.

Ignoring it, I went back to study three outfits lain out on my bed. So much had happened. I wanted to move forward. Jessica was out of the hospital. Detective LaSalle was going to be okay. Amber's fingerprints had been found all over my laptop, and while I didn't think we'd ever get an actual confession, we all knew how those Facebook posts had been made from my computer.

And in just a few hours, Chase and I were going to a movie.

It all felt so amazingly . . . normal.

But even as I reached for my favorite pair of skinny jeans, I couldn't stop thinking about the box. So I took my phone with me, telling Victoria that if I didn't text her back in five minutes something was wrong.

Odd. I know. But there you go.

The second I opened the door to the outside, something warm and pure whispered through me. Without hesitation I dropped to my knees, lifted the lid and saw her, small and emaciated and frightened.

But the moment I put my hand to the dull white of her fur, the small, white cat started to purr.